ASSASSIN

An SOBs Novel

IRISH WINTERS

Assassin, An SOBs Novel
Copyright ©2019 by Irish Winters
All rights reserved

First Edition

Cover design: Letitia Hasser, Romantic Book Design

Interior book design: Bob Houston, eBook Formatting

Editor: Linda Clarkson, Black Opal Editing

ISBN Paperback: 978-1-942895-89-3

ISBN eBook: 978-1-942895-67-1

Library of Congress Control Number: 2018914445

Irish Winter's websites: http://www.irishwinters.com and irishwinters.blogspot.com

Assassin

An SOBs novel

Angel – Chance's story
Assassin – Pagan's story

Coming soon:

Damned – Kruze's story
Lost – Julio's story

You can find Irish Winters
On Facebook
&
On Twitter

Sign up for Irish Winters' Newsletter at:
http://www.irishwinters.com/newsletter.html

For more information about all Irish Winters' books,
visit:
http://www.irishwinters.com.

Prologue

One month earlier

Some eighteen hundred miles east of Montana, Pagan took a knee outside one of two eight-paned rear windows of a townhouse in DC proper. Like row houses, the homes adjoined but their facades differed. Some were painted in federal blue with stark white trim, others in earth tones with dark brown accents. Gray stone and red brick decorated yet others, lending to the quaint appearance of American individualistic, independent spirits.

Yeah, right. This 'burb' was nothing but a cookie-cutter tract of over-priced housing for the upwardly mobile near-misses and abject failures in the District's dog-eat-dog, overly competitive business world. Inhabited by wannabe politicians who'd never been elected, it was made for men and women resigned to lesser ambitions because they weren't good enough for political office or the famed DC beltway, where overpaid lobbyists thrived. The faded paint and shabby lawns did look halfway decent by moonlight, though.

This particular home was special. John Wesley Mills lived here with his cat, and didn't that figure? Johnny-Boy was a cat person. Gallo, the hyperactive German Shepherd that belonged to Pagan's big brother Chance, wouldn't like that on principle alone. Neither would Lucky, the good girl who used to go by *Meine Liebchen*. Who in their right mind named a standard-size Schnauzer *love of my life?* An idiot like the recently deceased Mitchell Franks, that was who.

Dark had fallen hours ago, but Pagan had time. He now knew the intimate details of Johnny-Boy's alter ego. A lackluster insurance salesman who barely made his quotas by day, Johnny dabbled in illicit drug distribution by night. Didn't fall too far from the proverbial tree that had taken root in South America a long time ago, that was for sure. Well, not really that long ago, but back in the 1940s, when Nazis there thought they were safe from the reach of justice and truth.

Johnny's ancestors, two brothers, Richard and Zimmer Franks, both Nazi SS guards, had settled in beautiful Bogotá, Colombia, after the war. It was a nice place to live—then. But as sure as crusted dirty snow followed the freshly fallen, pure white flakes of winter's first storm, deceit, turmoil, and misery followed the Franks brothers.

Richard, the younger one, despised the lack of sophistication in his new country. In less than three months, he fled north to the United States, took on a new history, that of a used car salesman, but kept his old name. Zimmer, the older brother, was made of tougher stuff. After ingratiating himself to the governor of Bogotá, he began two businesses, one legal, one not. Zimmer married well and entrenched himself in wealthy Colombian society. The downside to his success was his only heir, a daughter, who in turn had married Diego Gonzales, the local crime lord. Not because she'd wanted to, but because Zimmer needed her to.

It was an arranged marriage of epic proportions, two criminals uniting their kingdoms and expanding their grasp, all accomplished in the time it took for innocent little Amanda to say two words: *I do.*

Zimmer lost track of Richard. To be fair, Richard had always acted as if he had a broomstick stuck up his ass anyway, and there were times Zimmer thought he'd detected homosexual tendencies in his younger brother. That perversion wasn't tolerated in their mother country, and Zimmer wouldn't tolerate it in Bogotá. Which explained how Richard had sent letters to his brother, but Zimmer had burned each and every one.

A staunch believer of all Der Führer stood for, Zimmer set his aims high and his means low during the war in order to acquire those aims on behalf of the Third Reich. He'd not only organized SS operations while in the Homeland, but architecturally designed several of the finest crematoriums. He was good at the death thing. That was how he did business. Efficiently. With measurable results. He said what he meant, and he followed his few words of harshly uttered direction with lethal enforcement. That was how a strong man ruled the world. A few beheadings, here. A dismemberment or two, there. All in a day's work.

Eventually, at the age of one hundred and one, Zimmer passed away in his sleep, but not before he'd trained his grandson, a darling, blond youngster to take over the family business.

Wilhelm Gonzales immediately executed every person in the city who owed his father or his grandfather as little as one peso. That was also the day Wilhelm learned he was not alone in the world. A long-lost relative surfaced in his fair but troubled city, another blond and blue-eyed man who reminded Wilhelm of his proud German heritage. That man was Richard Franks' grandson. Mitchell.

As for Johnny? Mitchell's sister, Celia Franks, had married Collier Mills, a Maryland banker. Not an important banker, but a hard-working nine-to-fiver who was never good enough for the rapacious, conniving dreams of one of Hitler's right-hand man's progeny. At least, that was the story John told his friends down at the local German tavern.

Pagan had done his homework well, not only online, but at the tavern as well. Men on the downside of life tended to gripe about the fathers they hated, especially after a few beers loosened their tongues. Johnny loved to complain. Pagan loved to listen.

It seemed that John Wesley Mills had just earned rank in the local fascist chapter, a group with violent tendencies toward murder, chaos. The usual. They went after anyone not of the pure, blue-eyed, blond-haired Aryan race. First lieutenant now, Johnny Boy had bigger dreams for America, dreams that paralleled Zimmer's dream for Colombia. Beheadings. Dismemberments. Hangings. Rule by terror. The tactics worked in South America. Why not here in the land of the brave and the free?

Hence Pagan took a knee, not to pray, but to aim his Sig Sauer P226 MK25, complete with SR09 suppressors. X-ray sights. Elite ammo. He didn't plan to use its very capable twin, but kept it holstered, loaded and just as ready. Like a brother who'd bail your ass out of trouble if things went sideways.

But that wasn't happening tonight. Donning black nitrile gloves that matched his leather jacket and his mood, Pagan ghosted into Mills' home without the OTC doorknob making so much as a snick as it turned. But the second—the very second—Pagan entered John Boy's space, his nostrils flared wide at the coppery scent of freshly spilled blood in the air. Damn it. Johnny wouldn't have killed someone in his home tonight, would he? Sure smelled like it.

When a silent shadow slid down the steps from Johnny's loft at his left, Pagan crouched low, his piece on target. He leaned into the act, anticipating it, needing to end this lowlife for the sake of the woman his brother loved. This was no sanctioned hit. Neither had it been vetted through the blackest of black operators, the SOBs. This was personal. Johnny was the last living descendant of the treacherous Franks brothers. Because of them, Chance's wife Suede had nearly died. John needed to die, and his twisted family's warped ideology needed to end.

Primed, Pagan had only to press the trigger, light up the night, and leave this house without waking the neighbors—until he realized he'd caught Miss Hex. Not John Wesley Mills. Damn it.

"Freeze," he growled, lifting to his feet and into view.

She halted, her right arm across her chest, her fingertips still on the handle of the pink-as-a-newborn-baby's-butt firearm she'd just holstered, her voluptuous breasts crushed and plumped inside that stretched-too-tight t-shirt in the process.

"Oh. Hi Pagan." She acted like they'd bumped into each other shopping at the mall. "What are you doing here?"

"You ended John Mills?" You'd think she'd have been a little surprised to see him.

The woman smiled. She knew she was eye-candy galore, from the tips of those buxom girls that all but spilled out of her shirt to the toes of her sleek, black designer boots. That she easily managed two underarm holsters with the size of her *assets,* amazed males everywhere. Not that Pagan minded. He just liked watching while she put those babies, meaning the pistols, away with those other, more succulent *babies,* in the way.

"'Course I killed him. Why are you here? To end me because I beat you to it?"

"Hardly." Pagan holstered his piece to prove his word, his heart thumping at the heady scent of cherry blossoms wafting from Miss Hex's slightly sweaty, yet very sexy, body. How could a woman so lethal smell so sweet and good, almost innocent? Hex was an enigma of the highest order, an ultra-feminine goddess, yet one of the best snipers in the business. But she was definitely not the nurturer all women were meant to be, and that was her downfall.

"You knew one of us Sinclairs would be coming for Johnny Mills. You should've let us end him." And she should have. Women just weren't supposed to enjoy killing. Pagan wasn't certain if Hex loved her work or not. She was just so good at it.

Victoria's deep brown eyes widened under delicate brows that made her look extraordinarily innocent. Which she wasn't. "I had a job to do, so I did it. And, oh yes, Pagan, thanks for asking. My fingers mended nicely, no thanks to your brother." Her palms fell to cup her hips. "So why are *you* here?"

Pagan's mouth went dry at the sight of all that exposed skin between the bottom of her tiny tee to the top of her low-slung jeans. Her belly. The creamy swells of her breasts above the bra. Her long neck. Of course, she'd dressed in black leather shorts that creaked when she walked, but those extra-long legs to heaven almost made a man believe in the hereafter.

Every drop of blood in his brain fled deep, deep south. But Hex was a tits-and-ass, *'play nice with me and I won't kill you'* kind of gal. A brazen female alpha. Possibly a dominatrix the way she wore that leather with an in-your-face confidence. Possibly with pride. He had no doubt she'd dominate any partner dumb enough to get too close to her, in bed or in a bar fight. But at the end of the day, she was still nothing more than Kruze's type, a dominatrix who liked to play. Didn't that reminder of who she'd probably been with last night—as in *slept with*—pump a gallon of bile into Pagan's already churning gut? There were moments Pagan truly despised his brother for the way Kruze treated women. Pagan refused to analyze what that meant about his feelings for Victoria.

He stepped away from Miss Hex, then took another step back for good measure, not sure why the thought of Kruze being with this woman irked him like it did. "Fine then. It's done. Goodbye." *And good riddance.*

Instead of turning in the opposite direction, Hex's chin went up. She took a step toward Pagan. "Would you like to double-check my work? I'm not proud. I'll show you, Pagan. One shot. He never felt a thing. Never knew I was waiting for him."

Pagan shook his head, as much to shake the notion of actually sharing the same air with this tantalizing but off-limits woman, as to distance himself from the scent of her lush and all too inviting body. For whatever reason, the delicate fragrance of cherry blossoms mingled with her uniquely feminine scent, made him unfocused and weak, two traits that could get a sniper dead. "No thanks," he told her, his voice uncommonly gruff in the darkness. "Gotta go." *As in right now. Before I do something stupid.*

"But Pagan," she breathed, her perfect lush lips drawn into a pout that made a man stop and take notice and wonder what those lips would feel like. What they'd taste like. From there, it would only be a hop, skip, and a quicker-than-quick jump to finding out what her other parts felt like. Tasted like. Probably salty and sweet.

His tongue licked a quick lap over his bottom lip before he bit it. Squelched the notion rolling around in his dumb head. Squaring his shoulders, Pagan intended to leave, and he would have, damn it.

But Miss Vicki wouldn't shut up. "You and I had a common enemy, Pagan."

And why he loved the way she kept saying his name the way she did—soft and suggestively low— Pagan had no idea. He just really, really did.

"I got here first, that's all. You would've done the same. Friends?" Miss Vicki extended her slender fingers, the nails painted pink, her trademark color, of course, reaching for him. Daring him to accept—

something that she'd no doubt bartered away other nights just as dark as this one. He was pretty sure it wasn't friendship she offered, but what was a guy to do, especially a lonely guy who just plain was not good with women?

Tugging his gloves off, Pagan stuffed them in his rear pocket, then made contact quickly. Succinctly. Barely squeezing those feminine bear traps. But sometimes, somehow, in the cosmic scheme of insignificant moments like this one, Karma intervened, and it only took...

One. Touch. A single brush of bare skin against bare skin. The melding of lifelines to lifelines. The matching whorl of fingerprint to fingerprint. The dizzying spark that sizzled up from her palm hit his brainpan like a bolt of greased lightning. It was a different kind of energy. Brighter. Crazier. Filled with promise and... So. Damned. Hot.

Miss Vicki pulled back with a hiss, a glint of shock in her sparkling dark eyes. "Pagan! Did you just—?"

"Shock you? No!" He leaped to defensive mode, because damn it. He had felt it—whatever it was. "The carpet's full of static electricity, that's all." *Liar.* He had felt some kind of weird energy arc between them, and he knew it. Pagan just didn't know what it was.

Her shiny black mane rivaled the shine in her eyes, even in the dark of a dead man's house. Vicki Hex, the Sicilian Mafia's number one killer, cocked her pretty head, and when she did, all that lovely hair swished over her shoulder. "I like you, Pagan Sinclair. You're... different."

Was that an insult or an attempt to be funny? Pagan wasn't sophisticated enough to play with the likes of Hex, and he didn't want to look like a fool. "I gotta go." Damned if his voice didn't sound rough and ragged instead of suave—like Kruze's would have, had he been here instead of his lamebrained little brother.

She moved in closer. "Let's go have a beer. Talk for a change. Just you and me. Maybe we can work a few jobs together. Please? I'd like that, wouldn't you?"

He shook his head, not ever—EVER—working with Hex, not in this kill-or-be-killed career they'd both chosen. It seemed wrong offing bad guys with a truly beautiful woman at his side.

"No," he told her, his lower back sore and his balls aching from standing at attention like he'd just realized he was. Least that was why he thought his balls ached. Couldn't be—*that other reason.* He wasn't attracted to her. No way. No how. Yes, he was hard as a rock, but that was just a side effect of the adrenaline thrumming through his system. That was all.

Again with the hair swish and the coy fluttering of lashes. Her eyes were blacker than usual tonight. Sparkly but deep and dark. Sultry and full of steamy promises he had no intention of fulfilling. Her full lips pinched. Deep inside, something sizzled. Pagan didn't dare blink for fear this was all a dream.

A dream come true...

"Aw, you're turning me down?"

Are you turning me on? "Yes," he damned near shouted. "Work. I've got work..." *Or something.* "...to do. Right now. Goodbye."

Miss Hex knew no boundaries in her specialty. In less than the time it took Pagan to draw in a belly full of air, she was in his face, her quivering girls plastered pleasantly against his wary pecs. Automatically, his gaze fell into the tempting valley between those girls. Soft. They had to be soft and warm. Femininely fragrant. A tempting place where a man could bury his face at the end of a long, hard day, right before he buried himself in her warm, wet folds and...

Umm, yeah. About that... Pagan knew damned well his brother had bedded Miss Hex at least once. That was his big brother's piggish style. *Love the one you're with and leave 'em in the dust when you're done. Never look back. Never bed the same chick twice.*

Suddenly, Miss Hex's elbows were on Pagan's chest, her fingertips teasing the curled hairs behind his ears, and her lips were within kissing range.

"I need a shave and a cut," he told her, not sure why that trivia blurted out of his mouth, but okay. His hair *was* shaggier than usual, and he hadn't shaved his face in a week. It meant nothing. An undercover operator had to be ready for short notice recall to the Mideastern countries where beards and unkempt hair were the norm. He might have to insert quickly.

Yeah. Insert.

Not on my best game here, he thought. *Mostly, cuz I got no game. Kruze is the one with game.*

Her lips pinched, and Pagan closed his eyes, not because she might kiss him, but because this was a dream, although one of his most favorites. Had to be. He'd wake up any second now, and he didn't want to embarrass himself when he did.

Instead, the softest lips caressed his firmly closed mouth like butterfly wings, brushing over his skin, asking. Just asking. Tasting. Not assuming and not taking, which surprised the hell out of him. He'd always envisioned Hex as a domineering wildcat in the sack. She surely dressed the part. Yet here in the dark where anything could go, and where no one would ever know if they did or if they didn't, her tongue flickered like a whisper and a promise, wetting his lips just enough to start a fire roaring in his gut.

He kept both eyes closed. God, she tasted sweet.

"Come on, big guy," she coaxed, her breath in his flared wide nostrils a heady hint of whiskey sour and forgotten good intentions. "Just one beer?"

And all bets were off. The beer could wait. Circling her with one arm, he cupped the nape of her neck with his hand, his other on one leather-clad cheek of her ass. Tilting her head for easier access, he took her mouth hard, mashing her lips against his, thrusting his ready tongue into the slick warmth of her eager mouth. All the while he imagined what other slick warmth her body offered, and what it would feel like to spread her legs and know her in every carnal sense of the word.

Victoria growled, but not in disgust. Giving back with passion and heat, her boots lifted off the floor when she wrapped her long legs around his hips, pressing her core to his belly and trapping him against her. What a rush. He now had both hands full of the most delectable ass in the world, and a painful hard-on in his pants.

"I'm not doing this with a dead man upstairs," he told her open mouth. *Kruze probably would, but I'm not made that way.*

Her fingers slid up his jaw and into Pagan's too-long-for-military hair, smoothed over his scalp, and set off every last milliliter of testosterone in his body. "I know a place," she whispered.

Suddenly he was nitroglycerin, unstable and ready to blow. Oh, yeah. If this was what she wanted, she was going to get it. Here. Now. He could push the thought of Johnny Boy out of his head for a few minutes. He could do this!

Until his common sense re-engaged.

Until he realized who she'd most likely been with at least once in the past.

Until he remembered what a real woman was, and what Victoria Hex most definitely was not. Wife material. All those family values and dreams he treasured most. Family. Babies. Sons and daughters.

His ardor expired as quickly as Johnny Boy upstairs probably had.

Pagan wasn't sure what had just happened, but he was certain he was not—NOT—going down this road with one of Kruze's used girls. Not in this lifetime. Not now that he was back in control.

Vicki Hex hadn't a motherly bone in her body. There'd be no kids in her future, and Pagan desperately wanted a family like the one he'd been raised in. A family required a real mom for his future sons and daughters, not some killer dominatrix with a leather fetish and a delectable but well-used ass. Pagan didn't do one-night stands, and he didn't do easy. If nothing else, the woman he married would be respectable and reliable from day one. She would gladly stay home where she belonged and raise his children, not because she had to, but because she wanted to.

Disgusted at his lack of control and his suddenly too-loose morals, Pagan uncupped his fingers from said ass, inhaled deeply to clear his head, then settled the soles of Miss Hex's boots back to the floor where they belonged, and where they should've stayed.

What was wrong with him?

With his heart jackhammering up his throat, Pagan stepped away from the hottest temptation of his life. He'd done crazy a time or two in the past, jumped off a couple bridges, driven too fast, hitchhiked, and downed too many fifths of Irish Whiskey in one sitting.

But this was more than his future on the line. This was his future family he was thinking about. Miss

Hex had no hold on that, and he wouldn't give her one now.

"I can't do this," he told her firmly. "Not now. Not ever."

Hex was a gorgeous mess of long, black hair, her just-kissed lips still wet from his tongue. She stood there with her boots spread, breathing hard, and her plump girls heaving beneath that tiny tee. "Pagan, I—"

He reached for those plump, moist lips and ran the pad of his thumb across the bottom one. Walking away from an offer of free sex that would've been out of this world, but would've also been so damned wrong. "I'm not that guy," he told her gently before he changed his still-considering-the-offer, red-blooded, all-male mind. "I don't go through women like Kruze does. I'm not made that way. Sex has to mean something for me. Sorry."

Her nose wrinkled. "Kruze? What's he got to do with this? With us?"

"There is no us, Victoria. I've got" —he ran a quick hand over his head, not sure what he'd just heard in her voice or why he'd called her by her full name— "I've got to go." *Before this night gets any weirder.*

Her fingers hit his wrist, clutching him before he got away. "I'm... I'm sorry. I... I didn't know that you...." Her voice trailed off to a throaty whisper.

That got his pride's attention. "That I what?"

Her head came up and her eyes flashed. "Never mind. Go Just go."

Pagan couldn't help but nod. If he lived to be a hundred, he'd never understand how the female mind worked. "Fine then. Bye."

Finally at Mills' rear doorway, it hit Pagan hard. Something was wrong with this picture, but damned if he knew what it was or how to fix it. Victoria had looked and sounded sad—or something. But turning back was not an option. No doubt, she'd read weakness into a weak-kneed, dumb-jock move like that. To Hex, love was nothing but a kill-or-be-killed game, and he didn't play that way. He just plain didn't have the heart for it.

Yet he couldn't stop his big mouth from asking, "Are you sure you'll be okay?"

Why wouldn't she be? She was every bit the assassin he was, and why the holy hell was he suddenly feeling protective? Of her? Of all the females in the universe, she needed no man on her six. Not unless he was there for a quickie.

Victoria stood there in the dark, alone again, but not as cocky as before. Her arms crossed over her magnificent chest, but her chin was down, her hair a thick black curtain hiding her face. "Yeah, fine. No worries," she replied without looking up, her voice unusually tight and—small.

Pagan slanted a curious look. What was that very un-Hex-like tone in her voice about?

"Tell your brothers hi for me. Later."

"Will do." And that was that. Pagan shut the door behind him. He had a flight to catch. Like the way it ended or not, this mission was over. He was on his way home to Montana—until his wide shoulders turned all by themselves. Until he found himself facing the door he'd just closed instead of the fast getaway he'd planned. Until his fingers turned Johnny Boy's backdoor knob one last time.

"Oh, hell. What's one beer?"

Chapter One

"Excuse me?" Pagan wasn't sure he'd heard Chance correctly. "You want me to end who?"

Chance Sinclair, his oldest brother and the leader of the SOB black ops team affectionately nicknamed Sin Boys, stared from beneath thick dark lashes. Unblinking. Unreadable.

At the moment, all three brothers were in different locations. Chance, in their Montana headquarters handling the business end of, well, the business of running the covert black ops team known as the Sin Boys. Pagan didn't begrudge his oldest brother that seemingly easier workload, not since Chance had recently married the only woman who'd ever turned his hard head.

After the tragic loss Chance had recently suffered in South America, when his SEAL team found themselves ambushed, Pagan didn't begrudge his big brother anything. He was just thankful Chance was still alive and finally back to being himself again. His pretty wife Suede had everything to do with that.

Pagan himself was hanging out in southern Alabama, waiting for his flight back home after a particularly distasteful job. But that white supremacist with subversive and perverse Al-Qaeda ties, the guy with the end goal of kicking off an American-style Islamic caliphate? The redneck with the big mouth and the bigger opinion of himself? The one who'd thought his merry band of assassins would further his cause if they bombed every school bus on the first day back to school? Uh-uh, no way. Not happening in Montgomery. Not in Chickasaw or Mobile, either. Bubba Dumb Butt was currently toe-tagged and blank-eyed on some morgue's freezer tray, alongside three of his best assassin buddies thanks to Pagan's dead-eye.

Kruze, brother number two, was on assignment in Houston assisting the SOB team known only as Night Shadows. Comprised of nobody knew precisely who, the Shadows did the dirtiest work of all the teams. They were the darkest of the dark, the covert empire builders and the destroyers of political kingdoms and ambitions. Think Pablo Escobar, Saddam Hussein, or Idi Amin. Think the various mystery assassinations on far-off continents that terrorists had yet to take credit for—but most definitely would if they thought there was a modicum of power or influence to be gained. Yeah, them.

The Shadows were the ultimate powerbrokers behind polished, politically correct and diplomatic scenes. They were the unseen guys and gals who toppled regimes and dictatorships. What Kruze was doing with or for them, Pagan had no idea. The call had come in way above his pay grade, and a smart man knew when to mind his Ps and Qs. If Senator McQueen Sullivan, the man who operated the SOB teams, had wanted Pagan to know Kruze's mission, he'd have told him. Plain and simple. M.Y.O.B.

"You heard me, brothers. Victoria Hex is our next assignment," Chance repeated, his tone deliberate, soft, and low.

Pagan jostled his laptop monitor, picking up on Chance's unease. It wasn't often the Sin Boys were called out to end a woman, much less a friend, which, like it or not, Victoria Hex was.

"As of noon today, we're the final vote of concurrence. All other teams have agreed with the evidence provided. She's gone rogue, and the CIA's provided adequate and substantive backup to support their request for an assist from Sullivan. We greenlight this kill and—"

"Is McQueen serious? He honestly thinks we're going to end Hex?" Kruze hissed all the way from Houston, his face lean and edgy and too damned close to the monitor, making the end of his nose look larger and wider than it was.

Took you long enough to engage. Pagan had expected that question long before now given his brother's perpetual dalliances with anything in skirts.

But really? Victoria? "Does Julio know?" Pagan asked.

Julio Juarez was Victoria's older and only brother, and the reason she was considered a friend in this nightmare scenario. In Pagan's opinion, Victoria was no real threat, just eye candy. He'd nearly taken her up on an offer to hang out and have a beer a month ago, but like the snake Julio's little sister was and always would be, Vicki vanished without a trace, left him high and dry. Not like Pagan hadn't seen that brush-off coming. Miss Vicki didn't care for him, and he absolutely never thought twice about her.

But really? Victoria? You want me to kill Vicki? WTF?

"Of course not." Chance shook his head at Kruze's question, but seemingly answered Pagan's unspoken doubt as well. "Sullivan doesn't run these kills by anyone but team leaders. You guys know that. And we've got another problem. JJ's been off the grid for months. Hasn't answered any of my calls or texts since he lost his son. I honestly don't know where he is. Do you, Kruze?"

Kruze ran a hand over his head. "Haven't kept track of him. Sorry. Been busy." *Well, shit.* "What'd Vicki do to merit a double tap?"

"Sullivan's got hard evidence she's turned." Chance's tone offered not one hint of enthusiasm for this job. If anything, he sounded as doubt-ridden as Pagan felt. "He's got multiple photos of Miss Hex with Vito Seranzino, others of her chumming with Dillon Roberto."

Pagan growled. "Isn't that her job, to swim with the sharks? Chumming, isn't that what—wait. Who's her handler anyway?"

"CIA Special Agent Dane Rich, but..." Chance murmured as another phone rang on his end and his gaze drifted from his screen. "Wait. I'll tell you two more later. I've got to take this call."

"Copy that," Kruze replied as both his and Chance's faces faded to black.

Unsettled and feeling like someone had just walked over his grave, Pagan kicked back from the hotel desk where he'd set his equipment prior to departure. It didn't matter what evidence this federal schmuck had on Hex, if assassinating women was what his future held, it might be time to rethink this whole black-ops SOBs team concept.

Yes, Victoria Hex was an outright paradox in the female gender and in the covert world of blacker than black ops. Maybe she deserved to die, maybe she didn't. But a long time ago, Pagan had drawn the line at offing children or anyone of the female persuasion. Assholes, yes. They were different, and, surprise, surprise. Most assholes were testosterone-poisoned males, outright psychotic narcissists, or sexual deviants who got off on torturing anyone weaker or smaller. Else they were whack jobs in powerful positions who thought they were above the order of law, truth, and justice because they had more money than God.

But deep down, Pagan hadn't ever met a woman he'd truly wanted to kill. Yet. He doubted, as vexing as Hex could be, that she'd be his first. Julio's sister wasn't evil. She just wasn't Pagan's idea of a real woman.

In the hard scrabble world he lived in, he and his former Navy SEAL brothers answered only to the dynamic Senator McQueen Sullivan, Texas. Known for getting the hard and impossible jobs done, McQueen managed six of the blackest black op teams on the federal payroll.

Funded from invisible money that didn't exist on any budget plan or forecast, each team operated outside the confines of the law. Yet all were comprised of special operators who'd honorably served. Whether former military, CIA, or FBI, none of the team members took this assignment lightly. Each decision to end a life required unanimous votes from the individual team leaders. At that point, the designated leader—this time, Chance—decided who on his team performed the actual hit.

No reports would be filed afterward. No evidence would be gathered at the scene of the kill. Neither would any records or audit trails be maintained. Once the selected agent—in this case, Pagan—reported job complete, the SOBs would all move onto the next in line, be that douchebag a murderer, rapist, or just another psychopath.

But really? Victoria Hex?

It seemed an unfathomable mission, not because he couldn't do it, but because Pagan truly loved women. Not like Kruze loved women, though. Hell, no. Kruze was the raunchy, bad boy in the family, the love 'em and leave 'em brother who ate women for dinner, but never for breakfast.

But Pagan was different. Born the third and last son of Scarlett Sinclair, the world famous, successful, and most-perfect mother on earth—God rest her soul—he didn't ascribe to the generally accepted, politically correct propaganda that women were created equal, either. True, if they worked the same job as a guy, they should be paid the same. But like it or not, politically correct or not, Pagan knew damned well that men and women had been created differently.

Men were like drones to the queen bee. They were the robots that lifted their sorry tired asses out of bed each day, went to work, and lived for the sublime joy of protecting that queen and any children that queen produced. Men did the hard, ugly jobs, so their women didn't have to. They died for their women and children. Least that's how it was supposed to work.

Not like Pagan had any life experiences with that kind of father in his life. But yeah, a woman's real job, her natural niche in society, was to bear children and keep the home fires burning, while that faithful—key word, *faithful*—male she loved, humped his sorry ass out the door every morning and brought home the bacon every night. Right?

Not that Scarlett had lived that way, but she would have if the deadbeat she'd married had been an actual man instead of a loser and a runaround drunk. That was the problem with this world. If everyone had stuck to the original program as Nature intended, if men were real men and honored their wives, then women would be real women and stay at home where they belonged. There'd be no equality crisis, because there simply wouldn't be a need for one. Children would grow up loved and sheltered inside happy families, and... and... everyone would be happy, damn it.

Ah, bullshit. The rant sounded good inside his head, but Pagan knew better. Life wasn't simple. Neither were men. And women were complex as hell. In so many ways, they were better than men, and his mother had proved it in aces the way she'd lived her life and raised three boys all by herself.

But if he ever married—and that *if* was a definite stretch into the far, far off future—Pagan's ideal woman would be a lot like Scarlett Sinclair. Damned straight. She'd put her man and her family first, and if that meant taking a back seat to the action in order to nurture the little ones at home, so be it. There was a natural order to things. Pagan damned well knew there was.

But really? Victoria Hex?

She was nothing like Scarlett. Wasn't even in the same universe. Hex wore plenty of leather and flaunted pink-handled nines, for hell's sake. She worked undercover for the Mafia. Covert or not, Julio's sweet baby sister or not, keeping up that twisted charade had to involve Vicki getting her dainty little hands not just dirty, but filthy, bloody dirty. How many men, women, and children had she killed for good old Vito Seranzino? Or for his aged father, the infamous Cabbrieli Seranzino of Black Friday fame?

Named after the bloody shootout in one of Chicago's upscale mall parking lots, and the grisly deaths of four FBI agents, one of them by garrote during that melee, the Black Friday Massacre remained unsolved. Old man Cabbrieli had never been indicted, though every lawman in the metropolis knew he'd ordered the hit.

Bastard should have fried for the ambush, but the guy and his family were Teflon-coated. Lo and behold, the mall's brand-new security system suffered an unrecoverable glitch that day. Go figure the odds of that happening. Then federal prosecutors lost track of their five—count 'em, five—eyewitnesses who'd previously sworn they could ID Cabb and a couple of his men. Still hadn't located any of those bodies. While three of Cabb's men were wounded at the scene and went into the federal prison system, not a one accepted immunity in exchange for inside info.

Pagan wasn't sure if Hex had been there in that Chicago parking terrace that day, but a couple of those FBI casualties were her style. She tended to aim for hands, shoulders, or ankles, as opposed to heads or abdomens when it came to the boys in blue. Or whatever the FBI agents wore that day. But still. How could any woman, undercover or not, turn her back on the country she'd pledged allegiance to?

He rubbed a hand over his hard head, sure he was missing something. And maybe he was. But one thing Pagan knew for a fact. He wasn't killing a woman, especially Victoria Hex, just because some federal dick said he should.

Chapter Two

"Because I'm tired," Vicki told her CIA handler, Special Agent Dane Rich.

Per some unwritten law only assholes knew and religiously adhered to, his gaze slipped down her neck, between the zipper teeth of her tight leather jacket, until it ended at the soft mounds of her very plump girls. As expected, he licked his lips, and an ugly, salacious smile cracked his oatmeal-toned face. The pasty white perv.

"Yes, they're real, and no..." *You dick!* "...you can't touch them," she snapped to get his wandering gaze off her chest and back to the *I-mean-business* glare on her *I-am-so-sick-of-taking-this-bullshit-from-you* face.

Dane had always been a sleazy creep, from the top of his Brylcreemed, perfectly combed, never-gonna-fly-away-even-in-a-hurricane dishwater-blond hair,

to his spit and polished, brand-squeaky-new Target—
or was that *Tar-zhe?*—penny-loafers. Argyle socks?
Go figure. There was a name for federal agents who
barely qualified for the government positions they
held—deadweight. But 'asshole' worked for this guy.

Vicki had been undercover inside the Sicilian
Mafia most of her career. When pressed, she'd often
passed herself off as working for the Drug
Enforcement Agency, Federal Bureau of Misfits, aka
the FBI, or the good old boys in ATF, the Bureau of
Alcohol, Tobacco, and Firearms. Actually, she worked
for an unnamed federal agency buried deep within
the muddled bureaucracy of the Central Intelligence
Agency.

But during her early years of damned tough
assignments and skillful misdirection, her brother
Julio lost his wife and child to a madman from South
America, one deranged psychopath named Domingo
Zapata. For five long years, Zapata had kept Bianca
and sweet little Tomas caged like animals inside his
private compound. He'd tormented, tortured, and
psychologically destroyed them with his demented
fetishes.

And for those same five long years, Julio had
faithfully served not only the President of the United
States as a deep undercover agent, but he'd served
two of Colombia's most sadistic drug lords, Viktor
Patrone and Benito Garcia, as well. Known as the
Godfather of all South American godfathers, at one
time Patrone ran a wickedly cruel cartel that

eliminated competitors by fire, gutting, or beheading. Crucifixions. You name it. Garcia hadn't been much worse, though he'd also dabbled in human trafficking.

But now they were both gone, their lives extinguished in a massive fireball off South America. Which was fitting. Death by fire. If one were a romantic, one could almost believe Satan himself had inhaled and sucked them back to Hell. Now that'd be something to smile about.

But Vicki knew better. The only Satan on this planet was mankind. It was the Sinclairs who'd ended Patrone and Garcia on an illegal and unauthorized infil into South America. But the total annihilation of the tiny island where Patrone, Garcia, and that diabolical Mitchell Franks had died? The hellfire that had effectively obliterated all evidence that the Sinclairs had been there? That was on Julio.

Watching him suffer these long, empty years had taken all of Vicki's heart and soul. Just doing his job. Just waiting for the intel he'd desperately needed to locate his wife and son. By the time he'd finally rescued them, they were no longer the sweet wife or happy son he'd lost.

Gone was pretty blonde Bianca's easy smile and sharp wit. One year to the day that Julio had taken them back to Southern California, she slit her wrists and walked into the Pacific Ocean. Tomas followed her in death a month later. That sweet baby boy had never recovered from the years of living on a steady diet of fear and starvation. Doctors termed what eventually took him as a profound failure to thrive. Vicki called it murder.

Which was why she'd smiled when both Viktor and Benito had died like they did. They were the puppet masters behind Domingo Zapata. Tried and found guilty of acts of terrorism, Zapata languished— she hoped—in an unnamed federal prison. What she wouldn't do to name that stronghold, then storm it to avenge her brother's loss. Maybe then she could sleep again. She knew for certain that Julio did not. More's the shame.

The only good that came out of that long five years of wasted time and hope was that Patrone's and Garcia's buddies were dead now. Among them Wilhelm Gonzales, the elusive behind-the-scenes Mitchell Franks, the playboy tennis player Lionel York, and the local wannabe-godfather, Johnny Wesley Mills.

But poor Julio was as broken now as Bianca had been when she'd set foot on United States soil the last time. It didn't seem fair that a man as good and honest as her brother should've drawn the short end of the stick in this wickedly cruel game called Life.

At the end of the day, it seemed to her that he was the one who'd truly paid for Zapata and his bosses' crimes in America. If she could, Vicki would dig up their dead bodies, resurrect them, breathe life back into them, let them believe they deserved a second chance, then gut every last one of them. Over and over. Again and again. Bastards. Soulless bastards.

On an intellectual level, she knew better. Every living, breathing person in the world today, especially the innocent victims caught in the drug and sex trades, benefited when evil died. Their parents. Their families. Everyone won when evil lost.

What was wrong with people these days? In barely concealed frustration, Vicki ran her fingers through her thick, black tangles. Even the very generic labels—drug and sex trade—reeked of political correctness. Those words whitewashed evil. They made marketing Death a tradable commodity on Wall Street instead of the degenerate human defilement it was. They trivialized the suffering of women and children the world over.

Let's call it what it is, people. Murder. Rape. Torture. Fix the real problem. Go after every last drug or porn pusher and end them!

So yeah. With news of sweet Tomas's death only months ago, she'd lost her perspective and her nerve. Her heart. Vicki was tired of fighting a war she couldn't win. It was five long years past time to leave this deceiver's life she'd chosen during her first year in college. Back then, she'd been filled with the patriotism and ideals of her new country, America. No more. She needed to come in from the world, and for once, Rich needed to not be the prick in her back who pushed her under yet another fast-moving train.

"Times are tough for everyone," he volleyed back at her. Sitting in his chair with one ankle cocked over his knee, he worked that mechanical pencil in his fingers like a cheerleader with a baton. Back and forth it ticked before he skillfully rotated it between his fingers and thumb. Cocky shit. He made it look easy, but it was his way of keeping her distracted.

Sorry. Not impressed with your digital skills, if you get my drift.

Because Dane had purposely not allowed any other chairs in his office, Vicki was forced to stand in front of his desk like a naughty schoolgirl about to be disciplined. Which was why he always stayed behind his designed-to-look-like-real-oak, government-issued, piece-of-pressed-wood. Or cedar or pine or— shit. She didn't know wood except for the block sitting between his taxi-cab-door ears. Damned things were big enough. He could make Dumbo's mother proud. Might even be able to fly.

Striving for patience, her gaze scrolled past his thick skull to the plate glass window behind him. Speaking of flying... She'd made a few of her 'jobs' fly. One didn't get deep inside the Sicilian mob without offing a few, ahem, unmentionable targets in the process. Yes, she'd carried out her orders like the soldier she'd been trained to be. What Mafia narc didn't? In her line of work, the *Seranzino familia* was everything.

But she'd made sure those targets were as dirty as the Don she supposedly worshipped before she'd followed through with her assigned hits. Not once had she killed an innocent, and she'd always— ALWAYS—found a plausible excuse for not killing any innocent bystanders. Never women. Never children. Uh-uh. Vicki was not a sloppy assassin. She abhorred collateral damage.

But the asshole men and women who'd thought they'd owned the world and everyone in it? Lying thugs willing to stab each other in back alleys or gun each other down to make a buck? To make a name for themselves. They were another story.

Up to now, Vicki had built a solid, albeit coldblooded rep inside the mob. She was their go-to girl for international contracts. When hits required a delicate touch, they called her.

You want a certain Monaco casino owner's head on a plate or in someone's bed? *Coming right up.*

You need a certain package delivered to a certain mayor or the dictator in a certain country, no questions asked? *Consider it done.*

People in the business said she was *'gifted'*. They said she had a *'way.'* All she wanted now was a way out.

Dumbo tapped the eraser end of his pencil on his desk. "Hey, Hex. You listening to me or what?"

She snorted, startled she'd actually zoned out on the man who could recommend her return to civilian life. "I'm always listening to you, Dane," she replied, keeping her tone under control and coldly professional. Anything else would encourage his wandering eyeballs.

"I might be able to help you," he said as he gave her cleavage another once over. "I know some important people. But you've got to make it worth my while, know what I mean?"

"And that means what?" *Lap dance? Blow job? Knife in your fucking throat?* That last one actually appealed to Vicki. It was certainly doable given her *gift*.

Agent Rich cocked his head as if appraising her talent, albeit the wrong one. He sniffed, then tugged a used tissue from his shirt pocket and blew his nose. At last, he tossed the extra-nasty tissue in the trash, leaned both elbows to the edge of his desk, and leered at her.

The Agency had to have been stone cold desperate when they'd hired this guy.

"I've got one last job for you."

She shook her head, and of course, he zeroed in on the jiggle that caused in her boobs. "Up here," she told him, fluttering her middle finger at him. Not like he saw that rude gesture from where his eyes were currently glued. The ass.

Still looking at her girls, he mumbled, "Bring Dillon in, and I'll put in a good word for you."

"Dillon?" she deadpanned. "Really? *Just* bring Dillon in. That's all?"

Dillon Roberto was the Sicilian mob's number one money laundering guy and the notorious owner of one of Chicago's largest casinos. The guy was rarely seen in public, but when he was, he traveled with an entourage of bodyguards that made the President's Secret Service look like a troop of Girl Scouts.

"You got a problem with following orders, Hex?"

She ran a fingernail down her jaw, struggling to keep her cool. "Let me get this straight. I ask you for a leave of absence, and you turn my simple request for time-off into a case of insubordination?"

Dane's jaw twitched as he dragged his gaze from her breasts, up her neck, and finally ended on her face. "No. You bring Dillon in, and we both get what we want." Which meant he needed her to make him look good, something he could never do on his own.

"This is the last time," she breathed. "I'm done after this job. I want out."

Dane nodded. Just once. Very deliberately. Like he held the power over her life and death in his sweaty hands. "Should be simple for a gal like you. Word on the street is Dillon's making a move to take over Vito's business. He's making waves. We bring Dillon down" —he fluttered his fingers like he was making stardust— "and presto, change-o. Your Sicilian boss no longer has an enemy in Chicago. Capisce?"

Capisce? Really? The temptation to roll her eyes was strong with this one. Instead, Vicki went with a solid, "Humph. Are you sure of your sources? Vito hasn't said anything to me about Dillon."

"Your boss may not know he's on his way out. I know you like Vito, but the guy's not a god, for Christ's sake."

Well, well, well. Agent limp-dick Rich actually got something right. Vicki did like Vito and his father

Cabb, but not for the perverse, older-man-with-a-hot-young-chick-on-his-arm reason Dane implied. Yes, her Mafia bosses always treated Vicki with respect. Yes, Vito could get unreasonably temperamental when she didn't apply the level of coldblooded force he'd requested while offing specific adversaries. But he'd always listened, and she knew he considered her more of a loyal friend—maybe even as a daughter—than just an employee. Hey, whatever worked.

Vicki studied Dane's instant acceptance of what she'd just stated, that she was close to Vito. Either Dane was as stupid as he looked, or he already knew how frightened she was of her Mafia association. And that was concerning.

Because Vito Seranzino was as close to being Satan as any man Vicki had ever met. He owned and personally controlled the Sicilian mob in Chicago from the ground up. He answered to no one except his aged father, Cabbrieli Seranzino, who now lived in Germany, since the Sicilian government had recently declared war on the Mafia in their homeland, for Christ's sake. Which in and of itself, was no great trouble.

Interesting side note: Cabbrieli was Sicilian for *Gabriel*. But the son of an angel of God, Vito was not. Still, at times, Vito was putty in her hands. At least he listened, which was more than Vicki could say for her handler.

Agent Rich snapped his fingers. "Yes or no, Hex? Wake up and spit it out. What's it going to be?" That damned pencil drummed nervously on the desktop as his round, piggish little eyes once more zeroed back to her cleavage.

"Yes," she hissed to get his attention off her boobs. "I'll do it, but know this, Richie Rich. I want out, and if you string me along like you did last time, I'll go over your head so fast, your ass will play hell catching up."

He nodded his chin at her, contempt flaring his recently cleared nostrils. "Get out of my office. People will talk."

She turned on her heel. "They already are." *Only they're all saying, 'You're a dick, Dane!'*

Chapter Three

Vicki woke up coughing. Make that suffocating. Wheezing! Make that dying. Choking! Frantic, with her mouth full of easily inhaled dirt instead of fresh air, the need to breathe pre-empted her innate sense of caution. This was one of those times when there was no try. Only do. And do it fast!

Clawing at the loose soil tamped over and around her, she made it quickly—if there were such a thing as quick enough when a person has just woken up in a grave—to the surface of wherever she'd been buried. Jesus H. Christ!

The night was thick and dark, cool and damp around her as she choked and spat out the dirt even as she inhaled deeply, sucking some of it deep into her airways.

Choke. Sputter. Breathe, breathe, breathe. Then choke and cough some more while waiting there in the dark on her hands and knees with her head down and her heart in the throat. Afraid to move. Praying that whoever'd done this to her was far, far away by now. He, she, or they, might be watching. They might've hung around to make sure she didn't rise from the dead.

At last certain she was alone in the dark, with her throat and gut tenderized from retching and vomiting mud, she collapsed face down. Breathing hard. But breathing.

Who could have done this? Who dared? And how? When? Fighting a number twenty migraine on a scale of one to ten, Vicki couldn't remember any details of a fight or a comeuppance or of being overpowered. Only the rude awakening to a dirt bath.

But someone hadn't done their job correctly or she would be dead. Obviously. Instead, that idiot had only injured her, then buried her in a shallow grave. Big mistake. For him.

Focused and actually able to breathe without inhaling more dirt, Vicki rolled to her back. She ran trembling hands over her heaving chest, down her aching belly, and then up to her neck and ended at her pounding head. Searching. Feeling. Praying she'd find no bullet or knife hole. Which she didn't.

She was still alive, and just touching her skin, grimy as it was, brought never experienced before sensations to life. Her fingertips were raw and tender, but warm. Her poor heart still pounded, but it was working and working overtime at that. Even her lungs were back online, inhaling and exhaling like they should. Wasn't it a true miracle to just lay here and breathe and breathe and breathe?

For once in her life, Vicki lay still, thankful for every beat of her heart.

The midnight stars overhead were bright. Sparkling. No moon hung in the sky, but man, those stars. She'd never looked at them before like she looked at them now, in wonder and gratitude. There were so, so many. Had to be the Milky Way spread above her like a magic carpet in a velvet black universe. Nothing dramatic as a star falling happened next, though, not that she needed to wish on a falling star or anything. No. She was alive. Alive! Just knowing she'd been given a second chance was more than enough.

The night air felt amazingly cool on her dry, burning throat. Her eyes watered, but not from the mud still filtering around her eyeballs. Nah. They watered because she was alive and breathing, and the gentle breeze wafting over her feverish skin was blessing than enough.

Swallowing hard, but not going to cry, damn it!—she dashed any hint of weakness away and took quick inventory. There were no knife wounds or bullet holes on her body, which would've ensured her imminent demise. No sign of a graze or flesh wound. Only the large knot above her right ear that testified to how she'd ended up here, wherever *here* was.

Someone had definitely bludgeoned her. How sloppy of her not to have fought back, not to have realized she'd been stalked in the first place. But whoever had gotten the best of her was an amateur. Any professional hitman worth his salt would've put a bullet in her brain instead of a bump behind her ear.

Growling to clear her throat, Vicki reviewed what she thought she knew. Last night, as were most of her nights, had been boring at best. Provided Vito didn't have her on stand-by for one of his jobs, downtime was just a quick combat nap between those illicit jobs and watching over her shoulder.

She recalled that she'd sent another quick, encrypted report to her handler in DC, that yes. This time, Phillipe Ventura, the elite and tremendously talented assassin from Madrid, was truly dead, thanks to her sharpshooting skills. Never again would the dirtbag kill another child for sport. Not that that was why Vicki had taken Ventura out. No, Vito ordered the hit because Phil refused to acknowledge the Seranzino familia's encroaching authority on Spanish streets. And everyone knew what happened to those who didn't kneel to the Godfather. They became gruesome examples of what *will* happen to others.

After that, Vicki had gone home to her penthouse apartment overlooking Lake Michigan, the one Vito Seranzino insisted she occupy at his expense. It made her look like a kept woman, which she was not, but Vicki had overcome her conscience and her strict religious upbringing to get close to Vito. Over the years, she'd created a strong working persona that defied who and what she really was inside. That was the life of an undercover operator. One had to play the part, dress the part, and be willing to kill or die for that part.

Which was why she hadn't contacted Julio since Tomas had passed. She couldn't. To reach out to anyone but a member of the Seranzino Familia, for any reason, would alter her current reality, and she couldn't let that happen. Too much blood, sweat, and tears had gone into her current *diva-hit-woman* reputation. To so much as hint that she had a brother would've brought down her house of cards, not only swiftly, but with deadly consequences. Not for her, but for Julio. And that simply would not happen. She'd do anything to protect Julio, even die.

After scanning through her mail, then checking her computer, the one she knew for certain Vito had bugged, she'd taken a hot shower to scrape the sins of her devious undercover life off her body. Which explained why she was now barefoot, wearing her black workout pants and what once had been a pure white tank top.

Frightened for the first time in years, Vicki rolled to her knees, then climbed shakily to her feet. Anxiously, she raked her thick, tangled hair out of her face and tossed it back over her shoulder. Someone meant to kill her. The second they knew she still lived, they'd be back. They'd try again.

With her heart pounding in her ears, she scanned the forest around her. Suddenly it wasn't so friendly. The stars had gone brittle and cold. Even the air slithered like a silent viper over her bare feet.

It was past time to move, but she couldn't go home. That was where she'd been before she'd woken up here. Vito had to be behind this take down, damn his conniving, lying soul. If Satan ever had a child, it'd surely be Vito Seranzino.

More sure of herself now, Vicki pulled her hair into an efficient, out-of-her-way ponytail, securing it easily with a strand of her own hair. She'd planned for this exact scenario. It had always been bound to happen. All she needed now was to catch a cab to the bus station and to key in the combination to the locker where she kept her emergency bug-out bag and a few bills.

After she paid the cabbie with that same money, she'd have him drop her at the downtown Denny's on Chicago's East Side, where Beverly, an actual friend, worked graveyard. Vicki's last resort, a bare-bones apartment with a fire escape out the window, lay five blocks east of that restaurant. After a quick meal and some coffee, and once she made certain no one followed her, she'd slip inside that apartment, shower, grab a quick nap if the coast was clear, then disappear for good. No one would ever know what happened here tonight. Not her brother. Not the man she'd once thought she could fall in love with. Not the bastard who'd thought she'd stay in that grave.

Vicki dusted her dirty, ragged hands on her dirty, ragged pants. Then she took off running, headed for the steady glow on the horizon. It wasn't Chicago, she was certain of that. But whatever town or suburb it was, it was good enough.

Chapter Four

The locked door Pagan couldn't break into hadn't yet been created. Once inside Victoria Hex's lair, which turned out to be nothing more than a crappy, nondescript couple of rooms in a tenement-style apartment complex on Chicago's East Side, he shut the sturdy wooden door quietly behind him. After making certain he was alone, he crossed the nearly empty living room and lowered to his haunches in the farthest, darkest corner beside the only piece of furniture, a ratty purple, green, and black plaid couch. He loosened the zipper on his black leather jacket, put both loaded and ready-to-go pistols on the floor beside him, and he did what he did best. Pagan took off his black nitrile gloves and settled down to wait.

This place was not what he'd expected to find Miss Hex living in, though. True, it was the address her handler, Special Agent Dane Rich, had on file for her, but the apartment had a barren, almost unlived-in feel to it. There were no pictures on the walls and no clothes in the closets. No magazines on the plain wooden coffee table. He'd found no toiletries in the bathroom and no sign that a woman had slept overnight here. No rumpled clothes on the floor. No nightgowns on the end of the bed. Even the sheets were clean and unwrinkled. Which basically told Pagan what he already knew. Hex didn't live here.

But if this place were nothing more than a misdirect that she maintained, a façade with no real substance behind it, where did the buxom dominatrix run to when the burdens of life and her chosen profession grew too heavy to bear? Pagan went to the wilds of Montana after completing an ugly job. There in the quiet solitude of the Sinclair high mountain retreat, stood the huge, rustic, family cabin where he had two brothers to confide in while he licked his wounds. Make that one brother. Chance was always ready to listen, but Kruze had never been big on brotherly love or conversation, unless it was about him.

With Julio missing, who did Victoria have? Anyone?

For some reason, the thought of her being alone and forgotten, maybe neglected by her brother, bothered Pagan. But no matter. Like her, he also had a job to do, and tonight he intended to make first, maybe last, contact with his target. If she didn't show, well, he'd have to dig harder to locate her. Maybe cruise over to the Seranzino mansion. Old man Cabb would surely know where she really lived. Of course, Pagan would have to go through Vito to get to Cabb, but that was doable.

He grunted to himself. That was probably where he should've started looking for Victoria in the first place instead of relying on what Agent Rich from the Agency had on file for her. There was something wrong with that guy, and Pagan intended to find out what that something was, but first, Hex. He had to locate and neutralize Vicki Hex.

Pagan waited patiently, a skill he'd developed during long missions on his stint with SEAL Team Three. Talk about a dream job. If not for the double hit his family had taken a year ago, when Scarlett Sinclair passed away from cancer at the same time that Chance had nearly died on an op in South America, Pagan would still be wheels-up and off somewhere in the world with his Navy compadres.

But yeah. The tragedy impacted Chance in ways Pagan hadn't expected. Suddenly, his very capable and overly confident big brother turned into a timid, reticent hermit who wanted nothing more than to be left alone. He took a medical from the Navy. If not for the out-of-sight job offer from Senator Sullivan to join his elite black ops team, coupled with the bizarre way Chance had met his wife, the former bad girl, Suede Tennyson, Pagan knew Chance would still be hiding out in Montana instead of managing the tightest covert ship in Sullivan's private fleet.

Which made Pagan more than a little jealous. Suede's sudden appearance in Chance's life had worked the miracle no amount of coaxing, bullying, or logic could have with his brother. Chance was himself again, running into the wind, full sails ahead, instead of running away from life and the battles of it.

Pagan wanted that same connection. Not with Suede, mind you, but with a woman just as worthy. Just as strong. He wanted a woman to look at him the way she looked up at Chance. He'd seen the adoration in her pretty eyes. It was as if the world stopped turning when he came into the room. Yeah, that was what Pagan wanted. A woman to serve and protect. To adore and worship. Someday...

Inhaling deeply, he shoved that very special thing that Chance had with Suede out of his head. He stretched while he waited. This could take a while. And it did.

The sun came up. The sun went down. Night fell, and another day was wasted. With it went Pagan's hope of easily locating Victoria Hex. He secured his weapons, arched his aching back, then lifted to his feet. Locating a mark on a first attempt was a long shot anyway. At best, it was a stupid idea. Knowing Victoria, she was probably out busting some guy's balls, maybe taking down one of Vito's enemies in a dark alley somewhere. Stalking her prey. Cleaning her pretty pink-handled pistols in preparation for another day. Or something just as professional.

Twisting sharply to the right to loosen the kink in his lower vertebrae, Pagan growled at the idea that he might not be as flexible as he used to be. He wasn't getting any younger. Damn it. Age and a lifetime of hard knocks, some of them intentional, were catching up with him. Suede might just be right. It was time to see that chiropractor she kept recommending.

Pagan had his gloves back on and he was at the door and headed out to find something to eat when he heard it. Someone was on the metal fire escape stairs outside Victoria's fake apartment. They'd barely clanked, but that one muffled thump against squeaking steel was enough. Silently, he drifted back into position as the only window in the tiny room slid silently upward. A slender arm, then an elbow, slipped between the closed drapes.

He cocked his head, needing to identify this infiltrator before whoever it was made him. It didn't take long, but damn. Victoria was sneaking into her own place—through the window? How interesting. Yet there the sassy dominatrix crouched. Her feet were bare, and her hands clutching the edge of the sill between her bent legs. She tossed her thick black hair out of her face. Like a spider testing the air before she committed herself to entry, her nostrils flared.

This was not how he saw a woman as glamorous as Victoria coming and going. What was up with her? Cocking his head, he waited to see what she'd do next.

Hidden in the darkened room like he was, Pagan had all the time in the world. After watching and listening for nearly five minutes, Victoria blew out a small sigh. Tugging a small backpack off her shoulder, she unfolded those long legs next. She lowered one bare foot—and that was another thing, where were her boots?—and slid noiselessly off the sill and into the room. The curtain barely moved behind her.

He knew then that she had never used the door. This apartment was a setup, just an address to satisfy her CIA handler, and the jerk had never followed up or investigated his covert agent like he should have. He'd taken her at her word, which meant Agent Rich had also never set foot inside this apartment. Pagan allowed a quiet breath. For whatever reason, that detail offered a heady dose of relief. Victoria and Rich weren't getting it on, at least, not here.

Turning sideways but keeping an eye on the exit door to her apartment, she turned around and lowered the window, locked it, and pulled the light-darkening drapes back into place. Only then did she press a light switch on the wall beside the drape— right before she launched herself like a rocket at him, one of her bare feet aimed at his face.

Jumping up, Pagan gave her his shoulder. When she struck, he reached out, grabbed and twisted her ankle, rotating her body away from him just as she'd made contact. Like some Ninja fighter out of a Jackie Chan movie, she flipped and landed on her feet, only to attack him again, this time with the lightning swift moves of a pissed off black-belt. Not like he didn't have those exact same skills.

Without any words of friendly greeting, they hacked at each other's biceps and forearms with the knife edge of their hands. Blow after blow, grunt after grunt, they parried as if they'd practiced a thousand times for this exact scenario. All the while, they delivered brutal, bruising kicks to the other's thighs and buttocks. Yet not once in this whirling dervish dance of two powerfully trained assassins, did either land a punch devastating enough to incapacitate the other.

Sweaty now, Hex blew strands of her hair that had come undone from her ponytail off her face.

Barely sweating at all, Pagan found the deadly dynamics between them refreshing in a weirdly arousing way. This woman was no lightweight, but her tank top was, and beneath that tank top, those girls of hers were unleashed and the tips were peaked as hard as diamonds. What a sight. He'd taken on Athena, the goddess of wisdom and war, and he was loving it.

Down boy. He was aroused like he'd never been before, and toying with her now. Throwing her purposefully off-balance. Chancing a sly grin when he wasn't getting his face slapped or his jaw smacked. She was just a woman. She'd tire soon, and then he'd—

WHUMP! Down he went. Flat on his back. The wind knocked out of him. He hadn't seen that combination kick coming. She *was* good.

Damned if she didn't climb aboard, her knees alongside his hips, and her overheated core plastered over his belly. It would've been a dream come true if she'd been naked, and if she hadn't pressed a knife to his throat, cutting the skin hidden beneath his beard. *Ouch.*

"You too?" she spat in his face.

"Me too, what?" he spat right back at her, his fingers curled around her wrist before she nicked him again. Which would be a cold day in Hell.

"Are you going to stab me in the back, too?" Man, she was pissed but what a glorious sight to behold when her temper was up. Her nostrils flared, but there was no let-me-spank-your-ass, dominatrix sparkle in her eyes, only the flat stare of a cold-blooded killer on the hunt.

Pagan began again, his fingers tightening on her slender wrist. "Shit, it's me, Victoria. Is this how you treat all your guests? Or just me?"

He could snap the tiny bones in his hand if he had to, but her wrist was so thin, so fragile, and her pulse was pounding like a mother. Yes, she was worked up. Who wasn't? But she couldn't already know there was a contract cut on her, could she? By the looks of her, she'd been in a war last night. Had that been a fight for her life?

He calmed and forced slow, steady breaths to get her to calm as well. There was still no hint of recognition softening the hard killer behind her features. Victoria had become the goddess Athena personified, as cold and as hard as marble.

"How'd you get into my place?" she bit out, then before he could answer, "Never mind. I don't care. Why are you here?"

He came clean. "Chance received orders to end you and—"

The knife dug deeper.

"And I was closer to Chicago than Kruze... Damn it, stop cutting me!" Pagan ordered before she sliced his jugular. "I'm not here to hurt you, Victoria. Chance voted no. He rejected the kill order on principle. We don't kill our friends, damn it. That's why I'm here in Chicago. I came to help you."

She sneered. "Prove it."

Could she possibly get any hotter? More breathtaking? Sexier? Pagan doubted it.

Strands of her hair hung into his face, catching on his beard, she'd gotten that close. As if she always threw herself into her job, the tips of her breasts mashed boldly against his chest. Sweat trickled down her neck into the hollow where her collarbones joined. If he didn't know better, he'd swear confusion and fear flash through those deep baby browns.

Never having been asked to prove anything before, Pagan blinked up at her. By then, he could feel warm blood trickling down both sides of his neck, but she was right. If he'd been her, he wouldn't believe what he'd said, either. Contract killers lied, and that was what he was. A mercenary who worked on the side of truth and justice. The American way. *Yeah, right.*

"Now how could I ever prove that Chance didn't send me here to off you?" he asked, keeping his tone calm now that they'd both stopped panting into each other's faces. "You'd never believe me, and why should you?"

Which was kind of sad, really. He'd been enjoying this woman's hot breath in his face. He missed it. Didn't that make him as big a horn dog as his brother?

"Not. My. Problem." She enunciated slowly, each word an ice bullet that spelled his upcoming death.

And enough! Because he was bigger, and okay, maybe just a little bit faster, Pagan slapped the knife out of her hand with one quick move. It flew off to his left, and then, one split second later, he'd rolled her over, had her pinned, and was sitting on her thighs. Capturing the flailing hands slapping his face took a little longer than he would've liked, but at last, he had her hands secured above her head.

"So, do it," she hissed as she arched her back to dislodge him, still fighting with all she had left. "Kill me now! Stop playing, Pagan. Just get it over with! Do it!"

Her neck stiffened and the cords in her neck stood out as her head came off the floor. He reared back, expecting to get his nose broke if she head-butted him. What he got was her hissing into his face, "Do it! Just do it!"

"Whoa. Just whoa. Settle down." The total fear in her eyes took the wind out of his sails. He'd never seen Victoria scared before. But she was now. Since the first time he'd met this woman, Pagan had been in competition with her. Damned if he knew why he'd always felt the need to make her submit to him. But not like this. He'd never wanted her to be afraid of him like she was now.

Women weren't supposed to be stronger than men. Smarter, yes. He understood that. Women held the power and the genius to think about everything in their universe at the same time, while men tended to be single-minded, one-track robots. Like right now. His all-male mind had definitely noticed the taut nubs under the grimy tank top of hers, and it was working a plan to get her out of her shirt despite the highly antagonistic position they were both in. Those nipples would be heaven to taste. Her plump, sweaty breasts would fill his hands, maybe overflow his fingers and his mouth and—

See? One track mind.

Earnestly, he refocused and once again attempted to gain her trust. Not her submission. Not like this. If it ever happened, it would have to be a gift. Not a duty.

"Victoria. Vicki. Honest. I'm not here to hurt you. Not sure how you made our hit list, but Chance,

Kruze, and I believe in you, okay? Now, if I let you up, honey, are you going to stick or kick me again?"

"Don't honey me," she hissed.

He blinked at the odd hysterical pitch in her tone. Oh-kay... Point taken. No endearments. But she was trembling like a leaf, and did her bottom lip just quiver? Was she really that frightened of him? Nah. Not the infamous Miss Vicki Hex, the Mafia's best-kept secret and the legendary hard-assed woman he'd secretly come to respect.

Without waiting for an answer, Pagan eased off her wrists.

But she'd been waiting for that. No sooner had he lifted his weight than the heel of her hand came up and struck him square in the nose. Hard. Made him bleed and made him mad. Damn it. There was no way she'd believe anything he said, so Pagan did the only thing he could do. He rolled to his butt, jerked his tee-shirt out of his pants, and used it to staunch the flow from his nose. "Great. Just great," he grumbled. "That'll teach me to trust you."

By then she was on her feet, her legs spread, her hands fisted, and bouncing on the balls of her bare feet like a feather-weight boxer ready to go another round. "How long you been here?"

"Twenty-four hours," he replied, still keeping his voice cool, calm, and staying as collected as any man who'd just been punched in the nose could. He noticed the dirt on her feet then, the black stain that could only be blood on the strap of her tank top. Her blood. "Where have you been all night, and what happened to you?"

Chapter Five

Man, his eyes were so green, a pure emerald green that instantly reminded her of the Sinclair Boys' mountain hideaway in Montana, where pine trees stretched to the sky, and where every last fragrant one of them reminded her of Baby Brother. She desperately wanted to believe Pagan, but he and his brothers weren't called the Sin Boys for nothing. He'd come prepared, the ass, wearing those black nitrile gloves, so he didn't leave any trace evidence behind while he did his dirty work. All former Navy SEALs, these brothers could kill without making a sound or leaving a clue. Each knew how to make explosives out of common household items found under a person's sink. They owned mad, hand-to-hand fighting skills that made other professional killers look like they were playing pat-a-cake and doing it badly when they fought.

That Pagan was here in her one safe place, the apartment she'd not so much as stepped one foot in before tonight, not even when she'd signed the rental contract, scared Vicki. Although she'd listed it as her domicile on her personnel files with the Agency, she'd never intended to live here. It was her bug-out place, her last resort should her cover come undone, and if all else failed. Only now, it wasn't safe, either. If Pagan could find her—her gaze darted over her shoulder to the single-entry door behind her—anyone could.

Not even that solid wood could save her if Vito had turned on her. How ironic. To die as she'd lived, struck down by an assassin she'd never see coming with a bullet she'd never hear. But not today.

"What's going on, Victoria?" Pagan asked patiently, his voice gone softer and lower than she'd ever heard before. Not that she and Pagan hung out much in the past or talked long enough to become familiar with each other's nuances. But his tone when addressing her was usually impatient and snarky, and she knew for a fact he didn't like her. He'd as much as told her that to her face.

So why was he being nice now? Only one explanation leaped to her mind. He planned to lull her into a sense of false security, then kill her without making a sound or leaving a mess. He could do it, too.

As if to prove her wrong, Pagan peeled off one black glove, then dug into a pocket. He pulled out a handkerchief and mopped his bloody nose, his expression a study in unhappy granite. Of both his brothers, he resembled Chance more than Kruze. Muscular in a heavyweight way, with broad capable shoulders that stretched over a thickly-corded chest and massive, muscled arms, Pagan was the baby of the three. His SEAL tag was, in fact, Baby Brother. And baby, he was one hot, darkly handsome, testosterone-blessed brother.

His dark hair had been shaved since the last time she'd seen him. The beginnings of a thick, black beard shadowed his chin and cheeks, no doubt because of his frequent flyer miles between Afghanistan, Iraq, Iran, Syria, and wherever else he went. The man had to be ready to travel at a moment's notice. But it was Pagan's brooding, green eyes that made the bad boy rep he easily maintained appealing to foolish women.

Fortunately, Vicki was not, and never had been, one of those dimwitted females. It was too bad for Pagan if he thought she was.

"You tell me what's going on," she ordered. "You're the one who broke into *my* place, remember?"

He shrugged as he stuffed both gloves into his rear pocket. That was not an acceptable answer, damn it. Not today.

"This isn't a game, Pagan. Answer the question," she demanded when he kept silent a moment too long. "Are you here to kill me?" *Because if you are, you'll die trying. But hurry it up. I don't have a lot of time. Because someone* is *out to kill me, and if it's not you, then...*

He gave her a totally Pagan-esque reply. Instead of obeying, he simply folded his long legs Indian-style. His hands, the same hands that could easily crush her skull like a glass Christmas ornament, landed on his kneecaps as he sat on the floor.

For the first time, she realized that if he'd wanted to kill her, he would've used one of the two pistols sitting loose and ready in his underarm holster. Neither were strapped in. He'd obviously been waiting for her. Man, he'd watched her break into her place. How embarrassing. He could've killed her the second she'd cleared the window sill. But he hadn't.

That had to mean she could trust him, didn't it?

Baby Brother stared up at her now, daring her, damn him, but daring her to do what? Relax enough to be overpowered and get her neck broken? To be knifed through the heart by the blade hidden on that massive body of his? To be softened up for the kill by revealing to her that he was armed, when he didn't need anything but those big hands to finish her off?

A shiver rippled up her spine at the killing machine she faced. In her apartment. Now, when she wasn't even close to being on her best game.

This was the double-edged dilemma to the double-agent job title. No covert operator could afford to believe or trust another covert operator. They were both trained liars, and since she and Pagan were still alive, they were both quite good at their jobs. But for once, just once, Vicki wanted desperately to believe in someone besides her brother. Julio had enough problems. He didn't need to worry about her.

Shaken but not ready to believe in luck or good fortune, Vicki asked again. "Why are you h-here?"

Why she stuttered, she didn't know. But a woman in dire straits could hope. The audacious Sin Boys were not only known for their excellent combat skills, but for their steadfast and very moral compasses as well. None of the three were Hollywood's twisted version of former military members gone crazy with bloodlust or the ever-popular and overly used post-traumatic stress disorder syndrome. The Sinclairs weren't mentally unbalanced, they weren't sick, and they weren't mercenaries. They were simply three good men who'd served their country in the past and who still did today.

Damn, she'd nearly convinced herself when Pagan lurched forward, grabbed her ankle, knocked her onto her butt, and bellowed, "Get down!"

Like she had a choice the way he'd thrown himself over her? The ass! She came up fighting and punched his throat before he could kill her. She'd almost believed in him, but no! He *was* here to kill her.

"Will you stop!" he growled as he captured her wrists in one hand and flattened her to the carpet with his entire body.

Already out of her mind, Vicki's nose betrayed her as it inhaled a gasping breath of Pagan. Man, he smelled good. Of whiskey and coffee and leather, her three favorite room fresheners. *But I don't care what he smells like! Wait. What's that noise? A chopper? Here?*

When an ear piercing "Brrrrrr-r-r-r-r-ttttt. Br-r-rt. Brrrrrrrt!" ripped the air and splattered debris from what used to be the building's outside brick wall over her and Pagan, Vicki stopped struggling. He wasn't trying to kill her. They were under attack. That was gunfire. Not just any gunfire, but the deliberate hellfire of fifty-cals peppering the brick walls of her apartment, shredding them like cheese.

"Move your ass! Crawl for the door!" Pagan yelled, even as he rolled her onto her stomach, put an impatient hand on her ass, and shoved her forward, all the while hunched over her like he meant to take a bullet for her if he had to. What was that about?

Reaching up for the doorknob put his arm in harm's way, but he swiftly got them into the hall. Not like they were safe there, not from the deadly rounds turning her empty apartment to dust, rubble, and so much noise. Without thinking, she clapped both hands to her ears. To block the noise.

"Jesus Christ, don't fall apart on me now. Move it!" he yelled. Grabbing her hand, Pagan pulled her onto her feet, and together they ran for the elevator. They made it maybe a dozen feet when the elevator doors opened, and two men dressed in military black camouflaged BDUs stepped into the hall, the massive rifles in their hands already up and on target. On them!

"Run!" Pagan bellowed as he swung the steel stair door open, and just in time offered a sturdy shield between them and the bullets fired by the men in black.

Vicki ran down the steps at a faster than fast clip, her heart up high in her throat, listening as Pagan growled behind her, "There. That'll slow them down."

In seconds, he caught up with her, his hand squeezing her elbow as he slowed her retreat and opted for the second floor exit instead of the basement where she'd been headed. "They'll expect us to run to the parking garage. Let's not."

"Right," she answered breathlessly. "Second floor. Plenty of windows. Got it."

Which told Vicki that Pagan had thoroughly cased her apartment building before she'd shown up. That he knew all second-floor units had balconies with sliders, that those north-facing balconies opened over a well-watered lawn instead of the streets to the east and west, or the concrete patio at the south. That they might actually survive if they landed on grass when they jumped.

Other tenants were out in the halls by now. The guys in black must've overcome whatever barricade Pagan had constructed, judging by the harsh slap of boots hammering in the stairwell.

"Hurry," Pagan urged as he barged past a woman just opening her second story door and ran into her apartment with his arm around Vicki. "Sorry, ma'am," he said as he gently pushed the startled woman back inside and closed her door behind them. "You need to call the police. Then lock your doors and windows and stay inside. Can you do that for me?"

Wide-eyed, the blonde nodded like she'd just met the most amazing man, and maybe she had. Pagan certainly seemed to have hypnotized instead of traumatized this female the way he'd handled her, all while they walked through her pristine apartment, headed for her balcony.

In seconds, they were on the ground and running, fully aware of the noise and mayhem they'd left behind. More rapid fire from that tiny chopper strafed the one side of the building. More gunfire and explosions came from inside the building. Women and men were screaming and shouting, and yeah. This was all her fault. But at least, Vicki wasn't running alone this time. She had Pagan, the man who thought she was brainless, at her side. What a joke these last twenty-four hours had been.

Once on the sidewalk, he shrugged out of his leather jacket. "Here. You're cold. Put this on."

With pleasure. He'd come prepared and still wore a layered look, an unbuttoned shirt over a tee, all in black, his signature color. Vicki let the warmth that Pagan left behind in his jacket lie to her that maybe she would live through this godawful day.

Two blocks west, they ducked into Van Luc's just-opening-for-business Vietnamese Noodle Parlor. Through the tidy little restaurant they ran while the cook and two oriental waitresses mumbled words

Vicki didn't care to understand. Pagan seemed to, though. He certainly said something to the cook that calmed the man as out the back door and into the alley behind Luc's they went. Five doors down but on the other side of the alley, Pagan steered her inside the rear entrance of Lucky Duke's Diner.

The tiny place was noisy and crowded with early morning commuters, leaving only two booths vacant, one near the rear where they'd entered, one by the front door. Without asking, Pagan shuffled Vicki toward the front booth instead of the back corner where they would've been less noticeable. Where she would've felt safer. What was wrong with him?

"They're expecting us to hide, remember?" Pagan explained as if he'd read her mind. "We stay in the open, they'll look right past us if they come in here. By then..." He patted the concealed firearm under his left arm. "They'll be dead. I'll cap them where they stand."

"Sure hope you're right," Vicki hissed as she settled low onto the well-worn green Naugahyde covered bench seat opposite him. She zipped his jacket up to her chin, then flipped the collar upright to cover the lower part of her face just in case.

"Trust me," he murmured. "I'm always right."

Said every liar and covert operator ever.

Vicki wanted to put her faith in this particular man. She'd forgotten how green his eyes were. Green, like a snake's.

Yet of all the people she hadn't expected to see this morning, Pagan was the absolute only one here, and because of him, she was still alive. She held back, not willing to put her life in anyone else's hands. Not even his. Not yet. Maybe never. The risk was too great.

She played it cool. For now, she focused on absorbing her new surroundings. The brown, water-stained ceiling tiles overhead looked like they'd been painted once or twice before. Also looked like they needed another coat. She studied the simple layout of the rectangular, greasy-spoon diner. The speckled gray linoleum floor that looked like it hadn't been mopped in days. The doorway into the kitchen. The height of the counter in case she'd have to sprint over it. The row of front windows, each of them steamy with condensation from the warmth inside the diner. That was what covert agents did. They planned how to escape a dozen what-if scenarios should the need arise.

What if those geared-up guys in black followed her? What if they came in through the back the same as she and Pagan did, while some other killer came through the front, spraying machine guns, killing everyone just to get to her? None of these people deserved to die like that. They probably had families, husbands or wives. Children. Friends. A life.

Man, this place was nothing but a death trap waiting to happen.

Vicki swallowed hard. She needed to run for better cover, far from this neighborhood. Yet she didn't. She held her tongue and gave Pagan his due. He *had* saved her life just moments earlier, and he'd risked his in the process. That *had* to mean he was on her side, didn't it? No gun-for-hire would be so courageous as to put himself in the line of fire for their mark, would they? Would he? Did he?

I hope so.

The nametag on the blouse of the grumpy, overworked waitress who asked if they wanted coffee while she ran a deprecating glare over Vicki's disheveled, grungy appearance, declared JOLENE. Pagan took that tiny info-byte instantly in stride with a polite, "Yes, Jolene. Good morning. Coffee would sure be nice. Do you have any flavored creamers to go with it?"

Vicki lifted one hand to her face. She'd nearly laughed out loud at his ridiculous request, although it would've sounded hysterical considering their predicament. Flavored creamers? Really?

But Pagan must've subscribed to the *'say their name to win them over'* philosophy. Jolene's thinned and graying brows narrowed, but a definite light flickered on in those steely blue eyes of hers at the sound of her name on his lips.

"Yes, young man, we most certainly do," she said crisply as she cocked her head and looked closer at him. "During the holidays, we've got eggnog and peppermint, but today all we got's French vanilla, hazelnut, and caramel. Which would you like?"

He nodded, not taking his eyes off Jolene's tired, wrinkled face. "I'm partial to caramel, ma'am, if it's not too much trouble." He was good at this choir-boy routine. If Jolene only knew.

"Hmmpf," she said as she hurried off without asking Vicki what she wanted.

That was Pagan's charm for you. When he focused on a person, the subject of his attention tended to forget anyone else existed. It was as if, for that singular moment in time, Jolene had been the only one in the world he cared about. His dark eyes had narrowed down on her like a sniper's scope. He'd blocked out competing distractions.

Vicki had seen him work his magical listening skills on Chance's new wife, Suede. Pagan had people skills that belied an extraordinary talent to focus. It was as if the person's life depended on him. Pagan could listen like no man Vicki had ever known. He was definitely worth watching.

Jolene returned quickly, her tray loaded with two steaming coffees, a saucer stacked high with tiny caramel-flavored creamer-filled plastic cups, and a sugar dispenser. As well as two menus.

Vicki couldn't help it. She risked a small smile at the deferential treatment Jolene gave Pagan. Looked like he'd made a friend. Also looked like she was having coffee.

"Just toast for me, ma'am," Pagan said before Jolene had a chance to ask what he wanted.

She finally acknowledged he wasn't alone when she set one coffee on the paper placemat in front of Vicki and asked with a sarcastic huff, "What'll it be?"

"Just this coffee. Thank you, Jolene. You're a life saver," Vicki replied, her eyes automatically skating beyond Pagan's beefy shoulder to the young couple who had just entered the diner's front door behind him. Both were in their early thirties, sandy-haired, rosy-cheeked, and dressed for the chilly morning, he in a leather bomber jacket that could easily conceal enough weaponry to murder everyone in the diner. She in a camel-colored, quilted jacket with deep pockets where knives, a pistol or two, maybe even a small brick of C4 or a grenade could be hidden.

Turning away from Vicki, Jolene greeted the couple with a surly, "Mornin', Robinsons. Sit anywhere you can find a booth. I'll be right with you."

"Hey, Jo! Good to see you today," the young man exclaimed cheerfully as he ushered the young woman toward the back of the restaurant.

Today. He'd said *today.* Which inferred that these kids were regulars, and regulars didn't have any idea who she was or that *today* she was on the run from the Mafia. Only then did Vicki take a breath.

Pagan reached across the table, startling her when he covered her hand with his. Make that, engulfed. Man, he was a big man. Broad in every possible way. Muscular from every angle. Thick-chested and thick-necked. Buying shoes, dress shirts, and gloves had to be a challenge.

"You're hurt," he told her as he rotated her wrist and examined her bloody fingers. "And you're bleeding. Tell me what happened to you."

"Yeah, well..." She pulled her hand out from under his. That was a first, him touching her skin to skin. "Where are your gloves?"

He shrugged. "Must've lost them. No worries. I'll get another pair later."

Of course you will. Because you'll need them to kill me, won't you?

Digging herself out of that grave hadn't been easy, and yeah. She'd broken a few nails, and her manicure was trashed. She looked like something the cat dragged in, and for certain, she wasn't on her A-game. What corpse would be?

But what'd he care? Even if he did, and even if he were sincere—which she doubted—she'd been on her own far too long in this dog-eat-dog world to buddy up with anyone—even him—now. Trust didn't come easy, and most times, it didn't show up at all. Crossing her arms, she trapped her tender fingers in the soft leather armpits of his jacket, immediately missing her pink-handled pistols. Vicki hated being unarmed. She didn't even have her bug-out bag. She'd lost it at her apartment when the shooting started. Could this day get any worse?

Discouraged yet on edge, she commenced tearing at the tender edges of the last of what remained of her gel nails even as she kept them out of sight under her arms. Gold and red matched her old life, not the one she'd crawled out of last night. Black. She'd need new gel nails to protect her damaged nailbeds. She needed them now, and she needed them to be black. Like her heart.

"What happened, Victoria?" Pagan asked again quietly, his eyes filled with what could be true compassion, but what was more likely a well-honed psychological trap. "You can tell me."

Pagan was the baby of the Sinclair family, the soft-hearted brother who took any assignment that called for ending the asshole-cowards in the world who harmed children. Be they dangerous pedophiles or the occasional Jihadist intent on teaching his son or daughter the proper way to hold a sword in order to behead Westerners, Pagan was known for his zealous protection of children. All children. Everywhere. When he wasn't on duty, he was somewhere in the world where children were in distress or starving. The Sudan. India. Cambodia.

She knew for a fact he'd been deep inside Russia, China, and North Korea aiding impoverished, unwanted children in those countries. He'd also been on Rio's brutal streets and alleys, feeding orphans and putting shoes on their feet. Instead of a Navy SEAL, Pagan should've been a priest.

Intently, Vicki watched the diner's entrance behind him instead of what seemed like concern welling in his eyes. The tender spot in his Navy-trained killer's heart didn't make him her friend.

"You've been on a job?" he probed, the brim of his cup at his lips as he took a long swallow. "Is that how, where, and when you were hurt?"

"Yes," she lied and left it at that. Chitchat would only reveal she'd been compromised, and right now, she didn't know by whom. Could've been any one of the dozens of people she'd crossed, guys and gals alike. Could've been Pagan now that she knew Senator Sullivan had also tossed her to the wolves. Or SEALs.

She suspected everyone, but Vito Seranzino was highest on her list, with Cabb running a close second. As often as Cabb claimed he adored her, she knew better than to trust him or his familia. The man was ruthless. Vito's snot-nosed, twenty-something, spoiled-brat son, Romeo, came in at number three. Her problem now was there were too many contestants in this game to know for sure who'd sent that chopper after her this morning and that killer last night.

She had to know. Vicki leaned over her tightly clasped hands, loving the feel and smell and false sense of security Pagan's leather jacket offered even as she asked him, "Why'd Sullivan send you after me?"

At least he had the decency to look her in the eye when he told her, "He has evidence you've turned rogue. Have you?"

"What evidence?" Of course there'd be plenty of evidence. She *was* deep inside the Mafia. That was her fuckin' job. Every day was filled with proof that she willingly served the Seranzinos. How else could she have gotten in deep enough for them to trust her, by selling Girl Scout cookies? At least, she had been in deep with them until she'd been made. It was very likely the Seranzinos now knew precisely who and what she was. At least, they knew she was dangerous to them.

But how and when had everything changed? What—or who—had she missed? She'd been so meticulous with her relationships. So careful in fact, that there'd been no close relationships since she'd gone undercover. She'd trusted no man or woman for years for this very reason, so no one could betray her. Then who was out to kill her?

Her hands came up, her palms forward blocking Pagan from answering. "Never mind. Don't care what evidence you think you have. Doesn't matter. Did Sullivan think to check with my handler before he sent you to kill me? Dane Rich would vouch for me." *He'd better. That's* his *one and only job.*

Pagan's eyes shifted past her to the other customers in the diner. "Shhhhh, keep it down," he cautioned as he shook his head. "Sullivan didn't send me after you, and I'm not here to delete you, Victoria. I came on my own volition. Once I got the call, I voted against it. All of us Sinclairs did. I told Chance something about the order didn't feel right. It was wrong, and Sullivan's evidence trail had to be bogus. He's not out in the field like we are, and yes, he worked through the unanimous-vote protocols we set up, but they're not foolproof, and obviously, they need more work. Chance and us opted to check things out firsthand. You know, confirm or deny."

"So what's your decision—" she stabbed a pair of air quotes at him to express how stupid she thought his line was "— now that you've *checked me out* first hand. Am I guilty as charged? Is this when you knife me?"

He never blinked. "You're still alive, aren't you?"

Like that heartless response made her feel better? The man was definitely lying. Vicki could tell. And why'd he keep calling her Victoria? It was obvious Pagan thought he could gentle her—right before he cut her throat.

Useless. This line of questioning was as useless as this man, and she needed to get far, far away from Pagan Sinclair to clear her head. She'd been running on empty since she'd dug herself out of that dirt bath. She needed a safe place off the gird where she could shower, catch a quick nap, and make a few calls. She needed to report into her handler, and to do that, she needed a damned phone! Dane needed to know her cover had been compromised. Not that he cared. He was just doing his job. She seriously doubted he'd do more than file an officer missing report when she failed to call in.

I have got to get out of here!

Lifting the coffee cup to her lips, Vicki sipped the steamy black beverage as her view narrowed down on Pagan. Two could play that gentling game. The second she lulled him into a false sense of security, she was gone. Caffeine would help.

Chapter Six

'She doesn't trust me, and I don't blame her. I wouldn't trust me either if I were her,' Pagan thought as he kept an eye on Julio's baby sister. *Victoria.* That she'd assumed such a Puritanical uptight name, then hooked it to a deadly sounding surname like Hex, fit her audacious style of undercover work. The woman was the promise of hot, heavy sex on two very long legs with a Kate Beckinsale in *Underworld* kick-ass attitude thrown into the mix. All that long dark hair of hers never failed to turn heads, but those *girls* were the main attraction.

Pagan caught himself before he licked his lips at the thought of all that soft female flesh in his hands or his mouth. It took a Herculean effort, but he managed. This wasn't a Hollywood stage, and that Boeing AH-6 Unmanned Little Bird gunship back at her apartment wasn't computer generated graphics filmed against green screens. *Uh-huh.* Victoria was in rough shape and limping. Someone had obviously beaten the hell out of her last night, then tried to finish her off this morning.

Not only were her face, arms, hands, and feet scraped and dirty, but that blood on her tank top strap came from a head wound. Damn Sullivan to the lowest level of Hell if he'd sent those remote-controlled choppers after Victoria, while Pagan was out here investigating whether she'd truly turned. Or not. At the moment, he was ninety-nine percent certain of Vicki's loyalty. But that one percent still niggled at the back of his mind. Miss Hex was damned good at what she did. If she'd fooled the Seranzinos all this time, she could certainly fool Pagan.

But if those were Sullivan's men back there at her apartment, good old McQueen would have another fight on his hands. He thought he was untouchable just because he was an elected official? *Guess again, Senator Dumbass. You come after me, and I'll make you wish you died in your sleep the day you were born.*

Personally, Pagan couldn't see Hex betraying her country, not the way she'd embedded herself into that multi-level nightmare with the South American cartel when they'd shown up in Portland, Oregon, last year. Yes, she'd shot Pagan in the ass during that convoluted operation, but he understood why. Hex was damned good at what she did, and she'd needed to maintain her cover. At that moment, that had meant maintaining her brother Julio's cover as well. Neither could afford to let the criminals they worked for discover who they really were.

Besides, that bullet in his backside hadn't hurt Pagan. Much. Not really. He'd just needed a few stitches on his rump. Chance took care of that minor surgery before the day had ended. Nothing serious. Hadn't even left a scar. Well, not much of a scar. More like a dimple.

Her undercover work inside the Mafia's Seranzino *familia* was more important than his ass. The intel she provided had already led to the arrest and conviction of Vito Seranzino's two filthiest right-hand men. Plus, she'd been deep undercover when the Black Friday Massacre in Chicago went down. If anyone could bring Cabb Seranzino to justice for that heinous crime, Victoria could. She was the man, err, woman, for the job.

Unless she was now as dirty as Vito and Cabb. Pagan hoped not. He might not like the promiscuous rep she maintained, or that she'd been with his brother Kruze for who knew how long. But Victoria was that one in a million woman in a throng of wannabes. Strong. Defiant. The ultimate femme fatale. She played a man's game, and she played it well. She usually won.

Pagan tossed his head back, and with one swallow, his coffee was gone, and it was time to move. Tugging a single bill out his rear pocket, he slapped a

Benjamin to the table while he held out his other hand to Victoria. "Let's go shopping," he said as he nodded toward the front door.

"I can't go anywhere like this," she growled indignantly as she lifted into the aisle. "Not even shopping, so don't ask."

"I'm not asking." He changed directions as smoothly as if he'd never planned to leave through the diner's entrance at all. Because he hadn't. "You're right. Restrooms first. Clean up, then shopping." He'd spoken loud enough for the customers' benefit anyway, not Vicki's.

Once far enough down the dimly lit hall, he opened the door on his left marked *Employees Only* instead of the one marked *Ladies*. There it was, overhead in the ceiling, their way out. The two-foot by two-foot painted-over panel to the ductwork and wiring in the crawlspace lifted with a creak. Certain that no one else had heard the noise, he turned to hoist Victoria up and out of sight.

But damn that woman. She was gone. Of course she'd run. What he'd expect?

Easing the panel back into place, Pagan went after Miss Hex again. Trusting his instincts, he hit the street, then jogged, dodging early morning foot traffic until he spotted his first clue. A bloody footprint on the edge of the curb she'd pushed off from. Poor thing was still running and doing it barefoot. She needed shoes as much as the jacket he'd given her.

But now he knew right where she'd crossed the street. He followed, and soon caught sight of a woman with thick, dark hair wearing his leather jacket and moving quickly up ahead. But Pagan had been around the block, so to speak, more than once. He recognized the ploy. Victoria had discarded his jacket the second she'd hit the street, probably tossed it at some brunette with long luscious locks like hers. Yeah? No.

He ran to catch up. Victoria had probably expected him to think she'd ditched the jacket when she really hadn't. She'd stay out in the open where a sniper could narrow down on her from any rooftop or open window along this gauntlet of modernization. What was she thinking?

"Going somewhere?" he asked nonchalantly as he fell in step alongside her. Man, it was good to be right once in a while.

"Figures," she hissed, not looking his way or breaking her stride. That a woman could be so stubborn amazed him, but that was Victoria's strength, her relentless drive. "What do you have, a hero complex that you can't mind your own business and leave me alone?"

He nodded, though he recognized sarcasm when he heard it. He'd rattled her plenty, but he also saw through her tough-girl façade. She wasn't pinging on all eight cylinders, and she knew it, too. That was her problem. She was truly frightened. Maybe this time, she needed a buddy on her six. "Sure, yeah. All us

Sinclairs have hero complexes. We're SEALs, remember?"

"You'd be smart to walk away, sailor-boy. I'm not a little girl, and I don't need saving."

Sailor-boy, huh? Like the boyfriend he most definitely was not, Pagan reached out and put his arm around her shoulders. He tugged her into his side while they kept walking. "Good to know there's no need for me to worry about you, Victoria. So, you can handle that dude in the trench coat who's been tailing you since the last crosswalk then, right? Without a firearm or a blade, you can take him out? Are you so sure of yourself? Shit, don't look now, but he's packing a sawed-off shotgun under that cheesy leather coat. Probably isn't even real leather. Damn, he's got a buddy on the other side of the street, and they're both fast-tracking you. Make that us."

Sliding his right hand under his shirt, Pagan passed one of his pistols to Victoria, sure to keep it out of sight. "Whatever you did to piss these guys off, I don't care. But make yourself useful, Hex. I'll take the tango across the street. You take Mr. Trench Coat. No collateral damage. One shot if you can make it. Don't miss."

She snorted as she gripped the firearm. "I never miss."

Pagan let that stupid comment slide. In sync with the Mafia's best girl, he spun to his right, aimed over the heads of the civilians on the street, and easily took out the scumbag across the street, the one aiming his weapon into the morning rush hour crowd no less. The idiot deserved to die before he hit any innocent bystanders.

As expected, people screamed, shrieked, and scattered. Some dropped to their bellies, but true to his word, Pagan had only fired once. Because once was enough. Mr. Scumbag dropped where he stood just as Victoria's single shot echoed Pagan's firearm's report. Neither shooter got a round off, but the police were already on their way, and Pagan was sure they'd shoot first and ask questions later. Cops in big cities like Chicago were always in combat mode. It was time to get lost in the crowd.

Tucking his piece out of sight, he let Victoria keep hers. That jacket she had on had enough bulk and inner pockets to conceal several pistols, a few knives, plenty of magazines, and a tube of lipstick if she'd had one. But if a loaded firearm helped her feel safe enough to trust him? Well, good, because Pagan trusted her. She could've used that weapon on him, shot him and made a run for it, but she'd hadn't. Instead, she'd followed orders, took out a dangerous man who was probably a known felon. The police ought to thank her for doing their job for them.

Pagan grabbed her elbow and together they ran with the panicked pedestrians even as some helpful person with a cellphone camera screamed, "There they go! They did it! Those two! That man and that woman killed those poor innocent guys!"

'Poor innocent guys? For hell's sake, shut your pie hole, you fool,' Pagan thought. Hailing the first cab that came along, he shoved Victoria inside and climbed in behind her, barely giving her enough time to scoot out from under him. "Could you drop us two blocks east of here?" he asked politely.

Without answering, the cabbie nodded, hit the gas, and after a few seconds, Pagan and Victoria were on foot again, still headed away from the hubbub. After three CPD cruisers roared by, their sirens screaming, he hailed another cab. Running for cover was all about diversion, dividing, and conquering. Illusion.

"Damn it, Pagan, these aren't hop-on, hop-off city buses," Victoria grumbled as, once more she found herself hustled into the back seat of another cab without explanation or warning or barely enough time to get seated.

Instead of answering, Pagan eased her butt out of his way when he handed the cabbie a business card and asked, "Could you drop us here, sir?"

"You bet," the cabbie replied. A wide smile blossomed over his face after he glanced at the address. "Be my pleasure, Mr. Sinclair."

The man's curiosity glowed through the rearview mirror. Yeah, Pagan got that *'Should I know you, and if I don't, can I get your autograph just in case you're somebody famous?'* look whenever he used that card. It paid to be the son of a popular, best-selling author.

In less time than most race car drivers could've rounded the track at Indy, the cab halted at the polished glass doors of one of Chicago's priciest high-rise hotels. The beaming and very attentive cabbie held his hand out, and Pagan shook it as he also deposited another crisp Benjamin. It was a small thing to overpay the real movers and shakers in America. The short-order cooks. The dead-on-their-feet waitresses. The round-the-clock cab drivers. The folks who did the minimum wage jobs and did them well.

"Gee thanks, mister!" the cabbie exclaimed and then handed over his business card. "You ever need a ride, I mean, ever, you call me, got it? I'm your guy, and I can get you anywhere you want to go, faster, with no questions asked."

Pagan left the grinning man behind as he lifted out of the cab and snagged Miss Hex's elbow. "Shall we?"

Chapter Seven

"Holy Schnikees," Vicki murmured as she stared up at the rows and gleaming rows of gold-toned windows on the face of one of Chicago's East Side iconic hotels. "You live here? Within sight of Navy Pier?" *In one of Chicago's priciest, most glamorous neighborhoods?*

Pagan grunted at her uncharacteristic euphemism for shit. "No, but Mom came to town often enough, and she wanted a place where she could get away from it all. This is it."

He called Chicago a town? What'd Pagan consider a big city then?

Like before, he latched onto her elbow like he needed to control, steer, or annoy her. Vicki shrugged away from his fingertips, intent on walking through the doors of this pretentious place without assistance and with her chin held high. It didn't matter how she was dressed or that she had no shoes. She was no meek, little housewife, damn it, and he needed to stop treating her like one.

Pagan had the good sense to follow her lead. For the first time since she'd caught him inside her apartment, he followed her lead. Smart man. Maybe he was good for something after all.

Breezily, she nodded at the silver-haired doorman. Epaulets, really? Intrigued, Vicki nearly reached out to finger those gold braids on Jobe's shoulders to see if they were real. She wouldn't doubt if they were.

"Good to see you again, Jobe," Pagan told the friendly, hunter-green uniformed man.

"You too, Mr. Sinclair," Jobe replied. "How are Chance and his new wife?"

"Doing well."

The older man smiled. "Any plans for babies yet?"

To which Pagan scoffed, "Now how would I know that?"

Jobe's gazed flitted over Vicki. "I meant with you and the missus." He coughed. "Unless... sorry. My mistake. I thought... Never mind. Just don't remember you ever bringing a woman here before."

Vicki waited to see how Pagan got out of this one. Was she his first or had he just been careful where he took his women?

"You know better than that," he replied easily. "Any mail for me?"

Relieved to be off the hook, Jobe nodded toward the front desk. "I do believe Sally said she was holding something for you. Will you be staying long?"

"Just passing through. A day or two at the longest."

With a polite nod, Jobe opened the wide glass doors.

Pagan nodded at Vicki, and she entered a world of plush comfort and money ahead of him. Who would've thought Pagan Sinclair knew about a world-class hotel like this, much less owned a room or a suite here? Man, the place even smelled rich.

Vicki forced her mouth shut before she drooled. The hotel trappings made her place look dime store cheap. Which it was. Neither Vito or Cabb believed in the lifestyles of the rich and famous, not unless it was for themselves. Or Romeo. Or one of the bawdy women they were currently seeing.

Pagan headed for the tall, platinum blonde at the front desk. "Hello again, Sally. Jobe says you're holding mail for me."

Vicki tilted her head. *Again? What else does she hold for you?*

"Pagan!" Sally Again all but gushed when she reached one elegant, manicured hand across the counter. "It's so good to see you!"

He engulfed that woman's hand within his much larger, very manly hand, shaking it gently.

Sally's eyes glowed at the contact and it seemed he held on just a millisecond too long. Why that simple contact with one of the hotel staff bugged Vicki, she didn't know. But if Sally Again's smile grew any larger or brighter, Vicki was going to slap it off her very lovely, creamy complexion. Maybe even leave a nice, big, red handprint for Sally to remember her by.

"Actually, it's a box from Montana. It's heavy. I'll have it delivered to your room if you'd like." Sally licked her lips when she said that. The subtext wasn't hard to read. *And I'll gladly deliver it in person. In a skimpy negligee. Coming right up.'*

Oh, no, you will not. Clearing her throat, Vicki stepped up to the counter and into Pagan's side, bumping his massive arm to get him to lift it out of her way and let her in closer. Which he did, like the gentleman he was. She could always count on the Sin Boys' manner. Scarlett Sinclair had raised them right.

Vicki turned sideways, bumping her *girls* against him, while she rested one possessive palm on his very fine chest like she owned him. Which she did in a fictional, fantasy-land kind of way. They were here in a fancy hotel together, weren't they? Miss Sally Again needed to back off and recognize her place in the grand scheme of things. And it was *not* by Pagan's side, *so drop the come-on, you troll!*

Pagan glanced down at her. Vicki looked adoringly up at him. His cheek pinched, and his lips twisted into a half-smile like he wasn't sure what was going on, whether he should grin or not. But at least his eyes were on the right person for a change.

"Let her send a bellboy with your mail, hon," Vicki told him, blinking up at him like an innocent girl to keep his attention on her. That worked on him in the past. "I'm tired, and I want to go to bed now. Don't you?"

There. That ought to set Sally Again straight.

His nostrils flared, and he huffed, but then he turned back to Sally and said, "Not this time. I'll take it now if you don't mind. Back room like usual?" he asked while he extracted himself from Vicki's clutches and headed around the counter.

"Yes, Mr. Sinclair," Sally replied, finally addressing him like she should've from the start.

Annoyed that she'd been rebuffed and left standing at the counter, Vicki watched Sally follow Pagan through the open door. Flexing his legs, he bent over and manhandled a large box to his shoulder while Sally stood there watching him. She didn't seem quite so friendly or so blonde anymore. She knew Vicki was watching her watch Pagan.

Boundaries. It was all about boundaries.

"Was this all?" he asked when he'd turned for the door. His gaze skated over Sally's shoulder to Vicki. Suddenly, his eyes turned molten. Her heart skipped a beat. His mouth twitched into a hint of a smile. It must've finally registered that she'd said, *'I want to go to bed now.'* Men. They might be tougher than a woman, but every last one of them could be brought down with the right encouragement.

"Yes, sir," Sally answered when Pagan gestured for her to go ahead of him.

Once back at her station behind the counter—where she belonged—Sally turned that brilliant, empty smile on Vicki. "Pagan's guests are always welcome here. If there's anything you need to make your stay more comfortable, please let me know."

Vicki smiled right back at her while she looped her hand through Pagan's free arm and rested her other palm on his wrist. "I can't imagine what it would be, but thanks for the offer, umm, Sally Duncan is it?" she asked, eying the woman's nametag.

"Sally Duncan. Yes, ma'am. Enjoy your stay. Next?" And with that, Vicki and Pagan were dismissed.

Pagan had the good sense not to say anything. Instead he gestured her toward the bank of brass elevator doors. Wait. Did he just kinda, sorta—bow like an old-fashioned gentleman? Even with that bulky box balanced on his shoulder? At least he'd lowered his head. He'd acknowledged her, hadn't he? This might be the best day ever.

Vicki let her long legs eat up the distance while he trailed behind like a good boy. She had to be dreaming. Pagan treating her like a lady? Yeah, right. The only things he worshiped were his collection of weapons, his former-SEAL brothers, and a shot of good whiskey after a hard job.

Julio had once said Pagan was the adrenaline junkie. Of all the Sin Boys, he was the ultimate risk-taker. The one to watch out for. Ha. If he'd been any good, she wouldn't have been able to shoot him square in the ass during that fiasco in Oregon last year, would she? No. Men came in two distinct flavors, the ones she could trust and the ones she didn't dare. Pagan was definitely the latter.

When the elevator door closed behind them, Vicki expected him to key in some code that would take them high into penthouse territory. Instead, he stabbed number two. She rolled her eyes as the bubble of Pagan being a smooth billionaire on the sly, burst. Second floor rooms were definitely safer, but they were just rooms, not posh suites where a famous author might have whiled away her hours between press conferences, book signings, or interviews. Vicki let out a sigh. It would be simpler to escape from a second-floor room. That much was helpful.

When the elevator pinged, Pagan once again did that head bow thing as he gestured her forward and said, "Hall to your left. Room two-thirteen."

All at once, Vicki froze. Her heart stopped. She couldn't breathe. The last two times she'd gone into what she'd thought was a safe place—her apartment— she'd been wrong. Dead wrong. Her feet refused to move.

Pagan must've sensed her reluctance. Stepping around her, he captured the closing elevator door, holding it open with one big hand as he leaned forward and glanced both ways into the hall. How embarrassing. She, the mob's top assassin, was afraid to step into an empty hallway in a high-class hotel.

"All clear," he reported quietly, "but let's be smart. You still have the piece I gave you earlier?"

She nodded even as her right hand remembered it was supposed to be wrapped around that pistol, her index finger ready on the trigger at times like this. But she'd been armed when she'd been drugged or knocked out, too. She still hadn't figured out how that went down, but the weapon she'd been carrying then hadn't saved her. What made this one so special that Pagan assumed she'd be safe now? Just because she carried meant nothing.

Like a gentle catcher's mitt, his hand landed on the cusp of her shoulder. He seemed to be holding her steady instead of shoving her out into the hall, which would've been one helluva fight at the moment.

"No one knows we're here, Victoria," he said calmly. "Come on. One breath at a time. One step at a time. We can do this together."

He made it sound easy, but man. She'd lost her nerve, and she knew it. In front of Pagan, no less. Him of all people. Why'd it have to be him?

Worse, she was shaking. Coming undone, not just her fingers but her entire body. Her arms. Her knees. Even her head bobbed like it'd fall off her neck and roll across the floor if it weren't attached. If she thought for one second that he'd allow it, she'd crash into Pagan and let him hold her instead of that box and convince her to man up. Yeah, that was what she'd do. Just for one tiny split second, she'd unravel enough to draw strength from him. She'd let him be the strong one for a change. Which he absolutely, positively was. But crap. Why was he the one who'd shown up, today of all days?

Sucking in a deep breath and her last ounce of courage along with it, Vicki took one extra-long step out of the elevator and into the hall. Then two steps. Then she speed-walked with her head held high to unlucky room two-thirteen. It took Pagan forever to key in his secret number on the keypad, which was an interesting hotel feature all by itself. Finally, the security lock buzzed, and the door opened.

But before he could palm the door open for her, she ran inside, her head pounding and her throat dry. "Shut it," she ordered hoarsely. "Close the damned door. Hurry! I'm... I'm cold and there's a draft and..." *Shit! I'm scared! Shut the damned door already! Before anyone sees me!*

He did, then slid the deadbolt as well as another sturdy looking lock. He activated the security alert device attached to the doorknob that would raise a notification in case anyone so much as touched it. That she recognized because she used one at her penthouse suite. At least she did before last night. Who knew what was going on inside her place today. Vito and Cabb might have already moved another woman in.

Who cared? "I n-n-need a drink. You?" she asked as she helped herself to one of the crystal decanters on the bar, trying to keep her fingers from trembling as she poured what had better be stiff and strong. What a day.

"Sure," Pagan answered smoothly as he deposited the box on the coffee table in front of a gray brocade couch. Then he walked through the lavish rooms and closed the drapes, turning on lamps as he went. Lighting the suite with a soft glow. Turning the cold hotel room into a welcoming home away from home.

There were framed pictures of the Sin Boys everywhere. On every wall. Some were of Chance, Kruze, or Pagan in their gleaming dress whites with rows of bright shiny medals on their left chests, the bright golden SEAL trident they'd each earned pinned above the rest. Other pictures were of them in casual clothes with Scarlett and an older, silver-haired gentleman beaming beside them. Family pictures. Vicki was looking at an arsenal of Sinclair family pictures that extended back in time to when the Sin Boys really were just boys. Man, Pagan looked so much like Chance back then. Kruze had the same coloring, but his build was more lean and wiry.

It seemed Scarlett Sinclair had created a home wherever she'd gone. At the sight of all that family togetherness, Vicki upended the lovely crystal highball glass, needing the burn. Quickly. Painfully. Anything to wash away the hollowed-out pain that was her life. When that drink was gone, she poured another shot of liquid fortitude. Damned straight. This was a two-shot morning. Make that a three. The burn felt just as good as her third Scotch went down smoother than the first. If this is what it took to get her head back in the game, she'd drink the whole bottle. Pagan could drink something else.

Until she realized what she'd done.

It hit her like a hurricane. One minute she was on her feet, thinking maybe she had a chance of surviving this nightmare. The next, she was on her way down. The glass fell from her limp fingers. The room spun, and she knew—damn it, she knew!—she'd fallen for the oldest trick in the book. The booze was drugged. It had to be to have hit her so hard and so fast. Worse, she'd trusted someone. Again. She'd let herself be handled and lied to. She, supposedly the Mafia's best go-to girl had never been more...

Wrong. Wrong. Wrong.

Chapter Eight

Pagan heard the glass thud to the carpet but managed to get to Victoria's side before she hit her forehead on the sharp edge of the solid oak bar on her way to the floor. That would've left one helluva red mark.

"Let me guess," he murmured as he eased to his feet with one sweaty, exhausted, and very unconscious woman draped over his arms. "You thought a drink would make everything better. Breakfast would've been smarter, Victoria. But I'll order that later. Right now, you need to sleep."

Man, she was a luscious armful. If he were a braver man, he'd undress her and give her a quick sponge bath before he tucked her into bed. Being clean always ensured a good night's sleep. Careful not to bump her head as he made his way into the master bedroom, he decided that was precisely what she needed, along with a bottle or two of water and a couple aspirin.

But he wasn't that brave.

Before he laid her on his mother's elegantly upholstered, silk, burgundy chaise lounge, he grabbed two towels from the bathroom and covered the lounge with one of them. It took him a second to situate Victoria so she'd be in the most comfortable position, but at last, she was sprawled with her head on the pillowed back of the lounge, and he was good to go.

Pagan filled the sink in what had once been his mom's bathroom with warm sudsy water, then traipsed back to Victoria with a warm, wet, but not too wet, washcloth. The poor thing was out cold, and no wonder. Three shots of pure Scotch on an empty stomach, on top of what had happened last night and this morning, had done her in.

She would still need a good soak when she woke, but for now, he ran the cloth over her face and neck, and down her bare arms. That was all he intended to do, just remove enough surface dirt to allow her to sleep comfortably. Honest. But her skin was so cold, and he paused a moment too long on her slender fingers. She'd washed them recently, but the nail beds were horribly trashed, some of her nails missing. Flecks of dirt were still embedded in her raw fingertips.

Pagan retrieved a blanket and covered her, then he lifted one delicate hand to better assess the damage to her fingers. Interestingly, her knuckles weren't bruised and bloodied like she'd been in a fight. Yet every fingernail... Damn. She'd scratched some of them off. Doing what?

"Where were you last night?" he asked as he rotated her wrist to better assess the damage. These poor fingers had to hurt. She'd been in some kind of struggle for her life. He got that, but where? In a mud pit?

It dawned on him then.

No. Not Victoria.

But yes. Victoria. He should've figured it out sooner. The flecks of dirt around the edge of her face. In her hairline. Her dirty bare feet. The dulled shine to her usually glossy black hair. Her once white, now rank and soiled tank top. It all added up. Some asshat had not only gotten the jump on Victoria, but he'd thought he'd killed her. He'd buried her alive.

"I'll kill him," Pagan growled softly as rage sprang to life in the deepest catacombs of his heart. This woman barely cleared five-six. Yes, she was in every way stronger and faster than most women. She was devious in ways men would never understand, but even on her best days, Victoria Hex was no physical match for an adult male. If an adult male had done this. Pagan knew a few women who could've taken Victoria down if they'd gotten the jump on her.

Incensed that anyone had dared hurt her, Pagan located a plastic wash basin from the master bathroom, filled it with warm, sudsy water and quickly returned to Victoria's side. If she woke now, she'd never let him get this close, so he worked quickly and efficiently. Dipping one of her hands into the water, he soaked a goodly portion of the soil out of her wounds.

They were totally off the grid here. They were safe. Victoria could rest long enough to regain her composure and her fierce lion heart. For that was how Pagan saw her, as a lioness on the hunt. Ever watchful. Ever ready to spring into action for her pride. Ever wild and free and untamable and...

Screech! Whoa, boy. Stop it. Just stop right there. Back that boat up and park it at the dock.

Kruze had certainly tamed this wild woman once or twice. That was how his brother operated. Love 'em and leave 'em. Love the one you're with. And Kruze had definitely been with Miss Hex in Portland last year. That was the only thing that explained why he'd gone silent at the same times that Hex had. They had to have been together.

Pagan snorted at the way his mind wandered. What did it matter if she'd gotten with Kruze? It didn't. Not really. Yes, Victoria was a rare woman and an even rarer American. She'd literally sacrificed any semblance of a normal life the day she'd signed on with the Agency. It was her job to end whomever Vito and Cabb told her to end, and if that meant schmoozing the pants off other covert agents, well, she certainly had the body to get the job done.

I mean, look at those girls...

Shit. Pagan jerked his gaze from Victoria's heaving chest and her very luscious and lovely *girls*. Yes, she was full-busted with a tiny waist that accentuated her figure. But this was no time to ogle an unconscious woman who'd unknowingly placed her life in his hands when she'd passed out. Ogling was not only stupid, it was an unforgivable breach of trust. It was unmanly. It was downright dishonorable.

Pagan shook his head and continued with what he'd been doing before his brain derailed. "You're safe here," he told Victoria in case she was listening at some barely conscious level.

Just because Kruze was the lady's past did not make Baby Brother her future. Pagan had no intention of going down that well-traveled road. He was only here to confirm, once and for all time, that Victoria had not betrayed her handler or her country.

"I shouldn't have kissed you that night at Johnny's," he told her as he applied a numbing agent to her damaged fingertips, then wrapped her hands with sterile medical gauze. "That was wrong of me. It won't happen again. You can trust me, Victoria. I'm on your side."

Not that she'd ever believe him. He didn't expect that. But what he'd told her was the truth. She was safe. *Safe from Vito and Cabb. Safe from Kruze, and safe from me.*

Chapter Nine

Buried alive! Not again! Vicki woke up startled and scared. Disoriented. Pissed as hell. But able to breathe. "Where am I?" she asked the empty room. Angry at the timid squeak that just came out of her sore, dry throat, she asked again with the full intent of kicking someone's ass if they didn't speak up. "Where the fuck am I? Tell me!"

"You're in my mom's apartment in Chicago with me," a quiet velvety baritone replied from the dark. When the back glow of a cell phone lit Pagan Sinclair's rugged face, it all came back to her.

"You drugged me," she accused, even as her gaze darted through the inky shadows, her heart pounding loud enough to wake the dead. Ha. That phrase wasn't even remotely funny given what she'd just lived through, but that was what her mind came up with. Wake the dead. *Not helpful.*

"Uh-uh. You drugged yourself when you downed two, maybe three shots of Mom's best Scotch without sharing."

Which explained the disgusting taste of dog hair crawling around the inside of her mouth. "I did do that," she admitted even as she ran her tongue over her furry teeth. *Eww. Not smart, Vicki. Not smart at all.* "What are you doing?" she asked to get the focus off of her mistake.

"Watching you sleep."

Great. Just great. "Well, you can stop now. I'm... What's this on both my hands? Bandages?" Those had to go. She would've clawed at the tape he'd circled each hand with if she could have, but no. Every last one of her fingertips were encased in clean, white gauze, swathing her hands like mittens.

"You were hurt. I cleaned your fingernails as much as I could, then I wrapped your—"

"Stop being nice to me, Sinclair," she bit out as she shoved out from under the blanket and shot to her feet—and immediately wished she hadn't. The room spun, and Vicki had to sit before she fell down. Lifting her bandaged hands to her face, she sank her nose into the clean, white gauze and breathed. Just breathed. Her fingers didn't hurt at all, but her head was another story.

Groaning at the blistering migraine rolling through her skull like some roller derby track, she eased her aching body back to a prone position on—

oh, look. She'd been sleeping on a very lovely, possibly an expensive French antique chaise lounge.

Doubting herself, she glanced at the man who had quite possibly been telling the truth when he'd come to her rescue. Maybe it was time to trust this particular Sin Boy. "I might need your help," she told him. "But not for long. J-just for the rest of today Is that understood?"

"Yes, ma'am," Pagan replied as he came out of the dark and straight to her side. Placing his hand on her forearm, he dropped to one knee. "What's wrong? Do you feel sick?"

"No, I feel..." Stupid. Exquisitely. Totally. One hundred percent stupid. Vicki raised a finger to her mouth, afraid she might just be stupid enough to say those words out loud.

"Here," he said as he eased one hand under her knees, the other behind her shoulder blades. "You'll be more comfortable in the bed. Hang on."

Vicki did. Closing her eyes against a sudden wave of nausea, she clung to Pagan Sinclair, her arms around his neck, and her nose in his ear as he easily transferred her from the lounge to another fine piece of furniture. Man, the luxurious softness of the quality mattress he laid her on probably cost more than she made in a month. The baroque headboard alone was worth a fortune.

"Please," she begged as ridiculous tears breached her eyelids and began to trickle down her cheeks.

"Don't kill me while I'm sleeping. Please, Pagan. Let me rest for a while, and then... And then..."

Vicki never got around to saying, *'and then we can fight to the death.'* The blanket Pagan covered her with was too soft, and his words were too sweet for the hard man she knew damned well that he was.

"Sleep tight, Victoria," he breathed against her cheek. "I'm not going to kill you. When you feel better, we'll come up with a plan to confront the Seranzinos, but for the rest of today and tonight, sleep. Just sleep, baby. You're safe with me."

A sob choked out of her at the tenderness in what was supposed to be a mean and gruff killer's voice. No one had ever called her baby before or said it the way he just did. She had to be really sick to feel so emotionally unstable.

"I'm just tired," she told him when he wiped the tears under her leakiest eye away with the pad of his thick, manly finger. Calluses abraded her skin at that intimate touch, but even they soothed her ragged heart. Maybe because they were his? Nah. More likely because she was weary to the bone. "I just need to sleep. Then I'll be ready to—"

He ducked in close and she was afraid he was going to kiss her. Instead, he just whispered against her forehead, "No one's going to kill you, Victoria. Not here Not with me standing guard over you. Sleep easy."

He almost sounded authentically sincere. "You'd do that?" she had to ask as she looked at his neck.

"For me?" *You really, really would stand guard over me? You won't kill me?*

"Shhhhh. Sleep. Just sleep. I've got your back." He pressed his lips to the middle of her forehead. His last words.

Her last conscious thought. *Sleep. Just sleep...*

*****

'And I've got your front, too,' Pagan thought as he stepped away from the gorgeous, but bedraggled princess sleeping in his mother's bed. He'd always been a breast man, but this fixation with Victoria's girls had to stop or he'd never be able to function around her. Not in a civil, gentlemanly manner. As it was, he had to continually adjust the hound dog in his pants. Just looking into her melted dark chocolate eyes compromised his mental acuity and his physical ability to react logically and sensibly. Those lush, plump breasts of hers forced every last ounce of his all-American-male blood southward. Into his other brain. The little brain with only ever one mission.

But damn. Victoria looked like she belonged there, tucked into that plush comforter on his mother's bed like she was. With her dark hair in tangles and those awful shadows under her eyes, she reminded him of his brother's wife the first time he'd seen her. Suede had been as close to death then as Victoria was now.

The first time Pagan had met Suede Tennyson, now Suede Sinclair, she'd been in bed too, recovering from having been thrown off the mountain in Chance's backyard by her former boyfriend and lover, America's most pretentious tennis star, the former Lionel York. Now deceased, York had once thought he could play with a couple of truly evil men out of South America. Bad choice in tennis partners. Cartel bosses did not make honest brokers.

But it was Chance who'd ended York. Pagan only wished he'd been there the day Lionel learned to fly. Too bad he never learned how to land.

With one last glance at Victoria, Pagan closed the bedroom door and palmed his cell. Thumbing in the number, he rang home base in Montana.

Suede answered with a cheery, "Sinclair Ranch. How may I direct your call?"

"We're a ranch now? Since when?"

"Oh, hi, Pagan! Yes, we're a ranch! Since Chance bought two Clydesdales for me. Isn't it great?"

No, it's not great. It's crazy. "Horses? He bought horses?" Pagan growled at the way Chance spoiled his new wife. "What does he know about taking care of horses?"

"Aw, how hard could it be? He's out with the crew he hired to build the barn right now, but you should see them. They're amazing!"

That was Suede for you. Enthusiastic. Kind as all get out. But spoiled rotten, and that was on Chance. He gave that girl everything. Literally. They hadn't even been married yet when he'd promised her that all he owned was hers. Falling in love had made Chance soft in the head, but Pagan had to admit. Of the three Sinclair Boys, Chance was the happiest. No doubt about that.

"Tell him I've got the package he sent," Pagan told Suede. Chance had sent extra weapons, ammo, holsters, and a couple burner phones in that box. In his line of work, he had the federal licenses and the means to transport whatever arms he needed to move. "Listen, can you help me buy some lady's clothes?"

That shut Suede up. For a second. "What? Women's clothing? For who? Please don't tell me you've crossed over into—"

"They're for Victoria Hex," he stated loud and clear and unmistakably gruff. "Not me, smart ankle." He would've said ass if he'd been talking to anyone but Suede.

"Oh good, because I'm not sure where to buy extra-, extra-, extra-large panties and—"

She giggled like a little girl, and as stern as Pagan intended to be, he couldn't maintain a terse demeanor with Suede Tennyson Sinclair. He rolled his eyes at the mischief in her tone, loving his sister-in-law with all his brotherly heart. "Seriously, I need to order, what'd you call them, women's clothes. Victoria's had a rough night. She'll need several outfits. Hell, she needs everything. Boots. Socks. Under, umm, things. Jeans. Shirts. All of it."

"Gotcha," Suede said as she shifted into her usual helpful mode. "I'm not sure of her size, but I'm a pretty good guesstimator. I'd be glad to place an online order for Vicki. Where should I have it sent?"

"We're in Chicago."

"Understood," she answered without needing further specifics. Since she'd married into the Sinclair family, she'd been read in at a certain, low-level security clearance. She knew administrative protocols. The number for the hotline to Senator Sullivan. The addresses for the various bug-out hides Chance, Kruze, or Pagan used when out in the field. But never anything about their missions.

Which explained the Clydesdales. Chance had just gotten home from three months in Bosnia. He was overcompensating in two very big, equine ways to make it up to Suede. What a sap.

"Will I be buying the usual wardrobe items for Miss Hex?" Suede asked. "Leather bustiers from Neiman Marcus? Black leather hot pants and see-through bras from Victoria's Secret? A riding crop from Cal-Ranch?" Could she get any more sarcastic?

"No. No crap." *Hell, no.* "Just clothes a decent woman would wear and..." Pagan started to say until he thought about it. Victoria would need to maintain her tough-girl image, and to do that, she'd have to project the same sassy, spitfire, in-your-face attitude as she had before. She'd have to dress like Vicki Hex, the Mafia's best assassin, because that was who she was. "Maybe one or two leather items would be okay," he agreed. "Boots for sure, but no crops or whips."

"Gotcha. No whip. No chair. Just lots of itty, bitty leather hot pants. I'll get right on this, Pagan, and I'll put a rush on it, too. You'll have everything within twenty-four hours. When are you coming home?"

"Not sure yet," he said as he looked over his shoulder at the closed bedroom door. "Tell Chance to ring me when he's done playing around with your horses. We need to talk."

"Will do. Take it easy, Pagan," Suede said as she ended the call.

He placed another call for room service, then stuffed his phone in his pants pocket. Two problems easily solved. One damned tough one to go. Who exactly wanted Victoria dead? Couldn't be the Seranzinos. They'd have popped her, and no one would have found the body. So who else was there?

Chapter Ten

Breakfast at midnight, if that was what you called two pieces of buttered toast and four ibuprofens washed down with a hot cup of the tastiest, rich, black coffee. "Thank you," Vicki told Pagan sincerely.

They were sitting inside his mother's hotel room, behind the sheer curtain panels at her wide picture windows, with the lights turned off as they looked out over the city lights of Chicago and Navy Pier jutting eastward into Lake Michigan. Chicago's major tourist attraction, the Centennial Wheel at Pier Park, glowed as it revolved, elevating its passengers to one hundred and ninety-six feet above the skyline. Go Navy.

Vicki had taken a shower after she'd crawled out of bed. Thankfully, the bathroom came stocked with high-end shampoos, conditioners, and moisturizers—everything a woman needed to make herself halfway presentable. She'd removed the bandages on her hands in order to shower. She'd also brushed her teeth until her mouth tasted squeaky clean.

The extra-plush mauve bathrobe she wore now was a nice touch since her clothes hadn't been worth saving. To send them out to be cleaned might have alerted her stalker. She couldn't take the chance. They went into the trash, and for now, she wore nothing under the robe. Nothing but disgust at the way her day had begun and ended.

Skunked was an embarrassing outcome for a supposedly intelligent woman. Factor in her failure to hydrate properly—Man, Scotch? Really?—multiply that by her underestimation of Pagan Sinclair's fortitude and honesty, and what do you have? One supposedly badassed undercover operator who'd failed—big time—in the badass department.

But something was up with Pagan. He'd grown quiet since room service delivered two steak-and-egg breakfast meals, toast, coffee, juice, and an array of sweet rolls. Why he'd ordered her the same protein-packed meal that he ate surprised Vicki. Not that she cared for that much cholesterol, but it was the thought that counted, right? And it had been an exquisitely kind thought to feed her so she could get her strength back. That was Pagan for you. Kind. Thoughtful. But too damned quiet.

"I can't eat all that protein," she explained. "My stomach can't handle it yet."

He nodded. Just nodded. He'd patiently rewrapped her hands after her shower to protect her fingers. All that gauze made her feel like she was wearing mittens. With anyone else, she would've told him to buzz off. On most days, she demanded total dexterity, her fingers unencumbered no matter how much her nailbeds bled. But Pagan had insisted, and since it was him, Mr. Nice Guy? Big, tough Baby Brother? She let him. Everything Pagan had done today had been nothing but thoughtful.

"I left my bag in my apartment when the shooting started," she told him over the rim of her steaming cup.

"I'm sorry about that, but we were lucky to get out of there alive."

"We were," she whispered, more to her coffee cup than to him.

Whoever'd buried her alive had also been behind that mini-gunship. It made sense. That person had obviously followed her. He'd meant her to die, ripped to shreds in a bloody, unrecognizable mess in her apartment. If she were a betting woman, she'd lay odds it was the same person—or persons—who'd made both attempts on her life. Maybe she'd been followed to her apartment. Maybe yesterday was a ruse to get her to reveal all her hiding places.

Vicki spared a glance at Pagan. It had been a long time since she'd been reliant on anyone, much less a man of his caliber. Vito and Cabb, yes, but that was different. She worked for them.

"I have nothing," she said pensively. "No clothes. No cell phone. No money." She didn't need to tell him she was naked beneath her borrowed robe. He was a man. He knew.

Pagan leaned forward in his chair and reached into his back pants pocket. "Here. To get you by," he said as he tugged a thin leather wallet up and tossed it to her.

Vicki caught it in one hand without spilling her coffee. Peeling it open revealed layers of green bills. "Cash?"

"A couple thou. If you need more—"

She tossed the damned thing back. "Keep it. I don't want your money. I need—"

"It's not mine. It's Sullivan's." Pagan tossed it right back at her. "I think he knows he screwed up, and he's trying to get on your good side."

Insulted because Senator Sullivan thought he could buy her after he'd sent Pagan to kill her, Vicki kept the damned money. Because of that high-level betrayal, she'd spend every last dollar if it was the last thing she did. "I hate you."

"I know," Pagan answered, not meeting her eye. *The coward.*

"And I hate this business."

"I know that, too."

Silence stretched between them like a tangible force field no words could breach. Talk was what got a woman killed, so Vicki sipped her coffee and let the night be what it was. Peaceful. Comfortable. Awkward and silent.

For the first time since she'd woken up in that grave, she could breathe without the simple, taken for granted mechanics of inhaling, hurting. That in itself revealed how safe she felt here in Pagan's mother's hideaway. How odd was that, an assassin feeling safe with another assassin? But she did. As long as it was Pagan.

Had to be because this suite had once belonged to Scarlett Sinclair, and those were family pictures of her boys on the walls. She'd filled these rooms with things that were important to her, pictures, snapshots, and portraits of the people who'd meant the most to her. Her three sons. The place didn't feel like a hotel as much as it felt like a home, and wasn't that another one of those crazy, weird things in life? Vicki had woken up today in a cold, dark grave, but had ended here in what was probably the nicest, most genuinely humble home of an honest to goodness mother.

Pagan arched in his chair, cracking several vertebrae as he twisted from side to side.

"Bad back?" she asked just to make conversation.

He grunted. "No worse than yours. I do need to check that head wound, though. Whenever you're ready."

Vicki set her cup to the table beside her chair. "Make it quick."

Pagan lifted out of his chair. The man was a study in quick obedience. He pursed his lips as he lifted a chunk of her hair out of his way. Then everything went from bad to worse. He'd gotten close. Too close. Vicki couldn't breathe. She grabbed his wrist to stop him before he touched her again.

Pagan looked down at her, the ambient light of the city behind him, his face shadowed and his eyes unreadable. Despite the cozy distraction of his mother's hotel suite, he was a hulking big man. Overwhelmingly big. He could still kill her, toss her body out the window, and no one would care.

Vicki stared up at him, her heart pounding at the possibility he would do such an atrocious thing.

He stood there in silence. Looking down at her. Breathing steadily. Waiting.

Her heart tripped up her throat. This particular Sin Boy was intensely gorgeous in a dark, ruggedly brooding way. Those lips. Heartstoppingly lush, not thin and cruel like Kruze's mouth. No. Pagan's lips were—dare she think it?—kissable. Full. They'd probably taste like the alcohol he loved. Bushmills Irish Whiskey, wasn't it? Her tongue slipped over her bottom lip at the thought of licking those lips. Mama Sinclair and whoever Daddy Sinclair was had made beautiful babies together.

Definite laugh lines bracketed Pagan's mouth as if he found life a joy instead of the trial she thought it was. As if he'd actually found reasons to smile in the ugly, covert world he lived and worked in. As if there really were such things as silver linings and lucky charms and all that cheerful crap. But he saved children, didn't he? She, on the other hand, earned blood money with every kill she made.

Yes, she practiced safe assassinations, if there were such things. Never had she killed a law enforcement officer, another undercover agent, or an innocent victim. Yes, she'd had some explaining to do when she'd gone home without offing her mark, and Vito wasn't high on sensitivity or understanding. But so far, she'd convinced him that good kills—a dubious concept in his coldblooded world—often took time. That sometimes it was wiser to let an enemy think he'd escaped instead of taking out an entire jetliner or a bus full of school children just to end one asshole.

Yet the differences between Pagan and her were as wide as the Pacific Ocean. Twice as impossible to breach. She really was a killer. A discriminating killer, but a killer nonetheless. And he was one of America's favorite heroes.

Once again, her tongue responded to his proximity, sliding over her bottom lip like the betrayer it was. Vicki caught herself before Pagan noticed her body's attraction to him. She'd thrown herself at him once before and gotten rejected. She'd never be that foolish again.

But damn, the man had big, gentle, soothingly warm hands. Without asking, he'd taken her head in his hands and was now running his fingertips through her hair, searching for the source of the blood on her tank top. He'd gotten close enough she could see his brows narrow when he located the bump. Gently, he tipped her head to the side and brushed her hair over her shoulder so he could get a better look. One hand slid into his front pants pocket where he could very well conceal a knife.

She stiffened, ready to bat him away if she were right. But he'd only brought forth a tiny LED penlight, and okay. She was overreacting and breathing heavy again. Damn. Her nerves really were shot if she'd suspected Pagan meant to murder her.

Of course, he noticed. "You doing okay?" he asked evenly.

"Yeah. Fine," she breathed. *Just fine.*

"You've got a nasty bump and a slice back here," he muttered as he pressed the pad of his thumb to the edge of the slice on her scalp. "That hurt?"

She winced even as her mind strayed back to Pagan-land. Carved was the word for his face. Carved from the prettiest tan granite. Pagan looked more Mediterranean than Californian. Possibly even exotic in a tough, rugged way. His nose was straight, his cheekbones high, and his jaw square.

"No," she told him breathily. "It actually feels..." *Good. Damned good when you touch me like that.*

"You could use a couple stitches," he said without ducking into her line of sight and making eye contact. His breath smelled of coffee and that chocolate after dinner mint from his tray. "Hey. You pass out or something?" He called her on her lack of response.

Damned if her heart didn't tap dance up high into her throat, reducing her airflow and muting her words into a whispered, "Yeah, well, no. This bump is nothing. Trust me, I've had worse. Let it be."

Lowering his head to finally look her in the eye, he told her, "This is serious. You could have a concussion, Victoria."

The rumbling octave coming out of his mouth shivered over her in waves. Through her. She melted like chilled maple syrup on hot buttered pancakes fresh off the griddle.

No man had ever handled her the way Pagan was handling her now. Combine his tender respect with his innate talent to read people, to see behind their masks and into their very hearts, and she was certain he knew precisely what he was doing to her. It had to stop.

Vicki pushed him back and away with a terse, "Leave me alone."

Man, when had this happened, this yearning? This unquenchable desire to lick his lips and bite his tongue? She needed Pagan gone before she ate him alive or got him killed. Before she climbed into his lap and kissed the hell out of him. Before this quiet, anxious flame fluttering to life between them roared into an out of control wildfire.

But obedient Pagan wasn't always known for following instructions. His hand came up to cup her jaw. In the ambient darkness lit by the light of the major metropolitan city outside this too, too quiet room, the pad of his thumb whispered over her hot cheek like a prayer.

"I'm sorry," he said. "I know you're hurting. Tell me what you need. I'm just trying to help."

And enough! Vicki eased to her feet to get out of his reach, her coffee cup empty but still in her hand. Her trembling, bandaged, sweaty hand. "I'm fine, so knock it off," she said brusquely before she dropped the damned cup and made herself look weak and helpless. "I don't need a doctor, so forget it."

Pagan still knelt beside the chair she'd vacated. His hand fell to his knee. His head dropped. Just that simple movement told her everything. He wasn't here to coerce or badger. In his way, Pagan was truly trying to help.

The steak. The over-easy eggs. His standing guard while she'd slept the day away in his mother's bed. It added up to an incredible partner who could get her killed. Because she—Vicki Hex—was beginning to like this man. He was kind and perceptive, and right now, she was vulnerable. It might be nothing more than the residual aftereffects from the adrenaline of having survived the day. Whatever it was, this—this whatever was going on between him and her—wasn't going to happen. No. Nada. Never. She'd as soon kill Pagan as fall in love with him. That was what assassins did.

Turning, she gave him her back as she set the empty cup on the room service cart and went to the window. Man, Chicago was a beautiful sight at night, but all she could see reflecting back at her was the warm light from Pagan's dark eyes. All she could feel were his fingerprints on her cheek where he'd touched her. Damn him for getting too close, and damn her for letting him. She should've known better.

Why, oh why did it have to be Pagan?

"I talked to Suede earlier. She ordered clothes and shoes for you. They should be here by tomorrow afternoon," he said behind Vicki's back.

"Stop it," she hissed. "Stop being nice. Stop pretending you care. I don't need your help. I don't need anything from you."

And suddenly he was behind her, the heat of his body reaching out with tendrils of aching comfort she wanted to wrap around her like a thick warm quilt. Because he would let her do that. He'd let her use him and take what she needed from him. She knew this kind of man. He was a sucker for needy women. Which she was not.

But for just for tonight…

It'd feel good to not be alone and afraid in the dark. Just this once.

No way!

Stiffening her spine, she resolved to be harder and better than she'd been before. Harder made for better, right? It had worked that way in the past. She could be that hard as diamonds, untouchable female assassin again. She could. She would!

Until two massive palms cupped her shoulders as Pagan pulled her against his magnificent chest. Until her ass hit his very muscular thighs.

"It's okay to cry," he told her in a gently rumbling whisper, his mouth against her ear and his nose in her hair. "Especially when it's dark. That's when I do my best falling apart. When no one else can see me."

"I'm not crying," she told him, her bottom lip trembling like it belonged on the face of a fool. Which she was not!

"I know, but maybe you'd feel better if you did."

I'll show you. Vicki whirled on him. "Oh, yeah? You want to know what I really need?"

She didn't give Pagan time to answer before she kissed him. Hard. Viciously. Forcing her tongue between his not very reluctant lips. Man, what a mistake.

The sweetest addiction slid over her tongue, filling her mouth with a flavor she'd not tasted before, but would forever crave. It was her meth. It was heroine. It was whiskey and spice. Coffee and peppered steak. Snips and snails and puppy dog tails. Of musk, something sinfully delicious and one hundred percent male. A bolt of white-hot lightning shot straight to her core, evaporating her intention to use him.

Wrapping his arms around her, he lifted her feet off the floor as his tongue swept into her mouth like a delectable all-day sucker with a mind of its own. Her best-laid plan fell into sensual chaos as his palms smoothed down her back and cupped her butt.

"This is a bad idea," he growled.

"Shut up," she growled back. "I know that, but for once, can't you just do what you're told?"

"What I'm told?" he asked around her questing tongue and foraging lips. "Not sure I remember getting any orders."

He wanted orders? That she could do. "Kiss me, damn you. Kiss me like you mean it. For once, Pagan. Shut up and kiss me like you want me."

"Not sure that's anatomically possible, kissing with my mouth shut, but…" He covered her mouth with his and groaned around her lips, "I promise I'll give it my best Navy try."

Vicki lost her mind as Pagan lowered his head and took control. He covered her mouth with deep, lingering soul kisses that melted what little common sense she had left. Caution flew out the window. This man could kiss.

Her achingly starved libido kicked into high gear. Needing more, she angled her head to keep him right where she'd wanted him for months now. In her face. In her mouth. Stroking deeper. Their bodies burrowing into each other.

She kissed him until his breath became her lifeline. His hands became her world. Would a big, brave hero like Pagan dare take a woman like her to his mother's bed? With him? Or would he consider it defiling his mother's pristine memory?

Groaning now, starved for the rest of this man's body, Vicki hooked an elbow around his neck and climbed aboard. Yes. This was where she wanted to be. In his arms. Her legs hugging his hips. Her heat pressed against his belly.

But all too soon, Pagan tore his mouth away. "No," he rasped. "What are we doing?"

Like he didn't know? "We're holding onto our sanity," she told him. At least she was. Just for tonight. Just barely. "This doesn't have to mean anything. We're just two people who need each other. It's a way to self-comfort. I screw you. You screw me. We go our separate ways in the morning."

But Pagan was breathing laboriously fast, not buying that total line of bullshit. He shook his head like he was shaking her off. Down Vicki went, her feet once more on the floor, her bubble burst, and the fantasy over. Rejected. She'd made a fool of herself yet again.

Well, no damned more.

Embarrassed for thinking he thought one iota about her, she stabbed her bandaged fingertips into his almighty chest. Who cared how handsome or masculine he was? Who cared whether he was a former SEAL? This was the last time she'd—

"Victoria," he growled. "I'm not done with you yet. Get your ass back here."

"Oh, yeah?" Damn, he was arrogant. "Well, I'm through with—"

"Like hell you are." His fingers captured her wrist. Like the bully he was, he pulled her against him. One hand clamped onto her backside, the other landed at the nape of her neck. His heart was pounding hard enough she could see his pulse throbbing in the hollow of his neck.

"Don't do this," she whispered. "Please, Pagan. You don't want me. Let me go."

"Are you sure?" he asked, his sharp eyes searching hers.

Yes. No. "Yes. I'm... I'm..." *I'm a fool.* Even as she rejected him, Vicki melted into Pagan, her strength gone and resistance futile.

Bending at the waist, he scooped her into his arms and carried her into the bedroom opposite his mother's. "You're tired," he said as he shoved the door open with one shoulder, then kicked it shut.

"I am," she admitted. *And I'm desperate. I'll do anything not to be alone tonight.*

"Tell me what you really want," he said patiently. "If you want me to leave, I'll leave."

"No. Stay. Just one night. I don't want to be alone. Stay with me. Please. Just pretend you like me and stay."

"That's the problem. I do like you," he said.

"Liar," she murmured, right before he eased her onto the bed.

Chapter Eleven

Victoria was killing him with that sad expression and those too-big-for-her-face melted-chocolate eyes. But her come-on signals were all wrong. Worse, she'd been sending those mixed signals all day, one second over the top confident enough to threaten him with a blade, the next cowering behind his jacket collar, glancing over her shoulder at any sudden noise, and afraid to step out of the elevator. She'd had no trouble taking out that joker in the middle of a busy Chicago street, but now she froze when Pagan finally had her where he thought she wanted to be, on her back in his bed.

He knew damned well there were no silk or satin barriers to stop him beneath that fluffy robe, but he'd expected Victoria to come onto him like some Playboy Bunny hooker now that they were alone. But the robe was still closed. Her legs weren't spread in wanton invitation. And her eyes weren't sparkling. She didn't look happy to be there.

What the hell?

So, he stood there at the side of the bed to get his bearings, because what was wrong with this picture? She'd said she wanted comfort. A screw. A one-night stand. A quick get some, then get out while the getting's good, and before the morning's regret had the chance to fester and ruin the night before. He could do that. He'd certainly done that with enough women in the past.

But this thing with Victoria was different. Pagan couldn't recall any of those other women's names. None of them were memorable or worth remembering. But how could anyone forget Miss Hex? The way she commanded an entire room by simply opening those come-hither, deep brown eyes and breathing? The way she commanded without a word.

Now he was thinking poetry and romance and—?

Oh, hell, no. This was just chemistry with an overload of adrenaline to top it off. Even if they'd climbed under the covers and shagged each other like rabbits, it'd still be over come sun-up. They'd go their separate ways and never speak of this night again. As for the romance and poetry happening in his head? That was because he was in his mother's favorite writing place, and yeah. That was it. Exactly. Yeah. That was precisely what the soft spot in his head was about.

But why'd Victoria look so unhappy? Was that because of Kruze? Had that son-of-a-bitch ruined her for other men? Or was she pining for Scarlett Sinclair's middle son, wishing he were here instead of his younger brother?

Pagan took a knee at her bedside. "I can't do this," he admitted. He was a man and a real man never infringed on his brother's territory. It wasn't honorable, and it wasn't right.

"Can't?" she asked as she lifted to her elbows, her voice as brittle as an icicle. "Or won't?"

"You're my friend, but you're also Julio's baby sister. I'll never be able to look him in the face if we... if we..."

She filled in the blank with a particularly nasty word.

"I would've said make love," he told her quietly, "but yeah. Okay. That."

"You didn't even know Julio or I existed until last year," she pointed out.

Pagan nodded. "You're right, but he's a friend now and—"

"And what?"

"And what about Kruze?"

She cocked her head. "What about him?"

Pagan dropped his gaze to the carpet, not about to disclose what he knew—or thought he knew—about what this woman and his brother had between them. It just wasn't done. "Listen. I got carried away out there, and I'm sorry I misled you. But this isn't going to work. You and Kruze—"

"You keep saying that. Me and Kruze." She bolted upright, her long hair softly shining over her shoulders even in the dark. "Spit it out, Pagan. What is it you think you know about me and your brother?"

"Nothing," he replied. *Nothing I'd ever tell.*

"Then get out," she told him. "Get out of my room and leave me alone."

"But you're in my room," he said timidly, for the first time afraid of angering a woman. At least, of upsetting this woman more than he already had.

"It's mine now." With a flounce of her ebony locks, Victoria rolled over and gave him her back. Again.

Pagan lifted to his feet. Well, okay then. The line was drawn. He'd have to live with it. Wouldn't that be fun, protecting a pissed-off woman from some unseen and as yet unnamed enemy, as well as from himself? Maybe from Kruze too if he were dumb enough to show, not that Pagan expected him to drop in for a quickie. Still. This was the audacious Miss Hex, and normally intelligent men were known to perform extreme feats of daring all because of a beautiful woman. They got irrationally territorial, possessive, and downright stupid. Look at all the trouble Helen of Troy caused.

"I'm sorry," he said one last time. "I'll be right outside. Good night."

A pillow flew over her head at him.

Yeah. This mission was going to be a real riot.

*****

Damn, she could smell Pagan on the sheets. In the air. On her skin. As un-mussed as the bedsheets and blankets were, he hadn't been in here very long, but he'd left behind a delectable combination of manly deodorant, body wash, and some kind of wonderful. Not musk. Not sweat. But somewhere in between Heaven and Hell. Whatever it was, she now had it all over her body and in her hair, and Gah! Vicki couldn't get away from him, nor could she get enough of him. She would've bathed in his scent if she'd known where to buy it by the bottle.

Only now she'd run him off. But honestly, every time this cosmically charged thing between them exploded... Every time she thought she had him where she wanted him—out of control—the dumbass opened his big mouth and dragged his brother into it. What did Kruze have to do with anything, anyway? Unless...

He wouldn't!

Vicki shoved Pagan's other pillow off the bed, her heart racing at the most outrageously and very probable explanation. Had Kruze bragged to his brothers about something he'd tried, but hadn't actually ever—not ever—not even close—achieved? How juvenile! Was that what this yo-yo act between her and Pagan was about, Kruze laying untrue claims on Julio's little sister like some lying teenage boy with a boner?

What a joke! Vicki would never. Not with Kruze. *Eww.* Sure, he'd made several over the top salacious offers in the past, but the never-gonna-grow-up party-boy of the Sinclair family was not Vicki's idea of a hero. The way he strutted around like he owned the world, she wasn't even sure he was a real man.

And Pagan! Was he dumb enough to believe everything his brother said? And why? Just because that was just what 'big, brave men' did? Brag up their conquests? Objectify women? Minimize a female's intellect, skill, and abilities because she was born with breasts that jiggled when she walked? Like she should dress like a nun or worse, wear a burka or a hijab, so weak-minded men wouldn't be distracted by the sight of quivering female flesh?

Get real. A man's failure to curb his mind or his appetite was not any woman's fault! And Pagan was no better than Dane if he'd believed Kruze's lies. The nerve! Damn those men for reducing her to just another idiot with a vagina instead of the gifted covert agent she was. Men were stupid. All they needed to satisfy their over-inflated opinion of themselves was tits and ass with a keg of beer and a slab of crispy bacon on the side.

Dogs. They were dogs. Weiner dogs!

Feeling righteous and with a full head of steam now, Vicki shoved her butt and back against the headboard and peeled the gauze off her hands and fingers. Yes, her fingers were sore, but she'd live, and these wounds were nothing. She'd been in worse shape before, once when Cabb had actually called his private physician to her penthouse to stitch her up. But she had work to do now, and money to do it with. Pagan could go play doctor with someone else.

Tugging the large bills, all five of them, out of that silly leather wallet of Sullivan's—what was he trying to do, impress her?—Vicki reached for the phone on the nightstand, and made two calls. One to her handler, so he'd know she was still alive and still on the job. Dane might be a horndog, but he tended to nag when she failed to report. That was the last thing she needed to deal with now, one more horndog on top of the others.

He was the reason her Class A weapons dealer façade worked as well as it did in Mafia-land. He supplied the guns she sold. She moved them like lightning, then the Bureau of Alcohol, Tobacco, Firearms and Explosives moved in for the kill. They didn't take down every sale she made though, just specific ones, and how they decided which to go after, she had no idea. But the cover worked, and that was all that was important.

The second call went to her product specialist at the local Neiman Marcus. Vanessa might be home at this time of night, but she worked on commission. She'd answer this call.

Sure enough. The phone rang three times before a groggy female voice answered, "Hello?"

"Vanessa? Hi, it's me. Vicki Hex."

"Oh, umm, hi Vicki!" See? That dull sounding voice turned sharp and alert in a hurry. "Man, it's awfully late, but wow, hi! What can I do for you?"

Enough with the small talk. "Remember that outfit I tried on last month? The one with the whalebone inside the satin panels? I think it was light orange or pink or something like that."

"I do," Vanessa answered, only she made it sound like 'I do-o-o-o-o-o-o-o-o-o!' "And it was sunset coral. It enhanced your natural coloring, and it looked like it was made for you."

Perfect. "Could you send that outfit along with my usual order of silk stockings, and a pair of those thong panties I like to my new Chicago address? A new pair of thigh high boots, too."

"Yes, ma'am. I'll do that first thing in the morning. What's the address?"

Vicki relayed her current location, then added, "I can't wait until morning. I'm sorry, but I need them tonight. Can you get them for me or not? I'll pay extra."

"Yes, ma'am, I most certainly can do that." Vanessa's phone hushed as if she'd covered the mouthpiece. "Get back to bed. You heard me. I'll be right in. Quiet."

A little voice grumbled on her end of the line, and wasn't that interesting? Until now, Vicki hadn't known the savvy saleswoman she relied on was married or had a family. Vanessa had always just been that eager, smiling face on the other side of the counter at Neiman Marcus. Blond and blue-eyed, she'd gone out of her way to assist her wealthy customers, and Vicki had been thrilled to toss a few extra dollars her way at the end of a hard day shopping.

Interesting. But uncomfortably interesting. Because Vicki had just mentally accused Pagan of treating her like a mindless object instead of a living, breathing human being, while she'd been doing the exact same thing to Vanessa. Not lumping her into the sex toy column, but certainly treating her as simply a means to an end, instead of as a human being with a family and a life and...

Oh, crap. She has a kid, and here I'm calling her in the middle of the night. Waking her and her little one just to pander to me. Vicki cocked her head as she listened to bits and pieces of the discussion coming over the line. Sounded like quite a little boy or possibly, a girl. It was hard to tell by just the petulant whining. Apparently, someone was spoiled and wanted Mommy to stay where every good mommy should be at zero dark thirty. At home. Like the rest of the normal world.

At last Vanessa came back on the line with a weary sigh. "Okay now, where were we?"

"I didn't know you had kids," Vicki said.

"Oh, yes. I've got two. One perfect little diva and another on the way, but Leena's back in bed now..."

She raised her voice and called out, "At least she'd better be if she knows what's good for her."

"I'm so sorry I've disturbed you. I never thought—"

"Oh no, I'm glad you called, and yes, ma'am. I can run to the store right now and have these articles to your door in an hour, maybe two. Will that work for you?"

Vicki shook her head though Vanessa couldn't see her. "I've changed my mind," she said quietly. "Tomorrow's good enough, Vanessa. Stay home with your family tonight. Go read to that little girl of yours. I can wait."

"Are you sure?" Vanessa sounded incredulous, and didn't that humble Vicki even more? That Vanessa couldn't believe a rich bitch would cut her this small portion of slack? Talk about a reality check.

I really am a bitch.

Vicki nodded, more at own her admission of guilt than the woman on the other end of the line whom she'd so blithely called friend all these years. But a friend was someone you knew and truly cared about, wasn't it? You put their needs ahead of yours. And Vicki had never gotten to know the real Vanessa. Until now, she'd just been a clerk with a pretty smile. An overzealous product specialist who'd acted as if she'd do anything to please her best customer. An act. Aw, damn. Vanessa was acting. That Vicki understood.

Vanessa was just like Vicki Hex.

I suck.

"Yes, I'm sure. There's nothing more important than family, so please accept my apology for bothering you so late. I've treated you badly, and I'm sorry. Sleep tight."

"But... but..." Vanessa sputtered. "Are you sure? It's no trouble. Really. I can be there in an hour."

Vicki smiled. "I believe you would, but please, not for me. Go snuggle that baby of yours. She's the important one." *Not me.*

There was a pause on the line. Then a concerned, "Miss Hex? Are you okay?"

"I'm fine. See you tomorrow." Vicki hung up the phone and looked at the door. No light crept underneath it, but she knew Pagan was out there in the hall. And he wasn't Kruze.

Chapter Twelve

He didn't go far. Pagan took up post, sitting with his back against the wall outside the bedroom he usually slept in when he came to town and his pistols once more alongside his thighs. He'd never been comfortable using his mother's bed. Mental note to self: *Probably ought to buy a new one. It's just furniture. Nothing special. Except Mom used to sleep there...*

The bedroom door in front of him opened noiselessly and there stood Victoria in that fluffy robe. She was a vision, her tangled black hair cascading over her shoulders and breasts, not that he could see them. But no male alive could miss the dips and curves hidden beneath even the fluffiest bathrobe.

Her head canted. "You're sitting in the hall? Out here? Alone?"

Well, duh. He grunted. No sense in answering the obvious.

"We, umm, need to talk."

Pagan slapped the carpeted floor beside him. "So sit."

Victoria knelt, revealing only her toned legs and her knees as she situated herself beside him. She drew her feet to one side, then made sure her thighs were concealed and the sash was tied snugly at her waist.

Pagan didn't dare glance her way. He'd tamped down his zest for a frolic under the covers the moment things got out of hand. This woman had once been Kruze's girl. Might still be for all Pagan knew. He was just here to get to the bottom of her kill order. Not to bang her into submission. End of story.

"So talk," he said to the wall across from him.

Victoria's hand clamped over his forearm. She tilted her head as if she wanted to see him better. It was dark in the hallway. "Hi. I'm Vicki Hex. I think we've met before."

He spared her a quick sideways glance, then went back to staring at the wall. *Hell, yeah, we've met. You shot my ass the first time, and this time around's not working out too well for me, either.*

She cleared her throat and started over again. "Hi, there. I'd like to introduce myself. I go by Vicki Hex when I'm working, but that's not who I really am, and if we're going to work together, I'd like you to know the real me. I'd like to know the real you, too."

He couldn't help the way his head cranked to the side as if its clutch had popped. "The real you?"

She nodded. "Yes, Pagan Sinclair. We got off on the wrong foot. I'd like to rewind that last scene, pretend it never happened, and start over. Good?"

Pretend *what* never happened? The way her mouth had tasted of Scotch mingled with some exotic honey? The way he couldn't get the warm, slick sensation of her lips against his out of his mind, much less off his mouth? The way his fingertips craved another touch of the satiny smooth hair they'd tangled in when he'd picked her up? The weight of her lush but lithe body in his arms? The handful of her delectable and oh, so soft ass? The smell of her, a cross between the Scotch on her breath and the perfumed body wash she'd showered with?

Even now, his nostrils flared for every last epithelial drifting off her skin and drifting out of her hair. And yeah, he'd give anything to lose himself deep inside her warm, lush body. What man wouldn't? But all she wanted was to be friends?

"Good enough," he said as he gave in and crossed his left arm over his chest to shake her hand. "Friends." *Now leave me alone, because that's the last thing I want to be with you.*

She had a nice firm handshake, but he didn't let the contact linger since they were nothing more than *friends.*

That handshake seemed to make her happy, probably just for a minute, though. "So tell me about yourself," Victoria said, a warm light twinkling in the corner of her eyes. "I already know who your mother and brothers are. Where'd you grow up? What were you like as a kid?"

A scowl seemed to have taken up permanent residence on his face. This was the dumbest conversation he'd ever had with another contract killer, but if she wanted to play Q&A, well, okay then. It beat sitting in the hall by himself. "San Diego. Joined the Navy straight out of high school. Became a SEAL. Learned to blow up things. Fought for my country. Resigned my Budweiser when Chance nearly died. Figured he needed me. There. The end."

A Budweiser was the special warfare insignia pin all members of the United States Navy received upon successful completion of BUD/S, (aka Basic Underwater Demolition/SEAL training) and the prerequisite SEAL qualification training. Didn't matter if they were officers or enlisted.

The Budweiser itself consisted of a golden eagle clutching a USN anchor, a trident, and an old-fashioned flintlock pistol, which had made turning his back on his Navy brothers one of the hardest things Pagan had ever done. But he did it because his real brother had been distressed at the time, and he'd do it again. In a heartbeat. That was what brothers did. They always had their brothers' backs, even when one of those brothers failed to live up to the Sinclair honor code. Once a SEAL, always a SEAL.

Victoria slid her left hand between his right bicep and his ribs and tugged herself in closer, using his arm as a lever. There were those mixed signals of hers again. She didn't seem to understand the rules of her own get-to-know-me-better game. One answer did not entitle the interrogator to familiarity, yet here she was, tugging her body against his, pressing the side of her breast into his arm like she wanted him to hold her.

What was a man supposed to do?

Pagan let her hang onto his arm. That was harmless enough. Like he'd already said. *The end.*

"How'd you become a SEAL so fast? I mean, you're only..."

"I was twenty when I passed BUD/S. Twenty-six when I left the Navy. Yeah. I was seventeen and a half when I signed up."

She cocked her head like she didn't understand. He got that a lot. He'd been young for a SEAL. All the Sinclair boys were young when they'd earned their tridents. Pagan didn't know for certain, but he suspected his mother's longtime friend, USN Master Chief Barrett "Bear" Knight, had some influence in them getting into the SEAL program as early as they had. But they'd earned those tridents, fair and square. Hell Week was no pushover.

He let Miss Hex think what she wanted. They were friends, not soulmates.

When he wasn't more forthcoming, she sighed and said, "Well, I guess it's my turn then. You probably already know that—"

"You were recruited out of high school by the CIA. The Agency needed someone inside Sicily, someone young and foolish, someone with a figure that could get her inside the Mafia during their not so quiet move out of Sicily into Germany. They needed a go-to pretty girl, someone the mob would trust on sight." He grunted again. "In other words, the Agency sent a teenage sexpot into Sicily with a cache of high-powered smart guns and told her to sell them to the biggest gang of killers on the planet. They wrapped up their little time bomb with a good-looking girl and tied her up with a leather bow."

"You mean a big pair of tits," she said evenly.

Pagan shrugged. "I mean you did your job well. It worked, didn't it? You're inside the mob."

"Is that all I am to you?" she asked as she did a Vanna White gesture over her very nice, very plump chest area. "These girls?"

Well, no. But yeah. Miss Hex was definitely endowed, and not just up top. The rest of the package was damned attractive, too. Of course his eyeballs followed her fluttering fingertips, and of course she noticed.

Her hand eased out from between his arm and chest as she drew her knees up to said chest and wrapped her arms around her girls and her knees. "I feel like Kermit the Frog. It's not easy being green."

Pagan hadn't a clue what she meant by that, so he kept quiet. No sirree. Miss Hex had nothing in common with a flat-chested, slimy green amphibian. That was more his department. He was after all, the Navy frog.

"I do good work, Pagan," Victoria said quietly. "You might not realize it, but I'm selective when I have to kill someone. I never endanger babies, children, innocent bystanders, or most women. If the man I'm supposed to kill has a family, I never take him out in front of them. Even if he's an abusive asshole, I wait until he's alone. I don't off him even if he's with his girlfriend when he should be at home with his wife. I don't double-tap him when he's beating his wife or his kids, either, although sometimes I think it would be better for his family if I did. But no, I wait, then I make a professional hit. I make sure he doesn't feel a thing, but I also make it so no one doubts that hit came from Vito or Cabb."

"You ever off someone just because Romeo told you to do it?" Pagan asked, his brows up.

She looked down at her feet and shook her head, her hair a soft ebony curtain falling into her face. "I don't work for Romeo."

That was interesting. "Just Vito? Just Cabb?" *Or is this just another coverup?*

"Mostly Vito. He and Cabb are tight. I suspect all Vito's orders are really Cabb's, though."

"The old man's still in charge." Pagan made that a statement.

"Yes. Don't ever make the mistake of underestimating him. Cabb might be over eighty, but he's very much alive. And he's vicious, Pagan. Damned vicious."

"Then how have you got close to the man and his sadistic son?" Pagan didn't dare let his eyeballs scroll even an inch lower than her mouth. She was different tonight, and he didn't want to spoil the tentative truce between them. "I've seen you on the news, hanging on Cabb's arm like some starlet, fifty years younger than him, but smiling like you're right where you want to be."

"I'm not sure I am close to him," she replied as one hand went into her hair over the bump. "I thought I was, only now..." She swallowed hard. "I really don't know who put me in that hole. I've made a few enemies in this job. It could be anyone."

"You think Cabb or Vito are behind your attempted murder?"

She nodded. "I did at first, but I'm pretty sure I would've woken up dead with two holes in my head if they were. Vito and Cabb don't play around."

"Tell me exactly what happened. What do you remember?"

Now it was Victoria's turn to grunt. "Not much. I woke up with dirt in my nose and inside my mouth. In my lungs. So I dug my way to the surface, which wasn't very far or very hard. The soil was loose. The idiot who buried me didn't tamp it down. But I couldn't breathe and I panicked and…" She lifted one of her hands.

Pagan grimaced. Once again, she'd removed the cushions of gauze he'd wrapped around those poor fingers to protect them. Silly woman.

"I couldn't get out of there fast enough," she said, breathing harder now.

"I can imagine. Someone buried you alive," he said to make sure what he'd suspected was fact, not an assumption.

"Yeah, the idiot knocked me out, then buried me in a shallow grave in some woods out west of Chicago. That's the thing that doesn't make sense. He only knocked me out. Whoever he was, he didn't shoot me while he could have." Her voice pitched higher and tighter. "He had to know I was still alive when he buried me Maybe he thought I'd suffocate."

"So it wasn't a professional hit," Pagan said evenly to get her to calm down. "Couldn't have been Vito or Cabb then."

"Unless they did it to scare me," she whispered, trembling like a leaf in the breeze. "It worked."

Instinctively, Pagan's right arm lifted. She ducked. The poor thing was still in PTSD land where every sudden move startled her. But slowly, his arm moved over her head, and he lowered it onto her shoulders. He let it rest there. Didn't move on her. Didn't use his hands. Didn't make any sudden other moves, either. Just let this tiny thing between them be whatever it was, which wasn't much.

She tugged her long hair out from under his bicep as he drew her into his side. Suddenly, ebony silk draped over his bare skin, tickling his arm hairs. This wasn't a hug or anything stupid like that. This was just a guy being friends with a woman. Being a real friend. That was all. But damn, did it feel good.

Victoria seemed to need the security of his tentative hold, and that was a nice change. Her fingers splayed over his right pec, featherlight as if she were afraid to really touch him. Her cheek turned into his shoulder. Softly. Carefully. The entire side of her plush body was touching him, but it didn't mean anything. Still just friends, see?

Pagan stared at the wall, waiting for what to happen next, he wasn't sure. This was the black leather, thigh-high-booted woman of his most forbidden dreams. For the first time, it dawned on him that while Miss Hex may have all the right equipment, she might not be a dominatrix after all. He cocked his head as that possibility sank in.

But she's so good at it...

Yeah, about that... Everyone had once thought Suede was a slut, too. She'd certainly acted the part, for all the press to see and take pictures of and to fill the gossip rags with. But once he'd gotten to know her, Pagan realized Suede was nothing more than an innocent, twenty-year-old woman caught in a twisted snare only the Sinclair Boys could've gotten her out of. And they had. They could do the same for Victoria.

The poor thing trembled, so he tugged her in a tiny bit closer. Kept her a little safer. Warmer. Still. Just. Friends.

"I keep asking myself why Cabb would've ordered a hit on me," she whispered. "There's only one way to find out. I have to go back."

Pagan about swallowed his tongue. She had to go back? To Cabb? To Vito? Into that mausoleum in east Chicago they called home? Oh, hell no.

But that wasn't Pagan's call, and this wasn't his mission. He'd only traveled here and intercepted Victoria to get to the bottom of her kill order. If another federal agency wanted her dead, they must have a reason. They wouldn't have sent their own covert agents after her just because Sullivan wanted more evidence first, would they?

But really? Go back to Vito and Cabb? She would do that? Pagan couldn't bear the thought. Not Victoria.

Chapter Thirteen

Wow. Way to man up, Pagan. Don't say anything at all. Just sit there like a big, dumb bump on a log after I've bared my soul to you and told you I'm probably going to my death. Vicki would've given anything if he'd told her 'no way in hell!' If he'd raised his voice and told her he was there for her, that he'd keep her safe. But that wasn't what was going to happen, was it? Because, bottom line, Pagan was just doing a job, and she was still on her own. *Alone again. Naturally.* Weren't those the stupid lyrics to some stupid song?

Any second now, she needed to distance herself from this stupid, stupid man. She needed to pull away, maybe shove him away. Maybe slap him for being so dumb, for being a man. She needed to scream and make him want desperately to get away from her. Any second now...

But she couldn't. Pagan smelled too good, and that massive arm around her felt like a very warm wall of solidarity. For once in her precarious, tempestuous, risk-filled life, she was safe within the circle of this particular and very sexy smelling male's arms. Probably for all the wrong reasons, but Pagan felt thick and solid and, damn it, he was here, wasn't he? When no one else came, Pagan did. And Vicki desperately needed someone to be here for her. Just this one time. Just a little while longer.

An image of Suede smiling across the Sinclair living room at Pagan crystalized in Vicki's mind. It had happened during their one and only meeting, when Chance Sinclair captured Domingo Zapata, the psychotic killer from Brazil. The trust radiating between Pagan and Suede that day had been palpable. They'd both just survived near-death experiences, though Pagan's came from Vicki. But really, she never would've shot him anywhere but on his very nice ass. But that day in the Sin Boys' cabin, you would've thought Pagan and Suede were brother and sister instead of soon-to-be in-laws the way they'd treated each other with respect and concern.

That was what Vicki wanted, the sense of belonging, of truly being an indispensable part of a real family. She didn't need to be suffocated by all that Sinclair machismo, but she wouldn't mind being missed when she was gone. Or someone worrying about her when she came home late or when she didn't come home at all. Someone running out in the middle of the night to look for her. Maybe rescue her. Maybe tell her everything was going to be okay no matter how awful it was.

Julio was her only living family, but he'd been out of contact since he'd lost his family, and Vicki didn't blame him. She'd wanted to crawl into a hole and hide when she'd heard about what happened to Bianca and Tomas, too.

But even in the best of times, she and Julio had never interfered with each other's missions or lives. It had nothing to do with their very different black operations. That was just the way they had always been. Fiercely independent. Never in touch with each other for too long. For years, they hadn't even lived on the same continent, and as far as the holiday get-togethers went, she'd never celebrated. Why start now?

Julio didn't need her. No one did. But suddenly, that kind of life wasn't good enough. Vicki had to know. She turned to Pagan and asked, "Why are you here?"

His dark brows clashed together. "Thought we already covered that."

She said nothing, just studied the coffee brown flecks in his green eyes. Pagan had vibrant green eyes, not the muted, washed out hazel that most people were born with, but truly, magnificent, lovely, and very peaceful greens that belied his gentle upbringing. He'd been loved as a child. How wonderful that must've been.

But past the green, she saw something else glowering. One could only hope it wasn't love, because love was the worst lie of all.

Vicki took a chance and asked the question she'd begun this cross-examination with. "Would you like to know my real name?"

He nodded, his brows still drawn into a sharp, pointy V, but his eyes glimmering. Glowing hopefully.

She let her gaze drop to his mouth as she whispered, "Paloma. My real name is Paloma. I looked it up once. It comes from the Latin word for dove. The symbol of peace."

Right on cue, his gaze dropped to her mouth and he grunted like that was the dumbest thing he'd ever heard. "Paloma Hex? Really?"

"Uh-uh. No, Pagan," she answered as she shook her head. "Paloma Juarez. Julio always called me PJ. Vicki Hex is a myth. A disguise." She let her tongue slip over the center of her bottom lip, moistening it just enough to keep his attention. "She's an act I put on to get the job done. That's all. She's part of my job. I'm not really Vicki, and Vicki's not me. She's an avatar."

"Oh, yeah, right," he murmured, his attention still on her mouth.

Paloma licked her lips intentionally, drawing him in. Using her Vicki skills to get what she wanted. What she needed just for tonight. "What can I say? My mother loved diamonds."

His gaze flickered up to her eyes then because everyone knew that sad story. At the turn of the century, Belinda and Pedro Juarez were gunned down by the Mexican police after they'd robbed a string of jewelry stores. They'd left two small children behind, and those small children had promptly been dumped into the care of wicked Belinda's aged grandmother. It wasn't long before Julio ran away. By then he was old enough to make his way northward into Southern California, where he worked days in the fields and scrounged for food during the night. A kind couple came across him one evening and took him in. Eventually, he attended school. He joined the Navy.

In the meantime, Paloma languished under her grandmother's harsh rules. But she also worked hard in school, hard enough that she was selected for the exchange program that took her also to Southern California. And that was that. The CIA had need of her, and she would've done anything not to return to her grandmother. So she lied about her age, joined the Agency, and went to Chicago instead.

"Paloma Juarez, huh?" Pagan snagged a thick strand of her long hair and let it coil around his finger. "That's a very pretty name."

Paloma looked up at him then and told him the truth. "Someone's out to kill me, Pagan, and I don't know who it is, and I don't know who to trust. I want to trust you, but if I do, I could get you killed, and I don't want that. I have to figure out who did this. If not Cabb or Vito—"

Pagan dipped his head to her forehead. "Shhhhh," he whispered. "Breathe. We're safe here. Let's tackle the problems of the world tomorrow. Tonight, let's just be—"

"Friends," she said as she kissed him.

He turned into her, his arm now circling her neck, his other hand cupping her jaw and holding her in place. "Very good friends," he growled, his breath a cross between coffee and whiskey, between Heaven and Hell.

She nipped his bottom lip, then licked it to soothe the sting.

His hands were warm, and his breath was like manna, full of promise and trust in what she was telling him. She bit him again, a little harder, just before she licked the inside of his mouth. This man made the earth stand still.

Paloma found her backside planted on his thighs as he deftly untied the sash and parted the robe, the palm of his hand instantly on her belly, his fingers caressing her. Distracting her. Nearly making her forget she still had a murderer after her.

Pagan took hold of her head with his free hand as he took her mouth by storm. Hungrily. Fiercely. His tongue swept against hers, tangling on its ways to the roof of her mouth. To the insides of her cheeks. Suckling and nipping at her lips, filling her mouth even as she wanted him to fill another aching part of her body. His teeth bumped against hers. Not jarringly hard. Just enough that he changed his angle and stroked deeper with his tongue. Wetter. Stronger.

Man, this guy could kiss, and she was losing her ever-loving mind, lost in the delightful sensation of an artful lover's kiss. His fingers tunneled into her hair, holding her head gently in place as he made a feast of her.

Her hand went around his neck, the other up the back of his head into his hair, holding onto him as well. She loved the bristly brush of her fingers over his shorn head. The hard sensation of his skull in her palm. The man was so much larger in every way than she was. Wider. Thicker. Longer.

"More," she whispered around his slick, demanding tongue. "I want more, Pagan."

He leaned her back onto the floor, carefully resting her head and shoulders onto the carpet as he knelt between her legs and spread both sides of the robe wide. Man, what she wouldn't have given to see his face. But it was too dark in the hall. As it was, he'd tilted forward enough that his eyes were hidden in shadow. But that sweet smile on his mouth? The glistening curve of his lips. Apparently, he liked what he saw.

Shy now that he'd exposed most of her bare body, Vicki, make that Paloma, reached for the two halves of the robe.

"Uh-uh," he purred. "I've been waiting a long time to see you like this. It's dark enough. Let me look, Paloma."

Her heart flipped a backward cartwheel, then stuck the landing. He'd called her by her given name. Her real name. It'd been years since she'd heard it, longer since anyone had called her Paloma with any degree of tenderness. And suddenly this was so much harder than she expected.

He fell on his face, his lips on her belly and his tongue lapping at her navel.

"S-stop," she whispered, shivering at all his intimate touch implied. If he didn't stop now, he'd move lower, and she'd be more out of control. If she were a weaker woman, she'd willingly succumb to the temptation of making mad passionate love with Pagan. She had no doubt he could make her sing and cry, then sing again. Probably alleluia. Wasn't that what she wanted? To be deliriously out of control yet safe at the same time? For him to demand she stay away from Vito and Cabb, that he'd take care of them for her? Yes? No?

Without badgering or denigrating her for teasing him or asking one single question, Pagan climbed up and over her bare body, his eyes locked on hers as his massive forearms settled to the carpet alongside her head, careful not to pull her hair. "You're tired," he told her, the tone in his voice the exquisite purr of a contented jungle cat.

Paloma wrapped her arms around his neck and pulled his head alongside hers, so he couldn't read her eyes. "I'm not tired, Pagan. I'm scared," she murmured in his ear. "Scared that whoever's trying to kill me will hurt you. Scared of this thing between us. That I'm not in a good enough place right now, and this is just another mistake I'll live to regret."

"Like Kruze?" he asked, his voice muffled in her hair.

He'd done it again! Damn him!

Paloma took hold of his hard head and pushed him up where she could look him in the eye. "Let me be perfectly clear," she told him in no uncertain terms. "I have never been with your brother. He's not my type. One, he doesn't light my fire; and two, I am not that dumb. Frankly, I'm insulted you think that I'm Kruze's type. He is an idiot. All he sees in a woman are tits and ass, and if you're dumb enough to believe everything he told you—"

A genuine smile crinkled to life beneath that thick beard, and Paloma prepared to hear something stupid-jock worthy coming out of Pagan's mouth. Something like, *'Oh really? You expect me to believe you over my bro?'* Or worse, *'That's not what I heard,'* or something just as asinine, pigheaded, or sexist. *Men!*

But Pagan only smiled that one-in-a-million smile of his and murmured, "Kruze never said one way or the other." Right before he kissed her again and again... and again.

Chapter Fourteen

She wasn't ready, and Pagan wouldn't force her into bed. Paloma Juarez, the assassin formerly known as Vicki Hex, was in over her head in this covert, mob-oriented nightmare, but she was also falling apart. It didn't take a rocket scientist to realize she was physically and emotionally spent. No way was she ready to begin a relationship. As difficult as that might be for most men to believe in, a relationship was what Pagan wanted more than anything. He didn't need another roll in the sack with a good-looking woman. He didn't want another temporary one-night stand or make-believe. He wanted *his* woman. The right woman.

But damn, Paloma was one helluva lady. If anything, she resembled Suede the first time Pagan had met Chance's new bride. Suede had one heck of a foul mouth on her back then. She'd dropped more fbombs than the entire seventh fleet when they'd dock at Norfolk after a year at sea. But the more he'd gotten to know Suede, the more her atrocious reputation and language had made sense. Neither of her politically charged parents had ever been there for her. Not once in her short twenty years had they stood up for her.

Because of that, she'd fought the world on her own most of her life, and she'd survived some atrocious crimes inflicted on her by adult males in positions of trust. While Pagan had no idea what that kind of loneliness meant to a young girl, he did understand how quickly Suede had blossomed into the sweetheart she was today and the best thing that had ever happened to Chance. All she'd needed was someone in her corner. Someone to truly love her. Instead of one person, she got the entire Sinclair family and a few of their friends.

The bottom line? Pagan wanted what Chance had, and he knew a man didn't get that kind of lucky without the right woman at his side. Was that woman Paloma? Her snarky declaration that Kruze was an idiot had more than bolstered Pagan's intentions to let her rest. It was the right thing to do. Licking her succulent lips one last time, he pulled his mouth away from hers. But then he kissed her one last time. Just because. Then one more last time. He swallowed hard, not sure he could make himself let her be.

The poor thing looked up at him, her eyes almost crossed, he was that close to her face. Pagan bumped noses with Paloma. Then he rubbed his nose down her cheek and into her neck. He would've gone farther south because he really wanted to bury his face between her plump, luscious breasts. Her girls. He wanted to drink in the warm, sweet, salty feminine fragrance that waited there. Man, he was as hard as a steel spike, but he was also smart enough to know that good things took time, and he had a feeling Paloma Juarez was one of those very good things.

Swallowing down a gut full of passion and need, he lifted his weight off of her and got to his knees, then climbed to his feet. He gathered the edges of her robe and knitted them together as he located the sash. Very carefully, he tied the sash, once again concealing the treasure that lay within those folds of fluff before he changed his mind and took her here on the floor.

Yes, it would be hard—oh, so hard—to wait, but he knew now. He'd been waiting for Victoria, make that Paloma, for a good part of his life. A few more days, maybe weeks or months—not years—would fly by. But SEALs knew how to wait. So, he would wait.

Was she anything like Scarlett Sinclair? Probably not. But maybe so. In her own way. There was only one way to find out. "Come," he murmured as he tugged Paloma to her feet.

She came off the floor like a ball of fluff. Pliable and willing. Light as a feather. She landed on the toe of his boot. "Oh, I'm sorry. I didn't mean to—"

"Shush," he told her as he pulled her into his arms and against his broad chest. Damn, she smelled good. This was where his woman belonged, snuggled in tight where he could take care of her. Who would've thought this sassy woman would ever submit to a man like him? He surely hadn't seen this coming. "It's time you went to bed."

She gave him a funny look, but that was probably because she'd never been part of a real family before. She'd get used to being told what to do once she lived with the rest of the Sinclairs. He nearly chuckled. They were a brash and bossy bunch of big mouth males.

Palming the bedroom door open, he nodded her inside with, "Bedtime."

"Excuse me?"

He shrugged, going for low key at the incredulous tone in her voice. "You need to sleep. We'll discuss our problems in the morning after breakfast. You'll feel better then."

"*Our* problems?" And suddenly Paloma turned back into Vicki Hex. "What has gotten into you? I'm not going to bed. I'm not a little girl you can boss around."

"But I thought—"

"What? That I was helpless? That I needed a big, brave *hero* to rush to my rescue and do all my thinking for me? Get over yourself, Pagan Sinclair. Yes, I appreciate knowing I've got you in my corner, but I'm not twelve, and these are not the Middle Ages.

You're a sexist and a male chauvinist, you know that?"

"I am not," he growled. Next thing, she'd be calling him a misogynist, and he knew for sure he wasn't that. He did not hate women, and he'd never—ever—hurt one of them. But a male chauvinist? No way. He did not gender assign roles—did he? He was just, what was the word? *Protective.* That was it. He knew plenty about keeping people safe, and that was all he'd ever done with Victoria, err, Paloma.

Her hands slammed onto her very lovely hips, and he was pretty certain he heard thunder clap when they did.

"Yes. You. Are," she said, each word a sharp staccato beat like the sound her stilettos made on granite. "But I've got news for you. When my new outfits arrive tomorrow, you will back off and let me do my job. I have to go back into Vito's and look him in the eye. If he sent a hitman after me, then I'll know for sure."

"What new outfits? Are you talking about the ones I asked Stede to buy for you?" Oh, oh, he shouldn't have told her that.

Her eyes widened. That wasn't a good sign. "You what? You bought clothes for me? How dare you! The nerve!"

"But yours were ruined, and you needed something better to wear, and... You can't be serious about going back into Vito's. There's no way I'd allow—"

"*'Better to wear?'*" There went that head bob and chin jut again. "*'Allow'*? Oh, my hell, do you even hear yourself? Do you *allow* Chance and Kruze the freedom to do their jobs as they see fit? Do you buy their clothes for them, too?"

"No, but they're—"

"Don't you dare say *'men.'*"

"But they are." He knew what he was talking about, damn it. "Men are bigger and stronger and—"

"If you say smarter, I am walking out that door!"

"Victoria, stop. I—"

"Damn you, Pagan. I can't believe what I'm hearing. My name's Paloma. I tell you my greatest secret, but you've got me stuck in one of your narrowminded male time-warps where my name is still *Vic-tor-i-a*..." She drew that name out like it was a bad thing. "Which it's not and never has been. But Victoria fits your Puritan fantasyland where all women wear flowery aprons, probably while they're nude—while they bake cakes, and they just can't *live* without a big, strong man in their lives telling them what to do!" That ended with another overly dramatic wave of her hand that ended in air quotes.

"But... but..." He stopped arguing because *'but Suede likes to bake'* didn't feel like the smartest thing to say at the moment.

Damn. Victoria, err, Paloma might be—right. But why did it feel as if admitting she was right somehow diminished him? That it made him less of a man?

Because you are a male chauvinist, Baby Brother.

No, I'm not. I just don't want to see women get hurt. Especially not the women who mean something to me. It's not right. I am bigger than they are and this is the one thing I'm good at. I protect them. I can and I will!

Pagan stared her down instead of sharing his mental argument. Was that how she saw him, just some big, dumb behemoth holding her back instead of cheering her on? His gaze hit the spot on the hall floor where he thought they'd both shared an intimate moment of pure bliss and understanding. Making love with this woman would've been incredible, but now, he wasn't so sure what had happened there.

"But I thought you and I... you know... Us. We had a moment where we both..."

"I thought we had a moment, too, but that doesn't mean I'm your property. This is the twenty-first century, Pagan, and our military men and women are right now, at this very minute, fighting a war against an archaic mindset where women are still being treated like mindless chattel. Like slaves! Where they get to *'live'* if some idiot male allows them to." Paloma made a lot of cutesy air quotes when she argued. "Where they can't even learn to read unless it's *'okay'* with their father and brothers. Where they can be stoned to death for falling in love with the wrong boy. I'm sure you've worked with female soldiers in the field. Were those female soldiers stupid and helpless? Inferior? Less capable of shooting, thinking, or making command decisions in any way, shape, or form?"

"Sailors," he corrected. "They were female sailors, and yeah, sure, I've worked with plenty of women before, but..."

"Let me guess. That was *'different'*?" Air quotes again. This woman liked to talk with her hands and fingers flying.

Her brow arched as she crossed her arms over her truly magnificent chest, one bare foot tapping beneath the hem of her robe. She looked like a stern schoolmarm dealing with a truant kid—a very sexy school marm in a fluffy robe with nothing on beneath it. From there, it was a short, erotic hop, skip, and jump for his all-male mind to conjure up Victoria, *err, Paloma,* in a plaid school girl's uniform with a short, short skirt, and her bare ass...

Assassin. Assassin. Assassin.

Pagan sucked in a deep breath and ran a hand over his head, then over his entire face, hoping she hadn't just read his mind like Suede seemed able to do sometimes. Except now his mind was off track and thinking about burying his face between her breasts and tossing that robe to the floor, so she could wrap those long legs of hers around his waist, and so he could...

Assassin. Assassin. Assassin. She's not the motherly type. Not even the wifely type. She's an assassin!

That did the trick. His mind switched tracks and headed back to the land of reality where she was the mob's best girl, not a helpless female by any means. He cleared his throat and charged back into the argument with, "But it *is* different. Those women I worked with are trained professionals who've—"

"And I'm not?"

"They weren't SEALs! And neither are you!"

"So what?" There went those hands to her hips again. She leaned into him like a prizefighter. An incredibly hot, sexy bantam-weight prizefighter with long silky hair that glinted silvery in the ambient light of the hall. "Just because the Navy hasn't caught up with modern times yet doesn't mean a woman isn't or can't be as good as those male candidates who go through Hell Week. How many of them wash out before that ends, huh?"

He had no idea a woman's bare toes could tap so loudly on carpet, but Paloma's certainly made a consistent racket that seemed to reverberate off the walls. Or maybe that was his stupid heart. This woman was one fiercely adorable Amazon warrior when she had her hackles up.

"Only around six percent meet the requirements," Pagan admitted as he swallowed hard. "I never said women were inferior to men."

"You don't have to come out and say it. You men imply it just by thinking you know better than me. That we women need to be told what to do, when to go to bed or what clothes to wear. Really?"

Ah, so now it was a *them and us* problem. Pagan was definitely outgunned in this war of wills. He lifted both palms forward and gave her what he thought she wanted to hear. "My mistake. I get it. From now on, hands off."

Damned if she didn't barrel inside his extended arms, shoving his hands out of the way, instead of asserting more independence as she crashed into his chest. The top of her head bumped the underside of his chin as she snuggled into him. Jesus Christ, he couldn't keep up.

"No, Pagan. Not hands off. That isn't what this is about. Just because I want you to respect my profession and my brain, doesn't mean I don't want this with you, too."

She wiggled in closer, flattening those girls of hers onto his chest. Man, her hair smelled good. It didn't escape him that her fingers barely reached all the way around his waist. Pagan had no idea where to put his hands in this new politically correct universe. He settled for neutral and cupped her fluffy shoulders.

She shook her head against him. "You don't understand what I'm saying, do you, big guy?"

"I'm trying," he growled, but no. He didn't understand this complicated politically correct mess of female Navy SEALs, and he wasn't sure he wanted to. He went to war, so women didn't have to join the military, so they and their children wouldn't have to deal with the horrors of war. It was his job to keep the world clean and safe for women like Paloma, so they could stay home and be housewives and do whatever they wanted to do. See, he could too remember her secret name, though he'd never call her that in public. She might want him to, but he would protect her because—

Damn. What if what she wanted to be *was* an undercover agent for the CIA? What if that was her supreme gift, her one true talent? What if she felt as strongly about doing her job as he did about his? What if she liked what she did?

I am a male chauvinist.

"I care about you, Pagan. I have for a long time," she murmured. "Please, I don't want to fight."

"I don't know what you want from me." He ran his hands down her arms and back up to her shoulders again, sticking to what he hoped were her safe zones. "I mean, I thought I knew when you shot me in the ass, but... Wait. You care about me? Since when?"

Her head bumped his chin when she nodded. "Since the little village outside of Tikrit. I saw what you did for that little girl and her mother."

Oh, that. Since the Second Battle of Tikrit, where Iraqi government forces recaptured the city from the *Islamic State of Iraq and the Levant*, commonly known as ISIL, many civilians had fled the city for the safety of nearby villages. An earthquake last year had destroyed all the mud-brick houses in one particular village, trapping families inside to suffocate or be crushed to death. No one bothered rescuing the inhabitants in one home however. He'd found out later the mother in that home had been an outspoken proponent for female education. She wanted her daughter to go to school like boys did. That was why no neighbors stepped forward to lend a hand. Letting her and her daughter die in that tumbled down mess solved their problem with the local zealot who'd targeted villagers when one of them stepped out of line.

Pagan eased his chin onto the top of Paloma's head, content to hold her if that was all she wanted. "It was nothing. They would've died if I hadn't gone in after them."

She nodded, the brush of her cheek against his chest an unexpectedly pleasant balm in the middle of their emotionally charged argument. "It was everything to them. You were very brave, Pagan. I was proud of you. The building could've come down and killed you along with them, but you just acted, and that mother and her child are alive today because you did. You even moved them to a safer home in Baghdad. That was kind."

"But that was a couple years ago. You were there?" The instant he asked, he wanted to call his words back. Of course she'd been there, or she wouldn't have known what he'd done. But why was she there?

"I was tailing Herr Goudier."

"Ludwig Goudier, the German banker?" He'd been executed, mob-style, in the Swiss Alps days later. "That was you who ended him?"

Another nod. "He cheated Vito when Vito transferred his accounts from Sicily. Cabb's finances arrived in Goudier's bank intact, but Vito's came up short by a couple million euros. When he confronted Goudier about the missing money, the man had the balls to tell Vito there was a cost to doing business outside Sicily, that he should be a man and get used to it."

Pagan grunted. "Vito obviously doesn't subscribe to the BOHICA philosophy of high finance."

She tilted her head. "What's that?"

"BOHICA. Bend Over, Here It Comes Again."

That got a genuine chuckle out of Paloma. "Ah, I like that. Yes, Vito didn't like the implication that he had to bend over and take anything Goudier offered. So he sent me."

"But why was Goudier in Tikrit?"

Paloma all but purred. "Because he was also Mohammed bin Hussein's banker."

Enlightenment arched Pagan's brows. "You ended bin Hussein, too."

Mohammed bin Hussein, a distant cousin of the former ruler of Iraq and now an ISIL commander, had also masterminded the genocidal killing of thousands in northern Iraq during the Sinjar Massacre of 2014.

One of Paloma's shoulders lifted. "Told you I was good."

Hot damn. This woman was not only good, but she'd rid the world of two truly despicable men. And she'd done it while working for the mob.

"I don't get it. It's okay that I saved that mother and her daughter, but it's not okay if I keep you safe and out of harm's way?"

He got a quick chin bump for that when she nodded. "It's not the same thing, and you know it. As you just heard, I'm fully capable of taking care of myself. Yes, I'm off my game right now. I ran into a little trouble, but that's why I need this—" Her hands swept up his back in a warm wave that shouldn't have made him smile, but it did. "—with you."

Pagan liked this truce with Paloma, enough that he relaxed and molded her body to his, her sumptuous breasts pressed flat—at least as flat as those voluptuous girls could get—to his chest, her hips cradled inside his. Her ear rested over his pounding heart and her belly pressed against his raging hard-on. *What do you know? She cares about me. She really cares.*

"Even the toughest assassin needs a friend," she murmured.

Wasn't that the truth. Since he'd resigned from his team, Pagan had struggled. His family had lost their cornerstone when Scarlett Sinclair died, and that mansion-like cabin Chance had built in Montana was more of a pitstop than a home. Pagan missed going home to his mom's apartment. He missed chatting with her and his brothers if they happened to be there at the same time. He'd been floating for months since Suede had moved in with Chance. Talk about a third wheel.

It didn't get any stranger—or tougher—than this. Holding a woman he wanted desperately to make love with. Talking to Paloma. Trying to understand where on earth her ideologies and her passion had come from. Realizing that he did tend to automatically minimize feminine strengths. It was, after all, easier to go with what he knew and understood instead of trying to figure most women out. Because of that reason, he did *sort of* pigeon-hole females into tidy cubbyholes, and maybe, just maybe, he did that for his peace of mind more than for their safety.

But it was true, and okay, yeah. Paloma was more than capable of taking care of herself—most days. He'd seen her in action. Yes, she was off her game right now, but most guys would be off their games too if they'd been buried alive. Men got hoodwinked, too. Shanghaied. Kidnapped. Probably even buried alive...

Okay then. Maybe it was a brand-new day. Maybe it wasn't about fighting the whole politically correct current liberal agenda as it was the right time to recognize the fact that women were as strong as he was. Not physically, but in so many other ways. And maybe—just maybe—it was time he admitted he was wrong.

"So, umm, about you going back into Vito's..."

Her back stiffened, but Pagan cut her off before she got her dander up. "How exactly do you see that going down? What's my role in this plan of yours? You do have a plan, don't you?"

Paloma tipped back on her heels to peer up at him.

Pagan licked his lips at the sight. Her sash had come loose. Her robe was undone. Damn, what a sight. Her softness mashed against his hard muscles. Even in the dim hallway light, he could see her big brown eyes and the quirk of a mischievous smile on her full, wet lips. The plump flesh of her voluptuous girls pressed against his t-shirt like pillows he wanted to lay his head on. Between. Whatever. Every last speck of blood drained out of his all-male head.

"I was hoping you'd come with me," she murmured, her lips glistening. The tip of her delicious tongue made damned sure her lips stayed that way.

He could not think! "Yes, ma'am," Pagan said meekly. "That I can do."

Chapter Fifteen

She couldn't resist. Paloma lifted up on her toes and kissed Pagan. Then she kissed him again as the wildfire she'd held back with her diversionary tactic on women's rights exploded. Suddenly, lips and hands were everywhere. She climbed Pagan as if he were her own personal tree, his thighs and knees mere footholds to get her where she wanted to go. Once in his arms, she wrapped her legs around his waist, and the next thing she knew, she was on her back in his bed again. Kissing him and loving every delicious, satisfying mouthful.

This man knew how to kiss with long sweeps inside her mouth and over her lips while he held her head between his hands. The sounds of a contented animal rumbled out of him, enticing her to open wider as their tongues made urgent, passionate love.

Easing back, he took a deep breath, which gave her just enough time to get him out of his pants. His shirt flew over his head, while she undid his belt and zipper. He took over then, peeling out of his boots, pants, and boxers. At last and alleluia! He was as naked as she was. Honestly, she had no idea where that robe went, and honestly, who cared which part of the bedroom floor was now graced by fluffy fur? She didn't.

"I can't wait, Pagan," she whined.

"Condom," he growled as he reached for his pants and dug into his pocket.

"Yes, condom," she breathed, her fingers straying to his groin. "Need help putting it on?"

That earned her a grunt and a gentle slap on her bare thigh, not like it hurt. "Never needed help before."

"Good, then..." She arched, every cell in her body on overload at the sight of him kneeling there in the dark, poised for action between her legs. Aimed at her. "Hurry," she breathed. "I need you. Now."

"Yes, ma'am," he replied, his knees spreading her wider still.

Paloma brushed thoughts of forever out of her head. Longevity had no place in the life of an assassin. This fling with Pagan was solely about giving and taking comfort when it came along, which was damned seldom in her line of work. Friendship. This would be a short-lived, but beautiful friendship.

Friends with bennies, yes, that was what this was. Nothing more.

Until Pagan waited a moment too long. Until he froze, still at the apex of forever, looking down at her with the most peculiar light glinting deep in his eyes.

"What's wrong?" She had to know.

"You're beautiful," he said, his voice as soft and deep as a jungle cat's purr. "I don't want to rush. This is our first time. Our only first time."

Could this guy have said anything sweeter?

"Pagan? I—"

"Don't you understand? Life is full of firsts, but none of them will ever be as perfect as this one." His heated gaze slid over her nakedness like warm caramel, saturating her body and soul in something incredibly sweet and tender. Gooey. She was no longer just the mob's best hit-girl. She was a woman. The complex, yet fragile feminine secret to Pagan's rugged masculine key. This wasn't just tab A sliding into slot B. This act they were in the middle of committing was something much more frightening. She couldn't put her finger on exactly what this was between them, and he didn't give her time to think when he...

Yes. This.

He slid into her, filling her with one gentle rush that made her breath catch and her heart pound. *This. Yes, oh yes.* This was what she'd needed. This rugged, mind-filling sense of connection. This wicked heat that warmed her from the inside out like nothing else. This incredible sense of fulfillment that chased away all thought and doubt, all fear and worry, and forced her to live with the now instead of the what-if.

Paloma closed her eyes and held on as she let Pagan become her world, and what a world he was. It had been so long since she'd been with another man that this time, she flew too high, too quickly. She soared. Arching her body back into the pillow, she bowed to meet his gentle assault, her head throbbing along with her burning heart as—

"Pagan, oh wow, Pagan!" she cried, her poor shredded fingertips digging into his shoulder muscles as her world exploded into light and life and just possibly...

No. Not love. Assassins did *not* fall in love with other assassins. This wasn't Hollywood. *But if they did...*

"I'm falling," she whimpered as the tectonic plates in her too serious world shifted. Sublime peace wafted over her like a veil, making her believe there could be more to life than living a lie. For once in her convoluted, tangled mess of a life, she felt—hope. How was this possible?

With an intense rumbling growl and another soul-searching push, Pagan rocked into her one last time as he joined her. Completed her. Filled her with fire and sparks and... *Damn, I do love this man. Pagan. It's always been Pagan. Why now? Why here?*

A choking sob sneaked up and out of her throat. Paloma clung to him while he gave her all he had.

Every last molecule of his masculinity. Every last beat of his mighty heart. The virile heart she'd seen in action over and over and...

Yes, oh yes. Oh yes. This man buried himself to his hilt inside her, and she took everything. Right then, she would've agreed to whatever he wanted.

Want to play pretzel? *Coming right up.*

Sex on the roof? *You're on! Race you to the top!*

Bake me a cake with chocolates sprinkles on top? *Would you like fries with that?*

Okay, so it made no sense, but neither did the tender way he eased one arm under her neck to cradle her, even as his sweat trickled between his cheek and hers. Even as her heart settled into a calmer rhythm that oddly, joyfully, matched his.

Hope and joy. Two wishes she'd never dared think possible, yet here they were, suddenly snuggled between her broken body and this gallant warrior. This man she so did not deserve.

Making love had never been like this before. She'd never felt so completely in sync with another human being, much less a male. And yes, Paloma fully understood the magnetic attraction fueled by adrenaline-filled events—such as being buried alive, shot at, then rescued.

But this sexual attraction was off-the-charts indescribable. Simply, utterly, indescribable.

Paloma couldn't keep her hands off Pagan. This connection, this sense of safety and security, of someone truly having her back, was what she'd been missing, and she didn't want this 'first' to end. She gathered him into her arms, her hands splayed across his broad back as if she could keep this moment from slipping through her fingers.

More... I want more time and more this *and more Pagan.*

Loving the salty, slightly spicy flavor of his shaving lotion splashed skin, she ran her tongue up his cheek to his ear. Relishing the prickly rasp of his beard on her lips. The decadent smell of him in her nose. Whiskey and leather. A definite hint of gunpowder. And sex.

More.

Her world stopped turning as a sob crept up her throat, strangling her. Making her think for the first time in years why she did what she did. For so long, she'd disguised her risky, death-dealing career under layers of patriotism, duty, and love of country. But what had propelled her all this time really was—and she knew it—fear. She'd been running all her life. Away from her heartless grandmother. Away from her pitiful past. Away from herself...

Until now, when the world had ground to a stop and forced her to face the truth. She was in love with a man she could never have. She wasn't good enough for Pagan, and she knew it.

"What's wrong?" he asked as he bumped his forehead to hers, his breath a warm, rich blessing in her face.

Paloma couldn't—just could not—let him see. Of all the people in her twisted excuse of a world, Pagan would take one look into her eyes, and he'd know. Damn it. He'd know, because he was one of those few people in the world who truly saw through disguises. That was how he'd connected so easily with Chance's wife. That was how he was able to save so many children. People in trouble saw him coming and instantly gravitated toward him. Pagan was trust wrapped up in a beefcake package, and she had to get away from him before she gave him too much of herself. Because she wasn't just falling. No, she'd landed in the land of Heartbreak and Hell.

"I'm just tired," she lied.

And wasn't that the truth? She was tired—of her life. It was a total lie. Even though Pagan was also a government assassin, his life had always seemed more honorable, because he was an honorable man to begin with. He'd never had to sell his soul just to look good enough for others.

"Talk to me, Pal," he murmured as he ran his tongue over her lips. "I'm here for you."

"No, you're not," she told him honestly, because *here now* did not equate to *here tomorrow* or *here forever*. It just didn't work that way. Not for her. As much as Paloma wanted to ground herself in the arms of someone decent and honorable and good just this once, it wouldn't last. It couldn't. They were assassins. The odds were stacked against them. "We're just friends with bennies, remember?"

"Hey. Friend with bennies," he teased as he rested his weight on his forearms and cupped her face in his impossibly gentle hands, the pads of his thumbs tender on her cheeks. "You're crying. What's up with that?"

"No, I'm not."

"Yes, you are." He proved it by wiping his fingertip under her eye, and okay. So she was crying? It happened. "Was I too rough? Did I hurt you? It's been a while for me, and I'm sorry if I lost control, but damn, woman. You're not what I expected."

She went for sarcastic. "Ha!" But ended up sounding sad. Probably because the lump in her throat was choking her, making her heart hurt like it might be breaking. Probably because Pagan was everything she'd expected he would be but could never have.

"Leave me alone," she ordered to get her mind off him and back into reality.

But when he eased away from her like an obedient sex slave she'd just used and abused, she wound her arms around his neck and jerked him back against her breasts with a strangled, "Don't leave me. I'm sorry. I didn't mean that. Please don't go."

Pagan dipped his forehead to her shoulder and kissed the soft pillowy flesh at the top of her breast. "I'm here," he told her again, "and I'm not leaving you, Paloma. I'll stay as long as you'll have me."

Ah! This man was breaking her heart!

Chapter Sixteen

As usual, Pagan couldn't figure Paloma out. One second, she hated him, the next she loved him, at least she kinda, sorta, liked him. But could he read her like a book? No way. The woman was as confusing to him as no woman he'd ever met. So, he held her extra carefully in case he had hurt her, and she wasn't ready to admit it. Yes, she had her pride, but he was a big guy, and Paloma wasn't as tough or as heartless as she pretended to be or as he'd once thought she was. It could easily have happened. He could've hurt her, especially if she'd been—

Oh, damn. What if she, somehow, had still been a virgin until he'd slam-bammed his way into her? A virgin assassin seemed an exquisitely unreal commodity in this insane world they both worked and lived in, but—what if?

"Are you okay? Do you need to, umm...?" How did a guy ask the woman he'd just had the most amazing sex with if she might be injured or bleeding in her most intimate places because of what he'd done? Pagan had no idea, so he opted to be gentlemanly first and foremost. "Would you like to take a bath with me?"

She held onto him tighter, trembling like a little girl. A lost little girl.

Okay then. If holding her was what she needed, that he could do. A bath could wait.

Pagan eased out of her as slowly as he could so as not to hurt her again. He slid to her side and made quick work disposing of the condom, then came back to bed. Because she shivered when he did, he tucked her sweaty body under his arm, where, damn, it felt like she belonged. Not only belonged but fit as if she were a part of him. A missing part. Like that puzzle piece you've been looking for, to complete the picture of—you.

Whoa, boy. No. Just no. Victoria Hex, aka Paloma Juarez, as in Julio's hot, sexy baby sister, was not his missing half. She couldn't be. No way. They were just—what'd she say—friends with bennies?

But his big, dumb hands didn't seem to know how to let go of her. Pagan tugged the blankets up and over them both, then went back to holding on, one arm draped around her shoulder, that hand cupping her soft, sweet breast, his other hand automatically pressed flat to her belly. Even that felt oddly familiar, his fingers splayed and cupping her soft abdomen, holding her like a man might hold his pregnant wife…

Oh, hell no. Pagan banished that thought, too. Condom, remember? And his condoms worked. Every time. He made sure to buy the sturdy, dependable kind, not the cheapies found in bar and tavern bathrooms. His mom always said if you wanted to dance, you had to pay for the music, and he plain did not dance. But every once in a while, he cavorted, and that was all this thing with Victoria, err, Paloma, was. A one-time thing, right?

You betcha. If Kruze could handle one-night stands, Pagan could, too.

But he couldn't seem to touch her enough or touch enough of her. Paloma's skin was the smoothest satin, so soft and warm and addicting. Her breasts overflowed his palms, and he had big hands. Her backside was another sumptuous paradise. Her hips. Her belly. Every inch of her was the most amazing softness over steel. And her hair smelled of flowers and spice that made him think of the breeze in the Orient. His lips found the smooth expanse of her forehead, and instantly, his tongue tasted perfumed honey that reminded him of tropical nights and sandy beaches. Of wind and rain and the peaceful surrender in a lover's arms.

Christ. Since when had he waxed poetic? That irked him. Of course, he spiked hard and heavy at the tantalizing temptation that was every inch of Paloma.

Her touch. Her scent. Hungry again, Pagan dipped his head and kissed her swollen, ruby lips.

She answered back with a sweep of her tongue inside his mouth and over his tongue, and Pagan knew. One night with this amazing woman might not be enough. Maybe they could stay in this hotel a couple more days and nights. Maybe she'd forget about confronting Vito and Cabb. They could order room service and just, what was the word? Play?

But no. Not going to happen. Paloma was no sweet, delectable female. Not really. She had a job to do. She was a killer with a killer's penchant for blood. He himself knew the demon of the kill, and the more kills, the more demons, and every last one of those demons was thirsty for blood. They plagued a man's daytimes, night-times, and his every in-between times. How much tougher would they be on a woman?

Each life he'd taken had likewise taken a toll on Pagan's soul. It left a blackness inside him as indelible as permanent ink, but twice as deep. Through his skin. Through his bones. Straight into his heart. Was it right that a man should suffer for protecting others by ending the predators in the world? Maybe not, but maybe, yes. The terrible yin and yang of the universe demanded a price for every decision made, didn't matter if that decision was made in defense of others or for self alone. Didn't matter if it was righteous or unforgivable. The cost always had to be paid.

Yet even as Pagan's mind strayed into the morbid land of regret and the perpetual need for repentance, the muscles of his buttocks bunched with need.

"Condom," she murmured, and damn. He'd gotten drunk on the woman in his arms for the first time ever, drunk enough he'd forgotten his one cardinal rule: protection. Anxiously hurrying now, Pagan rolled off Paloma and fumbled for another condom from his pants pocket.

She giggled, her fingertips teasing over his bare ass. "Nice view."

"I'm working here," he teased back even as goosebumps lifted where she touched. Tiny goosebumps that morphed into sparks that morphed into a desperate need to get right back inside her, where, damn it, he felt like he belonged. At last. He located the slick foil wrapper, tore it open with his teeth, and gloved himself with one swift downward slide of his hand.

"Aw, I wanted to do that."

Music to a man's ears.

"Next time, okay?" she asked in that adorable teasing way Pagan was just discovering that she had.

"Next time," he promised, his control slipping as he closed in on his lovely target again.

She welcomed him inside her open arms and legs, and Pagan sank quickly and deeply into Paloma's slick heat. So damned warm. So damned right. He cupped her lush backside as he buried his nose in the crook of her neck and let the sins of the day wait for tomorrow. He had a woman to make love to, and if this night was all they had, he wasn't wasting a second of it.

Like before, she ground against him, groaning her pleasure, and inciting him with every little sound she made. It took a little longer this time around, but once again, they climaxed together, and Pagan was fairly sure nothing in the world felt closer to paradise than lying replete and spent, sweaty and amazed in this woman's arms.

When aftershocks shivered through Paloma's body, he smiled. Each clench of her most feminine muscles on his manhood seemed to repeat, *'Don't leave me. Please don't go.'*

He didn't intend to.

With a sigh, he shifted to her side, separating from his own private heaven on earth just enough to secure the condom with a knot and set it on the floor beside his bed. Then back to her side he went, tugging her sensuous self under his arm where she fit and where he belonged. One petite hand came to rest on his right nipple, and man, what a gentle rush. This quiet intimacy with Paloma was unique and satisfying. Peculiar, yes, but—

He searched for the right word.

But all Pagan could come up with was... bulls-eye.

Chapter Seventeen

"So you're Baby Brother," Paloma said in the dark. It was early morning. Vanessa would soon arrive with the apparel that would transform Paloma into Vicki Hex one last time, and confronting Vito would ensure the savvy assassin's demise. Unfortunately, it would also end the sad story of one unknown and never to be remembered Paloma Juarez as well. But that was the way of this world. An eye for an eye. A tooth for a tooth. One life for another. Make that one life to save another. If nothing else came of this day, Paloma meant for Pagan to live.

His chest rumbled when he grunted, "Yeah. It's a handle I can't seem to escape. Once the guys in my boat squad heard it from Chance's big mouth, I was doomed."

"And Chance is...?" She let the question trail.

"They used to call him Priest."

"Priest?"

Pagan nodded. "He earned the moniker the hard way. At first, his guys called him Father because he acted like a doting old man with a pack of troublesome sons nipping at his heels. You know, always making sure everyone in his squad toed the line, ate their Wheaties, packed the right shit in their blow-out kits, stuff like that. But I guess it never felt right, especially when one of his guys said, *'Forgive me, Father, for I am definitely gonna sin.'* That's when his handle changed to Priest. His men said he was either there to save souls—preferably theirs—or to give his enemies last rites."

Paloma ran her fingers over the dusting of chest hairs evenly coating Pagan's pecs before they narrowed at his waist. He was an astounding male specimen who made professional NFL linebackers look dainty. He didn't just enter a room, he filled it and downright owned it like the star quarterback owned the end zone at a winning Super Bowl game.

Power radiated off wide, thick, and tanned shoulders that could hold up the world if he decided it needed holding up. She held off from trailing her fingers down his centerline though. That would lead to more sex, and while she loved sex with Pagan, she needed to talk. There were things that needed to be said. "But he doesn't go by Priest anymore?"

A sigh wheezed out of Pagan. "Not after what happened in Peru."

She held her breath, waiting for an explanation. A man who indulged in conversation after he orgasmed was rare.

"Karma really is a bitch, you know. Chance had it made that day. They'd tracked the package into the jungle, located her, treated and medicated her. All they had to do was make contact with their ride out of there, exfil like they were supposed to, and they were home-free. But they'd been forced to take a CIA agent along with them on that mission. Dick Card. You know him?"

Paloma shook her head. "No, but the Agency's got operatives all over the world. I don't know everyone."

He grunted. "Asshole took off when they needed him most. Ended up being a liability instead of an asset. Not that Chance wasted time looking for Card. By the time he and his men got the package back to the chopper, she was in bad shape, and Chance knew they were in trouble. His pilot was missing and the perimeter around the chopper had been chewed up by heavy equipment. He told his men to hold back a second too late, and—boom. I got a call from Chance's CO late that afternoon. There'd been an ambush. Explosions. Claymores. Two-thirds of Chance's squad were fragged and gone. It was a miracle he made it home alive. He sure wasn't in one piece when he did."

"How awful." Paloma spread her fingers over Pagan's chest to comfort him. "I'm sorry."

"Yeah, well..." He grunted again. Pagan seemed to do a lot of that when he was deep in thought. "Worst part is it happened the same day Mom passed. Only Chance never knew she was in the hospital the morning he touched down in Peru. Hell, none of us knew she was sick. Only she wasn't just sick. She was dying."

Paloma closed her eyes at this terrible tragedy. What could she say to a man who'd lost his mother and nearly lost his brother the same day? That had to have been terrible.

Pagan's hand came up to the nape of her neck as another deep sigh shuddered out of him. "They don't call us the Sin Boys for nothing, Pal. The day Mom died, we all changed. Chance gave up his team and became a recluse. He'd still be a hermit if Suede hadn't come along. Kruze went sideways, started taking the impossible jobs and banging every chick in sight."

"But not me," she reaffirmed strongly as she cupped his chin to get his attention.

Midnight dark eyes gleamed down at her, but Pagan said nothing.

"You believe me, don't you? I've never, not once, been with your brother." Why it was important that he trust and believe her, made no sense. Paloma didn't usually care what the rest of the world thought. Had to be the remnant traces of adrenaline still in her system.

So why, when he nodded and whispered, "I do believe you, Pal," did her heart squeeze like she'd just had an aneurysm? Why did her breath catch in her throat? And why—God, why—did her eyes tear up like this 'friendship with bennies' was so much more than a one-night fling? Rare and wild, passionate and incredibly satisfying, yes, but this moment was destined from the beginning to be short-term. Never permanent. She didn't believe in happily-ever-after anyway. No assassin alive did. They weren't in the business of fairytales, and if they were, they didn't live long enough to talk about it.

"And you?" she asked to keep him from reading her mind.

Another sigh. "Me? Nothing. Not really. I just keep trying to make this world a little better everywhere I go. I figure Mom would like that. If I have to kill someone to do it, so be it. Life shouldn't have to be as hard as it is for most folks out there, but it is. Just doing my part."

Which explained his self-imposed mission to save the world's children.

"You want to be a father." She made it a statement because it was obvious. Pagan did believe in happily-ever-afters. The fool.

"Yeah, I do. I want what Chance has with Suede. You know she's pregnant?"

"She is? No, I didn't know that. Great." But what was Chance thinking? A covert operator having a family? Getting his wife pregnant? Had some of Scarlett Sinclair's famous romance books rubbed off on her sons or were they natural-born idiots?

"Yeah. Think she's due in a couple months. Chance is over the moon about being a dad, but he's scared, too. Man, that'll be something. Him changing diapers and getting up nights with a fussy kid." This man actually purred when he was content.

"You'll make an awesome uncle," Paloma offered weakly. Because really. Assassins didn't live long enough to raise children and attend PTA meetings or bake cakes for their neighbors.

"Nah. Doubt I'll be around that much for the kid to know who I am." He shrugged her opinion off.

"So why'd you tell your friend Jobe downstairs that you didn't know Chance and Suede were expecting?"

Another shrug. "Because that's for Chance to tell. Besides, Jobe likes to talk. What about you? Any plans for a family or babies in your future?"

Paloma shook her head. He had to be kidding. She didn't mean to sound negative, but Pagan had to face facts. She was who she was. The Mafia's best girl. That wouldn't change even if somehow—and that was a far-fetched and impossible *somehow*—she got knocked-up. "I have no future, remember? Already been buried once. Walking dead now. Doesn't look promising."

That earned her a gentle smack on her ass. "I'm going with you. You'll be fine," he said as his palm smoothed over the cheek he'd just smacked, soothing the sting.

She shook her head. "No, Pagan. I've changed my mind. This is something I have to do alone." *Because I do care about you. I'd never forgive myself if you were hurt—or worse—today.*

"This is not me being a chauvinist, Pal. This is me being your support team. Your back-up. Your partner and your friend."

"No, this is about me being capable of doing my job and you respecting my decisions and my abilities."

"But even the biggest and baddest Navy SEAL gets assigned a swim buddy and a spotter. We never go out alone." Damn, Pagan really was one of those insistent SEALs.

"You go out alone now," she pointed out in case he'd forgotten he was a *former* SEAL, working for one of the government's most clandestine organizations ever. They both worked alone. It might be a tough way to live, but it was what assassins did.

That big warm palm of his cupped her backside, pulling her close. Instinctively, Paloma lifted one leg over his thigh, aligning her core to his hip. Wanting him more than she'd ever wanted any other man in her life. She swallowed hard.

"Again," he growled, his way of telling her what was going to happen next. Not that she could miss the sheet lifting over his groin.

"Hope you brought more condoms," she murmured as she closed her eyes and gave in to this impossible-to-resist alpha male.

"Eagle Scout," he breathed. "Always prepared."

'I love you, Pagan,' sprang to her lips, begging to be spoken out loud. But Paloma swallowed it along with her tears. Love was for fools and dreamers. Not someone like her.

Chapter Eighteen

Damn this woman! She wouldn't listen to reason, and now there she stood at the curtained window, looking down on Chicago like she owned the town. Her hands rested on her very lush hips, and her delectable backside was damned near hanging out of that hooker special the woman from some high-end department store had brought over at the butt crack of dawn. Vanessa What's-Her-Name. Did she have any idea what she'd set in motion when she'd shown up? Pagan had a good mind to turn Paloma over his knee and…

Shit. I am *the biggest male chauvinist ever.* The thought appalled even him. But damn! How could Pal go out looking like that? Dressed in an orange corset with blacker than sin silk stockings, tiny leather shorts that barely covered her ass, and thigh-high black leather boots. Man, she was every salacious degenerate dog in Chicago's wet-damned-dream!

Because she isn't Paloma Juarez right now. She's Vicki Hex.

Pagan groaned at the pain in his hollowed-out belly. She couldn't have gutted him any cleaner if she'd cleaved him open and taken a sharpened melon baller to his insides. And the only reason he knew what a melon baller even was, was because Suede liked to cook and bake—like normal women!

He ran a sweaty hand over his shaven skull, fighting the urge to argue. Yes, Pal had a job to do, and heaven knew she was good at what she did. Paloma wasn't your normal, everyday woman, and she never would be. A dove, nothing. She was more special than those pigeon-like birds. She did serve America, and she did protect the world. In her way.

But Jesus Christ! Did she have to expose herself to do the job?

Short answer, yes.

But Jesus H. Christ!

Paloma, err, Vicki Hex cast a simmering glance over her shoulder. She'd curled her hair. It now hung in tantalizing ebony spirals down her back, the ends of it lovingly fingering the bottom swells of her shorts. "It's nearly time. Did you come up with a burner phone for me? A couple of pistols? Pink-handled like I asked?"

He nodded, his throat gone dry and his heart no longer in this deadly game.

"So, where are they?" She turned to face him then. The cocky dominatrix was back. Her hands were on her hips. Her chin had a defiant, in-your-face tilt to it.

Pagan's chin nodded toward the bedroom where they'd made love a half dozen times, and where he'd come almost as often. With her legs wrapped around him, she'd made him believe in forever in that room. On that bed. What a joke. She'd used him, and he knew it now. She'd only needed comfort. Well, she had that in spades. Wasn't he the fool?

"Don't go," still slipped out of his big, dumb mouth.

She gave him that twinkling smile of hers even as she walked up to him like an alley cat, one booted foot in front of the other, her hips swaying as if she were walking a line. "Sorry, big fella. This is what I do. Now, where are they?" She fluttered her fingers. "Time's a-wasting. Give 'em up."

And enough! He grabbed her wrists and pulled her against him, grinding her belly into the hard-on from hell in his pants that he'd gotten at just the sight of her bare-naked assets. "I'm only going to ask you one more time, Paloma. Please. For me. For us. Don't go."

She had no choice but to look up at him then, her long slender neck leading the way to her over-flowing cleavage. The bra portion of that corset was tight, enhancing and lifting what didn't need any help in the enhancement department.

The woman was shorter than he was by at least a foot. Diminutive. Fragile. Enchanting in a way he hadn't seen coming. Kinder and more careful than he'd expected of an assassin. But certainly not built to take on the likes of Vito Seranzino's cruelty all by herself. Throw in the sadistic odd couple, Cabb and Romeo, and Pagan couldn't bear the thought of her facing them down. Not in that get-up. Not alone. If she'd only listen to reason.

Instead, she smiled her coy Vicki Hex smile. The one that had long ago convinced him that she was nothing more than the sassy dominatrix she'd portrayed herself to be. "There is no us, Pagan. There is only you and me, two very different operators doing our jobs. Now get out of my way and let me do what I do best."

"Sex? Is having sex with your Mafia boss one of the things you do best?" Pagan wanted to slap himself the moment those words flew out of his mouth.

"How dare you judge me. I'm no different than you. I do whatever I have to do to get the job done, and if I have to use my body to do it, that's what I'll do."

'No!' his heart screamed even as his mouth formed a semi-politically correct response. "Fine. Okay then. I get it. Okay, yeah. You do what you have to do. Fine." He was rambling, making a fool of himself, but he couldn't seem to stop. She would let a vile monster like Vito into that same warm haven

where Pagan had just found what had surely felt like peace? How could she?

She blinked those too-big-for-her-face windows to her soul, and for a moment, it was Paloma Juarez staring back at him again. He could see Pal in Vicki's eyes. She wanted him to stand with her, maybe even tell her that there was no scenario on Earth where she going out that door dressed like Vicki. That he'd protect her even if it meant protecting her from herself.

Her mouth opened, then closed. The tip of her tongue peeked out, wetted her lips like she had something to say, then retreated. And Paloma morphed into Vicki Hex. Once again, she was over-confident feminine temptation in leather boots, her get-up designed to distract, intrigue, and otherwise start a fire in the blood of any man with half a brain.

Pagan swallowed, strangled by the agony of utter defeat.

"Let me go," Vicki reminded him.

Pinching his lips tight to keep from telling her 'no way in hell,' he willed his fingers to uncurl and release.

Once set free, Vicki tossed her head and strutted into the room where they'd made love. Chance had procured and sent the same type of holster she used before. Ever proactive, he'd known what Pagan needed long before Pagan thought to ask. Those were the things in the box waiting for Pagan at the hotel when he'd arrived. Every last bit of it was for Vicki

Hex. For her to keep up her cover. To keep on keeping on...

Yet Pagan wasn't prepared when she strode out of that room with her head held high, her hair tossed back, and her killer game face on. Was she beautiful beyond words? Without a doubt. Vicki was that Amazon warrior come to life with a hardness in her eyes that could cut like a knife. Yet Pagan knew the real Vicki Hex now, and she was Paloma Juarez, the sweetest woman he'd ever met. And she was walking into Hell. Without him.

'I'm going with you,' needed to be voiced, but she wouldn't hear it, so he didn't say it. Like the dominatrix she was, all Vicki wanted now was his obedience. Strict. Blind. Obedience. She wanted him out of her way, so she could be all she had to be to serve her handler and her Agency. To serve Vito and Cabb. Maybe Romeo. The thought of her anywhere near those criminals made his flesh crawl.

Pagan watched Vicki unlatch the locks to the hotel room door. He watched her ass sway as she walked into the hall and leaned over and looked both ways. He held his breath as she closed the door behind her and left him without saying a word after putting on a show she knew damned well he was watching.

She'd left him without so much as an insincere, *'See you later.'* Not an offhanded, *'Don't worry, big fella. I'll be fine.'* Not even, *'Goodbye, dumbass. It's been fun, but that's all it was.'*

Just. Nothing.

Pagan rolled his neck to shake off the tension rising like a vise up his back and culminating in bone-crunching knots over his shoulders. To hell with what Vicki Hex wanted. She wasn't real anyway. But Paloma was, and she needed him. He damned well knew it.

Chapter Nineteen

Damn him for being so... so... so decent! It was past noon as Paloma stalked toward the hotel elevator, her vision blurred and her dander up. Pagan had nearly ruined everything with that foolish sentimental outburst. Us. Really? There was no us. What was he thinking, that this confrontation with the Seranzino's would be any easier for her than for him? One night together didn't mean anything. Comfort. It had only been about taking comfort from each other, damn it.

And yet...

She dashed away the single drop that overflowed the corner of her eye. There was no room for sentiment in this vicious dog eat dog world she lived and worked in. Weakness was a mortal sin, and she wouldn't allow it. Not today when she needed to be the baddest ass ever. Vito needed to know he'd crossed the line. Vito and Cabb both needed a lesson.

One way or the other, her association with them ended today.

Focused now and finally feeling confident, she passed the gleaming brass elevator doors and opted to take the stairs to ground level. She needed the exercise before her nerves got the best of her.

Pagan seemed to think this hotel was safe. She hoped for his sake he was right. Leaving him had been harder than she'd expected, but work was work. Either she maintained her alter ego with bright, smiling eyes that could kill, or she wasn't good to anyone, and it was time to retire.

Retire, ha! There was no retirement in this line of work. The only way out was a bullet behind her ear instead of the bump she currently carried.

Angry now, her stride lengthened with every step as she pushed the stair door open and hit the lobby. Of course, people turned and stared. They should. Half-naked women tended to draw attention. She raised one hand and turned to parade wave at the murmuring, self-righteous audience at her rear when...

She ran smack into one warm brick wall of a former Navy SEAL. Pagan had apparently taken the elevator. She didn't want to do it, but he seemed to not understand the 'friends with bennies' concept. Well, okay then. She could fix that. Shoving off and away from him with both hands and a curt, "Excuse me, sir. But you're in my way," she left him behind. Again.

He said nothing, just matched her gait as they both headed for Jobe at the front door.

"You're not coming with me," she ground out.

Pagan could certainly keep a tight lip when he wanted to. Not until they reached the exit did he say, "Morning, Jobe. What's the weather like today?"

The old man's eyes twinkled. "Sunny with a touch of lingering fog still. Should burn off by noon. Will you be needing an umbrella, Mr. Sinclair?"

"No thanks," Pagan answered jauntily. "Keep that for the ladies."

Of course Jobe turned to Vicki, his glance skating over her over-abundance of bare flesh.

She almost felt ashamed, but that was an emotion Paloma would feel. Not her. Not today.

"Thanks, but no thanks," she told him airily as she waved off the umbrella in his gloved hand. White gloves. Really? This old guy was too much! "Catch you later, Jobe. Don't wait up. I won't be back."

Chicago was chilly this morning, and Jobe was right. A fine marine layer of Lake Michigan mist hovered over the tops of the high-rise buildings. The sun would certainly burn it off in time, but it made a woman dressed to kill, shiver. She should've planned better. A coat would be nice.

That wish was no more than thought, when a black leather jacket settled over her bare shoulders. The warm scents of leather and whiskey filled her nostrils.

Vicki turned to her right and glared at the guilty party marching at her side, the one who'd also positioned himself between her and the street. Like a gentleman.

She swallowed hard. "You're not coming with me," she told him again in no uncertain terms.

He neither turned to acknowledge her presence nor answered her. Pagan just kept marching, his eyes forward, his arms swinging at his sides like he had someplace to go.

"You're incorrigible. You know that, don't you?" she snapped, exasperated.

Again with the straight-ahead glare. The squared-off jaw set with determination. The strong, manly gait she found herself struggling to keep up with. But not a word in reply. Damn him. He'd turned this into a male against female competition. Well, she'd show him.

Vicki slowed one step to get behind him, then dodged to the curb and lifted her hand, hailing one of the many cabs lined up in front of the hotel. It didn't hurt that she doffed the leather jacket to reveal her assets, the very girls that Pagan hadn't been able to take his eyes off. Of course the nearest cabbie all but fell out of his vehicle in his scramble to assist her.

"At your service, ma'am," he beamed as he opened the rear passenger door and gestured her inside with a cavalier wave of his hand. Dressed in a simple white shirt over denim jeans, and a dark blue corduroy jacket, he had a mouth full of crooked teeth, but an amazing smile. *'Smile all you want,'* she thought. *'All I need is a ride, and I don't mean that kind of ride.'*

"Thanks," she replied breezily, hoping he'd hurry and leave before—

Damn it! Pagan had already opened the opposite passenger door, slithered into the cab, and was now telling the cabbie to take *him* to Vito's. The nerve!

She cleared her throat and at last, Pagan made eye contact. His brows lifted as if he had no idea who she was. "Hope it's no trouble if I share the fare, ma'am," he said politely. "But I'm in a bit of a rush. Where'd you need to be dropped off?" The annoying shit!

Yet what could she say? "That'll be close enough to where I'm going. Sure. No problem."

The cabbie glanced from Pagan to her, then back to Pagan. Of course, he would defer to the male in the cab over the female. Just like a man.

Vicki ramped it up, pulling a roll of bills out from between her breasts. Sullivan's guilt money worked like a charm. The cabbie smiled, but so did that damned Sinclair brother at her side. Man, he was like that dog turd she'd stepped in but couldn't scrape off her shoe!

"I can pay more if you can get me there in twenty minutes," she offered with a salacious wink.

The poor cabbie peeled away from the curb, all four tires sliding on the slick, fog dampened road. "You betcha," he said with earnest glee in the rearview mirror.

In the meantime, Pagan leaned back into the seat, his right arm spread along the back of it, and the darkest, warmest smile playing over his handsome face. He scratched at his beard with his free hand. "You come to Chicago often?" he asked, still treating her as if he'd never met her before.

Vicki wanted to smile, but she growled instead. "I don't know you, mister, so mind your business. I'm sharing a fare, not my life story."

"That's too bad," he said softly as his hand strayed from the back of the seat to the nape of her neck. Man, his fingers were warm as they threaded between the chunks of her hair to her skin. He'd no more than made contact when the familiar lightning she'd come to expect at his touch sizzled up her neck, into her scalp, and down her arms, lifting goosebumps in its wake. The feminine part of her longed to succumb to his charms, because know it or not, this wicked man had charms. Enticing. Tempting. Irresistible charms. If not for the cabbie's watchful eye in the rearview mirror, she'd surprise Pagan and straddle his handsome ass.

But that wouldn't get the job done, would it? Acting irritated, because a part of her still was, she brushed his touch away and snarled, "Back off, or I'll mace you."

Damned if stars didn't twinkle in those midnight eyes of his as Pagan withdrew his hand like a naughty little boy, holding it to his chest as if she might bite him next. "Ooooh, you're tough. I get it. No touching. Works for me."

Ha! She knew better. Vicki couldn't resist. She smiled. Hell, she damned near laughed out loud at his pouty lips. She had to turn away to watch the scenery, but who was she kidding? With Pagan beside her, she couldn't concentrate. The outside scenery turned into gray blurs with splashes of red and green lights as other vehicles sped by, but all she could think about was the way he'd held her all night long. The way he'd tasted. The roughness of that hard, male body against hers as he'd filled her all those times.

If only he didn't smell so good. If only her senses weren't tuned to the nearness of him. The way he walked. The sound of his boots on her six. If only her nostrils would stop breathing him in as if her life depended on him. Because it did not! It couldn't. Life didn't work that way. Did it? Could it?

Vicki lifted one hand to her chest to silence the quiet thudding of her heart at the thought of having Pagan on her six while she confronted Vito. He didn't have to be right there in the house with her, but what if she went in with a tiny wire? Where she'd hide a wire in this get-up, she had no idea, but what if...?

The tight square of her shoulders sagged with a tiny glimmer of relief. This was still a dangerous thing she was about to do, meeting with Vito and Cabb. Neither were known for their humanitarian deeds. Both were cold-blooded killers in expensive business suits.

But she was their favored assassin. They'd either be happy to see her or shocked when she walked through their front door and asked Leonard, their subservient manservant, for time alone with them. That would be when she'd know if they were the ones who'd meant to off her. And if they were? Then she'd do what she did best. She'd end them both. After that, she'd call Dane, and she'd quit the Agency forever.

Slyly, she spared a quick glance in Pagan's direction and found him staring back at her. Watching her in that calculated way he had. Dressed in black as usual, he was a veritable vision in power and manly strength. He'd worn a button-up shirt today instead of a t-shirt, the top two buttons undone and the sparest chest hairs showing. The shirt stretched over his broad chest and it was tight on his biceps. He really needed a larger size, but Vicki doubted the change in apparel could hide the man he was.

The beard on his jaw seemed darker today. Thicker. She remembered the way it felt on her lips and mouth when he'd kissed her during their night together. She hadn't expected to like it. Clean shaven was more her style, but his beard was soft, not bristly. It didn't leave whisker burns on her mouth or chin like a five o'clock shadow, either. And it smelled like him. Tasted like him, too. All things Pagan were fast becoming things she didn't want to live without.

"So..." she started, not sure if what she was about to say and do was smart, but going to say and do it anyway. "How do you want to do this? Charge in with guns blazing or baffle them with bullshit?"

The handsome guy sitting next to her had the audacity to grin, and oh, what the hell. Her foolish heart somersaulted like an over-eager Olympic gymnast, then stuck a ten-point landing, grinning like a fourteen-year old fool. A crowd somewhere in the universe cheered for her. Vicki was sure she heard it. Banners waved and heavenly trumpets blared like she'd accomplished something wonderful just by letting Pagan back into her life.

Releasing his seat belt, he slid across the seat to gather her into his arms, his eyes full and rich and so damned warm that she wanted to cry. The minute his body surrounded her, she teared up.

"I say we start with bullshit," he whispered into her ear even as he drew in a deep breath of her hair. "If that doesn't work, we'll improvise. Sound good?"

Closing her eyes, Vicki breathed Pagan back into her soul. She needed this man. Might even love him. If they lived through the day.

Chapter Twenty

"Vicki! My princess! Where have you been? I was so worried when you didn't return home last night. I've got men are out looking for you."

Vicki cocked her head to make sure she'd heard the lethal hand of the Seranzino *familia* correctly. Vito almost sounded sincere. His eyes were clear. Still sharp and raking over her scant attire with glimmering lust, but straightforward. He hadn't blanched once since she'd been shown into his study.

The dark, polished wood paneling in the room combined with the heavily curtained windows, made his private study feel more like a corporate boardroom. But the moment Leonard had announced her with his stuffy, "Miss Hex to see you, sir," Vito had popped up from the chair behind that pretentious desk and come around to take her hand.

Dressed in a dark gray business suit with a matching tie and a gleaming white shirt, he looked the part of a vampire. Which he was in a way. As always, his hands were cold and moist like the dead. With his black hair slicked back and dark brows that peaked when excited, he could've passed for a creepy version of *Count Chocula*. Except there was nothing sweet about him. Still, there was genuine concern in his tone. Vicki knew that much.

So, she gave it to him straight. *Let the pieces fall where they will.* If Cabb or Romeo were the ones behind this assassination attempt, Vito needed to know. Maybe he could prove helpful for a change.

"Someone attempted to kill me, sir." He liked it when she addressed him formally. "It took me a while to clean myself up and..." She lifted both hands to reveal her damaged fingers. "I came back to you as soon as I could. Whoever's behind the attack wasn't very smart. The idiot buried me alive in a shallow grave, but he didn't shoot me. I dug myself out, and here I am."

Red-hot anger flashed in Vito's dark as coal eyes. His thin upper lip curled into a nasty snarl. "Who would dare?" he spat. "Did you get a good look at him? Them? What'd they look like? Tell me! I will paint the town with their blood!"

Okay then. Vito was not behind her attempted demise, but he'd sure make a perfect succubus.

"I'm afraid I saw nothing, sir. It happened so fast. In my penthouse. The night before last. Whoever did it was already inside when I came home. Perhaps I may stay at the main house until I'm sure my place is safe? Maybe it's time I moved here?"

She only asked because she knew how much Vito wanted what he couldn't have, for her to live under his roof. But wise old Cabb would never allow her to get too close to his son, much less live under the same roof with him. As old as he was, the elder Seranzino was erectile deficient, but extremely possessive and jealous. He wanted youthful, vibrant arm-candy, and she provided that illusion of a winter slash spring romance whenever he requested her company for a public event. He might kiss her on the cheek and whisper salacious words in her ear when others were near enough to hear, but he never wanted her in his room or in his bed. The poor guy couldn't get it up any more than he could walk without his fancy cane.

Vito blinked even as the muscle in his jaw tightened. "Absolutely," he growled. "It's time for you to come home where you belong." He reached for her, his long fingers stretched out to cup her jaw.

But no! Vicki turned her head and closed her eyes, hating this guy's touch more than anything. Only one man had ever made her feel alive, and that man had bailed out of the cab blocks away from Vito's estate. Vicki had no idea where Pagan was now or how he could possibly have her back when she couldn't see him.

Vito froze, and she knew she'd blundered by refusing his contact. Swallowing hard, Vicki blinked away feigned tears. "I'm sorry." She whined to achieve the right level of panic and fear in her voice. "I'm afraid I'm not yet myself, sir. The smallest things seem to frighten me." What a lie. Coughing to clear her throat, she lifted her head and stared into his cold, dead eyes. "But with your help..."

She let that suggestion hang. Staying in Vito's good graces meant a long life for a hired female assassin. He needed to believe she needed him as both a man and a boss. Ah, the games a woman played to survive in this world.

Vito's gaze softened as he reached again for her. This time she allowed the gentle grasp on her chin and the way he forced her head up to meet his eyes. "You are the strongest woman I know, Victoria." A truly sinister smile flicked to life across his cruel mouth. "I can wait for what is already mine, so yes. Take some time off until you are well. Do you need to see a doctor?"

"Yes," she said without hesitation. "I was struck here." She rubbed the bump behind her ear. "The bastard knocked me out. Can you believe that?"

Vito didn't so much as look at the injury where her hand directed him. Instead, his dark, thin brows clashed together. Elegant brows they were, and when they joined, so did the echoing wrinkles on his forehead, further accentuating his disapproval and his link to Transylvania. His hold on her chin tightened. "This was no professional hit?"

"No. This guy's either an amateur or an idiot."

Which sounded exactly like Romeo Seranzino. The twenty-something young man had an ego the size of Lake Michigan, but none of the family's business sense. Known for his wild carousing and jail time more than his work ethic, Romeo and his posse of like-minded friends dabbled in drunken fistfights, car prowls, drugs, and a revolving door of willing licentious women. He'd become a liability and an embarrassment to the fierce Sicilian father who'd raised him after his mother had died in a mysterious car accident when Romeo was nine. It was a classic case of the privileged son resenting the stern but gracious hand that fed him. Only Romeo had never grown out of it. He was a man now, but he was a man with no loyalty whatsoever to his heritage, and Vito knew it.

The temperature in the room shifted. Not by much, but enough that Vicki now knew Vito also suspected his son of trying to kill her. She backpedaled before Vito caught onto her suspicion. "I don't need a day to recover, sir. Trust me. I am ready for your next assignment. I can do it now."

His thumb stroked the hollow of her cheek as he studied her like an insect he could crush. Vicki never blinked under his scrutiny. Never wavered. That could get her killed. Either he believed her or not. She was the one with the pink-handled pistols.

"You have never let me down, Princess. I don't believe I understand why, however. No matter what I ask of you, you always come through. Maybe not right away—" He licked his bottom lip as his fingers turned what began as a caress into a vicious pinch that watered her eyes. "—but eventually, within a reasonable time of my orders, you comply, and then you come back for more. Like now. You stand before me a resolute warrior after surviving what you believe was an attempt on your life, while my own flesh and blood resists my authority at every turn. Yet you and you alone remain most faithful. Most obedient."

Her heart pounded. Vito was building up to something. She just didn't know what.

He turned her head from side to side, appraising her facial features as if trying to read her mind. "You are most certainly not Sicilian. There is no blood tie to hold you to this familia, only the pittance I pay you, which even I find a despicable reason for a woman of your talent to linger. You have no hope of ever being in my will. Romeo despises you as much as you despise him, so there is no hope of marrying into my family. Yet here you are again. Always ready to serve. Always ready to lay down your life for me. Always..." He paused. "What is the word? Willing? Why do you suppose this is, little one?"

*****

That didn't sound good. Pagan cocked his head to better hear what was going on inside the Seranzino mansion. Paloma wasn't wired, but her burner phone was open and reporting every word in this bizarre conversation back to him. Tucked into the holster Chance had sent specifically for her, she'd turned it on when she'd gone inside that whitened sepulcher of a building, where one of the most powerful families in America resided.

His life and his heart. Vito Seranzino sounded suspicious all of a sudden. He was baiting Paloma, err, Vicki. Testing her. Did she endure this type of interrogation often? Suddenly, Pagan wanted to know all that went on in Paloma's rich and infamous *'Sicilian'* lifestyle. The muscles in his back shifted as he prepared to storm that stronghold to rescue her. God bless the men who got in his way. If push came to shove, he would end them.

She wouldn't like his interference, but damn it. He'd interfere even if she were just a guy!

Just. A. Guy. He swallowed hard. Those three words magnified his problem. Vicki Hex was so much more than any guy he'd ever worked with. She was a goddess. His morning and his evening star, and damn it. He was waxing poetic again. But while the men on his SEAL team had been brothers, they'd been mere mortals, while she was...

Damn. She was everything. Wasn't that an incredibly ironic conclusion to this ridiculous mission he'd volunteered for. The woman he'd once disparaged because of her dalliances with his brother had now become the most important person in his life.

"Have you no answer for me?" Vito was asking, his tone icy.

Sounded like things were going sideways fast, but Pagan had no idea which room she was in. He knew the basic layout. Grand entryway. Marble statue of some Italian dude standing in the center of a tiled marble star on the entry floor. Probably Vito or Cabb in all their disgusting glory. Dining room and kitchen to the right. Parlor and bar to the left. He suspected Vicki was in what she'd called the study on the far side of the entry, but the last thing she would want was for him to barge in and interrupt whatever was happening between her and her 'Mafia boss.'

Pagan caved. He wasn't man enough to wait outside when she might be in danger. Fighting a wave of desperation, he deactivated the security system around the yard, rigging the very obvious laser beam so the circuit didn't break and send an alarm while he scaled the stone fence. Vicki's intel was spot on. Two men in business suits roamed the expansive lawn and driveway between the fence and the concrete walks around the home. Pagan used the rows of maple trees and shrubbery to conceal his path to the house. From there it was a simple matter of breaking and entering. Silently. Carefully.

He set one boot to the marble floor just as Vicki told Vito, "B-but you're all I've got, Mr. Seranzino."

Excuse me? That punch to Pagan's gut was nearly enough to make him think twice about saving her treacherous ass. *He's all you've got? What about me?*

"Familia," she murmured softly. Seductively. "To be perfectly honest, I have no other family than you, your father, and your son. Where else would you have me go?"

Ah, so she was giving Vito the old soft-shoe routine, a little truth mixed with lies. Damn, she was good. Wait just a minute. Were those lip-smacking sounds coming through the connection? Was she kissing Vito? How damned low was Vicki willing to sink to keep her cover?

Pagan was angry now. She already dressed the part. She had openly declared she would do whatever needed to be done to maintain her alter ego, to get her job done. Only what job was she working on now? Hand job or blow job? It was enough to make Pagan vomit. Just the thought of what she might be doing with—to—Vito...

He gagged. *Shit!* How far would she go? Was she right now straddling Vito's hips like she'd done Pagan's just a few hours ago?

His blood ran cold as doubt for his own sanity plagued him. What the hell was *he* doing, putting his life at risk for someone who played both sides against each other? He ducked into the shadow of the marble statue of some other stupid naked guy in Vito's grand entryway, just as Vito's stiff-necked butler passed by. Had to be Leonard. But what did Vicki think she was doing? After all they'd shared? Was this just part of the sexual games she played to get her job done? Was anything she'd said or done real? Had it meant anything to her?

Sweating now, he glided nervously toward the pair of massive wooden doors at the side of the grand centerpiece of the entry, the gilded gold staircase. According to Vicki, that room was Vito's office. Also had to be where all this 'business' was being conducted behind closed doors.

Pagan's palm had barely rested on the doorknob. He'd nearly turned it and burst in when everything Vicki had said to him before flooded his brain-pan. *'How dare you judge me. I'm no different than you. I do whatever I have to do to get the job done, and if I have to use my body to do it, that's what I'll do.'*

"Really Vicki?" he whispered to himself. "You'd have sex with Vito to serve your country?" It actually seemed like something Vicki Hex would do. After all, she killed for her country. Why would fucking a gangster or two—her word, not his—be different?

Because I like her. That's why. I like her a lot. And what we did is different, damn it.

Because he still termed what they'd done together as making love. Not... *that.*

Swallowing the bile accumulating at the back of his throat, Pagan blinked away the beads of sweat trickling into his eyes. He was no Kruze. He did not toy with women's hearts—their bodies, either. Pagan could count on one hand the women he'd been with, as in sexually with, in his entire life. Each and every one of them had been a mystery to him, but Paloma more than the others. Which made his decision simple.

Pagan withdrew his sweaty fingers from the doorknob. As silently and as stealthily as he'd breached the Seranzino stronghold, he left it. Once over the fence again, he walked away from the strongest temptation of his life, the inherent need to step on Vicki's mission in order to save her life.

This was her job. It was her talent and her craft. From now on, he had to respect that she knew what she was doing. He had to trust. Pagan decided to do the only reasonable thing he could do. If she were lying to him… if Vito Seranzino truly was all Paloma had in this world, she'd have to prove it the hard way. She'd have to throw it in Pagan's face and make him eat it.

He steeled his suspicions, knowing that to trust Vicki, err, Paloma, was to put his life in her hands and on the line.

Chapter Twenty-One

Vicki endured Vito's groping hands, his bad breath in her face, and his slimy tongue in her mouth. For two cents, she'd end him here and now, but that would only create more problems, and she had to think about Pagan. He was out there somewhere, listening. She was sure of it. He was that sunshine in her cloudy day, unseen but ever ready to spring through the darkest clouds with one of his scant smiles and save her from evil.

And Vito was one dark, ugly cloud. With a frustrated growl born of her unseemly hesitation in his arms, he set her back, his once gentle touch now cold and as hard as ice, his welcoming demeanor the same. The man had to be bipolar as quickly as he changed moods. "Go then. Rest," he hissed. "Come back when you're ready and able to play. Obviously, you're not in the mood."

"I'm sorry," she murmured, avoiding his brutal stare. "Being buried alive has shaken my confidence. I will be myself tomorrow, sir. I know I can do it. I will."

Before she could move away from him, his hand snaked out. Vito curled his long fingers around the nape of her neck, drawing her forehead back to his. "I don't know why you stay with me, Princess, but I'm glad you do," he whispered. "I will wait, but never forget who your true master is."

"You," she told him what she had so many times before. "Always you."

He had the balls to cover her mouth with his, the second time she had to endure an actual kiss from this madman. Closing her eyes, she played along, even slid her hand around his neck as if she wanted more of his creepy touch. Now was not the time to fight this snake. Now was the time to live to fight another day. To endure anything and everything for Pagan's sake. For him, she could do even this...

When the stifling kiss ended, Vicki knew two things. She would die before she let Vito into her bed, and she loved Pagan more than herself. He was worth waiting for. Worth dying for.

At last Vito released her, but then he wiped his lips as if he despised touching her. "That was as pleasurable as kissing a dead fish."

She lowered her lashes, thinking *'or a horse's ass,'* but said nothing.

Sticks and stones...

He turned his back on her, his signal that he was finished. "Go. Rest. We'll talk more later."

"As you wish," she groveled. "I'm going to collect my things from my penthouse later today. Which room may I shelter in when I return?"

He flicked his fingers at the wall dismissively. "Leonard will show you. Go now. Get that mundane chore done. Don't be long."

"Thank you for understanding, sir." And that was that.

Vicki exited the Mafia Don's office and quickly left the frigid welcome of the mansion through the front doors. She ignored Vito's two bodyguards stationed in the yard as she strode to the gate, punched in her code, and left the way she'd come, with her dignity intact, though she looked the part of a ferocious strumpet. Let just one of them snicker or treat her like a prostitute though, and watch what happened next. She was damned good with these lethal babies tucked alongside her breasts. She could take off a man's pinkie finger at a thousand yards if he so much as sneered in her direction. And she would. A woman didn't get noticed like this by the Don simply by spreading her legs. Uh-huh. Vicki had never spread her legs for any Seranzino, yet she'd proven her loyalty over and over. That was how she'd conquered this arrogant Sicilian *familia*. With blood and pain, loyalty and pink-handled pistols.

Breathing easier now, she fully believed the Seranzinos had nothing to do with the attack on her in her penthouse. They certainly weren't behind that mini-gunship that had strafed her apartment of last resort, either. Not unless they were suddenly working with the Feds. That just wasn't possible. Which meant someone else wanted her dead badly enough to have sent that gunship into the city after her. Which meant they had financial resources to blow and people inside the city's political powers to get the job done. They, whoever *they* were, could very well be watching her right now.

'Well, let them watch,' she thought as she flipped both middle fingers skyward to whatever hidden cameras might be following her progress away from the Seranzino estate. Breathing hard, she waited until she was far enough down the street before she tugged the burner phone from her holster and asked Pagan, "Did you hear all that? Crazy, huh?"

An impersonal "Copy," came back to her.

Removing the phone from her ear, she stared at it. Really? *'Copy.'* That was all he had to say after she'd risked her life to find out if Vito wanted her dead?

Of course, Pagan had also heard everything else, even that ghastly kiss. Vicki wiped her mouth again just thinking about it. But that had been the plan, for Pagan to listen in and come running if she'd needed help. Which she hadn't. Instead, Pagan sounded as if he thought the worst of her. He thought she'd liked sucking face with Vito? Kissing that vampire?

Gah, she wanted to wash her mouth out with nail polish remover to get the taste and sensation of Vito's lips and tongue out of her mouth. She settled for spitting on the grass alongside the sidewalk, then wiping her mouth with the back of her hand. Now more than ever, she needed to end this obtuse relationship with the pseudo-vampire cult from Sicily. Vito might as well have been from Transylvania the way he'd kissed. The man had no finesse, and he certainly wasn't Pagan. It was no wonder he'd fathered just one child. What woman wanted that monster for a lover?

"Where are you?" she asked Pagan impatiently.

"On your six," he answered, his tone still aloof and impersonal as if he'd answered with his nose in the air.

She cast a quick glance over her shoulder. There he was, a good block behind her in the shade of the tall stone fence lining the other side of the street. She was well past Vito's estate now. Lavish neighborhood homes had been built here with suburban streets and large front yards. "I had to do it, so stop sulking."

Instead of denial, she got silence for an answer. Well, fine. Her one link to the real world was acting like a proprietary asshole. *Let him. I never needed Pagan Sinclair anyway.*

Pissed that she'd ever thought she had real feelings for him, Vicki disconnected from what she'd thought was a lifeline, but had ended up being a temperamental male with a big ego.

Let him think what he wanted, because this was what she did to survive in her oh, so crazy Mafia world. Everyone thought it had been easy for her as a teenager to convince Vito and Cabb that she was worthy of joining their criminal forces. Well, it wasn't. If anything, it had taken more nerve than any young girl should have had to confront the suave, yet diabolical Vito Seranzino that first day on the waterfront. He'd been tailed by some past associate out for revenge. That was the day Vicki Hex was born. Dressed in her killer attire, Vicki had adeptly intercepted Vito's assailant just as he'd opened fire.

Yet she'd done it, hadn't she? She'd saved Vito's life and, in the process, she'd acquired his and Cabb's trust with that one frightening act of blood-letting courage.

It had nearly destroyed her, killing that enemy of Vito's. She'd been well-trained by then, well-educated in just how many enemies the Seranzino *familia* had, but just the same. Taking that first life had also transformed her. Did anyone ever consider the price of protecting others, even protecting men who themselves deserved the death penalty? Did anyone understand what it did to a person to turn themselves into a killer?

She licked her suddenly dry lips at the nightmare life she'd lived for far too long. It was no small thing to take a life. Every time she executed someone, another piece of the woman known as Paloma crumbled, and another piece of Vicki Hex kicked the dust of Paloma out of her way. Some nights, Paloma sat there in the dark of her penthouse suite with no lights on, just listening to her heart beat. Knowing that a killer like her was only granted a finite number of those precious beats. Knowing that one day, Vicki Hex would take over, and the girl called Paloma would be gone.

Unless someone else got to her first.

Yes, she'd used her sex to get inside the Seranzino inner circle, and she'd do it again. And again, if that was what it took! But Mr. Asshole Sinclair behind her was wrong. She'd never—not once!—been intimate with Vito, Cabb, or—perish the thought—that slug, Romeo. Until that disgusting kiss today, Vito had kept his hands off of her because Cabb doted on her in a weird, fatherly way. That was the loving connection—if men like Cabb truly knew how to love—that had sealed her fate. Vicki was now a part of the Mafia familia. But like it or not, the day would come that Vito discovered who and what she was. Someone would rat on her, or someone would concoct the perfect lie to discredit her, and Vito would believe.

Bottom line, there was no retirement plan for people in this business. Only a bullet in her brain, and Paloma knew she'd see that one coming. The Seranzinos make damned sure she knew precisely when her services were terminated.

Fighting the urge to run, she palmed her cell and called a cab. Let Pagan walk. He seemed to think he'd been wronged, the ass. Of all things, a tear welled in the corner of her eye, turning the landscape into twinkling stars. She dashed the damned thing away and wiped it on the side of her bustier, determined to be the strong, sassy woman she'd been before her dirt bath.

If only it were that easy.

It took ten long minutes of strutting like a slut through the neighborhood before she heard a car engine behind her. But before she could toss Pagan one last evil glare over her shoulder, he crashed into her. Cushioning her tumble to the sidewalk, he wrapped one massive arm around her shoulders, rolled on his side and then took her with him onto someone's lawn as a barrage of gunfire let loose over her head.

Not again!

"Stay down," he hissed as he returned fire while shielding her with his thick, muscled body.

No way could she lay there and play dead. Paloma was gone. She was Vicki Hex for hell's sake!

Shoving away from him, Vicki unleashed both pistols. Lifting to one knee, she braced herself for the recoil, and returned a healthy double dose of nine-millimeter rounds into the back window of that stupid SUV speeding away. New model Hummer. Black with darkly tinted windows. One shooter firing from the driver's open window. Black suit jacket. White shirt. Black glove on that hand holding the Uzi.

Pop. Pop. Pop.

Every hollow point round she fired hit that moving barn of a target, but it didn't slow.

Pagan's piece made a helluva lot more noise, so Vicki let him take over and finish the job. When the vehicle screeched away, he followed it into the street, blasting one hellacious cannon ball after another until the SUV roared around the corner and out of sight.

"Shit! Is everyone in the world after you?" he bellowed once he holstered the massive weapon under his jacket.

"You're packing a Desert Eagle?" she asked, dumbfounded that anyone could handle that specific fifty-caliber pistol, much less as expertly and as easily as Pagan just had.

He must've swapped pistols at his mother's place. Vicki was sure he'd carried SIGs before. But he'd made handilng that Desert Eagle look like child's play. Which it wasn't. Over four pounds, that was one damned heavy firearm to pack, much less fire with an measure of accuracy. A semi-automatic, it chambered the largest centerfire cartridge of any magazine-fed pistol in the world. Most men didn't bother with it because of its weight. Its recoil was mind-numbingly fierce and was usually the deal breaker. Why pack something you couldn't shoot more than once without injuring your firing arm?

"Which is it? A Mark VII Magnum or a XIX?" She damned well wanted to know. "Is it a three-fifty-seven Magnum or a forty-four?"

"Dammit, I asked you a question," he growled, his thick chest heaving and emerald green sparks flashing from his sexy eyes. "Answer me!"

Awww, he's angry. He really does care.

Vicki brushed the grass and dirt off of her knees and her backside as she sashayed over someone's front lawn to the handsome beast who'd saved her life yet again. Shoving her hair over her shoulders, she pressed her breasts into him. Placing both palms on that heaving, muscular chest, she could feel his heart pounding as fast as hers. She fluttered her fingertips, wanting to kiss this guy and a couple of his other body parts, too.

"No, the whole world isn't after me. But we need to move before the police show up, big guy," she told him breathily, eyeing his angry mouth, wanting to bite his lips and licking hers in anticipation of doing just that.

One hard hand reached out and circled her waist. Breathing hard, Pagan jerked her against him, lowered his face to hers, then slapped one massive palm on her ass while he devoured her mouth.

Vicki growled, loving the way her ass stung and adoring the way Pagan made her feel alive. Man, he could kiss. and this kiss was harsh and cruel, soooooo damned hot and…

Oh, hell. This was one of those alpha-male-claiming kisses that took a woman's breath away and maybe her soul along with it. At the same time, it swept every last logical thought right out of her head.

It seemed Pagan was pouring all his fear for her down her throat with that soul-searching kiss, nipping at her lips and licking the inside of her mouth like he couldn't get enough of her. As if he were demanding she acknowledge that he *was* superior and bigger and—harder. That he would always protect her.

Well, yeah...

He was all those things and more. By the time his kiss softened, she found herself pressed into one massive hard-on. There on the street in broad daylight, where any one of Vito's nosy men, if they'd followed her could see, Vicki wound her arms around Pagan's stiff neck and surrendered to him.

'Yes!' her foolish heart sang. Yes, she knew it was pure male ego fueling that kiss. Pagan needed more time to acclimate to the woman she was and the job she did. It might take him years to accept her as his equal in the black world of covert ops. But she knew right then and there. She'd loved him since that incident in Tikrit. She loved this pigheaded man who thought he had to fight the world on her behalf, because he *would* fight the world for her. And she'd die protecting him while he did.

At last the scorching kiss ended, but he didn't let her go. Which was just as well since her knees wobbled, and she would've fallen on her ass if he had. "You could've died," he told her huskily, his lips shiny wet from her mouth, and his big, warm hand still firmly cupping her ass.

She'd always thought she had a big butt, but he certainly seemed to like it. He kept grabbing it, and it did fit the palm of his hand like it belonged there.

"Me? You were the one lying there like a wall between me and—" She tossed her head in the direction the SUV had gone. "—whoever that was."

He'd palmed his cell with his free hand by then and curtly ordered a cab before he told her, "We need to talk."

She couldn't help the smile that blossomed over her face. Yes, talk, but he needed something more than just talk. This man desperately needed to make love to her. With her. For a long, long time.

Consider it done.

Chapter Twenty-Two

How many ways could a guy tell a woman he cared about her? Pagan had no clue. He was no poet or romance writer, so he told Paloma with his mouth and his lips, with his hands and his willing fingers until it was time to tell her with the rest of his body. He had meant to take this time with her slowly, but the adrenaline pumping up his spine at what she'd barely lived through, demanded a punishing pace once he had her undressed and on her back at the hotel.

Too bad they were still in the entryway of his mother's hotel room instead of in his bed. It was also too bad he'd torn her panties in his haste to get at her. Yet Paloma didn't seem to mind when he'd body-slammed her against the wall the second they'd cleared the door, peeled that form-fitting bustier off her girls, then licked and kissed, suckled and nursed them into pointy tips of submission. He was pretty sure he sported raspberries on his neck where she'd mauled him on their way to the floor. And he was proud of every last one.

Once again, he'd barely remembered another condom in time, and wasn't that near mistake telling? This woman made him forget all his rules. She made him crazy with some kind of out-of-control madness he couldn't overcome. One look. One belligerent order out of her sassy mouth, and he wanted her like he'd never wanted another woman in his life.

Paloma held some kind of magic power over him, and he loved it. Craved it. Like the whiskey he downed in one gulp after every comeuppance he'd meted out, he wanted every last sip and drop, every lick and swallow of all Paloma had to give him. She was his angel's share, that two percent portion of fine whiskey that distilled into the heavens from every wooden barrel ever filled, stored, and aged.

Flipping her onto her belly, he took hold of that luscious plump ass. "On your knees."

For once, she complied without arguing.

Kneading her hips as his palms and fingers slipped over her blushing cheeks, Pagan pulled her backside where he needed it to be. Dipping his head, he pressed his lips into the seductive hollow above the cleft where her cheeks joined. He breathed deeply of her feminine fragrance, loving the scent of her on his fingers and lips. On his tongue. This woman was one hundred percent that intoxicating angel's share, and he was an alcoholic, out-of-his-mind drunk on her.

"I... I..." she murmured, her ass in the air and her face to the floor.

He stiffened. "You want something, sweet cheeks?"

"Sweet cheeks?" She had the nerve to giggle. "What is this, a B movie?"

Running his palms up her trim waist, over her ribs, and all the way to her shoulders, he shook his head, though he knew she couldn't see him. He wasn't sure what was happening between them, but for sure it wasn't that off color-word she'd used before. Yes, this coming together was fierce and animalistic. It was as raw a lovemaking he'd ever demanded from his partner, but it still wasn't—that.

Even as his fingers drummed the cusp of her shoulders, he knew this wasn't just about sex. That, he could've left behind. He'd done it before. He could walk away from any woman, but not this one. Making love with Paloma was laced with binding tendrils of that indefinable *more* he'd seen between other couples, that symbiotic link that drew them to each other like magnets. Like the tiny brave Plover bird to the giant ferocious, man-eating Egyptian crocodile. That tiny bird that plucked the croc's vicious teeth clean and survived to do it again. Only Pagan wasn't sure which of them, Paloma or him, was the croc and which was the Plover.

"You don't like my nickname for you?" he asked when he finally found his voice.

"Right now…" Paloma ground her backside against him, inviting him to get on with it. "I like everything you do. So, do."

Pagan's very large, imposing body acted automatically upon her salacious invitation. His back arched. He gripped her plush hips, and with one thrust, he was in heaven. He growled, pounding her pillowy rump even as she stretched her arms above her head, palmed the carpet beneath her body, and met him every inch of the way.

It was happening again, that explosive fire that began in the soles of his big, bare feet and rippled up his spine in a flash of pleasure like he'd never known before. The world turned bright and brilliant and immeasurably perfect in those split seconds of total synchronicity with this woman. No, it wasn't just sex. This was a harmony of the rarest kind, the perfect coming together of two wandering stars that should've never been torn apart in the tremendous explosion when the universe began millennia ago. This was… this was…

Love?

Pagan honestly didn't know. Yet even as his eyes squeezed tightly shut, even as he pumped his heart and every last piece of his soul into this woman—his woman—he savored the rarest comingling of space and time, of her soul and his. Here was the warmth and understanding nothing else in the world offered.

Here there was a kind of safety where a man could reveal his innermost devils and saints. Here there was an uncanny acceptance. A quiet agreement.

Paloma's release had crested the precise same moment as his, and what were the bloody odds of that happening regularly between a man and a woman? Yet nearly every time they'd come, they'd come together. At the same time. Always in a rush, but always in sync. Always as one.

His thigh muscles quivered beneath his skin as the angst which began this feverish coupling deflated. He'd spent every last bit of his strength dominating this capricious woman, yet even as he hunched over her trembling body and captured the condom before it leaked, Pagan knew better. He had a snowball's chance of dominating Paloma Juarez or her alter ego, Vicki Hex. Either nemesis already owned him, body and soul.

If only his heart knew what to do. He tied off the condom and tossed it aside. Then, with his hands full of Paloma, Pagan buried his nose in her hair and rolled to his side, taking her lush assets with him.

"The bed would be softer," he murmured, his eyes still closed as aftershocks rolled through her body, clenching him as if her body didn't want to let him go any more than his arms wanted to release her. Yes, those greedy clenches were Mother Nature's way of ensuring the human species survived, that his seed had time to travel deep inside Paloma's body. But today it seemed different, as if her spirit needed him inside of her heart as much as his spirit needed her inside his.

He drew in a deep breath of Paloma's provocative scent. *I do really love her.*

Pagan gulped the frightening thought away, fighting the impulse to absorb this woman into his being before she suspected any such thing. There could be no loving relationship with Paloma. She was not the genteel, mothering type. She was Annie Oakley and Bonnie Elizabeth Parker rolled into one.

No woman who handled those pink pistols of death as adroitly as Paloma could ever be a mother of tiny sons and fragile daughters. Family, damn it. He wanted a family to call his own more than he wanted anything else, even more than he wanted Paloma. That was what made the world a decent and good place to live, all those mothers and fathers quietly raising their families in all those countries and on all those islands. Their religions and beliefs or nationalities didn't matter when it came to parenting. Loving families were what made the world a better place to live in. All those mothers and fathers who tended to their business of loving and growing the next generation of loving people.

He wanted a shelter like that in the storm that was his world, but there was no way two assassins could ever construct a lasting, loving relationship, much less build a home where children could play safely and grow and learn how to survive. It just wasn't possible, and as much as he yearned for this thing with Paloma to be real, it simply, absolutely, was not and never would be.

No. After all the yearnings of his heart, Pagan had to admit this interlude with Paloma *was* just about the sex. Uncommon, exemplary, and mind-blowing sex, but nothing more. This fling with Julio's baby sister—for that was all it was—was certainly not the 'more' a man could build a lasting future on. His children's futures on.

He crossed his arms over Paloma's overflowing breasts, caging her against his much larger body. Pagan closed his eyes and held on despite his resolve to distance himself from her. In truth, he couldn't seem to let her go. His arms just didn't work that way.

"Hmmm, bed, yes," Paloma murmured as she crossed her arms over his, trapping him like he'd trapped her and purring like a contented cat in front of a warm fireplace. "Soon. Very soon."

Blinking the sudden emotions leaking out of his heart away, Pagan buried his nose in the crook of her neck, and he held on. He. Just. Held. On.

Chapter Twenty-Three

Paloma knew she had to get him into bed. That was where he'd sleep soundest. Longest. And there she would desert the one man who seemed destined and determined to save a life not worth saving. To save her.

"Want to shower first?" He grunted, his deep baritone already thick and groggy.

She shook her head, bumping his nose still buried in her hair. "I'm cold," she lied. "Let's snuggle first. Shower later."

The man had the strength of a giant. Instead of pulling her to her feet when he rose to his feet, he lifted off the floor with her in his arms and had her tucked in bed and under the covers beside him in no time at all. God bless him if anything happened to him. She knew she could never lift him into bed that way, not even to save his life. Which was why she had to go. His heroics had to end. If she'd been marked to die, so be it, but she intended to do it alone. He was the angel in this relationship. She was the assassin, the liability he didn't need.

Squeezing her eyes tightly shut, she snuggled possessively into his arm, her head on his chest, her hair shielding her expression from his scrutiny. Hiding in plain sight. This was what she'd always done best. Hide her bruises from Julio's sharp eyes when she'd been beaten by their grandmother. Use plenty of flesh-toned makeup concealer after every girl-fight, man-fight, and in between fights. Vicki Hex was a master at disguising—herself. Or was Paloma the real master? Or was that mistress? Dominatrices were mistresses, right?

"You're quiet," he murmured, his voice thick and drowsy.

Paloma nodded. "I just need a short nap. A combat nap, isn't that what you Navy SEALs call it?"

"Yeah. Ah-huh." His breathing grew steady. His heart rate slowed. "Ten minutes. That's... that's all I ever need."

"Of course," she told him as she splayed her fingers over his chest, loving the coarse scrub of hairs under her hand. Worshipping the heat of his all-male body one last time, the warmth she would willingly leave if it meant saving his life.

"Sleep," he coaxed as his hand slid heavily to the middle of her back. His body went slack. He started to snore.

Paloma lay there in bed with her heart in her throat, tears stinging her eyes, begging for the release she refused to give them. The tender way Pagan had enfolded her against his rock-hard chest when he'd finally fallen asleep was breaking her heart now.

If ever there were a man worth dying for, he was it. Honorable. True blue to his country, his family, and his brother SEALs. Gruff as a much older, disillusioned man, but still loving and gentle in his adorable, reckless way. Pagan was one of the rarest breeds of men. One who never backed down from a fight or from doing what was right. Like today when he'd saved her life for, man, she couldn't keep track of how many times he'd done that. He seemed determined she live, and wasn't that an eye-opener for an assassin to not kill someone? To not worry that someone might kill you while you slept in his arms?

She snuggled her backside into the cradle of his hips, sore in all the right places and as warm as she had never been before. From the inside out, she was deliciously, sensually heated. Melted, gooey warm like a chocolate chip cookie fresh out of the oven. Fresh out of the oven of Pagan's very thorough love.

So, she cried without tears. Without sobs and without hope. After this latest near-death experience, she had no choice. Pagan seemed determined to forever put himself between her and her pursuers. He would take the bullet meant for her, and she couldn't let that happen. It was time to leave.

Stealthily and oh, so slowly, Paloma slid out from under his hand and onto the floor. She knelt there a moment, making sure he truly was as sound asleep as he looked before she eased to her feet, tugged the blanket up over his chest and left him. Silently, she dressed in simple workout pants and a matching black t-shirt, then slipped into the matching running shoes Vanessa had included in Paloma's order.

Hurrying before Pagan woke, Paloma gathered Vicki Hex's outfit from the entryway and stuffed the clothes into the black roller suitcase from Scarlett's closet. Pagan's mother wouldn't mind. She might even be relieved if this small theft ensured her youngest son's life.

In minutes, Paloma was back on the street with only the wind at her back. The single thing she'd taken with her was Pagan's jacket, and that only to conceal the hardware holstered under her arms. Flipping the collar up, she drew in a deep breath of the masculine scents he'd left behind: gunsmoke, whiskey, and freedom. That was how she'd remember the man she loved for whatever time she had left.

From now on, Pagan would walk these streets alone. Never again would she be at his side, and knowing that was enough to break her heart. Fighting tears, Paloma wound her massive wealth of hair into a messy knot, then tucked that under the plain black ballcap she'd borrowed from the Sinclair family apartment. Might've been Chance's. Might've been

Kruze's. Paloma didn't care. It offered the gender-neutral look she was going for.

Today her journey would end. She'd find the bastard who wanted her dead, and she'd set a trap to do it. She'd snare the son-of-a-bitch, and she'd end him. Or her. Never let it be said that women weren't as evil or twisted as men. She, of all people, knew.

Hailing one of the many cabs lining the street in front of the hotel, she set her jaw and her heart to her next task. It was better this way. Besides, what did her death matter in the grand scheme of things anyway? Not much. There might be a small line or two in the police blotter section of the Chicago Trib, but no one would miss her. Even Pagan would forget in time.

She'd always known she'd die in the line of duty. Ha. Duty to the mob. Wasn't that the richest lie she'd ever told herself? And believed.

Brusquely, she gave the cabbie the address to her penthouse, the place where her nightmare had begun. But this time she'd be smarter when she opened her front door. She'd be in control.

Paloma glanced over her shoulder at the grand hotel as the cabbie pulled away from the curb, striving to find the exact windows belonging to Scarlett Sinclair's suite. Seeking out just one last look at what could have been forever if she were a *'forever'* kind of a woman. Pagan might be standing there, watching her leave. He might be angry and waving, or... He might still be asleep. The window was too dark to see through. Even if he stood there bellowing at her, she couldn't see him. Paloma swallowed her last foolish hope.

We each make our own way in this world.

How well she knew. The deed was done. She'd left her fling with Pagan behind, and now she'd make the best of however many minutes or hours she had left. Setting her jaw with her unique brand of killer determination, she faced the busy street ahead. That was all it took to summon her alter ego to the fight. Paloma surely wouldn't survive this kind of day, but Vicki Hex might.

Only by then, there might not be any part of sweet, foolish, softhearted Paloma left.

*****

Pagan grunted, caught between the numbing states of half-sleep and half-wakefulness. He'd fallen hard, yet his internal clock still ticked down the seconds and minutes. Ten, he'd told himself before he'd closed his eyes, and ten minutes it would be. That was all he'd ever needed. Ten-minute power naps had been his mainstay for years. He'd learned that easily in his SEAL team. And yet...

Something was wrong. He could feel it. Sense it. The day had turned cold. Gooseflesh prickled up his bare arm where Paloma had just rested her sweet, tired body.

But she wasn't there now.

He jerked wide awake, his heart pounding at the sudden shift between sleep, anger and fear. There was no wondering where she'd gone. Pagan damned well knew. She'd left him behind like she'd always intended. Wasn't he the master idiot to have succumbed to her feminine wiles?

Putting both feet to the floor, he tossed the blanket she'd covered him with aside. Damn her stubborn self. What was she thinking? Of going out in a hail of AGN-114 Hellfire missiles? That unmanned baby bird that paid her *supposedly safe* hideout a visit could certainly end her. Shred her was more like it.

The damned aircraft easily handled a payload of over twenty-four hundred pounds, and that Hellfire missile, the one originally named 'Heliborne, Laser, Fire and Forget'? He'd seen them in action. Originally intended for anti-armor defense, the Air Force now relied on them for razor-sharp precision strikes against high-profile ISIL targets. They were damned deadly in the right hands, but in the wrong hands?

"Jesus Christ," he hissed as he located his pants in the entryway and jerked them on. Of course, her clothes were already gone.

Pissed and fighting mad, he didn't need his shirt, but neither could he locate his leather jacket. Well, good. Maybe Paloma was smart after all. If she'd taken his jacket, she had his arsenal, his extra pistol, and the three knives in his pockets. If she were wise, she'd acquaint herself with each of those multifunctional weapons before she faced down the asshat trying to kill her.

Pagan couldn't get out of his mom's place and on the street fast enough. He called home when he hit the pavement, glaring both ways, but not dumb enough to expect to see her. Paloma seemed to have a death wish, and he knew damned well she'd backtrack until she bumped into her killer. She had nothing to live for, but...

Me.

"Damn it, woman!" Pagan bellowed as he kicked one booted foot, scraping the sidewalk in fury. He'd given Paloma no reason to want to live. He should've told her what she meant to him. Damn, he should've told her he loved her. Because, yeah. He loved her, and he should've had the balls to admit his feelings to her face. What if there were no more second chances? What if—

A shiver raced up the back of his neck, and Pagan spun on his heel. The rule was that if you ever felt like someone was watching you, someone was. Yet he saw no one. Just the busy bluster of a hard-working city. Just rush hour at its prime. Too many faces. Too many eyes. But no Paloma.

"Where are you?" he asked the brisk wind whining through the canyon-like streets. "I don't understand. What are you thinking?"

Or was she the predator Vicki Hex today? Pagan ran a hand over his shorn scalp, needing to shave it though his beard was thicker, no doubt darker, too.

But he liked his bare head this way. People tended to steer clear of him when he looked like he did. Hence, the beard he maintained on his chin, the shaved skull look, and the dark scowl permanently etched into his ugly face. And he needed people to stay out of his way today.

At long last, Chance picked up. "Still in Chicago?" he asked without preamble.

"Lost the package," Pagan replied glumly.

"For the moment or for forever?"

Whatever that meant. Paloma's unexpected departure after their tender lovemaking had all the markings of forever. But once again, she was alone on the cruel streets of Chicago. Yes, she was tough and had always taken care of herself, but even the toughest of the tough eventually met their match or were outnumbered. Outgunned. Every day the obits were full of foolish heroes and heroines who'd thought themselves untouchable. Even those were only the bodies the police found.

"Not sure," Pagan answered his brother even as he scanned both sides of the street in both directions again. His gut clenched with his next words, "It's time for *Delta One*."

"Agreed," Chance growled. "Enough is enough." Wasn't that the truth? "Take her down, brother. Do whatever you have to do, but do it before this mess gets any more out of hand."

"Copy that," Pagan said as he sucked in a gutful of brisk Chicago chill. Part moisture laden breeze off the

Great Lake Michigan to his east, part breath off the cold concrete buildings hovering like walls above and beyond him, his heart froze along with his exhale. Shit. He didn't have to like it, he just had to do it. Paloma had given him no choice.

'Playtime's over, Miss Hex. I'm coming for you, and this time—' He hailed the nearest cab with an impatient flick of his hand. *'I won't miss.'*

Chapter Twenty-Four

Vicki heard him before she saw him. The gray trench coat made him an instant target. Her fingers on the triggers of her pink-handled babies itched to end him first and ask questions later. Romeo Seranzino. The lackluster bastard who lived off his old man and his grandfather was taking the fire escape ladder two steps at a time on his way up the side of her building. Romeo was no Spider-Man. More like Bozo the Clown in that *"Get Smart"* get-up. In broad daylight no less. What'd he think? He was invincible because of his name? That she wouldn't off him in public—like right damned now—just because she worked for his old man?

Swallowing hard, she kept the rangefinder she'd found in one of Pagan's many inner jacket pockets on her bumbling target. Not like that was hard. Romeo was no athlete, and he had no business climbing up that fire escape. He wasn't a monkey. The oaf wasn't even close to being physically fit. His ever-thickening middle made climbing difficult. He'd slowed to a crawl by the time he cleared the fifteen-story landing where he decided to take a nice long break, probably to catch his breath. His hands fell to his knees as he bent over, looking down. He was obviously in distress. The clown might have been afraid of heights for all Vicki cared.

For as long as she'd stood watching her penthouse window from across the street in the shadowy alley, her svelte body once again clothed in form-fitting black, Romeo had been the only one to show. Her nose twitched at the stink from behind her. Alleys in Chicago were where garbage of all sorts ended up, stacked or congregated.

That drunk passed out by the Dumpster turned on its side, the guy with his mouth open and snoring on his back, was one of those other kinds of garbage she usually stepped over while working. Not today. Everyone was suspect, so she kept a sharp eye on the guy. Pagan's six-inch blade made for a damned nice friend in her hand, cold, yet warm at the same time. Assassins were the best multitaskers. They had to be to survive.

Sure as hell, poor stupid Romeo leaned over the metal banister, then backed his extra-fluffy butt to the brick wall, his hands flattened behind him as if he were holding on. By then she'd watched him long enough to know he wasn't the one behind her murder. The man wasn't smart enough. He might've hired someone to do it, but this guy—kid—whatever—didn't have the balls to do his own dirty work.

So why was he sneaking—albeit hardly noiselessly—up that clanging metal fire escape?

Vicki inhaled through her mouth to avoid the stench permeating the air around her, her gaze focused on the klutz across the street. The tails of Romeo's trench coat whipped around him, baring his trouser-covered fat ass, and for a second, she debated shooting that ass to make her point. But no. She'd only ever left her mark on one man's ass before. That was her limit. Her brand.

"I do love you," she told Pagan even as she sighted Romeo in the crosshairs of her rangefinder, err, Pagan's rangefinder. "If you were here, I'd tell you. I've never said those words to anyone else. I'm telling you now, Big Guy. You are my one and only. My first. My last. My sun and my stars. But I wonder. Would you have believed me if I'd told you, or would you think I was lying?"

"There's only one way to find out," a gruff voice bit out behind her.

She whirled on Pagan. The ass! He'd sneaked up on her! The piece in his hand wasn't the Desert Eagle—thank God!—but it was pointed at her chest.

Vicki squared her shoulders. So, this was how it would happen. Body shot by an alleged friend. A lover. Not even the courtesy of a double tap. Just a gut shot that would blow her in two if that weapon in his hand was as lethal as she knew it was.

She pointed her weapon barrel up at the sky. It was time. She was ready. Sick and tired and oh, so ready.

At least it was Pagan ending her, not some random assassin whose name she'd never know. Whose face she'd never see. Whose bullet she'd never hear. It was better this way. Mercy killings didn't hurt as much when committed by friends or lovers.

There were no words for the tender look in his eyes. The hollow of his cheek as he lifted his weapon. So, she told him, "I love you, Pagan. Know that. Believe that. You're the only man I've ever loved. I'll take that to my—"

He fired. One shot. Straight into her chest. And Paloma fell, her arms opened wide in surrender. Even in death. Only to Pagan.

The percussion flattened her ass to the sidewalk. Her head barely bounced when it hit the concrete. For a split second, it seemed comforting, as if someone had caught her. The light of Chicago's weak midday sun faded as the shadow of Pagan's magnificent bulk blocked her view.

He stood over her, one boot on each side of her hips while she gave him all she'd ever had to give. Gasping now, because bullets don't lie and she really was dying, Paloma finished what she'd tried to tell the only man she'd ever loved. "I'll take that to my grave."

*****

Jesus H. Christ! He couldn't get out of there fast enough. He'd been seen, yet even as two police cruisers roared into view, Pagan hesitated. Paloma lay there glassy-eyed, her mouth open and her arms splayed wide at her sides. Dammit! This was not how he'd wanted this story to end. Not Paloma. God, not Paloma! How could he leave her now? Like this?

Simple. As usual, he followed the Sinclair plan. Heart pounding, he faded into the alley as two police officers scrambled out of their cruiser, barking orders for the EMTs who were already in transit to hurry faster. STAT!

Pagan stumbled over some drunk on his way, grumbled an apology the guy probably never heard, then prayed his way through the alley and into the next street. Tearing the bright green sweatshirt he'd committed the most heinous crime in, over his head— because he'd meant to be seen—he cleared the block. Running around the final corner now, he pulled the Chicago EMT hoodie he'd tied around his waist earlier this morning over his shoulders. Jogging and out of breath, he rounded the entire block, then came upon the grisly crime scene disguised as one of Chicago's first responders.

Jesus Christ, there was blood everywhere. But the body—Paloma—was already draped and covered, and son-of-a-bitch! He was having an anxiety attack. Pagan could barely breathe at the sight of her prone, lifeless figure beneath that gray tarp, knowing her last words had been words of love. For him! The bastard who'd shot her!

Why now? Why in Christ's holy name couldn't she have told him she loved him before? They could've worked things out, done things differently. Hell, they could've gone back to bed, where they both belonged.

Because I never told her first!

His heart hammered like a frantic troll determined to escape the cage of his ribs, shaking him from the inside out. Clawing at him. Tears filled his eyes at the despicable thing he'd done. He'd shot Victoria! Yet in that last second before he'd fully compressed the trigger, she'd turned back into Paloma. He'd seen the quiet transformation from killer dominatrix to his sweet, lost girl in those sad brown eyes. Always too large for her delicate face, she'd been scared there at the end. Scared, yet she'd also been resigned, as if she'd always known that he'd betray her.

Foolish woman! Why couldn't she have stayed with him? Why didn't she ever listen? Yes, he was just a man, but men were right as often as women. They knew things, too.

Fighting the greatest fear creeping up his spine that he'd ever known, Pagan railed at the injustice of his job. Yet even as his heart broke for Paloma, he knew better. He'd had no choice but to end her quest for justice. It had always been in the cards, end her before she jeopardized everyone and everything.

Sick at heart, he climbed into the still running ambulance, slapped the hunter green ballcap on the dash to his head, that cap with CHICAGO printed over the brim, then he gripped the wheel. Avoiding all eye contact, Pagan put his head down and faced his meaty thighs. To anyone out there watching this nightmare, he'd soon be just another reckless driver in the middle of controlled chaos. He was not the assassin. Not the shooter. Not the betrayer of one of the greatest, dearest women he'd ever known. Make that loved. Adored. Worshipped!

A tear trickled out of the corner of his eye and down his cheek, seeped through his mustache and went all the way to his upper lip before he caught it and swiped it away. This was no time for sentimentality. Things could still go so damned wrong.

It took a while longer, but at last the EMTs loaded the body bag onto their gurney and slid the gurney in through the rear door of the ambulance. One joked about this being just another murder in a long day. The other grumbled they should get hazard pay.

Pagan watched through the rearview as they stood there and chatted after the door slammed shut. To them this was just another senseless killing in the murder capital of the United States, one that might never end in a trial or justice served. To them this was just another day at work, a thankless job. But to Pagan... this was a sucking heartbreak. He. Could. Not. Breathe.

Chance had asked too much this time. Too. Damned. Much.

One of the EMT's smacked the rear quarter panel of the vehicle, jolting him out of his somber reverie. That was his signal to go, but it also alerted the real driver.

"Hey! You!" he bellowed, as, with tires squealing, Pagan gunned the engine, executed a sharp U-turn into oncoming traffic, then stepped on the gas as he swerved south onto Lake Shore Drive. The race was on.

Passing the famous *Bubba Gump Shrimp Company* at his left, he dodged traffic and executed a side drift onto Grand Street headed west. Seconds counted. He had to hurry. Speed became his ally as he laid on the horn and headed for the Chicago River. *Go, go, go!*

In a couple blocks, he flipped another U-turn, then came to a screeching halt at the mouth of another alley where—son-of-a-bitch! An armored car blocked his way. But wait. Was that man in the uniform...? Yes. Kruze. *Thank God!*

He jumped out of the armored vehicle, waving his arms for Pagan to step on it.

Pagan didn't have to be asked twice.

"You got her?" Kruze asked when Pagan exited the ambulance on a dead run, jerked open the vehicle's tailgate, and carefully lifted the body bag into his arms.

"Don't touch her," he hissed while he angled Paloma's limp body onto the rear of the armored truck, then, with trembling fingers, unzipped that damned bag. Another tear escaped, but Pagan was beyond caring what Kruze said next or what he thought. Pagan couldn't help it. Tears coursed down his cheeks as he looked down at the woman he'd loved.

Climbing into the truck, he gathered Paloma's body back into his arms and ordered Kruze to, "Get us the hell out of here."

Good thing his brother had the good sense to keep his mouth shut. Slamming the door and locking Pagan in with Paloma's body, Kruze climbed into the driver's seat and turned that pretentious looking ride away from the now-empty city ambulance.

But the deed was done.

At last alone with the fierce Amazon-like warrior who would never understand why he'd done what he did, Pagan sobbed over the limp lady in his arms, "I'm so, so sorry."

Chapter Twenty-Five

"I wouldn't go in there if I were you," Kruze warned as he closed the bedroom door behind him, his furry brown brows knitted, and enough worry lines etched across his know-it-all forehead to start a penmanship class.

For now, they were safe inside an undisclosed Sinclair brothers' safe-house, one of the few scattered across America's fifty states. It was late afternoon and Doctor Harding, the only physician in Chicago Pagan trusted, had already come and gone.

"What were *you* doing in there?" he snapped at his brother as his hand hit the cold brass doorknob. He'd seen enough bodies before, both male and female. He knew what to expect. This particular chore might be tougher than any other, but he had to face what he'd done.

"Just checking, you know, things," Kruze muttered as he walked down the hall toward the kitchen. "But I'd wait an hour or two before I—"

"Shut it," Pagan snarled at the man he'd once suspected of having illicit dalliances with Paloma. He had to work to relax his fists, uncurl his fingers, and not beat the shit out of this brother. Now was not the time to fight over Paloma.

"You ass!" she shrieked the moment he cleared the door. "I trusted you and look what you did! You shot me!"

Pagan nodded like the great dumb oaf he was. Why had he thought she might be a teensy bit happy to see him?

"Stay away from me!" she yelled as she backed her lovely ass up against the headboard of the bed where Doc Harding had treated her. The drug Pagan used had only rendered her unconscious for a couple hours. By the looks of it, Doc Harding had also changed her out of her bloody clothes and into a pair of navy-blue flannel pajamas with pink piping along the edges, collar, and both breast pockets. Or had Kruze done that? That'd be just like him to take advantage of Pal while she was down.

Shit. Pagan rolled his neck even as his blood pressure spiked into the upper atmosphere at the thought of his brother handling Paloma while she'd been unconscious. If he had...

Damned if Pagan's body didn't stand up and notice how lovely she filled that flannel top. Navy blue had never looked so soft nor so good.

She slapped one hand to said chest, cupping one of the very lovely girls he was ogling, jiggling it at him like a weapon. "Look what you did to me! My chest hurts! My boobs hurt too! For Christ's sake, Pagan! You shot my girls! I hate you!"

'But you're alive,' he wanted to remind her. *'And so are your girls, thank God. Your lovely assets are just bruised, and I can still hold you and love you for the rest of your life. And mine if you'll ever let me touch you again.'*

Still nodding like a blithering fool and unable to speak because his heart had swelled to ten times its size and was now stuck in his throat, Pagan marched straight into her clenched, angry fists to the fight he deserved. Brushing away her weak attempts to flail at him—*because the drug he'd used to 'kill' her was known to make a person weak*—he gathered her sweaty body—*another unfortunate side effect*—into his aching arms and smothered her under his chin, so damned thankful she was alive and pissed and angry and breathing and...

Just so damned thankful. From the moment he and Chance had devised this plan, then drew Kruze into it to tie up the loose ends and procure that getaway vehicle, Pagan had needed this sensation, this all-is-right-with-the-world feeling, right here. He needed her warm and alive instead of cold and dead like she'd been back in that alley.

He'd known all along he hadn't hit her with that pretend kill shot, but his mind had had a hard time differentiating what it looked like , from what it truly was. Looks were deceiving. Hence the tears he couldn't stop from dripping down his cheeks, making him look less than manly. A sob caught in his throat.

Pagan knew it then. She'd never forgive him. This time he had asked too much of Paloma. Threading his callused fingers through her hair and palming the back of her headstrong skull in his hand—though how she hadn't cracked it open when she'd fallen, spoke to the hardness of it—he flattened the other to the middle of her back and held onto the one woman he now knew he loved. Make that adored.

But if she never loved him again...? If she truly hated him the rest of her life?

It didn't matter. He'd do it again. Because of that shot, she was alive. What did the poets call it, unrequited love? *'Sign me up,'* he thought as he resigned himself to a life without Paloma. If giving her back her life meant she'd hate him forever, so be it. Let her hate him. He'd let her go.

If only he could.

"Paloma," he ground out, his voice cracking at all he stood to lose while his arms pressed her flat against his chest. It was just one word, but it was her real name, and he choked on it, so sure she'd never forgive him for overstepping her feminist boundaries and for making this awful decision *for* her instead of *with* her.

More than anything, Paloma wanted to be viewed as an equal, and she was. In every way that mattered, she truly was. He knew that now. He wanted her to know that he knew it. He needed her to believe him as much as she needed him to believe her. She *was* strong, self-reliant, and hands down, the best sniper he'd ever met. Well, except for himself, but that was another battle for another day.

Growling, she did the one thing he'd not expected. Paloma pressed her head under his chin and snuggled into him, rubbing her nose into his neck. "Kruze told me," she cried, her shoulders trembling. "Aww, baby, he told me how hard it was for you to d-do what you did, to sh-shoot me."

Well, yeah. Secretly delighted that she'd called him baby, Pagan bowed his lips to the crown of her head and kissed her hair. It had destroyed him to 'pretend' shoot her. He might never get over watching her fall to her back on that cold, Chicago sidewalk or the utter disbelief in her sad, brown eyes. The fake blood that came with the round that concealed the drug had made everything look a little too realistic, even for him. Yes, the round had disintegrated on impact like it was supposed to, leaving no trace evidence behind. But it had left an ugly bruise in the middle of her chest. And it had looked so damned real.

He choked remembering. Anyone watching would've believed she'd died. Even he'd second-guessed the wisdom behind the Sinclair *Delta One Plan* to take an operative out of circulation without actually killing her or him. Things could've gone so, so wrong. Chances were Paloma might've appreciated the sense behind the plan, but Pagan doubted Vicki Hex would.

But now Miss Hex was dead, murdered, at least as far as the rest of the world knew. Word of her demise was already on the streets. They'd all watched her die on continual replay, courtesy of this generation's quick thinking. Videos, some with selfies included, were right now being viewed all over *Facebook* and *YouTube.* The New York Times and the Chicago Trib had both carried front-page stories how one of Vito Seranzino's *'very best soldiers—and a female at that'* had fallen, with the overused caption: *'Those who live by the sword, die by the sword.'*

How dare they? Pagan grunted at John Q. Public's lack of critical thinking.

Everything on Facebook's true, isn't it?

Yet the widespread misdirection now ruling social media had served Pagan's purpose. America was off on another frenzy. Even now, a manhunt was on in Chicago for Vicki Hex's alleged murderer. Romeo himself had graciously offered to read her obit during her funeral at Holy Name Cathedral. Heaven forbid his Sicilian *familia* ever set foot in the awe-inspiring, and very Irish, Old Saint Patrick's Catholic Church.

If only they had her body...

Pagan sank to the bed as he spread his legs and gathered her much smaller body onto his lap. Damn, she seemed so fragile. So weak. But sometimes, touch was enough. Like now. He couldn't seem to let her go, nor could he breathe in enough of the slightly sweaty, yet antiseptically clean, luscious-to-die-for, scent of his woman.

"I heard what you said out there on that street, and you need to know that I *do* love you, too," he told her sincerely, his lips in her hair and his hand skimming up her spine to hold her in place.

The sassy former-dominatrix melted into him. "I should be angry," she murmured into his chest, "but now that I don't have to pretend that I like Vito and Cabb or..." A shuddering sigh wheezed out of her. "...Romeo. Now that I don't have to do what Dane tells me to do... Does he... umm, does he know?"

Pagan shook his head, his eyes closed as he absorbed this tender moment. He'd expected to get his ears boxed or his face slapped. Not this forgiveness. "No one knows but us Sin Boys, Paloma, not even Sullivan. He might call for the particulars of how it went down, but I think he's still feeling guilty for casting aspersions on your good name. If he calls, I'll let you be the one to tell him."

"I don't want to talk to him. I hate him, too," she mumbled.

"But you don't really hate me." Pagan could tell.

"Yeah, but I really do hate him," she whined as her head came up. "And I love you Pagan Sinclair. I have since Tikrit. That's why I shot you where I did. I own your ass."

He stared down into brown eyes so sad, yet twinkling for the first time since she'd awakened. Reluctantly, he moved one hand from her back to the dimple Chance had left behind when he'd dug that nine-millimeter round out of said butt. Pagan would have commented on her remark, but what was this new star-shine in her dark chocolate eyes? Could it be true...?

"Love?" Even as he asked, his heart closed around the word like the well-used leather of a catcher's mitt around the World Series winning pitch.

Solemnly, she nodded even as the shine dimmed. "I have no idea how this is going to work or if it will, but I wanted you to know. I love you."

Pagan closed his eyes and clutched her to him before his heart broke wide open. "One day at a time," he told her fervently. "That's how love works. We'll take at it one day at a time. One problem and one mistake and one success at a time. We'll fight. We'll make up. We'll have great make-up sex. We don't have to be perfect right now. We just have to..."

He was going to say *'try,'* but Paloma silenced him with a heartstopppingly perfect kiss that stole every last bit of his attention and filled the darkest recesses of his warrior's soul. With an enormous sigh of relief, Pagan circled Paloma inside the band of his muscled arms. They were strong and righteous, and God willing, enough to guard and protect this fierce feminine warrior chewing on his lower lip for the rest of time.

He flattened his hands on her arm and shoulder, hands that had dealt death in the past and would deal death again when called upon to do so. He pressed her warm soft body into his heart, sure that her pulse beat in time with his. Together, they made the music of life—a steady *kerthump, kerthump, kerthump.*

"We can do this," he said against her luscious lips. "We've fought harder wars before. This one'll be a cinch."

She grunted as she licked his chin. "Lock the door, Pagan. I want more."

"Now?" he had to ask even as his eyes scrolled to the steel bedroom door that could hold back a zombie invasion.

"Now. Please?" she begged.

Not like he could ever tell her no. Depositing her back onto the bed, he locked the door and ripped that *borrowed* Chicago EMT hoodie over his head and tossed it to the floor. He could take it back tomorrow.

Chapter Twenty-Six

Paloma woke extra-warm and much happier than she'd been in a long time. The room she and Pagan ended the previous day in, was windowless and dark this morning, and she was in bed with her man. The temperature in the room was cool, perfect for sleeping. The one steel door that hadn't opened all night, still remained closed. This room was a vault, but comfortably furnished with sheets and a down comforter on the bed, the comforter protected by a white satin duvet. The walls had been painted a delicate bronze tone that glimmered in the dim glow of a nightlight somewhere beyond the foot of the bed. No paintings adorned the walls, only two computer monitors, the screens dark at the moment.

She didn't remember them from her hectic yesterday, but then she didn't remember much after she'd been *killed*. Before Pagan arrived, she'd been out of it until some perky, young doctor woke her up. After Pagan had the nerve to walk in on her, she'd been emotionally distraught. Yes, that was the word for it. Emotional. She, the best hit-woman on the East Coast, had a touchy-feely-girly moment when she saw the man who'd shot her, followed by one heck of a meltdown because he'd looked so adorably devastated by what he'd done.

Paloma ran her fingers over the thick, muscular arms that had held her all night while that same warmth and happiness flooded her heart and leaked out of her eyes. Gah! For a woman with a hard-assed rep, she sure did a lot of crying lately. It was all Pagan's fault. He'd awakened the real woman inside her, and for once, finally, hopefully forever, she could put Vicki Hex to rest. If anyone needed to be buried, it was Vicki.

Dipping her lips to the back of his rugged, heavily-veined hand, Paloma kissed it. Her hand was such a tiny, child-like thing by comparison. Death had never before held the hope it did now. That hope swelled in her chest like a hot air balloon, closing her windpipe as more tears streamed over her cheeks. Summoning her alter ego, she wiped her nose and blinked the excess moisture away. If only it were that easy.

Of course, Pagan knew. He was so perceptive for a man. "It's okay to cry, Pal," he murmured into the back of her neck. "I've got you."

"I'm not crying," she told him, but he seemed to know the difference between her lies and her truths.

"Ah-huh," he whispered while his fingertips smoothed over her teary face and called her bluff. "Even big boys cry when they've had enough. Let it out and be done with it. You'll feel better."

She shook her head, her cheeks still wet and her false bravado revealed. "Crying can get to be a habit."

"It's a release valve, that's all," he whispered. "Go ahead."

And the dam broke. She twisted around to face him but buried her nose in his chest so he couldn't see. They were both still naked, but she was an ugly crier. This was going to get sloppy.

"You came for me," she sobbed, her eyes squeezed tight to stop the torrent unleashed from her heart, where, apparently, a well of tears had been stored for a long time. "Every time they tried to kill me, you were there. Even when I ran away from you, you followed. I deserted you, but you... you never deserted me." Her tone turned into a desperate, little girl's whine by the time she finished.

But it was true. Pagan was here, wasn't he? He'd followed her, protected her, and literally been at her side since the morning she'd dug herself out of her grave and returned to her safe place.

A gentle growl reverberated beneath her cheek. "Everyone thinks you're dead now, Pal. That gives us a little wiggle room to find out who's behind these bullshit attempts on your life. With you here and safe, we can do what we do best and unmask your attackers once and for all."

We?

Oh. The Sin Boys. Of course. That's why Pagan was really here, wasn't it? He'd undertaken an assignment from his older brother to track her down and... and what? Romance her into bed to get on her good side? To get her to talk? Wine and dine her until he knew for certain whether she was loyal to the Agency or not?

Kruze's presence yesterday confirmed her suspicions. This was just an assignment to Pagan. Damn it, and she'd fallen for it and for him. Her heart deflated just a little at that spoiler alert. She swallowed hard. "This was what you and your brothers planned all along?" *Please don't say yes.*

"No. *Delta One* was our go-to plan only if all else failed."

Somehow that adamant 'no' did nothing to relieve the doubts niggling at the back of her mind. *Delta One?*

He nuzzled the nape of her neck, his breath hot and moist, lighting all her feminine responses, and she very much liked it. Still...

Chance, Kruze, and Pagan had planned all along to shoot her and make the world believe she was dead, if she wasn't—what? Compliant? Obviously. Judging by this *safe room*—her fingers itched to stab a couple air quotes at him—Pagan had already been very well prepared to rush to her rescue after he'd shot her. He'd planned every step, every alley, and precisely where he'd rendezvous with Kruze before the police had the chance to whisk her body away to the county morgue. This was all part of another Sin Boys operation. Pagan's mission. Was that all she was to him, one of his targets or packages or endgames or whatever they called her?

The devil in her soul lifted its obstinate head and shook out its ebony tangles to reveal its horns. If she hadn't cooperated, would he have ended her? "You said if all else failed." A whisper of sarcasm crept into her tone. "What was that 'all else'?"

That got Pagan's attention. "Don't go there, Pal," he told her as his nuzzling ceased and his arms tightened around her. "What we did last night has nothing to do with this operation. I don't lie. When I told you I loved you, I meant it. This thing between us is something I never saw happening."

And enough!

She'd turned into Vicki when she jerked her body away from Pagan, needing room to think and air to breathe—not good morning sex.

"This *thing*?" she bit out. "What? You Sin Boys don't have a macho-guy contingency plan for this *thing*, too? What'd you think would happen when we made love, Pagan? That I'd tell you all my Mafia secrets, then drop and give you twenty just because you said all the right things and convinced me—?"

Vicki swallowed hard. "So you expect me to believe that you just *happened*—" She finally stabbed a pointed pair of air quotes at the testosterone swamped behemoth staring at her with his mouth open. "—to fall in love with the woman you were sent to—do what? Fuck into submission to make sure she did as she was told? You're as bad as Dane!"

Okay, that didn't make sense even to Vicki. Paloma either. Tired and confused, but mostly fed up with lying men's bullshit, she jumped off the bed. Her suddenly pounding head wished she hadn't, but that dizziness would pass. She was a killer, remember? Hard. Cruel. Supposedly smarter than her prey. Well, it was time to bully that prey into letting her go. Paloma and Vicki had a life to get back to.

Right now, Pal was Vicki, and Vicki was as angry as she'd ever been. She didn't know which part of what Pagan had said was real and what was not. Someone *had* meant for her to die, not only once, but multiple times over the last couple days. Yes, he'd intercepted every attempt, and, to be honest, he had fought for her at every turn. He'd protected her like her own personal bodyguard, but wasn't that what every Navy SEAL did? Protect his target or his tango or whatever she was? Infiltrate? Lie and cheat and—?

Vicki closed her stinging eyes and palmed her temples. Her head pounded like she'd laid it on the nearest L track while the pink-line train rumbled her way. Damn! She was beginning to hate pink. She'd moved on. Pink was for sweet little girls. Red was her color now, damn it. Blood red. The exact same color tinting the dim light from that stupid nightlight.

Heartbreak was all she'd ever known, and this thing with Pagan surely felt like another broken heart headed for her. How many times was a woman expected to get back on her feet after being steamrolled over by disappointment and lies? Was she an idiot to have ever believed this guy?

Her head buzzed. She couldn't think. She staggered. *What's happening to me?* Was Pagan the liar or was she... was she...?

Vicki dropped to one knee in what would be the last safe room of her life. Her chest hurt. Her pulse throbbed like a mother. She wished for just one of her pink-handled pistols as she clutched her swinging girls against her to keep those heavy breasts from toppling her over. They'd always been her best assets and her greatest liabilities. Too large. So heavy. Always in the way. Her back ached every minute of every day. There was no relief. What she wouldn't give for a shot of Scotch and... and...

"I'm so damned tired," she murmured as she face-planted and tasted the carpet.

Chapter Twenty-Seven

Pagan flew off the bed to catch her before she fell, but he didn't reach Paloma until she was face down. He'd been lying there with one arm behind his head, enjoying the show, and believe you me, she'd put on quite a naked-warrior-goddess show—until her eyes rolled back in her head and she dropped to her knees.

Angry at himself for not realizing she might still be physically compromised, he wrapped her into the quilt before he stabbed the emergency switch by the door.

Kruze knocked before he jerked the door open and asked, "What's going on?" His dark eyes widened as he took in Pagan's lack of clothing, but he was smart enough not to smirk or comment about it as he walked swiftly toward the lady in Pagan's arms.

"She needs a doctor," Pagan growled, sitting on the bed with her head tilted back, her body limp, and his heart racing. "Not sure what Harding did to her yesterday, but he should've checked her more thoroughly. What the hell, Kruze?"

"What's wrong with her head?"

Crap. Kruze didn't know what Pal had been through. That was on Pagan. Instead of regularly reporting and keeping Chance informed of every single thing that had transpired during these last few days, Pagan had assumed normal SOB protocol, which meant no unnecessary situation reports, no evidence gathering, no sniper logs that could be used against Senator Sullivan or his SOB operators, and no intel to share with Kruze. It kept their ghost status intact while the SOBs remained a figment of imagination to any congressional detractors of the elite blackest of black operators. But it had also kept his brothers in the dark as to Paloma's condition.

"She hit her head, hard, once when they buried her alive, then again when I shot her. Get Harding back here. Now."

Kruze palmed his phone, made the call, then slid his cell back into his rear pocket. "Talk to me. How'd it happen?"

"Whoever tried to kill her, knocked her out before he buried her alive." Pagan cradled Paloma against his chest while he combed his fingers through her hair, searching out that bump and the cut from her first attack. Only now, there was blood on his fingertips. Guess her head wasn't as hard as he'd thought. "This is my fault. She fell when I shot her," he admitted, his voice gone hoarse and gruff. "I shouldn't have—"

"She'll be fine," Kruze interrupted as he took a knee at Pagan's side.

The moment he reached one hand for Paloma, though, Pagan growled, "Don't."

Kruze pulled his fingers back. "What's gotten into you? I'm just trying to help. She's our patient until Harding gets here, and I'm in a better position to assist. Now come on. Back off and let me see how bad it is while you go put some pants on that big hairy ass."

"I'm not leaving." But begrudgingly, Pagan did let Kruze part Paloma's hair enough to check her head wound.

"Damn, you're right. We missed this bump back here, and, shit. There's a cut. It's pretty bad. She's bleeding." His eyes narrowed as he peeled one of her eyelids open. "I don't have enough light in this room. Hold onto her. I'll be right back."

Like Pagan could ever let her go? While Kruze hurried out of the room, Pagan hurriedly set her on the bed. Fumbling, he pulled on the pants he'd worn the day before, then settled Paloma back under his chin and told her, "I'm sorry, Pal. I should've planned better. I shouldn't have thought—"

"Knock off the moaning," Kruze chastised as he opened the door and returned to Pagan's side. "Christ, I could hear you crying all the way down in the hall. Things happen in combat, Baby Brother, and you know it. So what if you gave her a *widdle bump* on her head while you were saving her life? She'll understand. Don't wimp out on me."

"I'm not wimping out. I'm just worried, that's—"

"Yeah, well, wah, wah, wah. Stop crying over spilled milk and hold her steady while I..." Kruze shut up long enough to shine the light into Paloma's pupils. 'Good. She's not dilated or running a fever. Get her back into bed and make sure her feet are raised, just to be safe. I'll get an ice pack for that bump. She'll need fluids. Can you handle setting her up with a saline IV while I grab a painkiller and the lidocaine?"

Pagan nodded. This was all his fault. Paloma might be damned good at her job, but she was still a delicate thing. Her bones were slighter, her build more delicate, and obviously, her skull wasn't as thick as he'd thought. Instead of making love to her like a horndog last night after her alleged death, he should've double-checked that she was hydrated instead. He should've checked her from top to bottom and fed her dinner. But no. She'd said come hither and he'd come. A couple times. *Damn me. I'm as bad as Kruze.*

But Pagan had her now and a minor concussion was easily treated. He knew the rules. As long as the injured party could hold an intelligent conversation, sleep was good for the brain. Although, she hadn't exactly been making sense before she'd passed out, come to think of it. She'd gotten steadily angry over nothing, and she'd definitely had trouble walking and standing. Which started his panic all over again. What if this was more than just a simple concussion? What if—?

"I never touched her," Kruze said suddenly.

That jolted Pagan back to the situation at hand. "What?" he asked, not certain he believed anything his older brother said as far as it concerned him and Paloma.

Kruze met him man-to-man and eye-to-eye. "I said that I've never touched her, Pagan. Not like you think anyway." His chin pointed at Paloma. "Yes, we tangled in Portland last year. She caught me dead to rights. I'd just shot at Domingo Zapata, the psychotic killer out of Brazil. Missed the bastard. I was so focused on ending him that she came up behind me, had one of her damned pink pistols stuck behind my ear before I knew she was there. Could've shot me right then and there, but you know what she said?"

Pagan grunted, not sure he wanted to know what sweet endearment Paloma might have whispered in his brother's ear.

Kruze's emerald green eyes twinkled, yet there was a spark of sadness hidden there that Pagan hadn't recognized before. He did now. Kruze was— lonely? Nah, that didn't make sense. Kruze was the ultimate party animal whenever he came to town, any town. He had women lined up for miles. Pagan knew damned well he did.

"She told me I was the wrong brother," Kruze said quietly. "Guess she'd had her eye on you all along. Ain't that a laugh?" His gaze fell on the sleeping beauty in Pagan's arms. "She wants you, the family man, not me, the guy who's just like her."

"She's nothing like you," Pagan shot back even as he looked down at the woman he adored. With her long black hair tossed over her shoulders and draped to the floor, her normally olive-toned skin looked pale against his darkly tanned arms. "She wants out of this business. She wants to start over, fresh, like Suede did." Pagan didn't mean to censure Kruze like he had, especially not after something unexpected glittered in the corner of his brother's eye.

And it wasn't a tear.

It was despair.

"Yeah," Kruze said, his voice low and sounding uncommonly dejected. "I get it. You and Chance always were the smart ones."

"I didn't mean—"

"Forget it. I'll grab the first-aid kit and I'll set up the IV." Kruze lifted to his feet. "Keep her warm while I'm gone, Baby Brother."

What the hell was wrong with Kruze this morning? He'd never seemed as morose as he did now. Brothers. Who knew what went on inside their hard heads?

Kruze came back quickly. While Pagan bared Paloma's arm, he deftly set up an IV tree, then initiated the drip. With painstaking attention, he applied a topical painkiller to her head wound, then pressed a pad of gauze against her scalp before he bobby-pinned a chunk of her hair to hold the temporary bandage in place. Finally, he handed off a frozen gel pack to Pagan before he pushed to his feet. "That's for the swelling. Take good care of her, kid. Women like Vicki Hex don't come around often."

"Paloma," blurted out of Pagan's big mouth. "Her real name's Paloma. It means dove. Of peace. She's not who you think she is."

Kruze's head canted. His eyes darkened.

Pagan nodded. Did keeping Paloma's real identity matter? Kruze was always bound to find out, and Paloma wouldn't mind. "You heard me. Vicki Hex is her alter ego, but her real name's Paloma Juarez. She's Julio's little sister. Of course they have the same last name."

Kruze pursed his lips and said, "You're right. Guess I never really thought about it before. But Juarez, of course. Paloma Juarez. It's got a nice ring to it, don't you think? It makes sense. Paloma and Julio..."

"I'm going to marry her," Pagan declared righteously, his chin up for some reason he couldn't understand. But maybe he could. It was time Kruze knew. Pagan was staking a claim on this complicated, sometimes-dominatrix in his arms. She didn't know she was off the market yet, but Paloma Juarez was his. Vicki Hex was, too.

Kruze took it like a gentleman, but then he said something Pagan would never have expected in a million years. "Good on you, Baby Brother. Just remember what Mom used to tell us boys, when we were growing up and thought we knew it all. *'Working hard for something you don't care about is stress. But working hard for something or, someone you love—'"* his head dipped toward the lady, *"'—is passion. Always choose to live passionately, boys. Once you understand the difference, everything else comes easy.'"*

Pagan nodded as he heard his mother's words of wisdom again. It was almost as if Scarlett were in the room, telling him herself. God, how he missed her.

But what in the living hell was wrong with Kruze this morning? Pagan couldn't begin to understand. He opened his mouth to ask, but Kruze's butt pocket buzzed. He waved Pagan off as he answered his cell and walked out the door, telling Doc Harding, "Yes, she's awake, but she fainted. When can you be here?"

Just in time, too. Pagan looked down into the most beautiful dark eyes glimmering up at him. "I'm marrying you?" his strong little dove asked.

A tender smile breached Pagan's mouth. "I hope so," he murmured as he placed a gentle kiss to the middle of Paloma's forehead. "I truly, truly hope so."

"Since when? I don't remember you asking me."

"I'm asking you now, Paloma Juarez," he murmured as he kissed her again. "You are my passion and my heart. My reason to live and my will to survive. Will you marry me?"

But when he lifted his lips and looked at her again, her eyes were closed. She looked as if she'd fallen back to sleep. And that was okay. He'd ask again. And again, and again if he needed to because it was true. Paloma Juarez was his dove. She'd brought the peace to his heart that he'd lost when his mother died. He could breathe again. He had his heart back again.

But maybe that was the way it was always meant to be when a man took a wife. He'd always been a one-woman kind of a man. First, his mother. Now, Paloma. Maybe Scarlett had known her boys weren't smart enough to move on until she'd passed. Maybe that was why she'd never told them she was dying. Maybe that was all part of her Delta One plan.

Yeah, no. Not only no, but hell no. Pagan cast that notion aside as quickly as it hit his brain pan. Because one thing he knew for certain was that Scarlett would've loved being a grandmother. She had adored her sons every day of her life, and she would've adored their wives and their children, too. No doubt about it. That was the way Scarlett was.

Besides, there was never a good reason to die from something like cancer. It wasn't the same thing as dying in the line of duty or while defending another. Hell, no. She'd been smart enough that she'd prepared them even as boys to leave home and be men enough to do so when the time came. She'd been the force behind each of them joining the Navy and becoming SEALs.

Ever since he could remember, she'd been the encouraging, nagging, oftentimes bolstering patriotic wind beneath their wings. That she'd centered their single-parent, Sinclair home and raised her sons in Navy-proud San Diego, CA, had only made her job easier. The woman had been blindingly brilliant. Beautiful, too.

Which was why Pagan still missed her and always would. But that was what sons did. They loved their mothers, and that love prepared them in all ways to also love their wives. To treat them with respect and to do right by them.

"Yes,' Paloma whispered, her eyes still sealed, but her lips moist and lush. "I would very much love to marry you. I want to be Mrs. Pagan Sinclair for the rest of my life. When can we do it?"

Pagan grinned—right before he covered her mouth with his and gave the last piece of his heart away. Pagan and Paloma. Now *that* had a nice ring to it.

Chapter Twenty-Eight

Kruze stood on the street, a cigarette dangling off his lower lip while he studied the innocuous looking safe house in what the rest of the world would call every day, boringly normal suburbia. Doc Harding had finally returned, giving Kruze the chance to escape he'd been waiting for.

Someone in this family had to be smart. It was time to go.

Kruze wished he could've stayed with Pagan and Vicki. But life for the Sin Boys was never meant to be easy nor peaceful. Just because both Chance and Pagan had found the women they loved, didn't make any home safe. If anything, his brothers had just set everything and everyone that could possibly destroy them, in motion.

Every freak and terrorist, every betrayer and liar knew that an honorable man with a wife and family was a sure thing. He could now be tested and found desperately wanting. He could be swayed, coerced, and bullied into giving up his darkest most intimate secrets, hell, even the country's darkest secrets. He'd be tortured, and they could be tortured as well. All because he loved and would die for his woman.

If Senator Sullivan were half as intelligent as he thought he was, he'd factor that philosophy into the job offers he lured his super soldiers with. He'd insist they never marry, never date, and never fall in love. He'd make them sign on the dotted line to prove their allegiance to their country and to their country alone. Now there'd be a group of hard men for you. Hard in all the worst ways.

So be it. Kruze tossed his cigarette butt to the street and ground the dying ash with his boot heel. Pagan didn't need him around. Chance didn't need him in Montana, either. Anyone could see that. And Kruze knew damned well neither Suede nor Vicki Hex, make that Paloma Juarez, needed him.

Flipping the collar of his denim jacket up against the first of many oncoming winter storms, he lowered his head into the wind and walked away from his younger brother's first stab at happiness. Pagan deserved a good life, and if Vicki Hex made him smile, good on him.

Kruze sucked in a lungful of freezing air. An early cold front had stalled over the Great Lakes. Nature's phenomenon, the much-touted lake effect, ensured a large dose of snow and ice would soon be in the forecast.

He walked two doors down before he melted into the breezy shadows and paused. From now on, he'd do what he'd always done. He'd stick to the dark that he knew best. He'd play it safe. But he'd also keep careful watch over his brothers and their wives, his future nieces and nephews, too. If it took the rest of his life, he'd protect the family he loved. He could be that hard man standing fast against the world. He'd done it before, he could do it again. He would stand firm. If it was the last thing he did, he'd die for each and every one of his brothers.

Because there were things happening that neither Pagan nor Chance knew, but that Kruze had suspected from the moment he'd gotten the call that Chance had nearly been killed in South America. The annoying pain in his gut had only gotten worse when Kruze heard from Chance's torn and bleeding lips that an Agency operative had been on that mission with him. Some jerk-off named Dick Card.

But now was not the time for conjecture. Now was the time for fact-finding and filling in the blanks. And while he was at it, he'd get Pagan's leather jacket back for him, too.

Because that was what brothers did.

*****

"Where's Kruze? Thought he was there with you?" Chance asked over the laptop monitor sitting on Paloma's bed. Pagan had opted to use something portable for this discussion instead of the heavy-duty monitor on the wall. Just in case he'd need to do something drastic like slam the lid closed... or something.

Sitting safe and sound, downright comfy looking in his Montana office, Chance was dressed in his usual flannel shirt and jeans. Big brother looked plenty rested and content. Why shouldn't he be? He was home and safe with Suede, two rowdy dogs, and a home security system like no other in all of Montana and maybe the lower forty-eight. He'd probably just finished eating a home cooked breakfast, brunch, or whatever, after waking up late with his sexy wife. Suede cooked and baked like a master chef. What was not to like?

It was early afternoon. For now, Pagan sat at Paloma's side on an office chair he'd dragged in from the office across the hall, instead of sitting in bed with her. He hadn't shared the news of his upcoming nuptials yet. He'd been too busy making sure she was hydrating properly and eating the breakfast he'd cooked for her. They'd shared bacon and eggs, coffee, toast, and orange juice. Simple things like that. Nothing fancy like the walnut cinnamon rolls Suede had probably baked piping fresh this morning for Chance.

But now Pagan knew Paloma liked her coffee hot and black, while he liked his laced with enough whiskey to feel the burn. Too bad this safe-house didn't have any.

"Guess he went out," Pagan replied, not sure where Kruze had gone to. But that was how the middle Sinclair brother operated, here one moment, gone the next, always without saying goodbye or where he was headed. Kruze could be a royal pain in the ass.

"So who do you believe is after you, Miss Hex?" Chance directed the question at Paloma.

Pagan opened his mouth to correct his brother. Her real name was Paloma, but she answered before he could. "Not the Seranzinos. I've already met with Vito. I've stared into his soul. He's clear."

Chance nodded thoughtfully. "Cabb then? That'd be his style, stab you in the back and plead the Fifth. Or Romeo? He's got a drug rap sheet long enough to gag a horse. Could he be behind this attempt on your life?"

Her ebony locks shifted over her shoulders when she shook her head. "I'm thinking more along the lines of Dillon Roberto. I need to pay him a call. He's my next assignment anyway."

Chance canted his head. "Roberto, as in the Mafia's dry cleaner?"

"Yeah, him. We had a date to meet at his casino the evening all this started."

"Haven't you heard?"

Pagan's breath caught. "Heard what?"

Chance dragged a hand over his head and through his thick hair before he growled, "Shit. That makes everything harder. Chicago PD fished his body out of Lake Michigan the same night you say you were buried alive."

Pagan growled at Chance's word choice. "She was buried alive."

Both Chance's palms came up to stop the argument before it started. "Understood. Don't get your panties in a twist. It just looks suspicious, especially since—"

Paloma leaned into the monitor. "Since what?"

Chance pursed his lips, studying her as he asked, "Do you know where your pistols are?"

Pagan groaned when she shook her head and replied, "No, of course not. I woke up in a grave west of Chicago with dirt in my mouth and nose. I could barely breathe. How would I know? All my stuff was gone. Whoever stuffed me in that grave has it. Shit!"

"You think whoever did this would've left her armed?" Pagan snarled at Chance, knowing exactly where this line of questioning was headed.

Paloma knew, too. "I can take you to the place I was buried. If you don't believe me, I—"

"Never said I didn't believe you, Miss Vicki," Chance said as he shook his head. "But you need to know that both your pistols were found wrapped inside the plastic bag Dillon was suffocated with. They'd been used. Also, the rounds he'd been shot with but which didn't kill him, matched your pistols, both of them. And there were witnesses."

A breath hissed out of Pagan. "She's being framed!"

"Witnesses?" she snapped. "Really? I don't recall any witnesses watching me dig myself out of a hole in the middle of that fucking forest!"

Pagan cringed. Somehow that word sounded so much uglier when a woman used it. And yeah, that one hundred percent male opinion cinched it. He *was* a male chauvinist. He *did* have different rules for men and women. But damn it. Women *were* better than men. Every guy with half a brain knew that. And because women were better, they didn't need to act like or curse like men to be taken seriously. Men were the animals on this planet. That was why God made them first. Women came later. They were the angels. God's best work. Like frosting on a cake. You didn't add the best part until last, did you?

But the gloves were off now. Chance, ever the older patient brother, said, "I think it's time you took Miss Vicki for a ride, Pagan. Go to that forest she says she woke up in and find that grave. Validate her testimony. Take photos. Gather as much trace evidence as you can find. If she broke a fingernail digging out of that hole, I want it bagged and tagged and on my desk in two days. Make damned sure we've got every last one of our Is dotted and our Ts crossed, because we're going to need it."

"*I* don't need it," Pagan roared at the precise same time Paloma spat, "You think I'm guilty, Chief?" as she waved her still raw fingertips at him. "What? You think I chewed off my nails to make your brother fall for my lies?"

Chance inhaled a long slow breath, taking the hit of her calling him by his Navy rank with the professional grace of a man who'd been born to lead. "No, Miss Hex. I do believe what Pagan believes. However, someone *is* framing you for Dillon Roberto's murder, and whoever that someone is, he's done a damned fine job. We need to do all we can to prove you didn't kill Dillon, that you weren't even in Chicago when it went down. Who else knew you were meeting Mr. Roberto that night?"

Pagan turned to Paloma. She had a way of sliding her jaw off center when she was pissed. Right then, her teeth were grinding so loud he could hear them. The woman's tender fingers were curled into fists and her knuckles were white. He settled one palm over her joined hands.

Paloma brushed his offer of solidarity aside. "Do *you* keep an appointment book, Chief? A record of exact locations and landing zones where you send your brothers every time they go out on one of your *top secret* missions?" she asked pointedly, her fingers flashing those annoying air quotes at every word or phrase she emphasized.

Before Chance could answer, she hit him with a snarky head bob and snorted, "Well, neither do I.

That'd be rich, wouldn't it? Me keeping a Day Planner, marking off my kills with little tick marks like some upwardly mobile moron who wants to look good for the boss, while I leave an evidence trail a mile wide for the local DA to find? What kind of an idiot do you think I—?" She cleared her throat. Coughed. Choked. "What do you take me for?"

Concerned she might be on the verge of passing out, Pagan put his palm in the middle of her back to steady her. Impatiently, she lifted one shoulder and shrugged him off. "Leave me alone. I'm not an insipid little girl who can't hold her own in a fight, Sinclair."

No, you most certainly are not.

"I just had a thought, one of those déjà vu moments, and I need to..." She cleared her throat again. "I need to remember that... that thing I can't remember anymore because of you. Shit! Why'd you touch me like that?"

Like what? Like I love you and care about you?

Withdrawing his offensive hand, Pagan bit his tongue, fully aware that he was back to being *'Sinclair'* again. Okay. Stressed out woman in the room. Danger, danger.

But worse, Chance was watching, taking in the theatrics as only an observant former SEAL Commander could. Shit. All Pagan could come up with was to tell Paloma, "Think for a minute. You'll remember. I know you will."

For which he received a truly evil glare in answer. "What? You think I'm not trying to remember? You think I haven't been thinking all this time? Jesus! How stupid do you think I am?"

Apparently, he couldn't say anything right, so Pagan turned back to the monitor and asked his brother, "What else was on the body? Any trace evidence?"

Chance was definitely thinking and wondering. He pursed his lips again and replied, "Several long strands of Vicki's black hair. Her fingerprints on both pistols. A note written in her handwriting."

"Jesus Christ! Anyone smart enough to get into my penthouse could've stolen hair out of my hairbrush, and shit! My fingerprints are everywhere in my place, because—guess what? I lived there. What'd the stupid damned note say?" Paloma bit out.

Chance was a pro at keeping his cool. "It said, *'I'm on to you, Dillon baby. Bah-bye,'*" he replied smoothly.

Paloma cocked her head. "Wow, that's... weird." She combed her fingers through her long hair, rolling her neck at the same time as if she were fighting a migraine. Which Pagan had no doubt she was. He knew migraines.

Striving for patience, he asked his older brother, "Anything else?"

"The DA doesn't need anything else to file charges," Chance answered just as quietly. "One of Dillon's bodyguards witnessed Miss Hex confronting Dillon Roberto outside his casino the day before he was killed. He heard her tell Dillon that—"

"Hey, I'm right here, guys," she said tiredly. "Don't talk about me in the third person like I'm an idiot who doesn't understand English, when I'm sitting right here."

Pagan cocked his head at her. "You don't feel good," he told her, not asked.

"So?" she shot back at him. "What do you care?"

"So, you turned nasty like this before you passed out the last time. I'm calling Doc Harding. Something's not right."

"Oh, for hell's sake, Sinclair, shut up and—"

"And you keep calling me Sinclair like we've never—" He shut up on the verge of giving too much away.

Her hand went to her forehead. "Migraine. I just have a migraine. It'll go away. I just need..." With a stifled breathy wheeze, her eyes rolled back in her head as, once again, she collapsed.

Pagan shot to his feet, jerked open the door, and called out into the hall, "Doc? You still here? She needs you! Now!"

Chance was asking something, but Pagan only had ears for the doctor as Harding scrambled back into the room and ran to Paloma's bedside. "Damn it, Pagan, I told you she needs rest, not stress. You gentlemen have got to keep her quiet. Her brain needs to heal, and you're not helping."

"Understood," Pagan answered meekly as he met his brother's worried expression from the monitor.

While Doctor Harding double-checked Paloma's vitals, Pagan lifted the portable monitor off the bed and stepped into the hall with it. He sank to his butt on the floor to confront his brother. Thinking he could head Chance off at the pass he said, "She's got a concussion. My fault. She fell on the sidewalk when I shot her, and she hit her head pretty hard. She needs bed rest. All this bad news isn't helping."

"What else is going on?" Chance asked quietly. What he really meant to ask was *'why are you so broken up over the way Paloma's acting?'*

Pagan was no longer sure what to tell Chance. When he'd placed the call home, he'd wanted to share his good news, but now he wasn't sure if Paloma had correctly understood when he'd asked her to marry him. How stupid could he be, asking a woman with a brain injury to marry him when she was obviously impaired?

"Pagan?" Chance prompted. "Are you and Miss Hex—?"

"Paloma," Pagan replied wearily. "Her real name's Paloma Juarez. Vicki Hex is just her alias. It's not who she really is. It's like a stage name. A handle."

There went Chance's lips again, pressed together as if he needed to pout while he processed deep thoughts. Ha. There was nothing deep going on here, other than the deep divot in Pagan's big, empty head.

"The thing is—"

"You care about her," Chance astutely observed. "You like Vicki, err, Paloma Juarez, don't you?"

Pagan nodded. "I do," he admitted. "Never thought I'd fall for a woman like her, but... Yeah. I do."

"You're compromised," Chance said more clearly.

Pagan shook his head at that ridiculous conclusion. "I am, huh? Then who in Chicago are you going to get to replace me? I'm already here, aren't I? And I'm the one who can not only confirm Paloma's injuries and her state of mind on the morning she crept back into her hideout, but I was also there when that rogue helo blasted her out of her apartment. Do you even know who was behind that yet? I saw the dirt in her hair and the damage she did to her fingernails after she dug herself out of that grave. I was there damned near from the beginning of this nightmare, Chance. No one takes this away from me. Not even you!" *You smug ass!*

Pagan expected Chance to pull rank, but what he got was a clear and present, "Understood. I wouldn't have it any other way."

The oddest warmth swept over Pagan at that declaration of brotherly loyalty.

"I love her," he told his older brother honestly, a tear wending its way down his damned nose and into his mustache." But that was what brothers were for, wasn't it? To trust and confide in? To rely on? To cry to? And Jesus, this was one of those rare those times when Pagan absolutely needed at least one brother to understand the hell he was going through. "I'll die before anyone hurts her again. I will!"

"I know you will," Chance replied evenly. "Remember that op into South America when we retrieved Suede from Franks, Patrone, and Garcia? I thought I'd lost her, but you made it pretty clear you'd lay down your life for the woman I loved that day. I knew I had you on my six. Hear me now, Baby Brother. I'll do the same for you and Paloma. I'll be there in five hours."

"No," Pagan replied, though his voice cracked, and he sounded more like a crybaby little brother than a former SEAL known for getting the hardest jobs done. "Stay with Suede. Don't leave her alone. I have a feeling this could get ugly. Someone knows too much about Paloma's whereabouts the day she was buried. You know she never went anywhere without her trademark firearms. They were part of her mystique. Her disguise. Please. Take care of Suede. Let me take care of Pal. Don't let anything happen to Suede and that baby of yours."

Silence stretched across the miles between them. At last Chance hissed, "I could kill Kruze for leaving you like this."

Pagan wiped a callused hand over his face. "You know how he is. He hasn't been the same since Mom died."

Chance nodded, his lips pinched again, and his amber eyes somber. "That's no excuse. Neither have we, Pagan. It's been tough for all of us."

"Yeah, but Kruze..." Pagan almost said this brother was different. Which Kruze most certainly was.

He'd always held himself separate from the rest of his family. Instead of joining in at dinnertime or on summer picnics, he'd always sought the companionship of his buddies and friends. Long before he'd joined the Navy, he'd built his own team. He was the high school braggart in the parking lot, sitting on the hood of someone else's car, smoking with his juvenile delinquent buddies. Whatever devil rode him, it rode him hard and had been riding him for years.

"Let it go, Chance," Pagan finally muttered. "Kruze is who he is. If he's broke, he's going to have to admit it first." Wasn't that the truth? You can lead a horse to water and all that...

"I *will* find a way to help you," Chance said earnestly.

Pagan wasn't about to hold his breath and wait for the cavalry to come galloping to his rescue. Chance had his hands full with his new wife and those two horses he'd just bought her. No. Pagan and Paloma were in this alone. "Save some of those cinnamon rolls for me," he told his big brother instead of voicing agreement and thereby encouraging Chance to come solve his problems.

"What makes you think I've got cinnamon rolls?" Chance asked, his brows lifted over his amber eyes wide with mischief.

"Because your wife loves you," Pagan replied easily, "and that's how Suede proves it. She feeds you. A lot."

Chance smoothed a hand over his belly. How he maintained that trim gut despite all he ate was a mystery. 'Copy that. Take care, Baby Brother."

"Goodbye," Pagan said as he closed the laptop and ended the conversation. Wasn't that the worst way to sign off? With *'Goodbye'* instead of *'Copy that'*?

Made it sound kind of final, didn't it?

Chapter Twenty-Nine

"She still out?" Doctor Harding asked in his professional, cheery way. The young man was tall and slender with short wavy hair and grayish blue eyes. He'd taken care of Scarlett Sinclair until her cancer forced him to turn her over to the best oncology doctors in Southern California. Ever one of her closest allies, Harding had traveled with her until she'd decided she could no longer keep up her demanding pace during one particularly arduous book signing tour in Saint Louis. Then he'd accompanied her back home to the hospital.

The only thing Pagan had against the man was that, until the bitter end, Harding had kept Scarlett's confidences and her secret. Neither she nor Harding told her boys how close she was to dying until—Damn. Until she was already at Death's door. By then, it was too late.

However well-intentioned keeping that secret was, it was still dead-assed wrong of his mom and the doctor. Pagan understood the sanctity of doctor/patient confidentiality, but Jesus. They'd both known, yet they'd chosen to deny Chance, Kruze, and Pagan those last few months and days they could've spent with their mother. Unfair! Each of them had been out on protractedly long missions during that time, but they'd never failed to phone home or keep in touch however they could. The Navy made sure SEALs had enough downtime to carry on with their personal lives. But talking with Mom online or over the phone was never the same as a face-to-face, sit-at-her-kitchen-table conversation with her. The popular, too-busy-for-her-own-good woman would never think to FaceTime or Marco Polo. Now she was gone.

And shit...

Paloma was the one hovering between life and death, and Pagan could do nothing but wait. Without meeting Harding's eyes, he nodded. "Yes, she's still unconscious. She'll moan once in a while, but for the most part she lies there as if she's in a coma instead of just sleeping."

He'd been sitting with her since she'd passed out the day before, and he was worried. Harding assured him that these things happened, that time spent in a hospital bed wouldn't help her brain heal any faster than her sleeping in this safe-house.

But the fact remained. Someone was out to end her, and a worried mind came up with the most unlikely worst-case scenarios. Could this uncharacteristic weakness she was experiencing be yet another attack neither Pagan nor she had seen coming? For that matter, could his Mom's cancer have been man-made? Inflicted on her? He had no clue how that could've happened, but watching Paloma sleep, and remembering the way his mom looked the day he'd stumbled into her hospital room after he'd gotten the news, was killing him. She'd been as pale then as Paloma was now. So—mortal.

And once again, Pagan was in that exact same helpless place in time. Caught between waiting and praying and hoping this woman wouldn't leave him, too.

"Here. Listen," Harding commanded gently, his stethoscope in his outstretched hand. Eager. That was the word for Harding. Ever eager to assist. Ever eager to relieve another's pain, be it emotional, physical, or just plain because. "See for yourself, Pagan. Paloma has a strong heart. She's just exhausted. She'll pull through this. I can tell. She's a fighter."

'You have no idea,' Pagan thought as he plugged that stethoscope in and pressed the other end to the singular flat spot on her chest just above her girls. Man, he'd give anything to see them jiggle again. To see her open her pretty brown eyes and yawn. Something. Anything except this death-like sleep.

Ah, there she is. Pagan looked at the floor as Pal's heartbeat registered loud and clear against his eardrums. *Thank you, Jesus.* Tears welled in his eyes.

He blinked to keep them from spilling over. But at last his lungs opened, and he breathed his first deep breath in hours. Lifting his brows, he met Doc's steady gaze. "Thanks. I needed this."

A smile played over Harding's lips. "I'm very glad to be of service again, Mr. Sinclair," he said meekly. "You're so much like your mother, Pagan. You have her eyes and her coloring. Of course, you're a little wider, heavier, and taller, but she lives on in each of you. I can see her. I hope you understand what I'm trying to tell you."

"You should've told me," blurted out of Pagan's mouth before he knew what he wanted to say.

Doc Harding's lips pursed. His Adam's apple bobbed. He nodded. "She was so proud of you boys and the work you were doing," he said quietly as he met Pagan's glare. "So proud. And I was just her doctor, not her son. Please know I would've told you that she was dying of cancer if I could have, but she didn't want you to worry. She wanted you to live your lives and get out there and do what you do."

"You don't think we worried anyway?" Pagan bit out as he lost control of his tear ducts. Man, he was making a fool of himself, but so what? *Grown men cry. Get over it.*

"Pagan, there was nothing anyone could do. Scarlett went mercifully fast. She didn't suffer. You were there at the end. You know that."

Pagan nodded as his hand came up to cover his eyes. Taking his anger out on Doc Harding was not what he'd intended. Shit. Pagan dropped his chin to the floor. Talking about Mom was still hard. She'd only been gone a little over a year and a half, but it still hurt like a son-of-a-bitch.

Shit, I wish Chance were here.

Doc Harding cupped Pagan's shoulder. "You really should take a good long nap. You won't be any good to Miss Juarez if you pass out from exhaustion." His voice had changed from tender and caring to bossy and firm. "I'm here. Go. I'll wake you if anything happens."

Pagan *was* ten degrees beyond just tired, but yeah. No. "Not how this works, Doc," he said wearily as he lifted his head and stared the kind man down. "I'm on call until the next operator shows, and—"

A thunderous bang from the front room cut him off.

"Move her now!" Kruze bellowed as he ran into the house, slammed and locked the front door behind him, then came thundering down the hall. Decked out in green and black cammies, his right hand gripped an automatic rifle when he stopped at the bedroom door and ordered, "Get below. They're coming!"

Without a word, Pagan wrapped Paloma in her bed blanket, then scooped her into his arms. Harding grabbed the laptop from her nightstand and his medical bag. In very few minutes, they were out of the bedroom and inside the hall elevator that dropped them one level down to the panic room in the basement.

Only this panic room was like no other. Over-protective Chance had designed it with possible scenarios in mind. Like the one in the Sinclairs' Montana getaway, not only were these walls constructed of heavy steel, but the eight-inch thick vault door could only be opened from the inside once it sealed. Inside the room, a half-dozen adults could live for a month. Chance had also included a separate air filtration system as well as an escape route, a hidden tunnel that connected with the city's underground utility tunnel, just in case.

As Pagan now angled Paloma through that heavy door, the motion-sensitive ceiling lights flickered on. The climate control kicked on, activating the furnace, and the ice-maker dumped a load of cubes into the hopper of the stainless aluminum full-size refrigerator against the far wall. Recessed lighting flashed to life along the corners of both ceilings and floor. All this place needed was a friendly dog to greet them at the door with its tail wagging and the homecoming would be complete.

Doc Harding followed with Kruze behind him, walking backward as he covered their retreat.

"Close," Kruze commanded the in-home security system once he cleared the threshold. Breathing hard, he lifted the muzzle of his rifle to the ceiling and waited. As if it knew better than to disobey, the door swung inward, hissing while hydraulics engaged and sealed them in.

"Who's coming?" Pagan asked as he sank down onto the nearest Lazy Boy recliner. "How many?"

"Ten that I saw. Not sure who they are, but they're packing PGFs," Kruze muttered as he scouted the expansive panic room like he expected to find someone already down here, maybe hiding under one of the two triple-stacked bunk beds at the other end of the room. A floor to ceiling, portable noise dampening partition stood ready to be deployed at the end of one bunk unit. He searched under them all.

But PGFs, really? Precision-Guided Firearms were the absolute latest and greatest in military hardware. At least they would be if Congress ever got off their overpaid asses and actually funded a war to win it, instead of playing politics while young men died.

Pagan had witnessed the power behind those smart weapons a few years back at a shooting competition in Austin, Texas. The concept behind the weapon system was identical to the tracking technology found in the latest fighter jets. It wasn't any different than a soldier on the ground laser-painting a target for an A-10 Warthog flying overhead to zero down on and annihilate with its GAU-8, thirty-millimeter rotary cannon. That cannon itself was accurate enough to send over eighty percent of its shots into a forty-foot wide circle, and do it from an altitude of four thousand feet. Better yet, that already proven technology in combat made it possible for Air Force pilots to drop their ordnance in closer proximity to friendly forces than ever before.

Imagine that kind of firepower in the palm of your hand. Pagan could. He used a Precision-Guided rifle during that competition. All he'd had to do was line up his target in the crosshairs, squeeze the trigger just enough to engage the laser tagging protocol, and voila! His rifle—now called a weapon system—did everything a highly-trained sniper would've done. It just did it faster and better.

Not only had it tagged the target exactly where Pagan wanted his round to go, but its sensors automatically measured all the nuances a sniper would. Windage. Elevation. Spin drift. Air temp. Humidity. Barometric pressure. Rifle cant. It even tracked the Coriolis effect, the inertial force of planet Earth that acted on all objects in motion. Bye-bye ISIL.

Kruze stopped his wandering and stuck the butt of his rifle to the floor alongside one leg, his fingers fluttering on the barrel. "Who are we up against, Pagan? Do you even know?"

"Not the Mafia," Paloma whispered.

Pagan looked down on her. "Oh, you're awake. Nice to see you again."

Her eyes scrolled from side to side as she took in their new home away from home. "You guys sure get around. Where are we today?"

"Same house, but we're in the basement panic room. Don't worry. We've got company upstairs, but you're safe."

She rolled those expressive eyes. "I'm *safe*?" He almost expected air quotes to magically appear. "What, are you my hero again?"

Pagan nodded, smiling like a fool because she sounded more like herself. "As long as you keep fainting for me, you can bet I'm playing hero. Friends with bennies, remember?" he teased.

"Guyzzzzz," Kruze growled. "Critical situation here. Stop screwing around."

Pagan lifted his head to face his brother. He'd nearly forgotten Kruze was there. "Paloma's already been to see Vito. She's sure he and Cabb aren't behind this."

Kruze canted his head. "Then the son? What's his name, Romeo? Could he—"

"No. Romeo's into drugs. He wouldn't know how to tie his shoes without help," she replied as she snuggled against Pagan's chest and sighed, and yes. They were in the middle of Defcon Charlie. An attack was imminent, and he was grinning like an idiot because his woman was safe in his arms and happy to be there. Plus, those navy blue flannel pjs looked good on her. Life didn't get any better than this.

"Baby Brother!" Kruze snapped.

Pagan stared his brother down. "Yes?"

"Can you tear your eyes off Miss Hex, err, I mean Paloma, long enough to watch those jokers up top?"

"I'm on it," Pagan replied as he turned to Doc Harding and asked, "Could you hand me that laptop?"

"Sure," Harding replied, as cheerful as ever. The man was amazingly unflappable. "I imagine you've got a charging dock for this down here somewhere?"

"Sure do. Everything I need's right here." Pagan nodded at the cabinet serving as his side table even as he flipped the computer open with one hand, then set it on Paloma's lap so they could watch together. She wiggled around until she was upright, and didn't that get the rest of his body's attention?

Doc Harding offered a chin nod as he headed for the kitchen and asked, "Coffee anyone?"

Pagan didn't reply. He'd lost that wonderful, warm sensation growing behind his zipper when he saw the deadly team of professional killers moving like shadowy wraiths through the house upstairs. Ten of them, all dressed in the same black trousers and jackets, their faces were hidden beneath plain black balaclavas. But they moved like they were former military. Methodically. Efficiently. Silently as they searched each room, each closet, and drawer as if they'd done this before.

"Jesus, what are they looking for?" Kruze asked as he leaned over Pagan's shoulder, watching while the hidden security cameras upstairs caught everything.

Pagan shook his head. It did look like these guys were after something much smaller than the woman on his lap. The one who searched the bedroom Paloma had been in, studied the monitors on the wall longer than he'd investigated the en-suite bathroom where her fake-blood splattered clothes still lay in the hamper.

"Can't be the FBI. The Bureau's too cheap to buy PGFs for their agents," Kruze said as the team upstairs gathered silently at the entry, the front door still wide open the way they'd left it.

"True. They're constrained by the federal budget. Shhhhh. Listen." Pagan increased the laptop's volume just as one of the men asked, "Anything?"

One by one, the rest of the men declared, "Negative."

"Son-of-a-bitch." The guy who'd spoken first hissed a hearty, "We're wasting our time. He's not going to be happy."

One of the others grunted, "Since when are we paid to make him happy? He's a dick, and you know it. So we haven't found any proof yet. You ever think maybe there isn't any?"

"Proof?" Pagan muttered. "What proof?"

Another muttered, "Doug's right. I didn't find any drives or portables. Not even an SD card that can convict these guys. These assholes are good, I'm telling you. I say we blow this house and call it good. He sure as fuck can't complain then."

Yet another of the men nodded. "Fire's the only sure way to deal with them. No evidence, no problem, right?"

The leader of this odd covert ops team nodded, not what Pagan expected. These guys acted like mercenaries who didn't like their current job. Only these guys were out to deal with a 'them' not 'her.' They weren't after Paloma. They were here for the Sin Boys. Which sure felt like a clue, but he had no idea how it fit in with what he knew about Paloma's murderer. Until...

"Whoever buried you did a half-assed job of it, right?" he whispered, trying his theory on for size.

Paloma's throat worked as she swallowed. "Maybe."

Pagan nodded at her while he watched the goings on upstairs. "It had to be these guys. It's true. Think about how it went down for a minute. If he—or they, these guys—had been serious about making you disappear, they'd have executed you Mafia-style, two rounds through your head, then dumped you in a landfill or into Lake Michigan. You wouldn't have been able to dig yourself out then."

Mr. Team Leader grumbled, "Then torch the son-of-a-bitchin' place. Don't worry 'bout repercussions. I'll get back to him. I'll explain. You'll still get your hazard pay."

"Hazard pay?" Kruze hissed. "Who are these guys?"

"Not only that, but the chopper..." Pagan couldn't take his eyes off the man in charge upstairs. He'd taken his balaclava off. Tall, lean, and obviously nervous, his vivid blue eyes darted from one man to another as his team shuffled out of the house the way they'd entered—through the front door. The Sinclair perimeter cameras caught the last view of them as each faded in different directions and climbed into different vehicles instead of filing like a federal team into SWAT vans.

"What chopper?" Kruze asked.

By then Pagan couldn't answer. The assault team upstairs was gone. Mr. Team Leader stood alone in the hall. From there, he could see into the kitchen, straight out the front door, or down the hall to the bedroom where Paloma had stayed. Sliding one hand under the front of his jacket, he'd produced a dusky green cylinder.

"That's a bomb," Kruze growled. "Hold on, folks. It's about to get noisy and dusty down here."

Pagan cupped Paloma's jaw to press her to his chest and under his chin, but she wouldn't have it. "Knock it off. I'm not dead or dying here. I want to watch."

Alrighty then. Pagan, Paloma, and Kruze watched Mr. Team Leader set the bomb on the floor in the hallway, which was the dead center of the house. He rotated the metal cap enough to start what Pagan knew was a four-minute timer. Fast-stepping it to the entry, the guy closed the door behind him and nonchalantly walked away. On the sidewalk out front, he slipped out of his balaclava and jacket, then tossed them in through the open window of a nondescript gray sedan parked at the curb. As if he were just another guy out for a drive in the chilly weather, he climbed inside, started his car, and drove away.

By then, two minutes were left on the timer Pagan had set on his laptop.

"Are you sure this house can take it?" Doc Harding asked nervously from the sofa where he'd been sipping a mug of Kona's best.

"You bet," Kruze answered, his tone blithe and deceivingly confident.

But unexpected things still happened, didn't they? Ask Chance if you had any doubt of Murphy's Law. Hell, ask Paloma.

"Cover your head with the blanket on the back of the couch," Pagan told Doc Harding as he bowed his body over Paloma and wrapped his arms around her. Their two minutes were nearly up. He buried his face in her fragrant hair. If this was the end, he couldn't think of a better way to go than with her in his arms.

As the bomb upstairs ticked its final seconds, he whispered in her ear, "I will love you forever. If we live through this, let's get..."

BOOM!

"...out of here."

Chapter Thirty

They were on the run again, only Paloma was awake and running with the guys this time, not stuffed unconscious into a body bag. But something felt different, more urgent about this retreat. Pagan and Kruze had strapped up and packed on their gear without speaking, and they'd packed on a lot. Pistols and ammo, hand grenades and flashbangs. Knives. They each wore twin holsters over their shoulders, another on each thigh, and one at their ankles. Multiple belts slung over their shoulders or at their waists stored enough pouches to make her wonder how they carried so much weight and still did their jobs.

Pagan made it look easy. After he'd geared up, he tossed her a double holster like the one she'd had before this nightmare started. Then he made it better. Pink-handles first, he handed over two nine-millimeter handguns identical to the ones she'd lost. She could've kissed him, but that was a girly thing to do, and today, she was no girl. She'd summoned Vicki Hex to the fight.

At the moment, she was dressed again in running pants and shoes, but she had no clue who was behind the various attempts on her life, or the safe-house bombing. It still burned overhead, and she could clearly see the emergency vehicles and personnel that had responded on the laptop Pagan had left running on the kitchen table. It looked like Armageddon had come to this quiet little suburb.

"On my mark," Kruze cautioned Pagan from a wall panel between the kitchen area and the bunks.

Paloma hadn't noticed it until then because of the way it had been framed with the same molding as the cabinets. No wonder. Clever Chance had built in a secret panel to conceal an escape tunnel.

Shouldering his pack, Pagan tromped over to the panel with a pistol in his hand. "Ready whenever you are."

"One," Kruze said as he eased his fingertips into the groove where the molding butted up against the kitchen cabinet. "Two." Widening his stance, he leaned forward, and said, "Three." He jerked the door open, revealing a dark closet-like entry, which Pagan immediately stepped into.

"Clear," he said evenly, his weapon still up and ready. "I go first. Paloma, you follow. Doc, you're behind her."

"Move it, people," Kruze ordered, gesturing for everyone to do as they were told.

Hurriedly, Doc Harding secured the laptop in a backpack that went over his shoulder, while Paloma packed what little she had, most of it borrowed from Pagan. A man's winter jacket, black of course, as well as several pairs of black nitrile gloves, two bottled waters, what he called a blow-out kit, and the solid weight of a good supply of nine-millimeter ammo that felt damned good in her backpack. Now she was ready to go.

Pagan stood in the dark of that closet, his eyes bright as he watched her. She took his outstretched hand and followed. A draft met her with an icy chill. She disengaged her fingers from Pagan's and flipped the jacket collar up.

"It's breezy down here." She spoke louder than she'd meant to, but the lack of conversation was beginning to get to her. Even Doc Harding had stopped offering advice or help.

"The fire overhead creates a back draft once the panel's opened," Pagan answered as he led the way. "Once Kruze seals the door..."

The secret panel whooshed shut behind Kruze, and sure enough. The breeze reduced to nearly nothing. Track lighting in the corners of the floor and ceiling gave the tunnel enough light for them to see each other. They walked single file for the length of what felt like a block before Pagan said, "This is where it gets dicey. Whatever happens next, keep moving. Do not turn back, because the door behind us only opens from the other side."

Paloma nodded. She trusted Pagan.

"Wh-what's so dicey?" Harding asked from behind her.

"Entering the adjoining utility tunnel that this tunnel leads into," Pagan murmured. "It's no problem when it's clear, but if a city electrician or a lineman happens to be working down here, we'll have some explaining to do. I'd rather not deal with another problem today." He placed both palms against what appeared to be a solid concrete wall then, and—

Holy Schnikees! What a sight. The veins on his neck all but popped, he strained so hard. The muscles in his shoulders bunched against his already tight t-shirt and weapons vest. Bowing his head to the phenomenally heavy task, he grunted, then slowly lifted the entire concrete panel—all by himself. Panting, he set it aside and stepped over a bump of a threshold and into yet another tunnel. Wiping the sweat beaded on his brow with the back of his hand, he looked both ways, then muttered, "Hurry. I'll have to put this back."

Paloma hurried, glad to be out of that much narrower tunnel that Chance Sinclair had dug. "You should have let us help you lift that."

Pagan shook his head, breathing hard. "Nah. There's not enough room in here for anyone to help." With a smack on her ass, he told her to, "Scoot."

Grinning like a naughty little girl, Paloma did as she was told, which was really odd. Her being obedient? What was happening to her?

"Are you men always so underhanded?" Doc Harding asked as he pressed the laptop to his chest, ducked his head, and stepped through the tighter-than-tight entrance into what looked like another utility tunnel.

Paloma smiled. If the good doctor only knew how shrouded in mystery these brothers were. "It's what they do," she replied, winking at Pagan over Harding's shoulder. Even in the darkness, she could see the toothy grin that cracked his handsome face. "Well, it's true. You do what most guys won't or can't."

"Hey, I resemble that remark," Harding grumbled. "Not all men are meant to be superheroes, you know."

Paloma hooked her arm through his. "But you are a superhero. You saved my life, didn't you?" The problem with that friendly move was that her always eager girls mashed against the good doctor's bicep, and she was pretty sure he blushed. "Aw, come on, you already knew that, didn't you?" she teased. "It's a common fact. Doctors save people."

"Well, umm, yeah," he sputtered. "I guess I sometimes—"

"Oh, for shit sake, move out, you two," Kruze groused. "Play slap and tickle another time."

Paloma turned to look back at him. "Watch it, smart ass. I know your big brother."

"Yeah, well, I know yours, too. How is Julio these days? Have you talked to him lately, or are you too *'busy?'*" He had the nerve to stick air quotes in her face. "Do you even know where he is?"

Air quotes? Really? Overcome with the urge to slap the taunt off Kruze's smug face, she rolled her shoulder instead of following through. Kruze wasn't worth it. Besides, Pagan was watching, and she didn't want him to worry or be suspicious of his brother.

They ended up climbing the ladder to a manhole a block and a half away from the burning safe-house. Which was a good distraction in case anyone saw Pagan ease the manhole cover aside.

Paloma dusted her hands on her pants as Kruze led them to a black SUV with darkened windows parked near someone's driveway. "Your ride," he growled as he jerked open the driver's side door and cranked the engine. "Where now?"

These guys had thought of everything. Pagan opened the front passenger door and waved Harding to ride shotgun, then climbed into the backseat with Paloma. "Not the hotel," he answered his brother. "Just drive."

Kruze pulled away from the curb, his eyes sharp in the rearview. "Are you thinking what I'm thinking?"

Pagan nodded. "Those guys back there weren't after Paloma. I'd guess they didn't even know she was there with us."

"They're after us." Kruze adjusted the mirror. "Doc, if I tell you to hit the floor, get your ass down and lie as flat as you can, got it?"

Harding glanced over his shoulder. "Is someone following us now?"

"Not sure, but somebody knew that was our safehouse back there." Kruze's index finger tapped the steering wheel as he stepped on the gas.

"They were looking for proof," Pagan told his brother. "But proof of what?"

"My guess is they want the laptop Doctor Harding's packing," Paloma offered. "It's probably got lots of Sinclair secrets on it, doesn't it?"

Pagan's eyes narrowed, neither confirming nor denying what to Paloma seemed obvious. "This isn't about you or Vicki Hex," he stated, his voice low and menacing.

"Ha!" she scoffed, needing to argue like always. "Tell that to the back of my head and my shot-up apartment building, why don'tcha? Does nearly getting killed by that remote-controlled gunship ring a bell, Big Guy?" There went that audacious head swagger she couldn't seem to control. By the way his eyes glittered, Pagan was beginning to adore it, too. She added fuel to the fire glowing in those sexy emerald greens. "Or how about us being shot at by those dumb assed snipers in the SUV that nearly ran over us after my visit to Transylvania?"

Kruze's brows clenched. "What are you two talking about?"

She tossed her chin at him, too. "Vito's place, hot shot. You guys really think I like my job?"

He nodded in the rearview even as he said, "Well, yeah. You do, don't you?"

Pagan had the good sense to reach one arm around her before she slapped Kruze just for the fun of it. "Take it easy, Pal. We're just trying to figure out what's going on."

But he needed to know. "For your information, smartass..." She aimed that at Kruze's fat head. "I've hated my job since the first day I was hired."

Kruze stared back at her, his expression devoid of understanding or compassion or—

Oh, what the hell. He wasn't the Sinclair brother who mattered. Why bother explaining?

Thankfully, Dr. Harding turned halfway in his seat to meet her stare before she followed through on her need to punch Kruze. It was either that or cry. "I'm obviously not up to speed on every detail of this operation," Doc Harding said, "and I don't need to be. That's none of my business, but I also run a free-clinic downtown. You'll all be safe there."

The air in the SUV turned deadly quiet while Kruze and Pagan stared each other down through the mirror. Paloma held her breath. It'd sure be nice if they could catch a break and maybe a mug of coffee or two. "Sounds good to me," she said to get the ball rolling.

At last Pagan said, "Sounds good to me, too."

Kruze's agreement came with the slightest nod.

Paloma kept her relief to herself.

And away they went.

Chapter Thirty-One

"I'm not running again," Pagan announced as he shut the door to Doc Harding's tiny office behind him. It was well after midnight and he'd had it. "That's all I've done since I hit town."

The good doctor hadn't said this free clinic resided a block south of the toughest public housing project in Chicago, aka the Cabrini-Green complex of low-rent squalor. He'd already run to assist the on-call physician with a stabbing victim, or Pagan would've had something to say about their new 'safe' house.

"Agreed," Kruze bit out. "Enough's enough."

Pagan met Paloma's dark gaze from her vantage point across the room. Like any other experienced sniper, she'd chosen well. Sitting in a wooden swivel office chair like the one behind Harding's desk, she'd backed herself into a nice, neat corner where no one could get at her from behind. From there she also had a full view of their cramped quarters. One pink-handled pistol rested on its side on her knee, the other was still holstered.

He rubbed his bearded chin, sad he'd missed watching her pull those pink-handled babies from the holsters alongside her voluptuous girls. That was a secret dream he'd crushed on for years.

She cleared her throat, and damn. Heat spread to his groin as quickly as it warmed his bearded cheeks. He'd been caught, yet he grinned, hoping she couldn't see him blush like a girl.

Tossing a quick glance at Kruze to make sure he wasn't watching, she sent Pagan a sly wink. Pagan breathed easier. Yes, she knew he loved all of her, not just her girls. He pinched his lips in the barest air kiss back to her. A small part of him was disappointed that he'd acted no better than most other men, but damn. *Those girls...*

Rolling his left shoulder, he crooked his neck to get his head back in the game. As much as his fingers twitched to fondle those soft and lovely girls, sex with Paloma had to wait. Speaking of sex, he now needed to remind her they were engaged to be married. After her last fainting spell, he wasn't sure what she remembered.

"Those guys were after us, not Paloma," he told Kruze steadily. "Until today, this game's been about keeping her safe. I thought we'd have time to track the people who tried to kill her now that everyone supposedly thinks she's dead, but—"

"What I want to know is how anyone knew where we were." Kruze cocked his head accusingly at Paloma. "None of our safe places have ever been breached until today."

Her brown eyes blazed at the insinuation. "Don't look at me like that, Sinclair. You guys killed me, remember? I'm dead."

Pagan intervened before she launched out of her chair and slapped Kruze. "First things first. Yeah, Kruze, we need to know who was behind the hit squad that burned our safe-house, but first, we need to know who was behind Pal's murder attempts."

"Besides you and your brothers?" she asked, just the tiniest hint of snark coloring her tone.

Pagan had to give her that. He had 'killed' her. He'd like to give her a lot more than just his agreement, but a tumble under the sheets with her really had to wait. "Hate to say this but my killing you probably saved your life. Let's stick to the plan," he said to Kruze as he palmed his cell and placed a call home.

Chance picked up with an impatient, "It's about damned time. Where have you been?"

"Ah, running for my life," Pagan offered sarcastically.

"You know what I meant," Chance growled even as a sigh of relief breathed over the connection. "Damn it, I've been watching the safe-house burn.

You should've reported in by now. Jesus! Who were those guys?"

"That's what we want you to find out," Pagan answered. He could picture his oldest brother perched on that stool in his command center, running a hand through his thick hair, maybe tearing it out in frustration that he hadn't been contacted sooner and he'd been worried.

But hey. Pagan was calling now. "Who else are you watching? Anyone suspicious? Anything pop since we last talked?"

"I haven't had not one single SitRep from you since we put our plan in action!" Chance bellowed. "Not one!"

"I was following standard protocol," Pagan reminded his oldest brother.

"Well, stop it. From now on I want updates, morning, noon, and night. Understood? Jesus!"

Pagan smiled at Kruze across the room. Kruze nodded back, but the smile on his lips didn't reach his eyes. Yeah, something was definitely going on with that guy this morning, and Pagan meant to find out.

"Hell, yeah I'm pissed, and I'm not the only one. The senator called to express his concern that you offed Paloma after he told you to stand down. He was mad as a hornet, wanted to know what in *'Sam hell'*— his words, not mine—you were thinking. Once I explained our plan, he cooled down, was just pissed we hadn't kept him in the loop to begin with."

"Anything else?" Pagan asked indifferently as he toed the shabby green carpet underfoot. This clinic had seen better days. Rundown and over-used, he made a mental note to spruce up the place once the dust of this operation-gone-crazy was settled. Doc Harding was a good guy. Looked like he could use a little help on this side of town.

But the bottom line? Pagan might work for Senator Sullivan, but Pagan was not a forgiving guy, not the way this kill order to end Paloma had come down from Sullivan. He still couldn't get over the Sin Boys getting the assignment to end Vicki Hex. What in *'Sam hell'* indeed. Although now that he thought about it, that was precisely what he'd done. He'd ended Vicki Hex, which left Paloma Juarez alive and free. Interesting how Karma worked.

The barest chuckle tweaked his lips. *Sam hell* instead of *Sam Hill*? That faux pas was new. Sullivan must've been spitting mad. *Good. Serves him right.*

"You bet," Chance muttered. "For one thing, the media's all over the playboy, Romeo Seranzino. Someone caught him outside Paloma's apartment with their cell camera. He told the local reporter who interviewed him after that coverage hit YouTube that he usually came in the back way whenever he visited Miss Hex. Then he said he and she were tight, that she liked when he did risky stuff. And get this, Romeo had the balls to tell that reporter that he was her Dom, that he'd do whatever he damn well pleased with her, to her, and to her place. Lying bastard sure can conjure fake tears when he wants. Is Paloma with you?"

Pagan's head came up as he met her stare at that unexpected question. "Where else would she be?"

Chance blew out a breathless, "Thank God. Kruze there too?"

"Kruze too," Pagan replied evenly.

For now, Pagan stood near the door, while Kruze sat behind Doc Harding's desk like he owned the place. He couldn't hear the conversation, but he had to have known his name would come up.

"You know where he disappeared to before the shit hit the fan?" Chance murmured like he didn't want Kruze to hear.

Shaking his head, Pagan said, "No, but I'll ask." He tossed his chin at the middle Sinclair brother. "Where did you go when you left the safe-house?"

An insolent "Out" came back to Pagan.

"Put me on speaker," Chance ordered, right before he bellowed, "Out where, damnit?"

Kruze's lashes fell to the pen he was fingering on Harding's desk. Cocking his head at the closed door, he finally looked up and asked, "You ever think about Dick Card?"

That shut Chance up. He coughed. Cleared his throat. Coughed again. At last he said, "No. Why should I think of that jackass?"

Kruze's nostrils flared. "Because I happen to know he's back in town, as in Chicago. I saw him the night before last."

"You sure it was Card?" Chance asked.

"Positive. I know everything about the jerk-off. Trust me. Ever since you—" Kruze sucked in a gut full of air like he'd said too much. "Never mind."

"You've been following him?" Chance asked. "For how long? Really? Since—?"

Yeah. Even Chance couldn't verbalize the exact moment he'd nearly died on that op in Peru. The investigation as to what precisely went down that fateful day he'd lost most of his SEAL team was still ongoing, not an easy thing to accomplish in a country overrun by Shining Path rebels. Also not simple when one of the operatives had mysteriously vanished during the infil before all the shit went down, was a cloak-and-dagger CIA operative.

A small smile cracked Pagan's lips. He might not understand the Sinclair middle brother, but this right here was what counted. "You want to avenge Chance," he stated, not asked.

Kruze's eyes locked onto Pagan's like the Green Hornet's lasers on a man about to die. "Don't you?"

Pagan had never thought about offing Card for what happened to Chance and his SEAL team in Peru. But he was thinking about it now. "No. I've been a little busy cleaning up the world. Where and when'd you see him?"

"The first time, near Mom's hotel, the one off Navy Pier the day you arrived."

Pagan nearly swallowed his tongue as he realized Kruze had been watching out for him. Incredible.

"After Paloma and I were strafed by that mini-gunship? After we ran for our lives? He was there while we were inside Mom's place?"

Kruze nodded. "Don't worry. I kept track of him, and Card never made me, but yeah. It was Card in the silver trench coat that day. I'm sure of it. He turned and walked away when you pulled up in the cab, but he didn't go far. He watched you talking with Jobe from the crosswalk."

"Where were you?" Pagan wanted to know.

"Close enough I could've air conditioned his fat head." Which meant Kruze had a sniper hide across the street from the hotel or up top on any one of the high rises in the area. He'd had Card in his crosshairs. No wonder Pagan had that sneaky sensation he'd been watched. Because he had.

"What else did Card do?" Chance asked.

"That was all," Kruze replied more evenly. "He just stood there and watched Pagan and Paloma go into the hotel. He didn't call anyone, and I didn't see him back there again over the next couple days."

"Which doesn't necessarily mean he wasn't there," Chance muttered.

"You were there the whole time?" Pagan had to ask. "You stood guard outside the hotel in the cold while we were inside?" His fingers raked over his beard at the thought of Kruze watching out for him like that.

"Well, yeah." Again with the green laser beams and the accompanying death ray. "Soon as I could, I left Houston and flew into O'Hare to assist you. You're my brother. Why wouldn't I?"

Pagan cocked his head at his brother. He'd asked a fair question. Pagan just didn't want to answer it with, *'Because I never thought you cared.'* Instead he said, "You could've let me know you were out there. You could've come inside. I'd have liked that. We could've talked."

Kruze shook his head. "Not when I saw you with Paloma. It was obvious she'd been injured. She needed you, not me."

Pagan wiped a hand over his eyes, remembering what Kruze had told him about Paloma. He had two brothers again. Finally. "What else do you know about Card's whereabouts?"

"Only that he was there at Seranzino's the same day Vicki, err, Paloma met up with Vito. I saw him talking with Romeo."

"Damn it, Kruze, you should've told me," Pagan murmured.

"Why didn't you?" Paloma asked as she stalked to the desk and leaned over it, using her girls to distract Kruze. Pagan was very afraid what she'd do if Kruze dared look down her shirt.

Out of character, Kruze maintained steady eye contact with the exotic tigress in the room, the one on the hunt. For him. "Because I've got no proof of what Card was doing here in Chicago or at Vito's place," he answered quietly. "He was there before you guys even showed. All I've got is conjecture and a raging hard-on to kill the bastard. Unfortunately, that's not enough. I need solid evidence before I rip his head off and stuff it down his throat. I've been following him, putting out feelers, and waiting and watching. Just don't have what I need to act yet. Actually—" Kruze rolled one shoulder like it was killing him. "—I've got nothing on Card, nothing at all. Not yet."

That seemed to satisfy Paloma. She nodded, folded her arms over her girls, and returned to her corner.

"You never left us, did you?" Pagan had to ask. "Not at the hotel. Not at the safe-house. That's why you knew someone was coming. You were waiting outside for that hit squad to show, weren't you?"

Kruze's head bobbed even as he swallowed hard. "Don't," he growled. "I'm no hero, Baby Brother. Don't make me something I'm not. Chance almost died, remember? I. Wasn't. There."

"You meant to make sure I didn't die?" Pagan asked. Of course. That was what was eating Kruze. He blamed himself for what happened in Peru. Didn't they all?

"But how could you have been with me in Peru, Brother?" Chance asked quietly. "You were in California that day, running drills and hounding SEAL warnabes to hurry up and ring out, so you could go to dinner. You were doing your job. I was doing mine."

"Leave it," Kruze ordered his big brother as if Chance were suddenly an obedient dog. With one quick hand, he swiped at his eyes, then blinked because they still glimmered.

"But that's what SEALs do, their jobs. Their very difficult, dangerous jobs," Paloma added gently. "You can't be everywhere at once, Kruze."

Pagan persisted. "And you knew someone would come after us in the safe-house, didn't you?"

Swallowing hard with a tic in his jaw, Kruze nodded. "I didn't. Not for sure. Not with Vicki Hex supposedly dead. The attacks on her should've ended. Only my gut kept telling me it wasn't over, not to get lazy. I went out for a smoke."

"And you didn't come back. You went out to watch out for Paloma and me."

"I couldn't just leave. I couldn't take the—" Kruze's dark green eyes scrolled to the phone in Pagan's hand, "—chance."

It was suddenly crystal clear. Kruze had a flaming case of survivor's guilt mixed up with a little something called brotherhood. Might not always be pretty, and it might not show up until the last minute. It might not even materialize until after all hell broke loose, but there was nothing like it in the world when it did.

A deep sigh eased out of Pagan. Walking over to Doc Harding's desk, he laid the phone in front of Kruze and asked his older brother, "Do you think Card is behind all the attempts on Paloma's life?"

"It'd sure make sense," Kruze replied. "He's Agency. He's got access to firepower like that Boeing

AH-6 Unmanned helo. Plus, he's qualified. He'd know how to work it."

"Was he there at my apartment?" Paloma asked.

"He wouldn't have to be there to operate that gunship, not if he had a drone overhead."

"The bastard," Paloma hissed. "Do you mean this Agent Card could've sent that piece of shit chopper after me and ordered some other asshole to shoot me down like... like in a video game?"

"Yes," Pagan told her. "Modern warfare has become very much like a video game."

And all those operators working the controls on those clever drones were racking up mega guilt points over every last target they ended. Because killing another human being was no game, and Death still played by the same rules it always had. Sliver by tiny sliver, target by target, it sucked an operator's soul out of their body, no matter how removed from the action they thought they were. Be they lying on their bellies out in some Third World desert behind a sniper scope or sitting in a nice comfy office chair watching a computer screen and working a joystick, Death still exacted the same high price. For every life you took, Death took a piece of you. Then another. Until...

Pagan growled to clear his throat as well as shake off the disturbing image of the Master Reaper hovering over him with a scythe. "Okay, umm, so see what you can dig up on Card, Chance. We'll work the Seranzino angle from here."

"But I'm telling you Vito and Cabb aren't behind this," Paloma insisted yet again.

"And I'm telling you they'd off you in a heartbeat," Kruze told her as he leaned over his clenched hands on the desk. "Seriously. They would've ended you the second you stopped being useful, and you know it."

"Only now I did it for them," Pagan finished. "Let's get back into their estate, Brother. Let's plant a few listening devices in Vito's office to see what's going on behind that closed door."

Raising her brows, Paloma breathed out a deep breath through her nostrils. "You're right. I might be wrong. I'll go with you."

'I'm always right,' Pagan wanted to tell her, but it'd hold way too much sexual innuendo if he said it the way he meant, so he kept his lip zipped.

"No. You stay here," he told her in no uncertain terms. "You're dead."

Her head swagger was almost comical the way she answered, "Oh, yeah, I am, huh. I forgot."

Oh, you crazy wonderful woman, you. How could you forget what's going to give me nightmares for years to come? Pagan wanted to mash his mouth to those wet, full lips of hers in the worst—and best— ways.

"I'll check with Sullivan. Maybe he knows something," Chance offered.

"About Card?" Kruze piped up.

"About anything. Keep me informed."

"Copy that," Pagan and Kruze said in unison.

Chance signed off with a husky, "Later brothers."

Chapter Thirty-Two

"I don't wanna go like that!" a shrill male voice screeched from beyond Doc Harding's closed office door. "No cops! Where is she? Where'd that bitch go?"

"She's safe, Lamont. Honest. She's somewhere no one can hurt her." Harding's reply came through firm and steady, like he was standing right outside his office.

Which he was. When Pagan cracked the door to see what was going on, Paloma jumped off her chair to peek around at the cause of the commotion.

A single, very stout black man stood in the narrow hall pointing a handgun at Harding. Doc had both hands raised, palms forward as he repeated, "Honest, Lamont. You know me. I've treated you since you were a kid. Why don't you go home and sleep it off? Come back in the morn—"

"I don't wanna come back in the morning! I want Lisbeth! She oughta be home with me 'stead of running her mouth to you and your nurses and telling white folks how I beat her when I didn't do no such a thing. No, sir, it ain't me what done that to her."

"Then explain how she broke her arm again," Doc demanded as his hands sank to cup his hips. "This is the fourth time I've treated her for the same type of break in the same arm, Lamont. If she's not safe in your home—"

Lamont's eyes went white around two angry black orbs. "But she is safe! I done told you, she safe with me!" The handgun in his right hand flicked up near his forehead as if he were batting at a fly. "She always safe, only that woman liezzzzzzzzz like you wouldn't believe, Doc. She do! She always telling folks who got no business knowing what goes on in my house my business. She sneaky that way."

"Can I help?" Pagan said as he stepped into the hall and alongside Harding.

'No!' very nearly leaped off Paloma's lips. But talk about the kettle calling the pot black. Suddenly she knew how Pagan felt when she'd disregarded his overprotective need to hold her back from doing her job. At the time, she'd thought it was sheer male ego, his innate instinct for her to obey and let him do the manly work. Let him be the he-man.

But it was nothing so trite as that. Paloma never knew how much loving another took. She'd never had anyone to live for like she did now. She'd never had anything to lose. Or anyone. Keeping her mouth shut and not dragging him back where he'd be safe, was incredibly—shit, it was the hardest thing she'd ever done. Her heart raced. It felt lodged in her throat. Stuck. She could barely force a swallow. Or breathe. Pagan had to stand down and get his ass behind this door, right damned now. Only that wasn't how it worked, was it? The man wasn't capable of hiding. From anyone. Even from some unpredictable addict with a pistol.

"Mr. Sinclair, meet Lamont Dupree," Harding said out of the corner of his mouth without taking his eyes off the handgun pointing at him. "Lamont, I'd like you to meet a very good friend of mine, Pagan Sinclair. It'd be nice if you didn't shoot him."

As if he hadn't heard Doc Harding, Lamont's handgun turned on Pagan. "Who're you?"

Only Pagan didn't lift his hands. They remained steady at his side, his fingers spread and relaxed as if he weren't talking with an armed and angry man. "Name's Pagan Sinclair, Mr. Dupree. What's the problem tonight?"

The barrel of the handgun scraped the side of Dupree's gleaming, sweaty forehead. "I ain't got no problem. It's Lisbeth. She done run off again, and she's lying 'bout me, and what's a man s'posed to do, huh? Let her do whatever she wants? That ain't right. I'm the man of the house, ain't I?"

Pagan nodded even as he said, "Sometimes the man of the house needs to step aside and let his woman do what she wants, though. Sometimes women are smarter than all of us guys put together."

"Say what?" Lamont's neck crooked into a ninety-degree angle. His big square head tilted sideways and his eyes widened until the whites showed. "You let your woman do what she wants? All the time?"

"I do," Pagan answered quickly, his hands still not raised even as he managed a half-step forward. "I'll bet your woman's as smart as mine. Why'd she run off?"

"Cuz I hit her, whatcha think?" Lamont said even though he'd accused his wife of lying about him doing that. "She come at me with that frying pan of hers, and I let her have it."

"With what?" Pagan asked, still as calm as if he weren't talking to a monster.

"With these two hands, whatcha think!" Lamont shrieked, all at once irritated and even more unpredictable. As if to prove his point, he raised both those massive hands he was so proud of and...

WHAM! Pagan punched Lamont square in the face. The firearm went flying. The big guy's eyes rolled back in his head. He dropped to his knees, then rolled over onto his back, one hundred percent dead weight. Lamont was out like a light, his arms splayed at his sides and his mouth open and drooling. His handgun now resided safely in Kruze's hand.

Paloma threw the door open and ran to Pagan's side. He wasn't even breathing hard. Man, she needed to hold him, but restrained herself. What was this sudden overwhelming need to kiss him? She dragged a hand through her hair and tossed it back over her shoulder. Where was a hair tie when she needed one?

"Way to go," Kruze muttered as he tucked the loose weapon into his belt.

Paloma took a hesitant step into Pagan's side, secretly thrilled when he pulled her under his arm and crushed her against his hip. Her hand slid instantly over his taut stomach while the other circled his back.

So, this was how he'd felt when she'd walked into Seranzinc's death trap all by herself, skimpily dressed like Vicki Hex. So arrogant. So proud. So sure of herself. He hadn't been as near to her then as she stood with him now. Things could have gone so, so wrong that day.

This feeling right here, this gut-wrenching feeling as if her world had ended, was why he'd been angry. She understood now. There was no living without him. Paloma swallowed hard as she forced her throat muscles to relax enough to let her breathe. Ashamed at how she'd treated her very own personal hero, she pressed her head against his chest just to hear that tremendously kind heart of his. He'd only wanted to protect her like he'd just protected Harding.

"We good?" Pagan asked Doc Harding, who was sweating up a storm and looked like he needed to sit down before he fell down.

"Yes. Good. Thanks to you, yes," Harding replied hoarsely. "Not sure what I would've done if you hadn't been here."

Pagan reached out and steadied Harding with one massive hand to his shoulder. "So tell me. Where is Lisbeth? Is she really safe?"

"Quite safe. She's at a women's shelter across town." Harding put his hand to the wall as he breathed more evenly. "One of my nurses drove her just minutes before Lamont arrived. Her children are with her."

Pagan growled. "You get trouble like this guy very often?"

Harding's head bobbed. The man had gone scary pale now that the threat had passed, and Paloma knew exactly how he felt. She fell apart after a hard kill, too. Only Pagan hadn't killed Lamont Dupree, but now the police would arrive, and damn. She was tired of running.

"Yes," Harding admitted. "If you didn't notice when he drove through the 'hood, this is a tough neighborhood. For the most part, people leave us alone. They know we're the only help they've got, that if they run us out, some of them will die of things as simple as the flu. But Lamont's not most people."

"He is a big guy," Pagan noted as he stared down at the passed-out gentleman at his feet. "Want me to restrain him before we leave?"

"We're leaving?" Paloma asked.

Pagan's gaze narrowed down to the death grip she had on his bicep. Coughing to clear her throat but not yet ready to admit to him that she'd been scared, Paloma released him and took a step back from the situation.

"Yes, we're leaving," he told her. "We're going home."

"To Montana?" she asked at the same time Kruze asked, "We are?"

Pagan nodded, the light in his green eyes gone dark and somber. "Chance and Suede are alone. Whoever's behind that bombing might target them next. One of those unmanned Little Birds could be hovering over the cabin while we stand here and talk. If we leave now, we can be there in five hours, six at the most in case these bastards hit them."

A strangled growl ripped out of Kruze. "They wouldn't dare. Not Chance."

Paloma swallowed hard as it hit her. Yes, they would. Whoever was behind her attempted murder and the attack on the Sinclair safe house had most definitely proved they had the money and the means to attack that incredible hunting lodge Chance had built in remote Montana. They'd have no problem murdering him and Suede, their dogs and horses, too. Like they'd done with the safe house, those unnamed assailants would level the place, probably firebomb it off the planet. Leave a crater. Chance and Suede were so far from the nearest town that no one would ever know until it was too late.

"Let's go. Hurry," she told Pagan. "Call home and warn your brother. Let him know we're coming his way and to take extra precautions until we get there."

A gentle smirk and a bob of Pagan's head told her he was one step ahead of her and didn't exactly need to be told what to do. But he nodded obediently, even as he turned back to Harding and extended a hand. "You're welcome to come with us."

Doc shook his head while he returned the handshake. "One of these days, I might just take you up on that generous offer. Until then, take especially good care of your family."

And suddenly, Paloma found herself crushed in the warmth of Pagan's arm as he told Harding, "I intend to. But first, I need to cuff this guy while you call the police. Then we're out of here."

Chapter Thirty-Three

Paloma stepped away from Pagan as he rolled Lamont onto his side, then tugged a pair of flex-cuffs out of thin air to restrain the man. Pagan was a magic act all by himself. He carried more gadgets, ammo, and weapons on his handsome, capable body than any street magician Paloma had ever seen.

She found herself looking into the clinic's overflowing waiting room. Parents huddled with sick kids. An elderly couple, both with portable oxygen tanks at their sides, sat reading magazines and waiting their turn. A too young to be out at this time of night teenage girl sat alongside a younger man with an obvious bloody, probably broken, nose.

This wasn't simply a clinic. Looked more like one of those twenty-four-seven emergency rooms. You name the injury or illness, it was probably here. But never did she expect to see a familiar face in this rag-tag crowd. The green and red beanie with dangling knitted ties was what caught her eye. Why was Cherry Goodwin sitting out there?

At the same time Paloma spotted her, Cherry looked up from her bandaged hands and across the sea of needy people between them, her brows narrowed with surprise. Dressed in black slacks, a matching black turtleneck sweater beneath a camel-colored double-breasted peacoat, she almost looked professional. But those smears of what had to be blood down the front of her coat gave her away. She mouthed, 'Vicki?'

Instantly, Paloma transformed into her kick-ass alter ego and walked over to where Cherry sat waiting. She greeted the woman she barely knew indifferently as her gaze automatically skated past Cherry though the plate glass window behind her and out into the busy street. Nothing was ever as simple as it seemed on the surface, and Cherry being here was no coincidence. Agency operatives didn't simply run into each other on the street. Uh-uh. Not unless one was driving an SUV with a sturdy grill.

"You're out late. What's up?"

Cherry's gaze zeroed past Vicki to the hall. "That your mark? That big guy you were standing with?"

Now why'd she have to say that with so much condescension? Like Pagan was somehow a lesser life form?

"You could say that," Vicki replied as she tossed a quick glance at the broad back blocking most of her view of the hall. Kruze stood at an angle beside Pagan, talking while Doc Harding faced them both and nodded. It looked like those three had everything under control.

"You got a minute?" Cherry asked quietly, her blue eyes extraordinarily soft and glimmering from beneath her long blonde bangs. Were those tears?

Yeah, right. Something was up, and Vicki intended to find out what or put an end to this charade. "Sure. You in trouble? Hurt?" *Or playing me for a fool?*

Slowly, as if she were dealing with pain in her back—which could be just another act—Cherry lifted to her feet. "Always. You know how it goes."

Vicki snorted at that very vague answer. "Who hurt you?"

Cherry answered with a groan and a whispered, "Don't worry about it."

The woman was convincing, but Vicki knew better than to trust someone she knew little about. Careful not to touch one of her few friends in the business—if you could call someone she seldom bumped into a friend—Vicki palmed the clinic's glass door open, then gestured for Cherry to exit ahead of her. Call it calculating. Call it shrewd. Call it outright cold and uncaring. But sometimes letting another lead the way could save a life—as in hers. "Small world, Cherry. Now what's going on, and why are you following me?"

Cherry seemed to be hurting from more than just those bandaged hands. "Because I'm in trouble. I've been looking for you a long time," she whispered, her gaze fixed on the sidewalk. "Never thought I'd run into you here."

"Yeah, well..." Vicki glanced back at Pagan, still preoccupied with Doc Harding's drama. Her chin came up. "Now you found me. What do you want and what's it going to cost me?"

Cherry sniffled.

Great. More tears? This was getting old. Vicki blew out a hiss of exasperation. If this woman didn't man up and explain why she was here, Vicki was out of there. She had more important things to worry about, and that handsome man back there was one of them. She sent another glance Pagan's way, wishing he were out there on the sidewalk with her instead of chatting with Harding.

"Talk to me or I'm walking," Vicki ordered.

Goodwin was obviously not having a good night. She shook her head, her blonde tangles spilling out from beneath that ridiculous red beanie. "I... I can't. I'm sorry, Vicki."

"About what?"

"About this," a conniving male voice declared at her left.

Vicki turned at that familiar voice. Damned if it wasn't... "You," she hissed at the interloper she'd never expected to see at a free clinic, at the same time that poor, sweet, lying Cherry Goodwin stabbed a needle in Vicki's neck.

"Ouch, shit! What's going on?" One hand came up. Fisted. Ready to strike back. But so damned blurry. Stumbling, Vicki turned back to the clinic door, needing Pagan to notice that like an idiot, she'd left his side again. That she needed his help. Now!

But Pagan was no longer there. Neither was the clinic or all those poor people. Everything in the neighborhood had changed. The night was darker. Colder. The clinic had faded away. But not the sidewalk. It came up like an ocean wave, and the lights went out.

*****

Pagan rolled his neck, edgy and irritable at the constant running away that he and Paloma seemed to be doing. Retreat was not his style of combat. He rubbed the back of his neck, sure someone was watching him. Through a scope. "Down!" he bellowed mere seconds before the plate glass window in Doc's waiting room exploded and sprayed glass over everyone sitting out there. Everyone but Paloma.

Hunkered over both Harding and Kruze, Pagan glanced over his shoulder at the screaming mayhem the single shot had created. "Where's Pal?" he asked, his heart hammering up high in his throat when he couldn't spot her.

Kruze shot to his feet, pistols in both hands and his eyes wide open. "She was just here. I swear."

"Paloma!" Pagan bellowed as he pushed off the floor and headed for that shattered window and the asswipe who'd just tried to kill him. Whoever he was, he'd better be good, as in good and gone.

Squealing tires confirmed the coward had left the scene. Might've been a drive-by shooting. Might've been nothing more than this neighborhood's usual quota of gangbangers out to make their nightly trouble. But then again...

Kruze ran back from the hall, shaking his head. "The exam rooms are clear. I can't find her."

"Look again! She's got to be here," Pagan growled, his temper flaring. She wouldn't have just walked away, would she? No way. That gunshot would've brought her running. Like it or not, the truth was staring him in the eye.

The gunshot was just a diversion.

Paloma was gone.

Chapter Thirty-Four

"Shit! Stop! S-stop it!" Paloma sputtered as some asshole turned the cold-water faucet running into her face back on. Damn, it was frigid in this dank, dark wherever she was. Her head still pounded from whatever had been in that needle. It was so hard to think, much less comply.

"Then talk, bitch," that same snarky voice ordered just as he'd ordered several hundred times already.

She couldn't keep her eyes open long enough to be able to identify him in a lineup—or a dark alley. Hell, she could barely draw enough air into her spasming lungs to stay conscious, much less think what he might want to hear.

Cough. Gag. Cough, cough, cough. Trying to catch a breath without inhaling or swallowing more water, she croaked, "What... what do you w-w-want to..." *Spit. Choke. Choke.* "...know?"

The water poured into her face relentlessly. The metal plank she'd found herself strapped on when she'd come to, was just as unyielding and plenty frigid. Her poor heart pounded with fright and confusion. She was dying of hypothermia while being drowned!

"Whatever you want to talk about, Princess. Just talk." The guy leaned into her face and bellowed, the water still running. "Tell me everything or tell me nothing. When you finally say something important, I'll stop the lesson."

Princess? The pet name was familiar, but that was not Vito's voice. Someone sure wanted her to think it was, though. Who, she didn't know, but if she was Vito's Princess, this jerk in charge of drowning her was the Village Idiot. What'd he want? To extract a confession about Vito or to frame him? Or just to play with her while he tortured her to death?

Each breath became an excruciating effort. Each second, harder and harder. Living through this became a very real impossibility. She couldn't struggle with her arms and legs bound as tightly as they were. Couldn't even turn her head to escape the deluge.

The Village Idiot had thought of everything. From her feet to her head, he'd caged her entire body in some kind of brace. Tilted, with her feet higher than her head, the water drained, leaving most of her shirt and all of her pants dry.

But there was no way to escape or fight back. No way to win this fight. All she could do was lay there and take it. She'd already inhaled and swallowed so much ice water that her belly ached and her lungs burned. Her insides felt raw, as if she'd inhaled nails, and they were right now shredding her lungs to ribbons.

Damn it, she wasn't supposed to go out like this! Her throat clenched shut even as her need to breathe won out yet again, and she inhaled another dose of living hell. Panic struck. She inhaled again. She sputtered as the Village Idiot squeegeed a rough hand over her face. Rubbing her nose painfully upward enough to make it bleed, he palmed the water into her hair. Like that helped.

Coughing and choking, she could barely open her stinging eyes, much less see who the guy was. Squinting, she made another attempt, then another until, at last, a blurry square blob came into view. But the stark, white flood light behind this guy offered no identifying features, only a black silhouette of total anonymity. All she knew for certain was that the Village Idiot was medium build, probably close to one-seventy pounds, and dumber than shit.

Arching her back as far from the plank as she could—which wasn't much—Vicki gathered a mouthful of water and spat her defiance into his face.

Reprisal came swift and hard. Ouch. The big, tough bully wore a ring. Her left eyebrow was now bleeding. Like that was unexpected. She knew the drill. Mafia torture didn't usually end with happily-ever-afters. *Might as well make the best of it.* She gave him her favorite line from *The Sandlot.* "You hit like a... a girl."

The Village Idiot grunted—right before he grabbed hold of her hair, twisted it until her scalp screamed, and he turned the faucet back on and up.

Vicki held out as long as she could, but her body's automatic instinct to survive betrayed her. One last gulp. No air. All water. And she was dying. A freakishly calm sense of complete disassociation enveloped her.

'*So this is how drowning victims feel at the end,*' she thought, '*when they finally realize no help's coming because no one knows where they are or how deep they've sunk. Out of sight, out of mind...*'

Bullshit! Pagan knew! She didn't know how or when, but he *would* come for her. He had in the past. He would again.

'*Just hold on!*' he'd tell her if he were there. '*I'm coming!*'

Struggling with a chest full of lancing pain and no way to fight back, she sent one quick prayer for a miracle that couldn't possibly arrive in time, into the universe. The odds of her survival were slim. She sent it anyway.

Pagan!

*****

Pagan stood in the street in front of the clinic, his fists clenched and his heart hardened. Thinking. Weighing what he thought he knew against all that had happened over the past few days. Whoever'd taken Paloma had to have been someone she knew. She wouldn't have left the scene with just anyone. Of that, Pagan was certain. Unless this was what she'd planned all along, to lure him into trusting her. To lull him into believing she loved him, while... while what? She ran for her life?

No. That made no sense, and he knew she loved him. She might not remember him asking to marry her, but he chose to believe Paloma over the evidence staring him in the face. She hadn't lied when she'd told him that she'd loved him since Tikrit, so yeah. Despite the fact that she was nowhere to be found, he chose to believe every single word she'd ever spoken. All of it. About love. About Julio. About her grandmother, and about how she'd come to work for the Agency at a young age.

The Agency... Now there was a fine group of self-serving liars for you. What were they thinking to hire and train someone as young as Paloma was to be an assassin, when she'd joined out of sheer desperation. All she'd wanted then was to stay in America. Didn't that smack of brainwashing and coercion of a tender innocent? If he could go back in time, he'd rescue her before she'd ever met her first federal operator. Why not? When had the CIA ever come through for him or his brothers? Easy answer, that. Not. Ever.

Canting his head, Pagan listened to the night noises in the low rent neighborhood even as he drew in a belly full of the crisp cold front hovering over Chicago. Snow was the last thing he needed. It covered things up and slowed things down. It muted sounds and obliterated evidence. It made everything harder. Colder. But it was imminent and, damn it. Paloma wasn't wearing his leather jacket. She'd left it behind when she... *left me.*

Even that forlorn thought rang false. She hadn't left of her own volition. No. She was taken. Yes, that was what happened. Someone lured Paloma out of the clinic, where she'd been shanghaied and hauled off to who knew where.

Sure of himself, he tugged a pair of nitrile gloves out of a back pocket, then over his fingers before he stretched and snapped them at his wrists. The police were on their way to take Dupree off Doc Harding's hands. Pagan knew he and Kruze couldn't be here when they arrived. Yet he couldn't leave.

This was where Paloma had last stood. She had come out that front door. She would've walked right past him since she couldn't have gotten past Dupree passed out in the hall like he'd been. Like he still was. Lamont was a big guy, and he took up a lot of space. Paloma had been on Pagan's right before he'd let her go to cuff Dupree. That had to be when it happened.

His throat went dry at what she might be going through while he stood there doing nothing. Pagan swallowed hard. Trusting her still. Knowing in his heart she hadn't left his side voluntarily.

Then where was she and who had her? She'd been so sure Vito wasn't behind her murder attempts, and yet... Maybe Vito knew something Paloma didn't.

It was time to hunt that bastard down and find out. Because he had no other leads, and because Kruze had just rounded the corner of the block after what looked like another fruitless perimeter search in that dangerous neighborhood, Pagan called out, "Let's roll."

His brother set a long-legged lope toward Pagan. "Where we going?" he asked as he ducked into the passenger seat of the SUV they'd arrived in and slammed the door.

Pagan climbed aboard. "You got our laptop?" he asked instead of answering the question.

Out of breath, Kruze slapped a hand over the backpack hanging off his shoulder. "Haven't let it out of my sight since Harding handed it over."

"You trust him?" Pagan asked as he depressed the ignition button and the SUV purred to life.

Kruze's green eyes narrowed. "Yes, don't you?"

Pagan didn't step on the gas and lay rubber out of there like he'd initially planned. "I can't help thinking about what Paloma said, that maybe those guys were after our laptop. It was obvious they were looking for evidence before they torched the safe-house."

Kruze snorted. "Like what? You know the automatic protocol Chance installs on all our portable devices. Every file we receive automatically self-destructs within minutes of receipt. This laptop's just a way for us to keep in touch. Hell, the only thing I keep on mine is my Christmas list."

Pagan's brows crinkled at that very un-Kruze-like info-byte. He kept a Christmas list? Of who? His one-night stands?

"But no one else knows about that protocol program," Pagan reminded his brother instead of delving into crap he didn't care to know. "Not even Paloma. She alluded to all our Sinclair secrets, remember? That's why most operators keep electronic devices with them when they run. Not us."

Kruze nodded, his lips pursed. "So, what are you saying? What do you want me to do? Override Chance's program and plant some kind of bogus *Eye-Only* file for someone to find?"

"Exactly. Can you do it?"

There went Kruze's lips again as he flipped the laptop open and began fingering a series of commands.

"You know how to write code?"

"I know a little." Tap, tap. Tap went Kruze's long fingers.

But what the shit? Pagan hadn't noticed before how his brother couldn't use the index finger on his right hand, or that he was missing every fingernail on his left hand. How each nailbed was a roughened pink gnarled scar.

"What happened?" Pagan had to know.

Kruze barely lifted his gaze from the screen. "What? You mean with my fingers? Nothing. Don't worry about it."

Didn't look like nothing to Pagan. "You do know you can always talk to me, right?" he asked quietly.

"And you know I would if I wanted to, but I don't, so knock it off. Leave it alone," Kruze answered as he nodded at the screen like he agreed with it, then slapped the cover closed and tucked the laptop into the backpack. "There. I've planted an encrypted file marked SULLIVAN ONLY. I also buried a tracking signal inside the program no one'll be able to find. That ought to do it. What do you want me to do with this now?"

"I didn't know," Pagan said softly, wishing this brother wouldn't keep everything to himself like he did. But that was Kruze for you, ever the wayward sort who declared he needed nothing and no one, when the truth was—he did.

Kruze drummed his fingers, those poor damaged fingers, on the backpack's flap. "Focus, Baby Brother. Encrypted file, remember? Your idea. Do I stash it here at the clinic or take it with us? You tell me."

"Leave it. Go back into the clinic with it, but don't bring it out with you. Make it look like you forgot it."

"Consider it done," Kruze murmured as he scrambled to his feet, whistling as he headed back into Harding's clinic. Didn't take long.

Pagan watched as Kruze waited at the waiting room's restroom door. In seconds two little boys came out, and within just seconds more, he was back in the SUV riding shotgun, and they were on their way to the Seranzino estate. Only this time, Pagan intended to knock.

Because Kruze seemed indifferent, Pagan avoided the whole concept of brothers sharing war stories. Instead, he aimed for the only lead they had. "Seems damned interesting we were targeted by a sniper at the same time Paloma goes missing from Doc Harding's free clinic."

"Not Doc Harding," Kruze said evenly. "He's been too good to Mom and us. He wouldn't betray us. Not Doc."

Pagan dared to disagree. "Then who? He was at the safe house when it was bombed, and right after, he offered up his clinic. It's almost as if we're being pushed in the direction someone else wants us to go, and I'm sick of it."

Kruze's jaw clenched. "It's not Harding. Trust me. I know the guy. He'd never betray us."

Pagan knew better than to argue the point. Like everything else in his life, Kruze obviously wasn't going to share how he knew that Harding was solid. Scarlett Sinclair had always trusted Doc, and that was enough for Pagan. "If not him, then who's hunting us and who took Pal? Because I've got to tell you, we've got not one damned clue to go on."

"Then exactly where are we going if you're clueless?"

Pagan nodded his chin straight ahead. "Back to Vito and Cabb."

"Are you fuckin' kidding me? They're the bad guys."

Pagan spared his belligerent brother a sneer. "In case you haven't noticed, we're not so squeaky clean ourselves. Just want to talk to one of them, you know, get a feel if I can trust them like Pal does."

Kruze huffed a breath through his nostrils. "But Mom always said—"

"Can it!" Pagan slapped the wheel, frustrated that Kruze wouldn't open up and talk to him, and angry that Paloma was missing. Pissed that he hadn't protected her like he'd said he would. Scared at what she might be going through while he hadn't a fucking clue where to begin looking for her. "You think I don't remember every word Mom ever said about prayer, about swearing, about what happens when we lay down with dogs? Jeez, Kruze. I carry every story she ever told us right here." He slammed his fist to his chest. "But she's not here, is she?"

"But Baby Bro—"

"Don't Baby Brother me! We've got nowhere else to turn! Call home."

"Call Chance?" Kruze shot him a totally snarky glare. "Why should I? You gonna tell on me?"

Pagan could've slapped the shit out of him. Older brothers were supposed to be smarter. Guess Kruze missed that memo. "No, but if someone's after us, they might be after him and Suede, too. We need to warn Chance. Shit, they've got a baby on the way. You ever think of that?"

Kruze had his cell to his ear in a heartbeat, "Sorry, no. Damn. On it."

Thank God for small favors and pig-headed brothers who finally stopped thinking about themselves and did what they were told. By then Pagan was one big raw pulsating nerve. If whoever had Paloma laid one finger on her, he'd flay that son-of-a-bitch alive. And if Chance, Suede, or that tiny little baby inside her suffered so much as a hangnail, the bastard would die. After Pagan gutted him, strangled him, shot him, and killed him. Okay, so that didn't make sense, but Jesus! Nothing about this mission made sense.

Where the hell is she?

"Chance is on his way," Kruze replied when he ended the call.

"No, no, no!" Pagan shook his head and bellowed, "That is not okay. I never said for you to tell him we needed help. Jesus! Who'll stay with Suede?" Was Chance a total idiot? How could he put his wife in danger like that?

"He's umm..." Kruze cleared his throat. "She's coming with him."

Pagan nearly choked. "Is he crazy?"

"No," Kruze said evenly. "He's married, so shut up and deal with it."

"Call him back," Pagan ordered. "Suede's pregnant. Tell him to stay put. Somehow we'll manage—"

"You call him," Kruze argued. "This is why I'll never get married. Wives never listen. They think they know better than men. Every damned time! Uh-uh. Not me. Not ever."

Pagan could barely see straight by then. "Unacceptable!"

"What? Me not getting married, or Chance playing *Father Goose* and *Father Knows Best* and all that other bullshit he does whenever things don't go like he expects?" Kruze shrieked back at him. "Jesus! He's worse than you are!"

It took a second for that info-byte to settle into Pagan's seething brain. He'd just turned onto Vito's street, and he'd actually slowed the SUV down to residential speed instead of eighty and screeching around corners. But say what? Kruze was pissed at Chance for being over-protective? "You don't think he trusts us?"

"Me, Pagan. Not you. It's me he doesn't trust. I'm the reason he's coming to town. Don't you get it?"

Apparently not. "Chance is just being Chance," Pagan explained as he slammed the SUV into Park and climbed to the street. "Ever since Mom died—"

"Yeah, yeah, ever since Mom died, nothing. Chance always thought he had to play dad. He's lorded it over us ever since I can remember, and shit, Pagan. He isn't our father, and news flash. He never was. He needs to knock it off and back off, take care of himself for a change and leave us the fuck alone!"

"Like you?" slipped off Pagan's tongue before he knew what he'd said.

Kruze's nostrils flared. "Yeah. Like me," he chuffed. "The worthless brother. Yeah. Just like how I desert everyone. He needs to think of no one but himself, like the selfish bastard son that I am. Shit, let's get this meeting over with. I've got other places to be."

Wishing he were a smarter man and could think of some way to get through to Kruze, Pagan offered, "How'd you want to do this?"

His brother shot an evil glare over the roof of the vehicle at him. Direct hit. "Me? Oh, no, this is your show. You tell me. Should we knock politely like two widdle boys who need Daddy to tell us what to do, or go in guns blazing like the men we are?"

Pagan scratched his head. He'd meant to go through the front door like a gentleman. But now that he was standing at the end of Vito's gated driveway, it felt wrong not to make a statement of superior firepower and strength. Especially after Kruze's taunt. Two against an army of bodyguards might not be smart, but he and Kruze had both faced tougher odds before. Not together, but on their own teams. They were SEALs. They could do it. Only...

"Paloma might be in there. We knock," he replied as he rolled one bitch of a tension headache off the back of his neck and prepared to act civil. Act being the key word. He swallowed hard as he hit the call button at the gate.

"I seen you assholes out there. Beat it," some foul-mouthed monster with a heavy Brooklyn accent answered. "We got nothing to say to yous guys."

"Put your Boss on," Pagan demanded. "I'm here to speak with Vito Seranzino, not you."

"The boss know you're coming?"

"He does now." What Mafia Don didn't know precisely when a fool set foot on his property?

Brooklyn grumbled, then reluctantly said, "Come on up."

The gate opened, and the con was on.

Chapter Thirty-Five

Paloma woke stiff and wet and aching, the ice coating her brow melting into her eyes. Blinking, she took a shuddering breath, then exhaled a cloud of frozen vapor through her mouth. Not her poor swollen nose. It had to be broken. It hurt even if all she did was blink. *Ouch.*

Salty, stinging tears sprang unbidden to her blurry eyes. Not like she'd expected anything less. Every part of her body hurt, not just her nose. There was no relief anywhere, and no way to move, even just a little, to keep warm. Not unless flexing her arms and legs or the uncontrollable shivering rattling every last one of her bones counted. Which it did in a small way. Shivering meant she was still alive instead of catatonic at Death's door. But it wasn't enough.

Forcing the agony in her spine, neck, and head back for that singular moment in the near future

when she'd be back on her feet and able to stretch—
and trust me, that day would come—she focused on
her surroundings. Today's morning-after-breath
tasted thick and nasty on her tongue. Rank and
coppery. Like blood. Her blood. Swallowing hard, she
blinked the remaining ice crystals off her eyelashes. It
was a helluva way to wake up.

She knew she'd been slapped, but she couldn't
remember getting that broken nose. Or her fat lip and
loose teeth. No doubt the Village Idiot who'd been
brave enough to waterboard her, had also roughed
her up after she'd passed out, the chicken shit. Like
beating a defenseless woman was soooooo hard to do.
From the first, he'd seemed like the kind who'd kick a
person when they were down. Man, was he going to
get his.

There was no way out of the restraints binding her
to the icy plank like a dead fish to a block of ice.
Random thought: how many other men and women
had lain on the same plank and suffered like she was
now? Yeah, not going there. But she hadn't revealed
anything, had she?

Man, I hope not.

Fighting the panic sidling up her body from her
nervous belly and her twitching legs, she focused on
getting her mind in the game. Breathing in. Breathing
out. Staying calm enough to think. To endure. To wait
for that one last chance. To kick ass and escape from
wherever she was at the first opportunity.

But could Vito be behind this? Could he have planned to make it seem as if he were being framed, so she'd think he was innocent? So she'd continue to trust him? Or was this torture Romeo's idea to break her? He knew she had no use for him. He knew she thought him weak. Because he was.

She doubted everyone now. All except Pagan. His gruff, tender voice grumbled inside her head like a loose cannonball. There were no words to decipher. No secret message to decode. Just that sexy, deep masculine growl that rumbled up his throat when he came in her arms. When he purred and kissed and loved every inch of her body, and when—

A great big hand reached out of the darkness and slapped her, jolting her head to the right in that narrow brace where she lay imprisoned and unable to fight back. Yeah. Good times were about to commence again.

Steeling her inner bitch, Vicki resolved to be just like Pagan. Strong. Silent. The predator that this fat ass running his hands over her girls would never see coming.

Unfortunately, the Village Idiot was back. Chuckling, he squeezed her left breast extra hard, like it was one of those gel-filled stress balls and he needed to strengthen his fingers. "'Bout time you woke up, Princess." *Squeeze, squeeze, squeeze... and enough already!* "You ready to talk some more?"

She refused to flinch at his disgusting touch even as his fingernails dug into her tender skin. *Talk some more? Did I do that?* But no startling memory of her spilling anything she knew about Vito or Cabb, Pagan or his brothers, sprang to mind. She was certain she'd said nothing.

Yet he said I did so maybe I did. He said...

Lies. All lies. He wants me to think he's smarter than me, that I'll fall for intimidation just because he says so. Just because I'm female. Just because I'm smaller. Just because I've got breasts and I can't fight back at the moment. Well, guess again.

Lifting her chin, Paloma took a deep breath as she stared at yet another murderer dressed in a suit. White shirt. Black tie. Definitely not Sicilian, not that the mob only hired their own. This guy's face was too long. Like a horse's. His lips were too full. And he'd missed shaving a spot just above his upper lip. The whisker hairs were long there.

Silently, Paloma recalled her in-your-face alter ego to the fight. It'd take more than that pathetic attempt at brainwashing to push Vicki Hex over the edge, or to make her believe she'd revealed anything under the previous day's vicious interrogation. She'd been mentally trained for this kind of crap, remember? Emotionally prepared. Tested. By. The. Best.

Blinking up at the smirking moron leaning over her, a random thought intruded. After this was over, Dane would probably be called to the CIA Director's office to accept a medal on her behalf for her above-and-beyond brand of bravery and endurance. That was his style. He'd grin like it was his medal, and he'd love standing in front of his peers, taking credit for her refusal to buckle under extreme pressure. He'd brag about her by the time this power struggle was over. He'd claim she'd only ever acted under his direction and guidance, that this was all a part of his master plan.

She would've stuck air quotes in his face if she could've.

But yeah, he'd probably watch over the stone carver who'd add her star on the Alabama marble CIA Memorial Wall at Langley. Like the other one-hundred twenty-nine employees who'd died in the line of service, Vicki Hex would finally rest beneath the proud words: *IN HONOR OF THOSE MEMBERS OF THE CENTRAL INTELLIGENCE AGENCY WHO GAVE THEIR LIVES IN THE SERVICE OF THEIR COUNTRY.*

And in that little black *Book of Honor* in the steel display case below the field of stars, Dane would add the year of her death to the list of other American heroes. Just not her name. Or the date. Not good old conniving Dane. He'd go to his grave with that secret, if only because outing how she'd died would also out him.

Then, because he'd never been allowed in real life, he'd run his hand over her star. He'd tap his fingers nails over every engraved corner and crevice. He'd smile that creepy, salacious smile of his, and he'd probably lick his lips too, imagining he was finally fondling her girls.

"Go to hell," she croaked, instantly denying Dane as much as the lie the Village Idiot had spouted. *You think you're big and bad and mean enough to break me? Me, Vicki Hex? Vito's very best assassin? I don't think so. The Agency might've trained me first, but Vito trained me last. When I kill you, you're going to wish you'd never laid a pinkie finger on me.*

Closing her eyes, Vicki Hex wrapped her warrior's heart in steel for another day. That was what made her weak, a heart that could be broken. Not anymore. That heart had always belonged to Paloma anyway. Conjuring up a mental image of Pagan and those tender green eyes of his, Vicki cast the final weakness of hers into the universe and sent that too-soft-for-the-world heart to him. He'd know what to do with it.

Big, Bad, and Stupid leaned into her, his breath in her face as he rattled the steel cage surrounding her. "You want to try that again, Princess?" he threatened as he palmed her breast again and squeezed it tighter. "Only this time, say it with feeling."

A groan almost escaped her lips under that demoralizing assault. Almost. But she wouldn't give in. Not to the Village Idiot. There was no reason to. Her heart was safe now.

Let the son-of-a-bitchin' games begin.

Chapter Thirty-Six

"You're either exceedingly brave or you're the dumbest men in Chicago," Cabb Seranzino said evenly from the couch where he sat nearest Vito's desk.

"Yeah, I get that a lot," Pagan replied nervously.

It was early morning. The sun was barely up, not that you'd know it from this vault they'd been ushered into by some guy dressed in some kind of a shorty tux. Could've been a butler's uniform, but Pagan wasn't sure mobsters hired guys like that.

At the moment, he and Kruze filled the two wooden chairs in front of Vito's desk in his very large, very dark office. Heavy curtains prevented any light from creeping into what felt what Pagan had always thought a Mafia den would feel like. Soulless. Helpless. Hopeless. Yeah, all of that and more.

Dressed completely in black from his tie and suit jacket to his shirt and shoes, Vito sat behind the desk, his elbows planted in front of him, his thin fingers steepled beneath his narrow chin. His face was long and narrow, his frame thin to the point of being bony and gaunt. A receding hairline accentuated his wrinkled forehead. Sitting here very nearly in the dark gave Pagan the impression his skin lacked any pigmentation. The man had no discernible facial hair, either.

Cabb on the other hand, had taken a comfortable, I-couldn't-care-less posture in the corner of the leather couch nearest Vito, where the only lamp in the room was. With one arm sprawled across the back of the couch and the other relaxed on the armrest, his bright blue eyes sparkled out from an evenly tanned, almost wrinkle-free, playboy's face. White-haired, he acted as if he hadn't a care in the world. And he smiled when he'd been called to attend this meeting.

But of all the outfits Pagan expected a Mafia Don to show up in, it was not the burgundy and gray tartan plaid jacket and gray slacks that Cabb wore. The colors were muted, and the suit looked pressed and high-end, but still. What'd he think? That people would mistake him for a Scot instead of a Sicilian crime boss in that get-up?

"We're here because we need your help," Pagan said, clearing his throat as he corrected his statement. "Um, that is, *I* need your help. My brother's just here to make sure nothing happens to me. I'm looking for one of your people, a gal named Vicki Hex. Have you seen her recently? We know she works for you. Has she been here? Do you know if she's okay or—or not?"

Vito's steeple collapsed as he leaned farther over his clenched hands. His knuckles went white, probably not a good sign. "Why would I tell you anything about one of my employees?"

Pagan rolled his neck, debating how much to tell this guy about him and his brother. Vito hadn't seemed interested during introductions, and honestly, mobsters weren't trustworthy. Who didn't know that?

He cleared his throat again, then boldly went where no smart man with half a brain in his head would've gone before. "She's my fiancée," he admitted as sweat beaded at his temples. Why did this feel like he'd just betrayed her, when all he wanted was to save her life?

Vito's face wrinkled as he pursed his lips and said, "No," very definitely.

No what? "You haven't seen her?" Pagan had to ask. "Or you're not going to help us?"

"No, she is *not* your fiancée," Vito hissed. "Definitely not. You're obviously a former soldier of some sort, but she... she..."

"She's familia," Cabb inserted diplomatically as he tilted forward, both hands cupped his knees. "She knows better than to stray." He grunted as his gaze shifted over Pagan's bulky body stuffed into this confining little office chair. "Especially with someone like you."

Okay. That explained the creepy sensation of betrayal Pagan felt the moment he'd sat down in this office. Of course, the Mafia wouldn't accept that one of their own might actually choose to marry outside the *familia*. He remembered that from *"The Godfather."* The *familia* was everything, and the women caught up in its web were treated well—as long as they didn't step out of line. Which meant they were pretty much chattel. Possessions. Paloma must've hated this job considering her views on feminist rights.

Shit. What to do now?

"Things happen," Kruze said. "Guys and gals fall in love. Even the most powerful man in the world can't stop Mother Nature."

"No, but I can stop my daugh..." Cabb cleared his throat now. "Err, my employees, from being stupid."

Pagan caught the blunder. So Cabb thought of Paloma like a daughter, huh? He could work with that. Turning his attention from Vito to the elder Seranzino, Pagan zeroed in on his target.

"I just want to make sure she's okay," he said honestly. "We were hanging out yesterday, and she had to leave, and now I can't reach her, and..." *Damn, I hope this guy falls for this line of BS.* "I think she's in trouble. To be frank Mr. Seranzino, I have nowhere else to go, and no one I trust more with her welfare than you. I can't contact the police because she's involved in some kind of criminal activity. I don't know what and I don't care. I just want to make sure she's alive. If she's left me of her own accord, if she never wants to see me again, fine. I can live with that. I just want her to be happy and alive and…"

Pagan swallowed hard at the lies spewing from his mouth at the mere thought of someone hurting Paloma. There was a difference between leaving voluntarily and being kidnapped. His fists clenched and his heart was banging against his ribs like a troll that wanted out. Whoever held Paloma against her will might be hurting her again. Right now.

'God, help me find her!' his soul screamed. *'I really can't live without her. I've got to do something!'*

"Don't let my brother fool you," Kruze muttered quietly from his chair. "Pagan's head over heels in love with Vicki. It'll destroy him to lose her, but hey. That's the breaks. All's fair in love and war, right? But we really would like to make sure she's okay, and we've got no one else to ask for help finding her."

Vito's lip curled. "Exactly who are you that I should tell you anything?"

Good question. Intros had been names only. Pagan had purposely left out any mention of time served or Senator McQueen Sullivan. Stuff like that.

The room had suddenly grown stifling, the air in it unbreathable as despair settled in. His lack of finding any clues back at the clinic and not being able to take fast action now suffocated Pagan. Here he sat chatting, starting over at Point A again instead of running to Point B, which was wherever Paloma was.

Drawing in a shuddering breath, he debated telling Vito and Cabb the whole truth. Everything. Who he was. Who he worked for. What he did for a living and what he could—would—do to them if they failed to help him find Pal.

He'd never known this hellish level of desperation before, Pagan knew he'd literally do anything to get Paloma back. Fight any army. Stoop to any level. Kiss any Mafia Don's ass.

Humbling. Truly humbling. But this was that day.

Yet even as he prepared to bare his soul to these murdering bastards who killed their enemies without compunction or worry that they'd be caught, he knew coming here to beg a favor of Vito and Cabb had been a rookie mistake. What had he thought, that these two cold-hearted thugs actually had the capacity to care one iota about Vicki? That she was personally important to them, maybe even favored by them? Yeah, no. Guys like these two sharks chewed women up for breakfast and spat them out before lunch.

Pagan swallowed hard as that migraine kicked into overdrive. How stupid—?

"We're former SEALs, Mr. Seranzino," Kruze interrupted Pagan's self-doubt as one of his brother's big hands settled heavy and warm on Pagan's left shoulder. "Both out of Coronado. Both decorated and battle-hardened. We've been to the sandbox and the jungles. We know how bad this world can be. Right now, we're between jobs or we wouldn't be in Chicago. You might've known our mother, Scarlett Sinclair. She stayed at a hotel over by Navy Pier when she came to town for book signings and interviews. You might've seen her. She loved your Windy City."

Cabb's mouth dropped open even as Vito asked Kruze, "Scarlett Sinclair was your mother?" He turned to his father, sputtering in Sicilian, his fingers flying. Apparently, he talked with his hands as much as Paloma.

When Vito turned back to Pagan, his eyes were bright with a different kind of interest, but it was Cabb who spoke. "I am so sorry for your loss, boys. Scarlett was a dear friend of ours. She cared about her three sons more than you'll ever know." A hand went to the middle of his chest. "It hit me hard when she died so suddenly. I miss her."

WTF? Dumbfounded at this totally unexpected about-face in the conversation, Pagan asked, "You... You knew Mom?"

Cabb nodded as he licked his lower lip and placed one palm to his chest. He actually teared up. "You have no idea how much she meant to me," he whispered.

"To us," Vito boldly declared. "She was our guest every time she deigned to visit Illinois. My father and I begged her many times to stay with us where she'd be safer, but she always found a reason to decline. Either she expected one of her boys to visit or her schedule was too busy. But I think she believed in this arrogant country of yours, that no harm would dare befall a mother whose sons served."

Relaxed now, he tipped back in his leather chair, the starch gone out of his shoulders and the baleful glow in his black eyes soft, almost friendly. "I knew who you were the moment you pulled up to my gate. Why would I not follow the heroic exploits of my favorite author's three Navy SEAL sons? Why didn't you just tell me you were Scarlett's boys? Yes, a thousand times yes, I will help you."

Pagan nodded though he probably looked like a flummoxed deer caught in the headlights of a speeding racecar on the Autobahn in Germany. WTF indeed. Mom knew the Seranzinos. He hadn't seen that one coming.

Again, Kruze interceded. "When did you last see her?"

Cabb cleared his throat. "A couple months before she passed. She came to Chicago for some librarian conference and then stopped in for dinner on her first night in town. I could tell something wasn't right. Her eyes were without their usual spark. When I asked if she was feeling okay, she brushed it off and said it was nothing, that she'd simply caught a cold on the flight out of San Diego. But it wasn't that simple. It was cancer..." He let that hang as if he couldn't bear to go on.

"Thank you," Pagan murmured, his own heart aching for that 'one more day' with his mom. She really had spread sunshine wherever she'd gone. Even here. Who would've ever thought?

Kruze coughed. "I meant Vicki. When did you last see her?"

"A couple days ago," Vito promptly replied. "She was in rough shape. She'd been ambushed in her penthouse then buried alive. She wanted to stay here for a while. I told her it was time she moved in, to go get her things."

And then you kissed her, you maggot.

Vito shrugged as if he felt indifferent, though Pagan knew he cared more about Paloma than he let on. "It was time. She's lived on her own since she came to work for me, but this was the first time she seemed shaken."

"For us. She came to work for us," Cabb murmured, one silvery brow spiked.

Vito's chin came up at the blatant reprimand, and wasn't that interesting? This son and father were both vying for Paloma's loyalty—or to get into her pants.

Pagan refused to let his shoulder roll in disgust at the notion of Pal being intimate with either of these guys. So what if they'd loved his mother? Paloma had too much class for this familia. Too much self-respect. She was just plain smarter than either of these guys.

"When was the last time *you* saw Vicki?" Cabb asked as his brows narrowed thoughtfully. He'd sunk back into the couch again, his arm extended on the armrest like a panther ready to spring, his fingertips tapping at the rolled leather edging that accentuated the armrest.

"This morning," Pagan replied honestly. "We were downtown at the free clinic because she keeps passing out. She has a concussion." That much was true, but neither Vito nor Cabb needed to know Pagan had shot her, and she'd fallen, thereby contributing to the concussion she already had. Remorse for hurting her quelled the shred of hope he'd been hanging onto up to this point.

"Now that I think about it, she was quite pale last time I spoke with her," Vito said thoughtfully.

Because you had your tongue down her throat!

Cabb cocked his head at his son. "When was that?"

Vito shrugged as if it were insignificant. "A day or two ago."

Cabb didn't seem to think so. The glare he sent his son was downright frigid. "You should've told me. She needed our help," he said pointedly. "Who'd you send out with her?"

"No one."

"Why not?"

That got Vito's hackles up, though the only evidence was the tick in his jaw. "You know why. Vicki never asks for help..." *That's my girl.* "There was some trouble in the neighborhood right after she left. My guys thought we were under attack. They locked the gate and prepared for trouble."

"That never came." Cabb tsked, censure pinching his cheeks.

"They did what I pay them to do," Vito snapped. "The police came, but by the time they showed, the uproar was over, and the perpetrators were gone."

"They came here? Into my house?"

"Yes. Like any other time there's trouble beyond these walls, they came to me first."

This was like watching a lethal game of tennis between two men who didn't appear to like each other.

"You didn't check to make sure Vicki wasn't involved?"

Vito volleyed right back at his old man with, "I never have before."

"Someone dared bring trouble into your neighborhood?" Pagan asked, more interested in what Vito had to say about that shooter than the Seranzino father/son dynamics.

"Just another random drive-by, I'm sure," Vito muttered as he tore his barely suppressed anger off his father and gave Pagan his pointed chin. "And it's not *my* neighborhood, Mr. Sinclair. I don't care what goes on beyond these walls."

Point taken. *Why would you? You're probably the cause of most of it.*

Pagan eased his back into his chair even as Cabb leaned forward, rested his elbows on his knees, and said, "But you should care. The more care you take with our nearest neighbors, the better your reputation becomes, and the farther that good reputation travels. People tend to protect the smart man who watches over them. They talk. That is how legends are born. Their influence alone can bring your downfall or your exoneration when you need it most."

Pagan let his gaze drop to the floor. This was not the first time these men had locked horns, and Vito bristled accordingly. Apparently, Cabb had no problem humiliating his son in front of strangers. Pagan wanted nothing to do with that.

"I'm worried one of your enemies has taken her," Kruze said, drawing everyone back to the reason for the visit. "You wouldn't be having issues with any business associate in particular at the moment, would you?"

"A man makes many enemies," Vito purred. Typical Mafia response.

Kruze never batted an eye. "Would you mind if we kept in touch? Called, texted, or something? You know, in case either of us hears from her we could let the other guys know?" He made it sound so easy, like everyone texted their local Mafia Don like they were BFFs.

"Not at all." Vito reached for the crystal tray on his desk, thumbed a business card up, and tossed it across the desk at Kruze. "I'll have my men ask around. They also have many contacts. We'll get to the bottom of this."

Cabb's gaze zeroed in on Pagan. "I will personally cut the throat of anyone who's harmed her."

"Not if I get to him first," Pagan promised as he lifted to his feet. *Even you.*

Chapter Thirty-Seven

Vicki lay struggling to stay alive, but still thinking about the inherent flaw hidden deep within the tangled psyche of thugs, rapists, wife-beaters, and men who liked to drown people who were weaker. Every one of them thought that just because they were bigger and meaner that they were in charge. Guess again.

It took one helluva lot of self-control and willpower while she was being drowned, but Vicki managed. She kept her wits and shoved her panic down deep in her gut at the same time she lifted the folding pocket knife out of the Village Idiot's front trouser pocket. The ass. While he'd copped a feel and drooled over her twitching body, she'd picked his pocket. That was what happened when a woman's arms were restrained, and she had only the use of her fingers. She got creative.

But the moment she had that knife concealed in her left hand, she went slack and pretended to pass out. Predictably, he turned off the faucet before he cursed, then backhanded her. Once. Twice. In an act of utter depravity, he lifted her off the metal plank by her shoulders, then licked her mouth like the dog he was.

Eww. That was beyond disgusting, and it took every last ounce of willpower to not react or gag. But Vicki maintained focus. Never twitched or growled or allowed one single instinctive reaction. Like puking. She just laid there and took one for her team while her restraints dug into her arms, wrists, thighs, and ankles because the Village Idiot forced this unyielding position.

Patience. Most of being a good sniper was about a finely-honed sense of patience. She'd learned that level of control early in her career. The early bird might get the worm, but the cat who lay in wait in the bushes got that fuckin' bird.

At last the creep dropped her back onto the table. "You're not as good as I thought you'd be, Hex. Tits, yeah, but not smart enough to know when you're beat." He slapped her head to the side one last time, then bellowed, "Goodwin!! Get in here!"

Cherry Goodwin? Here? Oh yeah. It came back to Vicki. Kind of. Sort of. Cherry'd been there at the clinic that night when... *when what?*

Once again Vicki drew a blank attempting to recall what had happened to her before she'd shown up here. The details were elusive. Cherry. Clinic. Doc Harding. Pagan. And... and... and what?

Nothing showed up to explain how she'd ended up waterboarded in this cold room by the Village Idiot. It was as if she'd simply woken in this nightmare after... after what? Not being able to remember was frustrating.

A door somewhere beyond the metal plank opened and closed. "Yes, sir," Cherry said meekly.

"You see this?" the Village Idiot demanded as he stabbed a pointed finger into the soft skin at the hollow of Vicki's throat. She nearly allowed a reflexive swallow but caught herself in time.

"See what?" Cherry asked from somewhere not even close to the plank or the faucet. The coward. She'd certainly had no trouble betraying Vicki, but she hadn't the stomach to witness what her betrayal had cost?

"Get over here. Look. Hex keeps passing out. Thought you said she was tougher than shit?" He ran his finger up from the hollow of Vicki's neck to her chin.

"She is." Cherry's voice had gotten smaller and weaker, if that was possible. What was she, a mouse? "But he said all I had to do was bring her to you. I don't have to watch, do I?"

Vicki held deathly still, the small knife adeptly hidden in her left palm. One idiot was easy to fool, but two? And who had told Cherry to bring Vicki here? Who had the nerve?

The Village Idiot must've turned his back on her. His voice wasn't as loud when he scoffed, "What? He promise you a promotion, too?"

"No, my, umm, he said that he'd get my husband back for me. That he'd put in a good word and he'd make sure Dick came home."

Vicki almost cocked her head. *Dick who?*

"Yeah, well, he promised me this bitch's job, only she keeps passing out on me. How am I supposed to get any inside information on the Seranzinos like this?"

He slapped Vicki's cheek again. Only this time, he'd put more force in it. Her eyes watered, and she had to catch her breath before she cried out.

Shit. Every inch of her skin had been tenderized from the cold and the previous beating. This was getting old. The knife in her palm felt warm and ready. It might be time to—

Patience.

Cherry squeaked when the door opened and closed again. Three against one? Not good odds.

Vicki's heart hammered with every passing second. It had gotten harder to control her breathing. Her one window of opportunity was about to close. It was now or never.

The Village Idiot snapped out a proper, "Sir!"

Cherry Goodwin whimpered.

Who else was out there? Who held the kind of power these two were afraid of? Vicki flexed her left hand as she slid her thumbnail up the safety guard along the top of the knife's still concealed blade and—

"Hello, Vicki," a familiar voice purred over her.

She had no choice. Her eyes flew open. "You!"

He nodded, as smug as ever as his gaze took in the condition of her face, lips, throat, and—of course—her girls. His tongue moistened his lower lip. What she wouldn't give to slap that smirk off this guy's ugly face.

"How's it feel to finally get knocked off your high horse and fall flat on your snooty face for a change? Bet you didn't see that coming," Dane said as he fingered her fat bottom lip like he cared. "Humbling, isn't it?"

All she could do was blink up at him in disbelief as the link she'd forgotten flooded back. He was the subject of that fleeting attack of déjà vu she'd had when she'd accused Chance Sinclair of thinking she'd kept a Day Planner. That was something Dane did. Religiously. He kept track of every last detail of every day because he needed to prove he was the indispensable one. Dane was behind everything!

He winked. The ass winked! Then her conniving handler twisted her lower lip and said, "Trust me, Hex, you haven't seen anything yet."

*****

Cranking the steering wheel to the left, Pagan shifted the SUV around Vito's circular driveway and headed for the heavy metal gate, which opened automatically on approach. Once back in the residential neighborhood, he peeled rubber, anxious to put as much asphalt between them and the Mafia Dons as he could. Talking with stone cold murderers always gave him the willies. The farther away from men of their caliber, the better.

The dynamics between that father and son were interesting. In no way did Cabb act like an eighty-year-old. The man still had all his faculties, and he obviously kept a tight rein on his family business. Yet Paloma was right. Cabb and Vito truly cared for her. It was just as clear they only knew Paloma as Vicki Hex.

Mental note to self: *Don't out her. She's Vicki whenever these guys are around.*

While he maneuvered through traffic, Kruze put in a call to Chance. "You're on speaker," he said without a *'hello, brother, how are you doing?'* Which pretty much summed up the rift between these two older brothers. Pagan honestly hadn't noticed how Kruze bristled at Chance before, but he paid close attention now. The Sin Boys had a solid rep in the covert world. It needed to stay that way.

"Hey, Kruze. I'm good. Real good. How's life in the fast lane?"

"Fine. What's up?" Kruze stared out the window, shutting Pagan out now, too.

An audible sigh hissed over the connection. "What's up is I've got two monster horses eating me out of grass hay faster than I can haul it up the mountain and put it in their loft. I might have to get creative and build a fence. Then they can roam free and graze instead of staying corralled and working my ass off."

Kruze grunted like he could care less, so Pagan interceded. "Probably should've thought of that before you bought them."

"Now you tell me," Chance joked good-naturedly.

Speaking of which, "We've got a barn?"

Pagan could see his big brother rubbing a hand up the back of his neck and over his head with some level of weariness, maybe chagrin. But hey. The big guy was a sucker for Suede, and she generally got whatever she wanted.

Of the three, Pagan resembled Chance. While Kruze was strong in an athletically lean and toned body, Pagan and Chance were both beefier with wide shoulders meant for hard labor and thick, muscular thighs for heavy lifting. Dark-haired, they could've passed for twins until that failed op in Peru.

Chance had gotten torn up pretty bad in that mess. As a result, scars pocked his face and permanent skid marks marked his scalp where the nails packed inside that hidden IED had ripped into him. When he'd left the Navy, he'd gone off to Montana where he'd grown reclusive and shaggy until Suede came along.

She wouldn't let him hide from the world, so he'd cleaned up his act, and he'd finally shaved. Which meant a lot in the grander scheme of things. Those scars didn't matter, not to Suede or Pagan. He hardly noticed them anymore. Chance was just and always would be Chance. They shouldn't have mattered to him, either. All those jagged scars were not only a small part of his history, they were a lasting testimony to his strength of fortitude and his will to survive. His and Suede's.

"Yeah. Raised it the day after the horses arrived. Had to. It's supposed to snow later this week. Wish you guys could've been here to help, though. It's just a pole barn, nothing major, but I could've used the muscle. You know Montana, when it snows—"

"You'll be stuck on that mountain until spring thaw," Pagan finished for him as he steered toward Harding's clinic to see if the good doctor needed a ride. "What are you going to do, shovel a path from the house to the barn to feed them?" Winter snows could get just that high during a good water year. Last year's snow level had been record-breaking. It could happen again.

"Not sure," Chance said. "But wait until you meet them. They've got as much personality as the dogs. Maybe more."

Pagan grunted, doubting that. Gallo, the German Shepherd pup that Scarlett had left to her oldest son, was as human as any animal could get. Those big puppy ears, and the way he cocked his head like he understood exactly what you were telling him, made him just another one of the Sin Boys in Pagan's book.

The other dog they now owned was the standard-sized Schnauzer Pagan rescued on the same mission they'd rescued Suede from Mitchell Franks. Originally tagged *Meine Liebchen* by the bastard Franks—Pagan still wanted to gag at that pretentious moniker—she now went by Lucky. The way she and Gallo tore through the nearby woods and ran up the steep incline behind the Sinclair home was a thrill to watch.

"When will you be here? You talk with Sullivan yet?" Pagan asked.

"We just landed and yeah. Just got off the phone," Chance replied. "Paloma's handler finally got back to McQueen. Guess Rich isn't happy with Sullivan since he refused the kill order on Hex. He had some hard words for McQueen. Said his teams have too much power, that we need to do what we're told before we lose our federally funded paychecks."

"Ooooh, I'm shaking in my boots. What's he going to do? Tell on us?" That'd be the day. No one knew who Sullivan's SOBs were. Not their names, blood types, or their DNA. They were the invisible, blackest of black operators. Unlike the Agency, they were legally designated to operate on United States soil as needed. They'd been vetted by the President, something Special Agent Dane Rich obviously didn't know. Which was just as well. He needed to stick with his own federally authorized mandate and let the Sin Boys stick with theirs.

"Would you believe Rich threatened Sullivan's leadership as Chairman of the Senate Finance Committee?" Chance asked, slightly out of breath since he was most likely fast-walking through the concourse with Suede close at his side.

Pagan grunted. "Who does he think he is, God?"

The Senate Finance Committee held the largest jurisdiction in either House of Congress and oversaw more than fifty percent of the federal budget. Whoever ruled that Committee was a powerful man to piss off. "Bet Senator McQueen Sullivan had some hard words for him, too. What the hell? A kill order on Paloma? Now that I know her better, I'm thinking maybe we need a reverse kill order. You know, on Rich."

Kruze had yet to engage. He still stared out the window, but at least he grunted at that comment. Pagan wanted to smack him for pouting.

"I've been thinking about what you asked me, Kruze," Chance said. "You know, about CIA Card. I keep going over what I can remember of him from that op into Peru. None of us SEALs wanted him with us. That was a given. We weren't told why he had to tag along in the first place, then he was late on arrival, which kept us sitting on our thumbs on the tarmac waiting for his ass to show. He infilled along with us fine like a pro, but he split the moment we closed in on Gillian Enright's location. One second we had eyes on him, the next—poof. He was gone."

Pagan knew this story by heart. Reed and Gillian Enright were two naïve American missionaries who'd mistakenly thought they could deal intellectually and reasonably with the belligerent Shining Path guerillas terrorizing the farmers in the countryside of Peru. That stupidity earned Reed a quick and bloody death by machete, which was when Chance and his team were sent in to rescue Mrs. Enright.

Unfortunately, she died during the exfil when *Gun Powder*, aka Stokes Remington, triggered one of the several IEDs the guerillas planted around their ride, an Army stealth-modified Blackhawk. The chopper was lost in the ensuing battle.

Thankfully, the Night Stalkers, the 160th Spec Ops Aviation Regiment out of Fort Campbell, Kentucky, were on stand-by nearby. Within seconds of the first explosion, they sent their MH-6 light helicopters, aka Little Birds, to rescue what was left of Chance's team. If not for those mini-gunships pounding the immediate area and laying down suppressive fire, Chance wouldn't have made it home. Two-thirds of his team, as well as Special Operator Petty Officer First Class Stokes Remington, hadn't.

From Pagan's perspective, Chance was one lucky son-of-a-bitch to have gotten out of that debacle alive. If only he could find a way to let go of the survivor's guilt that came along with living when most of his men hadn't. He'd been team leader that day. He'd been in charge. Everything that went down still lay hard and heavy on his shoulders.

So, yeah. Where was that spook Card now? And why had he been outside the hotel precisely when Pagan arrived with Paloma? He couldn't get over Kruze covering his ass that day like he'd been, but Card stalking him? That was no coincidence. Somehow Card was square in the middle of Paloma's attempted murders. He had to be involved in the team that bombed the Sinclair safe-house, too. Pagan damned well knew he was.

"You there, brother?" Chance asked quietly.

"Yeah. Here," Kruze replied indifferently.

"Do you know why Card's in Chicago? Is there something you want to tell me?"

Now was the time for Kruze to open up and contribute to this latest lost cause they'd undertaken. But like the spoiled brat he could be, he kept his head turned, staring into space.

Pagan wanted to reach out and knock that hard head into the window. Maybe then Kruze would engage. At least he'd be pissed and fight back. That'd be better than nothing.

Chapter Thirty-Eight

Kruze kept his gaze fixed on the streets and sidewalks, the cars and pedestrians passing by him in a whir. Truth was he didn't see anything out there on the streets. Just her. Just them.

Civilians didn't have a clue what it meant to strap on the weapons of a warrior, to join up and put your life on the line under the pretext of keeping America safe. Then to come back home only to find the media spouting half-truths and fiction about what went on overseas, when those reporters knew nothing about what it took to walk the fine line at the edge of sanity after you'd offed someone. To *have* to kill, even the psychotic bastard who'd very much deserved what he got after what he'd done to—her.

Kruze's hand came up to brush the fuckin' tear out of his eye before Baby Brother caught sight of it and pulled him into one of his strangling bear hugs. Hugs were Pagan's answer for everything. He was a hands-on kind of guy, but the time for togetherness was long past. Kruze didn't want a hug, and he didn't want comfort. He wanted his brothers to stay as far from him as possible. They were the important ones in his life, and it was important they lived, damn it. Not him.

More than anyone, Chance and Pagan needed to live long enough to be fathers and to be happy. If it meant sacrificing one life to make their lives so, Kruze meant for that life lost to be his.

"Are you still there?" Chance asked again, dragging Kruze back from the edge of a melancholy so deep neither alcohol or sex could numb it into submission. He ought to know, He'd certainly attempted both.

Kruze knew what his older brother was doing. Interfering. Keeping his thumb on the pulse of the best black ops team ever, the Sin Boys. Kruze hated that label. They weren't boys, and God knew they weren't heroes. It was a struggle to face his cell phone and grumble like the moody asshole everyone thought he was. "Yeah. I'm listening. What do you want?"

"I asked if you know why Card's in Chicago. Also want to know if there's anything you want to tell me and Pagan that we don't already know."

Like how I can't sleep at night? Like when I close my eyes, I still see the fear shining in her dark brown eyes? Yeah, big brother. She knew she was going to die. Like every time I look at Hex, I don't see Pagan's girl, only the one I lost? Like I can't stand the sight of Hex or Juarez or whatever her name is today because she looks like her!

Instead of truth, Kruze coughed and settled for, "Nah, I'm good. As far as why Card's in Chicago, your guess is as good as mine. Maybe that's his schtick, to screw up every Sinclair life he touches." Then Kruze thought twice. "Have you ever wondered why those Little Birds arrived so quickly after you went down? You ever ask yourself who called them? For sure you or your guys didn't. So, who do you think had advance notice that op was going to go sideways like it did? When it did? Do you ever stop and think why you're still alive, Chance?"

That shut everyone up, and Kruze knew he'd said too much. Shit, he had a big mouth.

"Okay, enough!" Chance snapped. "Stop beating around the bush and tell me what's going on with you. Now!"

Kruze would've laughed in his brother's face if he'd been sitting there in the SUV with him and Pagan. But Chance was safe. He'd already been targeted and survived his hell on Earth. Or had he?

"I have a theory," Kruze said more to himself than to his two edgy brothers. "But you need to get Suede somewhere safe before I say anything more."

"You talking conspiracy?" Pagan asked as he smoothly maneuvered the SUV into tight parallel parking.

Kruze nodded. "Exactly."

"Between Sullivan and who?"

"Not Sullivan. Stop and think. Whoever sent that unmanned gunship into Chicago has influence and power. He thinks he's above the law. He's untouchable. Sound familiar?"

"Mom's place," Chance snapped. "In thirty. Can you guys make it?"

"On our way," Pagan replied as he pulled away from the curb.

"Yes," Kruze agreed. It was time the Sinclair Boys talked. It was time he revealed his theory and let the dice roll.

Guess Harding would have to catch another ride.

*****

"Now you've got it. Good girl. Now go. Clean yourself up. Take a nice warm shower. Get out of those dirty clothes. Then we'll chat."

Or I'll kill you. Vicki stifled her urge to strike back at her handler since finally, she'd been allowed to climb off the colder-than-shit metal plank. She sat at the edge until the room stopped moving, and she was sure she wouldn't pass out. Being upright after the night she'd had was difficult. That last slap had rung her bell.

Unsteady on her feet, she let the Village Idiot who'd beat her, lead her three metal doors down the hall from the torture room to a concrete cell with a cot, a stainless-steel toilet, and an open shower. No shower curtain. One dingy white towel on a hook beside the shower spout. Great. Life didn't get any better than this.

"You got ten minutes to shower and get into your new *outfit*." The Village Idiot stuck air quotes at her as his long chin pointed to the black clothing on the cot. "Step on it. I got things to do, bitch."

'You have no idea how bad a bitch I can be,' she thought even as she promised herself that she'd never make air quotes again. Ever. Pagan should've told her how ridiculous she looked when she stabbed them at him.

Swallowing hard, she stepped into her concrete cell. Stiff and sore from lying too long on the frigid plank, it took a minute to strip out of her clothes. Her fingers were numb and every other body part was stiff and aching.

After she showered in plain view of the perv ogling her from the exit, she toweled as quickly as possible, then dressed in the simple outfit someone had left folded on the cot. At least they were warm and clean. But the sleeves were too long, and the black flannel pajamas made her feel like a prisoner of war in the old Hanoi Hilton. Snapping the towel, she tipped her head forward to wrap it turban style around her wet head.

"Drop it," the Village Idiot demanded.

Too tired to argue, she let the towel fall. Already water-logged, it was too heavy anyway.

Wherever this place was, it wasn't legal or sanctioned. But it was secure. No one, not even Pagan, would be able to find her. She was Dane's prisoner. He just didn't know she'd taken special care to conceal Village Idiot's knife. It had never left her hand.

By now, she knew it was less than twelve hours since she'd fallen for Cherry Goodwin's simpering naiveté. It was mid-morning, but all that time lost had been sheer hell. It had to have been the same for Pagan, him not knowing where she was, whether she was alive or dead. Her heart ached. What she wouldn't give to be back in his arms.

He'd be angry and frantically searching, then frustrated enough to do something stupid, like charge into Vito's place and demand, '*Where is she?*'

But Vito wouldn't know and going to him would only raise more questions. Vicki hoped for his sake that Pagan wouldn't do something that rash. That risky. Vito and Cabb were not men to go to war with, not over her.

Slowly and methodically—because it seemed to piss the Village Idiot off—Vicki rolled her long sleeves over three times, bringing the cuffs to the middle of her forearms where she could stash the knife if needed. It was small enough that for now it stayed in her palm, nearly in plain sight if her guard had paid attention to detail.

She licked her swollen bottom lip to disguise the sad smile thinking about Pagan brought to her mouth. She could almost see him and feel his rage. For a moment there, her world had been different because of that man. He'd brought a rugged kind of light into her world. In his way, he'd made her a better person. Her future had looked brighter. She'd been foolish enough to believe she could actually leave Vicki Hex behind. Guess not.

Somehow Dane had known she was alive all along. She needed to get to the bottom of this nightmare before he hurt the man she loved or anyone else.

"You ready yet?" her jailer asked as he stepped inside the cell and jerked her by her elbow.

Fed up with this moron, she whirled on him, aimed for his crotch and...

Nailed it!

He dropped to his knees, cupping his man bits. It would've been easy to yank his head back and cut his throat, but patience won out. Instead, Vicki bent over far enough alongside him that she could peer into his face. "You ever lay a hand on me again, and I'll kill you," she promised. "Now get off the floor and take me to your son-of-a-bitch' leader."

Not that she couldn't find Dane by herself, but now she was one up on the Idiot. He'd never tell anyone he'd been assaulted by a woman, and she wouldn't tell Dane that she'd kicked him in the nuts.

Groaning, her new buddy crawled over to the cot, then used it for leverage to get to his feet. "I... oughta kill you for that," he whined.

She planted her feet, her arms akimbo. "Then bring it on if you're still man enough," she taunted, fluttering her still tender fingertips at him. "You are, aren't you, tough guy?"

"Tsk, tsk, tsk," Dane muttered from the door. "Stop fighting, children."

"She hit me," her idiot friend declared even as he wheezed like a baby.

Ignoring him, Vicki glared over her shoulder at Dane. The ass stood there smug and too sure of himself, a black leather collar dangling on two fingers. "What's that?" she asked, daring him to come risk his family jewels and put it on her.

He tossed it through the air at her, but she let it fall.

"Put it on, Hex," he said calmly. "Be a good girl for once. Do what you're told."

"Why should I?"

"Because you're my bitch now, and you'll do what I say, when I say, and you'll ask, *'please, sir, can I have some more?'* when I'm done with you."

That'll be the day. Keeping an ear out for whatever the Idiot might have planned, she faced her handler. "First, I want to know how you knew I was at that clinic? I want to know where this place is and why Goodwin's scared to death of you."

The Village Idiot was on his feet by now, red-faced and winded but smart enough not to clutch his crotch in front of his boss. Not that Dane didn't know what just took place. Of course, there'd be hidden cameras in this secure place he'd created. The jerk had probably watched her being tortured and showering, too. Assholes. She was surrounded by assholes.

He folded his arms, still blocking the exit. "That's where you're wrong, Hex. I didn't know you were still alive, not after the dramatic and very convincing death scene you pulled off in the alley across from your penthouse. Man, what a dive. Good old Vito can't afford to set you up somewhere a little classier?"

"Then how?" she demanded, not letting herself be distracted. "How'd you know I was even at the clinic? How'd Cherry know where to find me?"

His shoulders lifted. "She didn't. Like the rest of America, we both fell for that death stunt. Never would've guessed you were that kind of smart. But then you showed up on some surveillance I had running, and..." A truly evil smile slithered over his lips. "It dawned on me that I could kill two birds with one stone. Maybe three. You, the Sinclairs, and Senator Sullivan. So yeah, I've got you right where I want you, and soon, I'll have the senator, too."

"You've got nothing," she declared even as her heartbeat soared. Could he be right? "You've been surveilling the Sinclairs? What do you have against former SEALs. They're heroes. They served." *Unlike you.*

His face puckered into lines and wrinkles. "See that's the thing. I don't care what happens to the Sinclairs. Those losers are just a means to an end. They're in my way."

"You're after Senator Sullivan then." She made it a statement.

Dane neither denied or confirmed, but he'd already said enough. Vicki knew she was right, but now she needed details. What did Sullivan have on Dane, and why did he want the senator of Texas dead?

Dane's salacious gaze slid down her body to the collar on the floor at her feet. "Put. It. On," he ordered, his eyes had gone dark. Almost made him look lethal. But Vicki knew better. Dane Rich was that pathetic schoolyard bully who lorded over other weak kids.

Stooping to retrieve the collar, Vicki considered her chances, then obeyed. Discretion beat out valor for the time being. Sliding the leather beneath her wet hair, she fastened the buckle behind her neck.

"Uh-uh. The leash loop goes in front." He twitched his index finger in a circle. "Turn it around. Yes. like that. I want it where I can reach it."

She stood there defiant, then dropped her arms to her sides, the knife still safely hidden. Let him just try to snap a lead rope on her and her deliberately chosen discretion would go right out the window.

He tossed his arrogant head at her. "There. Now you'll come when you're called, understood? You'll wear that collar everywhere you go. Make up whatever excuse you need to tell your buddies Vito and Cabb why you like it. If you don't, I have another collar, one I doubt you'll, ahem, appreciate as much as this one." He pursed his lips, then licked them again. "Come to think of it, maybe you'll like that one better. You're into all that stuff, aren't you." It wasn't a question, so much as a threat.

She never blinked. He thought he could intimidate her into believing he was into BDSM? Him, the one and only milquetoast boss she'd ever had to work for in the CIA? He thought he could control her whenever he wanted, just by saying, 'Heel?' Like she'd submit to a worm like Dane Rich?

Never.

He had yet to put the 'fear of Dane' into her, something a real Dominant knew from birth. Alphas weren't made, they were born. It wasn't a skillset one learned at the hands of a Master. Pagan had it. So, did Chance and Kruze. Either you were born with it or you weren't. Dane most definitely was not.

Now that she was dressed and warm, her confidence was back. So was her alter ego. Vicki Hex knew collars and whips, what to do with bad dogs who failed to keep their mistresses happy. Oh, yeah...

She pursed her swollen lips, then opted to run her tongue enticingly over them instead of arguing. Her mouth was still too sore for even an air kiss. But this was a dance of seduction. And she meant to win.

"Okay, so you've got me now," she admitted with a coy head tilt. "What's up with numbnuts? Why's he even here?"

"That's Agent Morton Hermes to you, bitch," the Village Idiot muttered.

Tapping her bare foot, Vicki shot him a baleful look that he immediately dodged, because, well, he was the only submissive in the room. The poor baby's hands went to his zipper. Like she wanted anything beneath it? Funny, stupid guy.

But Hermes? Really? How he came to have the surname of the Greek god of sports, travelers, and athletes, also known as a trickster and a faster-than-light messenger of the gods, baffled Vicki. Hermes had the body of, well, a god. Muscled. Athletic. Strong. But Morton Hermes was all flab with a flaccid double chin. If anything, he was a clone of the weak but cocky bastard who thought he was now man enough to be Vicki's master.

"You ambushed me at my penthouse, didn't you?" she asked pointedly.

Had to be him. Only a coward would've done that to another agent.

"You knocked me out, then you buried me alive," she declared, her bare feet spread wide and her hands on her hips again. "I'll bet you hurried back to your boss as fast as your legs could carry you. And he told you he'd give you my job when you killed me, didn't he? Did he also tell you I'm a tough bitch to kill?"

She cocked her head at her handler. "I'll bet he told you he killed me, didn't me?"

She turned back to Hermes. "

Dane didn't have to say anything. Vicki knew she was right, and the sheepish shadow that flickered across his countenance before he suppressed his features confirmed it. That was precisely what Hermes had told Cherry, that he couldn't get insider information on the Seranzinos, never mind that Vicki kept passing out when he hit her too hard. That Dane had promised her job away if Hermes would only kill her, as if the Seranzinos would allow just anyone inside the *familia* once she was dead

Which once again proved how much Agent Rich thought of himself, but how little he truly understood *the job*. She nearly smiled. That'd be a sight worth seeing, this non-godlike Hermes jogging up Seranzino's long, winding drive. Maybe knocking on their elegant front door, all sweaty and panting his guts up—if he made it past the guards without being shot. What'd he think, that she'd filled out a job application to gain entry into this Mafia familia? That Vito and Cabb were stupid? The fool.

Back to Dane. "Who's Dick?" she asked him point blank. If ever there was a time to find out how Cherry's husband fit in this diabolical scheme to kill Senator Sullivan, it was now.

He shook his head. "Uh-uh. That's not how it works. I'm in charge, not you, Hex." Extending his right hand, he beckoned her to come forward. When she'd gotten a few feet from him, he had the nerve to point to the floor at his feet. "On your knees. Here. Now."

She sucked in a breath. *He wouldn't...*

Hermes let out a long snort through his nostrils. "Now you'll get what's coming to you."

Vicki's head came up as she shot him her most lethal stare.

His jaw ticked, but yeah. He closed his big mouth. He knew who was boss.

Drawing what was left of one tender thumbnail under her nose like a prize fighter, she looked to her handler. Had she underestimated him or was he just the prick she'd always suspected? It might be time to find out.

Her hair hung wet and heavy down her back and over her shoulders. Because of it, her flannel outfit was soaked through in some places. But all of that hair had also allowed her to conceal the blade Hermes still wasn't aware she'd taken. If Dane wanted her to do what she suspected, expected...

If he wanted her on her knees because of... that. *Eww.* The thought of her turning him on with her mouth, even a little, turned her stomach.

Never! Her defiant self shrieked.

But for Pagan...

This could be that day. But first...

Vicki walked straight up to Special Agent Rich and stared him in the eye. It never ceased to amaze her how so much pasty oatmeal could be stacked so high. That was Dane through and through. Weak. Bland. A coward with no backbone. A bully with no real power to back up his mouth. She called his bluff.

"You called?" she quipped as sarcastically as she could.

"On your knees, Hex," he hissed, that annoying, prissy index finger still pointing down.

It'd take less than a second to break it off. By then, Hermes would be within range. He'd been asking to have his throat cut. Vicki knew she could end both of them right here and now, maybe Cherry too if she were brave or stupid enough to intervene.

But Vicki needed more intel on this plan to off Sullivan, possibly the Sinclairs too, before she struck back. She needed exact details, dates, and schedules. The glory-mongering Dane had set in motion had to be stopped, and since she was here? Why not?

But of all the assholes in the world, Vicki had never suspected that her cowardly CIA handler would be the mastermind behind all of her near deaths. It seemed he was smart enough to have built, ahem, blackmailed, an army of unwilling Agency operators who all wanted something.

Mousey little Cherry Goodwin wanted her husband Dick, aka Richard—whoever he was—back. Morton Hermes wanted the praise and respect of his peers that he didn't deserve and wasn't willing to earn. He wanted what Vicki had, the notoriety that came with working undercover inside the Mafia. Vicki still didn't know what Rich held over the operator of the unmanned gunship that had ripped her apartment building to shreds, or who the shooter in the SUV was. But she'd find out. If it took the rest of her life, she would find out.

And Vicki Hex, aka Paloma Juarez? What did she want badly enough to obey Agent Rich? Only the life of the man she adored. For Pagan, she'd do anything.

"All I have to do is wear this collar and go back to work for Vito and Cabb?" she asked, even as she'd doubted every word that came out of Dane's lying mouth.

"That's all." Air whistled through his nostrils, and that was when she knew. The man didn't have the balls to fuck her in front of his subordinate. He really was a coward. Which on one hand was very good for her, but on the other hand...

She could work with that. Audacious now, Vicki Hex laid one palm on Dane's scrawny chest, right over his palpitating heart. *Man, can you feel that? This boy's on the verge of cardiac arrest.*

Her confidence soared. She slid the other hand down low enough to cup him through his pants. That let him think she was willing to do just about anything. It let him believe she was weak and willing. Pliable. Stupid.

"Knock it off," he growled, then nodded, his oatmeal-toned skin oddly gray under the fluorescent lighting in this concrete room. The man needed to get out in the sun more. He was as pale as Vito, just not as strikingly handsome in the scary, unpredictable, Seranzino way. And in no way, shape, or form was Dane the alpha male that Pagan was.

He cleared his throat, obviously uncomfortable with her fingers clutching him where she could do the most damage. Not that she would. After all, she was—patient. Cunning. More devious than he'd live long enough to understand.

"Since you proved harder to kill than I, umm, anticipated, I've changed my a-agenda." And now he was stuttering. "You're back on the job. Hermes will have to be content with the job he's got."

"B-but boss—" Hermes sputtered.

"Can it," Dane growled huskily even as his eyelids grew heavy under Vicki's continued massage. But he wasn't kidding anyone, and she wasn't a fool. He was behind her kill order, she damned well knew it. Which meant Senator Sullivan must've somehow put the fear of God into this weaselly, conniving little man during the last few hours or days, maybe when he'd refused to hunt down an innocent Mafia assassin—if there were such a thing—just because Dane said so. She had the Sin Boys to thank for that.

Which also meant, despite her tenuous hold on the, umm, situation, Dane Rich was now running scared. The wimpy, wannabe was afraid he'd get caught. Which made him malleable, yet unpredictable.

She could work with that, too. She'd have to proceed cautiously, but yeah. He was after all, just a man with a wimpy hard-on. "What do you mean, you've changed your agenda?" she breathed into his face as she released him but continued stroking him through his pants.

He stuck his weak chin at her, his eyes bright. "I just might tell you now that I've got you sufficiently collared. What could it hurt?"

As if she didn't hold his whole world in her hand? It could hurt one hell of a lot. The need to strike back was strong, the need to avenge what Dane had done to Pagan, Paloma, and timid Cherry, fierce, and oh, so tempting. Vicki could end this farce here and now, before it went any further. She could!

She could save Senator Sullivan, Pagan and his brothers, maybe Cherry Goodwin and her hubby, too. Saving Morton Hermes was off the table, but Rich needed to die. One clutch. That was all. Just one strangling tight grip on his testicles, and he'd be the one on the floor on his knees. Wouldn't that shock Hermes? He'd thought he'd get a front row seat to her humiliation and degradation. He'd thought he could get his rocks off watching her get hers. Wasn't that—rich?

But before she proceeded with her better plan, Vicki Hex leaned into her handler and whispered, "Please, sir. May I have some more?"

Chapter Thirty-Nine

Pagan couldn't drive fast enough to the other hotel his mother had once loved in the rowdy town Carl Sandburg, the American poet, had romanticized all those years ago.

Hog Butcher for the World,
Tool Maker, Stacker of Wheat,
Player with Railroads and the Nation's Freight
Handler;
Stormy, husky, brawling,
City of the Big Shoulders...

He knew only the first few lines of the famous poem because his mother had spouted them often enough, only she'd spoken them with drama and flair. He thought of them now with a fierce determination to not let this wicked, wicked city swallow Paloma down its yawing throat, too.

Until Kruze's butt pocket buzzed, and with one word, the world turned upside down yet again. Kruze turned and stared wide-eyed at Pagan as he asked, "Julio?"

He nodded, listening instead of asking the questions Pagan threw at him. "Where is he? Where's he been? Has he heard from Paloma? Does he know where she is? Talk to me, damn it!"

Instead, Kruze told Julio, "Copy that," and he hung up. He! Hung! Up!

Pagan could barely catch a breath by then. "Speak," he ordered his older brother.

"Julio's in town," Kruze answered even as he thumb-dialed another number and said, "Change of plans, big brother. Can you meet us over at the loading docks?... Yeah. The Iroquois Lakefront Terminal and... That's right... No, we can't swing by and pick you up. Take a cab... Ah-huh... We're already on our way." He gave Chance an address before he said, "Copy that," and hung up. Again!

Pagan nearly shrieked, "Where are we going?"

"Calumet Harbor," Kruze said calmly. "Take a right at the next intersection. Chance will meet us there."

"The Port of Chicago? Why? That's—"

"I know. It's close to an hour from where we are now, which is why you're going to hook into I-90 and head south. Hurry." Kruze's narrow lips pinched tight. "We may not have a lot of time."

"Why? What'd Julio say?"

Kruze chin nodded at the heavy traffic snarling the lanes ahead of them. "He said he's located CIA Agent Dick Card. Will you step on it?"

Pagan floored it. Where Card was, he'd find Paloma. He had to!

*****

Vicki sat across a small round table where Dane Rich sat with Hermes at his right. The big tough guy still hadn't gotten up the nerve to look Vicki in the eye, but he was walking straighter. Kind of. Timid, mousey Cherry Goodwin sat stiff and darn near comatose at Dane's left. She looked like she was afraid to breathe, and she hadn't spared even a quick glance in Vicki's direction.

Until Vicki asked her handler, "Who's Dick?"

Bingo. That got Cherry's attention. "My husband," she answered even as her eyes scrolled sideways to her boss. Her small white teeth bit down on her quivering bottom lip. This woman was the most pathetic agent Vicki had ever had the misfortune to meet. Dane sure knew how to pick them.

"Is he an agent? For the Agency?"

Cherry's head bobbed. "Yes, he's assigned to the San Diego office. The last time I talked with him, he was on his way to Singapore. Something about a bank robbery. International jewel thieves."

"Where is he now?"

The woman's throat worked extra-hard as she forced a swallow. "I... I honestly don't know."

"Interesting," Vicki replied to that silly goose answer. "How can a wife not know where her husband is?"

Dane huffed, shaking his head while he stared Vicki down. "Do not play with the mice, Victoria. It's cruel, even for a cunning bitch like you."

At least he got that right. She was one bitch of a predator on the prowl. Make that a sleek black jungle cat. A leopard. "It's Vicki, not Victoria," she corrected her handler. "You ought to know that by now."

Ignoring her correction, he flipped open the gray folder lying in front of him. "Ah, yes. Vicki Hex. Not Victoria. Let's see what else we know about you, shall we? It says here you were trained by the CIA. Several good conduct medals. An overachiever. Doesn't like to kill federal officials. Hmmm..." His index finger skimmed the comments in her service record. "It says here you only wing police officers, federal agents, and former military. You haven't killed one yet." His head came up as he asked, "Why's that?"

She gave him her chin. "You ought to know. You're my handler. You tell me."

Grunting, Dane slapped the file closed. "That professional courtesy ends today, Hex. From now on, you'll end who I tell you, and you'll do it when I want. Understood? Now answer me. What are the Sinclairs to you?"

"Nothing," she lied intelligently. Dane already knew she'd been at the clinic with Pagan, but she doubted he knew much more. "I ran into one of them late last night. The youngest, Pagan, remember? I shot him during that Portland op last year. Never expected to see him again, but there he was."

Dane's head bobbed as if he remembered that detail from her previous after-action report. "Why were you there?"

"Because some asshat..." She cast a glare at Hermes. "Hit me over the head, for one. Then, when I *died*..." She could have slapped herself as her hands came up automatically and performed those ridiculous Morton-esque air quotes. That really had to stop. "I fell and hit my head. Got a concussion. I'd passed out a couple times, so I scoped out the nearest clinic for a few meds. Do you have a problem with that?"

"Who pretended to shoot you?"

"How should I know? I was dead."

Dane leaned into the table. "Here's what I think happened. Pagan Sinclair came to town. You two hooked up. By then you knew you were on someone's hit list. Hell, he probably came to Chicago just to rescue your sorry ass. You stayed at the same hotel his mother used to stay at before she kicked the bucket, right?"

"There's no need to be coarse," Vicki said. "Scarlett Sinclair was a rare woman to raise those boys all by herself. She deserves nothing but respect."

Crossing his arms over his chest, Dane kicked back in his chair. "Answer me. You stayed in her personal hotel suite, right?"

He had her there. "Yes. Pagan intercepted me after I dug myself out of the shallow grave where numbnuts left me. Pagan helped me, okay? That's all. Is that so bad?"

"What else do you know about Scarlett?"

Vicki paused to reevaluate the decidedly unexpected turn this conversation had taken. For once Dane knew something she didn't. Maybe it was time to let him talk for a while.

"Have you been following me?" she asked.

"What would it matter if I had?" he shot back at her. "But truthfully, no. Not you. Now tell me, have you ever seen Scarlett Sinclair with Vito or Cabb Seranzino?"

Vicki rolled her eyes. "No. Never," she said, meaning it. "What on earth do you have against the Sinclairs?"

"I told you it's not about them."

"But you want to use them to get at Sullivan."

Dane's eyes glittered as if she'd finally understood. "This is what's going to happen, Hex. You're going to put on that tramp costume you usually wear, and then you're going to pay Sullivan a visit. I've already made the appointment. No one needs to know you're there. No one needs to see you. Just get in and get out. Keep it simple. Know what I mean?"

"And then...?"

Dane never flinched. "Kill him. Put one round in his head behind his right ear like you do in a Mafia hit. That's all. End him, and you'll end several other problems. Maybe then I'll bring you in from the field. Wasn't that what you wanted, to come in?"

She kept her cool, drumming her tender fingertips on the tabletop as if considering her options. Which were nil until she was out on the street. "Why?" she asked finally. "What's Senator Sullivan ever done to you?"

His lips thinned. "Because everywhere I go, I run into someone connected to him, and I'm sick of it. His people are ruining all my... my plans."

"His people? The Sinclairs are *his* people?" It took some restraint, but she conquered her urge to make air quotes. "What plans?"

The light in his eyes went out as if she'd flipped a switch, and suddenly, Vicki was looking at a flat-out psycho. Agent Rich cocked his head, looking at her as if she were a worm on a hook, when he said, "My plan to kill everyone who gets in my way. In case you're thinking of double-crossing me, think again." He slid a black and white glossy across the table to her.

Shit. He had a picture of her and Pagan kissing in the dark. Double shit. That impromptu kiss happened the night she'd offed John Wesley Mills in his home. Pagan had come to do the job, not knowing she was already there.

"You had me followed," she declared.

Dane shook his head. "No, but I've been watching the Sinclairs for some time now. They work for Sullivan. I know they do. Just haven't figured out exactly what they do for him." He cocked his head at her. "Your choice, Hex. Kill Sullivan or I end that boyfriend of yours. Either way, I win."

Which meant Dane had Sullivan under surveillance, too. That was how he'd linked Pagan and his brothers to the senator from Texas.

"Sullivan," she said swiftly, her heart hammering. This would be an unfortunate first. She'd never deleted an honest man before. "When do you want it done?"

"After you honey-up to Vito, so he gets his ass back to work."

Vicki understood completely then. Dane had gotten involved in something illegal that Vito unknowingly handled, probably drugs, cash, guns, or women. When Vito got *his ass back to work*, whatever deal Dane had working on the side would go down smoothly. Which meant someone was also watching Dane, waiting for him to deliver. This nightmare kept getting better and better.

Scoffing as if this kill order were a no-brainer, Vicki pushed back from the table. "Sullivan'll be no problem. Sure. Yeah, I can do that easy. Where're my clothes?"

"In your penthouse. Morton will drive you." Dane slid a brown envelope to her. "Here's a phone. Call me when it's done."

She opened the envelope and a small white appointment card fell out along with the burner. Great. Looked like she really had a date with Sullivan. "He's meeting me at nine in three days?"

Dane stuck his arrogant chin at her. "Be there."

Chapter Forty

The sun had barely set when Pagan turned off his headlights and coasted the SUV up to the square concrete warehouse abutting one damned tall loading crane. But winter was coming. The sun set earlier every night. He flipped his collar up and slipped one pistol out of his underarm holster. Already armed and dangerous, Kruze had bailed out of the SUV a block back when they'd spotted Chance waiting beside the road. Pagan now had the two men he trusted implicitly at his back as he faced the breeze blowing off Lake Michigan. Big, fat, wet snowflakes that would turn everything to ice before morning, began to fall.

Climbing out of the vehicle, he hunkered into the wind and stayed in the stark black shadow the crane had created. Industrial halogen lights lit the loading platform ahead. Beyond the crane at his left, rows upon rows of containers stood stacked for transport, either waiting on semi-trucks to come get them, or waiting on ships. The Port of Chicago at Calumet Harbor handled tons of deliverables and consisted of several major facilities, one of them abandoned and directly in front of Pagan. Off to the side of that building, a long pier jutted out into the murky whitecaps of Lake Michigan. The tethered ships alongside the pier bobbed like giant corks in the choppy water.

This particular terminal hosted several transit sheds that were more like monstrous, mile-long warehouses built to accommodate both big ship and wide barge berthing. The storage facilities down the pier had the capacity to store the hundreds of metric tons of grain transported across the lake daily. Busy place, this side of Chicago. Must be why Carl Sandburg named it the *City of the Big Shoulders*. Only the place wasn't so husky or brawling tonight. Stormy, yeah. But quiet. Might be because of the winter storm moving in. But it might not.

Pagan kept walking, his firearm drawn, his footsteps muffled. There he was, hunting for Dick Card when he'd rather be searching for Paloma. If Julio were here, he had yet to make himself known. All Kruze knew was that Julio said come, so they came.

The softest rustle caught his attention as a door up ahead opened and a wide, shadowy, male figure in a trench coat stepped into view. A slighter figure without a jacket came out of that door next, her head down as the wind whipped her long dark hair.

Paloma?

Pagan froze where he stood, watching. Waiting. Hoping.

He had to allow those people to get close enough before he confronted them. Before he got Paloma hurt. All at once, the big guy at her side cocked his arm back. Before Pagan could shout a warning, she took the guy down with one lightning swift roundhouse kick, then climbed on top of his fluffy gut, her nose in his face. Pagan fast-tracked close enough to hear her order the guy, "Give me one reason not to cut your throat, Morton."

"Answer her," Pagan growled, his pistol levered at this fool's forehead.

"Pagan!" she squealed as she jumped to her feet and barreled into him. "You shouldn't be here."

Ah, the warmth that spread through his heart just holding her again. He could barely speak. "Yeah, well, you shouldn't be here either," he said as he kept his weapon aimed at the sputtering fool on his back. "What's going on? Why'd you leave? Why aren't you wearing my jacket?"

Tossing her head, she shoved him back. "Leave. Now! This is none of your business. Go!"

He cocked his head, not understanding. Her hair looked wet and her lips were bruised and swollen. More mottled bruises darkened one eye. Her poor nose was swollen, and her left eyebrow was cut. His inner caveman roared to life. "I'm not going anywhere!"

Damned if she didn't pull a pistol from those black pajamas of hers and point it at him.

"What's going on?" he asked.

"Nothing," she snapped, her heretofore tender eyes now gone hard as diamonds.

He played along. "Vicki? I... I thought we were friends."

Her lips pinched. "Were, Baby Brother. Good word, were. Now beat it. Not sure why you're here, but I've got work to do, and you need to take off."

"I'm following a lead on some gunrunners," he said, intent on maintaining her cover in case she needed it. "What are you doing here?"

By then the guy she'd kicked was up on one knee and pushing to his feet. Breathing hard he pulled his badge as he wheezed, "CIA Agent Morton Hermes. Clear the area, Mr. Sinclair. Scram before you fuck this operation up, too."

What did that mean? Pagan cocked his head at the guy he'd never met but who knew his name. He swallowed hard and nodded, about to do the hardest thing he'd done in a while. He tipped two fingers in respect to Paloma, even as his heart screamed, *'Run to her. Hold her. Protect her. Never let her go.'*

Her eyes glistened, probably from the biting cold. But it could've been the emotions playing across her beautiful, battered face. As slight as she was, she looked sadder than ever before. Lost.

Against everything he believed in, Pagan took a step back. Unable to make his eyes move from her, he muttered, "See you around then."

"No,' she said very definitely, her chin up and her sad eyes bright. "You won't. This is goodbye. Tell your brothers goodbye for me as well. Tell Julio and Kruze I'll miss them."

Pagan nodded at the bizarre farewell, then turned his back on the only woman he'd ever loved this hard, leaving her behind while his heart shattered. WTF? Julio and Kruze? Did she know her brother was here, too? Was that what the breadcrumb she'd just tossed at him meant? That Julio was already in play?

With the wind at his back, Pagan lifted his cell to his face and speed-dialed Kruze. "You made contact with Julio yet?"

"No, was that Paloma?" Kruze asked as he and Chance advanced from the shadows toward Pagan.

He tossed a backward glance over his shoulder, but Paloma and that agent were nowhere in sight. Shit. Wasn't that the bleakest sight in the world, her not being there watching him leave? "Yeah, but she's in trouble."

"So, you left her?" The sheer disbelief in Kruze's snarky voice warmed Pagan's soul. His brother cared.

"Her choice, not mine. She said to tell you and Julio goodbye. Made it sound like you and he were my brothers."

"Where is that rat bastard?" Chance growled, now standing directly in front of Pagan.

"On your six," a rumbling baritone murmured from the shadowed doorway Pagan had just passed. "Don't turn around. Keep walking, guys. I'll follow."

As Chance and Kruze marched alongside Pagan, Kruze hissed, "What the fuck's going on, JJ?"

"Patience brother," Julio murmured. "I've got a man inside."

"Patience my ass," Pagan growled as he pivoted and ran back the way Paloma had gone. Chance, Kruze, and Julio thundered behind him. It took mere seconds to breach the doorway he'd seen Paloma and Agent Hermes exit from. Down a long dark hallway he ran, his heart stuck in his throat. It was hard not to bellow, 'Paloma!' but he resisted the urge.

At last, the hallway ended at a T. Pagan took the corridor at his right, his lips dry and his blood on fire. If that guy had hurt her...

He slammed open the first closed door he came to. Nothing. The room was cold and empty. The next was the same, but those clothes on the floor, those were Paloma's. He left them where they lay along with a wet towel. "She was here," he told his brothers over his cell.

"Get your ass in here," Chance ordered grimly. "We found Julio's inside man."

"Only she's not a man," Kruze added.

Quickly exiting what was nothing more than a jail cell, Pagan ran down the hall until he came to Chance and Kruze. "Where the hell is Julio?"

Chance shook his head, nodding to the floor where a blonde woman lay on her back in a pool of blood. She'd been shot in the chest. Kruze was on his cell contacting 911.

It no longer mattered where Julio was. Pagan secured his firearm and knelt to begin medical treatment. He tore her blouse open as Chance knelt beside him, handed over a ready bag of QuikClot, and said, "You pour. I'll pack."

Swallowing hard, Pagan poured the anticoagulant over the massive hole below her collarbone while Chance applied sterile surgical gauze to staunch the flow.

"She's going to make it," Pagan told his brother even as the odds of a woman as slight as this gal surviving that kind and size of a hit, told him differently. Yet, Pagan knew better than to quit. He'd seen strong men die from lesser wounds. He'd also seen lesser men—and women—pull through when everyone had said, *'all is lost.'*

All was never lost, and who was anyone to declare a situation hopeless? Like he'd done with Paloma, Pagan chose to believe in miracles and the power of indomitable spirits. That was what made America great. People who never gave up when everyone else said they should. People who followed their hearts instead of public opinion.

"I could use a little help down here," he prayed earnestly as his hands grew slippery with blood.

"I'm doing all I can," Chance answered just as earnestly.

Pagan almost smiled. He'd meant for God to answer, but Chance's reply was just as good.

The woman coughed, but unfortunately, a red clot dribbled off her lip. Again—not good.

But there, in an icebox of a concrete room at the end of another hopeless day, he labored with every last fiber of his tender warrior's heart to save this unknown woman's life. Even as the woman he adored was lost to him, Pagan strove for a finish line that seemed farther and farther out of reach. He couldn't save Paloma, but he might save this stranger. It didn't seem fair, yet he never hesitated. Wouldn't even think to slow down or quit. This was what he'd been trained for and what he lived for. Saving the helpless. Honoring his mother. Being all he was born to be. To never—ever—quit.

"I love her," he told his older brother as his vision blurred.

Chance's big hands clamped over Pagan's as together, they applied pressure to slow the blood loss. "I know. Trust me, I know."

Kruze took a knee alongside the unconscious woman. "I know who she is," he murmured as he smoothed a chunk of honey-blonde hair off her face and tucked it behind her ear, his touch uncommonly gentle on a night so dark. "This is Dick Card's wife."

"How do you even know that?" Chance asked as he put his weight into it, clamping down tight over Pagan's spread palms.

Kruze inhaled a long breath. "Told you. I've been checking into Card for a while. Julio thought he'd be here tonight because of her. That's why he called when he did."

"He's following Card too?" Pagan had to know.

Kruze shook his head. "I think Julio's been working with Card."

"You're shitting me?" Chance spat. "Julio's in league with that bastard? How long's he been with Card? Jesus Christ! Was he in Peru when—?"

Both Kruze's palms came up. "I honestly don't know. I haven't seen JJ long enough to talk with him about Peru since I started putting two and two together. Shit, Chance. Don't you think I would've told you if I knew for sure that Julio and Card were working to kill you? How big of an asshole do you think I am?"

Both Chance's bloody hands flew to cup Kruze's face. He bowed his forehead to the center of his belligerent middle brother's forehead and said, "Never. Not once. I never thought you were an asshole, Kruze. You've been to hell and back with me. You and Pagan, now Suede and Paloma are all I've got left in this world. Don't. Just don't give up on me like you've given up on yourself."

Kruze shrugged out of Chance's grip. Lifting his arm to his face, he wiped the bloody smears, making them worse. "I haven't given up on myself. I've just got... things to sort out, and one of those things is what happened in Peru. God, I don't sleep most nights, just lie there thinking about... things. Like how lucky you were that those Little Birds arrived as quickly as they did. But even that good fortune seemed odd. Unlikely, you know?"

"I've been thinking more about it, too," Chance agreed. "Contacted a buddy who knows one of the Night Stalkers out of Fort Campbell. He verified that a call for an assist came in ten minutes before me and my team even scoped in on that Black Hawk before exfil. He didn't have a name back then, and for a while, his CO opted to disregard the distress call. We were on a covert mission. No one knew we were out there, not even the Little Birds working a massive cartel drug bust two miles south of our LZ." The Landing Zone.

"I think Dick Card was behind that distress call," Kruze said quietly, his gaze still on the lady who lay dying at his knee. He coughed, then cleared his throat. "Her name's Cherry. She goes by Goodwin when she's working, kinda like Paloma goes by Vicki Hex, only..."

A real, no kidding tear rolled down Kruze's cheek. *Son. Of. A. Bitch.* Pagan saw it before Kruze shoved the back of his wrist over his eye and banished that drop of weakness into oblivion. "They've got two kids, a boy and a girl."

"How long have you been watching Card?" Pagan asked as a siren finally sounded beyond the concrete walls.

"A while. At first, I went out to end Card. I wanted revenge for what I thought he did, only the bastard was never home, and his home was so—nice. Kept up, you know. The trees were trimmed, and there were all these rose bushes. I mean, Jesus. The man planted roses everywhere. It was obvious he took care of things at home. The wooden fence around his yard was painted, and the more I looked and waited and watched..."

"That's when you saw his wife," Chance stated.

Kruze's head bobbed. "Yeah, Cherry and his two kids. They looked so... normal. Shit, they looked loved. I really started thinking then. I mean, the guy never came home. Why not? He had a family waiting for him. A good family from what I could see. Fair question, right? So where has he been all this time?"

The questions and answers ceased as Kruze lifted to his feet and ran to guide the paramedics through the maze of concrete hallways that led to Cherry. As they took over emergency treatment, Pagan stood over the dying woman now surrounded by his brothers.

Life was hard, damn it. Too hard sometimes. Those two little kids were about to become orphans, never an acceptable outcome in Pagan's book. Two children. What was God thinking to take their mother away from them like this? And Paloma. Where was she, and why had she pushed him away? His fist clenched. His heart ached to know the answer to that one.

At last the medics had Cherry Goodwin-Card ready to transport. She was hanging on by a thread, but she was still alive. Maybe God would work a miracle after all. Pagan could only close his eyes and hope.

Overcome by the loss of the day, he grabbed both his brothers in tight for a group hug. It was either that or break down in front of them and bawl like a damned baby. "Thanks," was all he could grind out as the thread that Scarlett Sinclair had knitted between them all those years ago tightened and pulled them back together. They were brothers again. Like she'd meant them to be.

For once, Kruze didn't shove away. Mom had to be smiling down from heaven to see her three boys hanging onto each other and getting by. Maybe she'd even shed a tear or two. Pagan sure was.

Chapter Forty-One

It took three days for Dane to get through to Senator McQueen Sullivan. Or so he'd said. Now on her belly on a conference table deep inside an empty room inside a closed, ground level office building, Paloma stared at her designated target through her rifle's top-of-the-line M5B2 Leopold scope. She didn't need to meet the esteemed senator from Texas to end him. She couldn't miss. This scope boasted the most precise mil dot reticle available. All she needed was for Sullivan to be where he said he'd be at precisely nine AM this morning.

And there he was, seated at the little sidewalk café just off Independence venue in Washington DC. Right on time. McQueen bore all the marks of an old time cowboy. Tall, trim, and agile, he made that tan, western cut business suit with its chestnut front and back yokes, look good. The customary black bolo tie beneath it was one of his distinguishing looks. As were his denim jeans and leather cowboy boots. For an older guy, he was good-looking with a distinguished air about him.

Unfolding his newspaper, he looked up and smiled at the waitress on his right. She chatted back, one hand on her hip as she pointed at the menu in his hand with the other. Probably telling him what the daily specials were. Or what her favorite menu item was. Simple stuff like that.

Paloma panned her scope's crosshairs over the young woman. Blonde. Perky. Great big smile. Genuinely happy. Blushing under the prestigious senator's attention. Even as old as he was, Sullivan could still pour on the charm. The waitress looked a lot like timid Cherry Goodwin, except this woman had nothing to worry about. She had no way of knowing that an assassin had her sighted, or that her life could end just as easily as Sullivan's. Like him, she'd never hear the round that ended her, either.

That thought alone raised a tender lump in Paloma's throat. It was hard to breathe. Harder to swallow. She wasn't here to end some perky waitress who probably had little ones at home like Vanessa. But Paloma had been there when Dane ended timid Cherry.

It happened so fast, the night of the same day Hermes had nearly drowned Paloma. One minute Dane was chatting with Cherry, telling her to go home and take it easy for a couple days. His voice had been lighthearted. Almost friendly. He said she deserved a break. 'Go be a mom for a day or two. Come back to work when you're ready.'

She'd brushed a delicate hand over her forehead, moving her bangs out of her way. She'd been relieved. Her eyes had lit up as if she couldn't wait to leave. She'd actually thanked Dane for thinking of her kids. She'd smiled at the rat bastard.

And like the lying asshat he was, Dane had sounded sincere. He'd turned his back on Cherry to tell Hermes and Paloma to hurry up and leave. They had a senator to meet. They couldn't be late.

Paloma bit her lip to keep from remembering. *But the music played on...*

Dane whirled on Cherry and... BANG! He'd fired point-blank. Damn, the noise! But it was the shock and hurt in Cherry's sad, blue eyes that would haunt Paloma forever. Like the fool Cherry was, she'd believed Dane.

The impact blew her into the concrete wall behind her. She'd hit so hard that her head bounced, but she hadn't said a word. Didn't even whimper. Just crumbled like a spineless rag doll to the floor. Which was precisely what Cherry was. An innocent woman caught in a treacherous spider's web.

And every time Paloma closed her eyes, Cherry Goodwin fell again and again...

"Enough!" she commanded herself. Seeing someone die shouldn't affect her like it had. Vicki had personally offed more than a dozen of Vito and Cabb's cronies and enemies. She'd been just as quick, just as cold-blooded as Dane. That was what assassins did—their jobs. And if they were good, they lived to see another sunrise while their marks did not.

But Paloma was no longer Vicki, and simpering Cherry Goodwin's death was different. She had to have been some kind of administrative assistant instead of a trained killer. She hadn't the strength of character for that job title. But there'd been no reason to end her. Unless Dane had never intended to bring her husband back. Unless Dick Goodwin was already dead. Unless Dane had intended to kill Cherry all along to prove he meant what he'd said, that he would also kill the Sinclair Boys to get at Sullivan. To get Vicki to fall in line.

"God, what have I done?" she asked. For her, it was too late. Once she dropped Sullivan, she was done being a stone-cold killer. She'd either suicide by cop with her rifle in her hand, or she'd flee the States and never come back. Special Agent Rich could go to hell.

Because Paloma was no longer the invincible, risk-taking Vicki Hex. She hadn't the heart. Those few moments of utter safety she'd found inside Pagan's strong, virile arms had ruined her. But watching Dane murder an innocent like Cherry was the last straw, and she, Paloma Juarez, was that poor camel with the broken back.

"I don't want to kill you, Senator," she whispered to McQueen, "but Dane will kill Pagan or one of his brothers if I don't end you today. I'm sorry, but I love those Sin Boys more than you. I do."

Yet again, she hesitated. The simple job ahead of her seemed incredibly difficult this morning. What a waste, to end someone as noble and patriotic as Sullivan. She licked her dry lips and wished there were a way to summon Vicki Hex one last time to complete this ugly, despicable act of betrayal.

But Paloma hadn't been able to transform into her evil twin since she'd told Pagan goodbye. A part of her died on that dock in Chicago. She never would've guessed it'd be Vicki Hex, though. Karma really was a bitch.

"I will do this. I have to. For Pagan's sake," she told herself sternly.

Like that meant anything. Dane had used the burner phone in her inner jacket pocket only hours before when he'd called to tell her Sullivan was on his way, to make it clean and fast. His last words were, "Don't miss."

Her problem now was her conscience. She'd never killed an innocent man before., and McQueen Sullivan was innocent. She knew for a fact that the handsome, older gentleman sipping his coffee black, just the way she liked her coffee, was also incredibly kind. Yes, he'd sent the Sin Boys a kill order to end her, but the very fact that he'd hired good men with morals just like him proved her point. Good men still made mistakes, but if they surrounded themselves with enough other good men, well... chances improved that they'd make fewer mistakes, and the ones that got through would be caught. Fewer mistakes meant fewer agents like Cherry dying in the line of duty.

Paloma squeezed her eyes to stop the continual instant replay of something she'd had no part in. *Cherry Goodwin is dead. Move on. Take a deep breath. Eyes back on target. Get it done. Do it fast. It doesn't matter if you die today. Just finish what you started. Once and for all time, save Pagan. He's who matters. Not you.*

Fortified by her somewhat motivating, though also somewhat depressing self-talk, she zeroed back on Sullivan. There was no sense stalling. That only made this hard job harder.

Even at this distance, he exuded the calm power of a man who stood for something other than greed and gossip and the customary morals of a few politicians. Silver-haired with an impressive mustache, he wore the prestige of his Senate office like an elegant kingly mantel. Texas should be proud of him.

Sucking in one last breath, Paloma held it as the crosshairs settled on Sullivan for the last time. "Do or die," she whispered as her index finger pressed against the fine-lined grooves inside the curve of her rifle's trigger. All she had to do was depress that tiny lever to actuate the firing sequence. Because of the double action design of her rifle, once that trigger reached a certain point, it cocked the weapon. From that point on, there'd be no turning back. The power she held at the top of her still healing finger awed, humbled, and frightened her this morning. Senator Sullivan would slump forward and die the second she released the kinetic energy behind the massive round in her chamber.

If only she could.

*****

Pagan grunted as once again, Vicki Hex stalled. Which was both good and bad. The longer she waited, the harder this call to action became. Waiting gave a sniper too much time to think about their target. It messed up their psyche and forced them to see their mark as a human being instead of a bulls-eye. It was smarter when a sniper took care of business efficiently and quickly. Before he had time to think.

Because Pagan was thinking now. If he were smart, he wouldn't stall like Vicki. He'd end her, pack his gear, and vanish. End of story.

Yet there he lay flat on his belly in a closed-for-business service station across from her location, his eye to his scope, and his finger on the trigger of his own rifle. Stalling. Hoping against hope that she wouldn't carry through with the cold-blooded assassination attempt against Sullivan.

If only she knew she'd been set up, and that Metro PD's finest were already primed and waiting to move in on her the moment she fired. If only she knew that her son-of-a-bitchin' handler had outed her the same night she'd told Pagan goodbye.

Because now Pagan knew everything. He knew how Agent Rich had contacted Sullivan directly, and how he'd bragged he finally had solid proof Vicki Hex had gone rogue. Said he had a taped confession, but also video footage of her stalking Sullivan. He claimed he had an eyewitness, Agent Morton Hermes, though Pagan doubted Hermes was still alive. Rich also claimed Vicki Hex had a vendetta against Sullivan, that she had sworn she'd kill him.

Of course Rich knew the day and time. He'd set the whole thing up. The bastard had even gone so far as to arrange this early morning meet-and-greet with Sullivan to hand over his alleged *solid evidence* against Vicki Hex, substantiating his initial kill order.

If only Pagan knew where Hermes was right now. If only he'd gotten to Vicki sooner. He wouldn't be poised to kill the woman he loved now.

"Don't," he commanded her from his location across the busy thoroughfare. "I don't want to have to end you, Vicki." He had to think of her as Vicki. Thinking of her as Paloma hurt too much.

Pagan now knew Rich had been behind Chance's near death in Peru as well as the attempt on Cherry Goodwin's life. Which was why McQueen had stepped up to the plate to act as bait. Rich's hands were dirty. Bloody and dirty.

If only Vicki knew that Goodwin was still alive and talking. But she'd been on the wind since she'd fled

Chicago days ago, and the location she'd chosen as her sniper hide this morning was one of many good choices in the area. It didn't take a genius to convert an empty room or a dark corner into a last stand.

Chance and Kruze had also come to DC to take her down, Chance from his position atop the Savings and Loan across the street. Kruze from inside the utility van parked at the curb. The magnetic sign on its side panels might declare PEPCO for Potomac Electric Power Company. But it was FBI down to its wheels.

Damn. She'd just snugged her cheek against the butt end of her rifle. Her shoulders lifted with a gentle inhalation as that weapon in her hands became an extension of her body. Game time.

"Vicki, no," Pagan begged even as he steadied his rifle to end her. Sullivan would not die today. That he'd been brave enough to maintain a visible, very public profile proved the man's dedication to his SOB teams and his trust in Pagan's ability as a sniper.

Damn, I hope he's right.

"I love you, Pal," Pagan whispered as his index finger squeezed the hair-trigger of his sniper rifle. Deep breath. Let a small breath of it out. Then...

"Don't shoot!" Kruze bellowed in Pagan's earpiece even as—*BOOM!* Vicki fired.

She did it! She shot Senator Sullivan!

Panicked now and out of his mind, Pagan panned his scope to the left, searching for confirmation of Sullivan's hit, even as Kruze repeatedly bellowed, "Don't shoot! Don't shoot!"

Pagan bellowed back, "I never fired! Stand the fuck down!"

But who was the man slumped forward on the table opposite a very calm McQueen Sullivan? Pagan shook his head, not believing what his scope was telling him. *Is that... Was that... Could it really be...Dane Rich?* Blinking hard, he looked closer. *It is Rich. Son-of-a-bitch. Vicki ended her handler, not McQueen Sullivan!*

Pissed at himself for losing focus and his target, and rattled at this unexpected change in mission, Pagan panned back across the street to Vicki. *Please be there!*

And she was. Still prone on that long conference table, she lay there with her forehead pressed to her forearm, and her rifle on its side. Her shoulders were shaking. Hell, her entire body trembled, even her boots.

So damned relieved that she hadn't killed Sullivan, Pagan told her to, "Run!" even as sirens blasted their swift approach from all four corners of the District. Over the years, DC had seen its share of assassinations, bombings, and murders. Metro PD, Secret Service, FBI, and Homeland Security would have every available asset on scene within seconds.

"Run, Hex! Get your ass out of there!"

Yet she made no effort to save herself. She lay perfectly still now. Panic lifted up Pagan's spine. She meant to die. That was why she hadn't moved. This was the end.

"No, no, no!" he bellowed. Yet he couldn't simply run to her rescue this time. He wouldn't leave his weapon behind, and an armed man dashing across any busy District street after shots fired, would only create more chaos. Sucking in a steadying breath, Pagan disassembled his rifle as fast as he could. By the time he'd finished, it fit the ordinary looking briefcase he'd brought with him. But he was all thumbs, and his heart felt ready to explode out of the top of his head.

"Please run for your life, Pal," he begged one last time. "Save yourself. They won't take you down easy, and if you're still holding that rifle when they get here...God! They'll kill you on sight."

But it was too late. Squealing tires and roaring engines announced the arrival of every law enforcement officer in the District.

"Shit!" Pagan hissed as his and Pal's single window of opportunity closed.

Digging into his jacket pocket, he pulled his rangefinder up for one last look at where she'd been. But the table was empty. Her rifle was gone. MPD officers in blue and FBI agents in black swarmed the entire ground floor of the building she'd selected. *Shit, shit, shit!*

Maybe Chance or Kruze had gotten to her in time. Maybe they'd already gotten her out of there. But hope died quickly on that District street when Pagan zeroed in on his brothers, both standing on the sidewalk outside the now cordoned-off office building where Paloma had made her last stand. Chance stared up at the window at Pagan, the wind ruffling his shaggy hair but his sharp eyes betraying nothing. Standing away from Chance, Kruze puffed a smoke like he had nothing better to do.

"Do you have her?" Pagan asked his brothers over the wire in their ears.

Chance offered a barely perceptible headshake.

"Then where is she?"

"She's gone, Baby Brother," Kruze said under his breath, his gaze still on the busy street.

Which offered the smallest frisson of relief. Vicki had finally fled the scene. She might be on the run, but she'd been alive when that army of FBI agents stormed the building.

Pagan sucked in a breath of hope as he watched the drama unfolding outside Vicki Hex's last stand. Metro PD now pushed folks behind their hastily erected police barrier. More men in black suits with earpieces arrived. More SWAT. More Metro PD. Even DC Fire and EMS were on scene, as well as three ambulances, one hook and ladder engine, two unmarked cars, three K9 officers with their dogs, and a partridge in a damned pear tree.

Hurriedly, Pagan descended the stairwell to the street. Jesus H. Christ, it looked like a first responders convention over there. All very professional. All very armed. But no Vicki Hex.

Which told Pagan what he'd suspected from the start of this final charade. Vicki Hex hadn't pulled that trigger today. Uh-uh. Paloma Juarez did that. She'd ended Dane Rich, which was why it took her so long to line up her shot. Vicki wouldn't have had a problem zeroing down on him. She would've been confident and professional. Lethal. But Paloma wouldn't have been so sure. She wasn't a killer at heart, and she would've taken extra care to miss Sullivan.

Paloma was the softer side of Hex. She was the lover, not the fighter. Yet somehow, she'd known Rich would show today, which made Pagan wonder if she'd known all along that Rich had and would again betray her, that he was in the business of taking care of himself first and always? That offing Cherry was just him cleaning up loose ends? For that matter, did Paloma know where Hermes was?

Not like it mattered now. Paloma Juarez had just offed the real predator in the District. In doing so, she'd not only saved Senator McQueen, but she'd rescued every Agency employee who'd been caught up in Rich's insidious web.

"These guys will be working this crime scene for days," Kruze muttered as he blew a puff of nicotine into the wind. "Want to bet what they'll find?"

"Nothing," Pagan answered, his voice gone uncommonly husky and quiet. Thoughtful. Because it was true. If Vicki Hex were finally gone, so was Paloma.

She'd left nothing behind but his broken heart.

Chapter Forty-Two

CIA Agent Richard Card looked happy. Content. He also looked different than Pagan expected. He wasn't the spawn of Satan, and there were no horns curling out of his head. Go figure.

Instead, Dick was a real Brad Pitt look-alike if ever there were one, instead of the snake the Sin Boys had thought he was. As blond as his wife, he was what women might call Hollywood handsome. Tall, tanned, and a capable agent, he was also a died-in-the-wool patriot who truly loved his country. He'd actually accomplished one helluva miracle that day in Peru. He just hadn't performed it fast enough. In hindsight, which was always twenty/twenty vision, he'd told Pagan he wished he'd confided in Chance Sinclair the first moment he'd laid eyes on the brash Navy SEAL.

Cherry Goodwin had just been moved from the Intensive Care Unit to a normal patient room, where she could receive more visitors. Chance and Suede had just left. Pagan wished he'd been a fly on the wall for that conversation between Chance and Dick.

Pagan just wished he were as happy as Card, but he wasn't. Might never smile again if things kept going the way they were. There'd been no sign of Paloma for days. No phone calls. No texts. No nothing.

Reaching across the foot of the bed, Pagan took firm hold of the extended hand of the man he'd once thought about killing on sight. "Hey, Dick. How's the Missus doing today?"

Cherry hissed a breathy, "Hi, Pagan," around the oxygen cannula in her nose.

Like every time Dick Card shook Pagan's hand over the past days, the man's eyes teared up. "She's alive. Because of you and your brothers, she's alive, and I have my family back, and I can never thank you enough."

"Well, good," Pagan replied as he nodded at the poor woman who had survived two surgeries to remove bullet fragments from her chest and lungs over the last week. "That's what I like to hear but knock off the gratitude. It was my pleasure. Just glad I was there."

"I should've trusted your brother," Dick said yet again as he released Pagan's hand. "You have no idea how sorry I am that I chose Dane Rich over Chance that day. None of this would've happened if I'd only told Chance who and what I was up against. He would've believed me. I know he would."

Pagan shrugged Dick's self-condemnation off as he settled his bulky frame into the crazy-small, molded-plastic chair at Cherry's bedside. "We all make mistakes," he said, "so climb off the cross. Someone else needs the wood."

Dick clasped his wife's frail hand and brought her fingers to his lips. "That's what I should do, but Pagan..."

His eyes teared up again, and damn it. Pagan had to look away when the real hero in the room kissed his wife's knuckles.

Rich's hold on Dick had been as lethal as his hold on Dick's wife. They'd both been leveraged. Rich had used one against the other. If Dick had failed to comply, Rich swore he'd torture Cherry and Dick's children. Conversely, if Cherry had failed to locate Vicki Hex, she'd been told she'd never see her husband alive again, that Rich would send him on every dangerous mission that came along until he died or was never heard from again. Which was precisely what Rich had done.

That day in Peru? Rich had sent Dick to meet with the despot currently leading the Shining Path rebels in that area cease. Rich wanted them to cease and desist fighting with the local authorities. Only by then, Dick knew Rich was running guns and drugs in Peru. What he hadn't known was that the two alleged missionaries, Reed and Gillian Enright, were at that moment cutting into Rich's drug sales. They were Christians all right, Christians and capitalists who'd grabbed onto an opportunity to get rich quick, but ended up dead when Rich paid the local guerillas to shut them up. All with taxpayer money.

By the time Dick figured out Rich's real intentions, Chance's SEALs were already in the river, underwater, and incommunicado. Dick had never run so far nor as fast as he did that day to get to the Night Stalkers on stand-by nearby. He'd damn near belted that snooty Spec Ops Army captain in the nose after he'd refused an order to activate his chopper pilots to intervene.

That was when Dick pulled rank and became the hero of the hour as far as Pagan was concerned. He'd jerked that smart-assed captain's rank right off his shirt and declared, "You're fired!" Then he'd ordered the pilots standing there watching the fracas to, "Get your dumb assed in the air, and do it right now! American SEALs are dying out there! Do your son-of-a-bitchin' jobs!"

In seconds, the several pilots at that location not only had their asses in the air, but several fully-equipped and loaded-for-bear Little Bird helos as well. Which explained how Pagan still had two brothers today. Because Dick Card was one of those behind-the-scenes heroes no one ever thought about, knew about, or would ever hear about. Even if the press knew that he'd died in the line of fire that day, he still would've been an anonymous statistic the press would never pass along to the American public. Patriots just weren't that sensational.

As far as why he'd been outside the hotel that day in Chicago? It wasn't because Pagan was in town. No. By then Dick had turned on Rich. He'd been following Morton Hermes, the idiot agent Rich had assigned to surveil Pagan. That Pagan had hooked up with Vicki Hex had only made Hermes's job easier. If things had gone as Dane had planned, the unmanned gunship and the hunter/killer team he'd called down on Vicki's apartment would've killed two birds with one fifty-cal stone. As it was, Rich only pissed off the most lethal team of black operators on the planet—and a sassy dominatrix who was one helluva shot.

Cherry reached her free hand from under the blanket and stretched it to Pagan. "Thank you," she whispered. She was a pretty little thing, and Dick looked like he'd never let her go.

Damned if Pagan's eyes didn't get a little misty. "You're welcome, ma'am."

"You'll find her. I know you will. Keep looking. She's out there. She needs you."

"Yeah, well..." He let that kindness slip away the same way Paloma had slipped away. Finding her wasn't the problem. Letting her go was.

Chapter Forty-Three

Months later...

Another day, another dollar. Paloma swept the stray chickens and their feathers out of her shack yet one more time as the warm Mexican sun began its climb into another bright, cloudless sky. Robin's egg blue was now her favorite color. It bespoke of light and energy and life. It spoke of peace and quiet, too. All she had to do was lift her weary face to the sky, and she was energized and ready for almost anything.

Oh, crap. Except him.

Blocking the sun with one hand, she spotted Julio at the edge of the leafy green jungle that relentlessly invaded her corner of the world. Why was he here and what did he want? As much as Paloma loved her brother, she craved distance from him more. He hadn't healed from his losses any more than she had from hers. They had nothing in common but the pain and misery of their past lives. There'd be no reminiscing today.

Yet, like a dutiful sister, she waved him forward. He might as well join her for coffee. Then he needed to leave and never come back.

"Paloma," he said in his quiet, understated way. No brotherly hug. No tender smile. Never a hug or a hello peck on the cheek. Not even a handshake. That was his way of keeping his distance. If you never held the people you loved, it couldn't hurt when you lost them. Stupid man. Didn't Julio yet understand that love always hurt? That was how you knew it was real.

But there was nothing rambunctious, spontaneous, or sweet about Julio. Never had been. Their lives growing up together had been filled with too much harsh reality for anything soft or endearing. No sentimentality. Pretty much nothing. Just blood.

Paloma wished that were enough, but truthfully, it wasn't. Even as Julio rested his lean square frame onto one of her rickety, second-hand barstools, she wished he hadn't come.

After pouring another coffee, she placed it on the woven mat in front of him and finally breathed, "Julio."

He nodded, his eyes dark as he cupped the mug and took a long hit of the steaming hot beverage. Black. Everything about him was as black as his coffee. His eyes. His hair. His shirt and pants. The shadows forever lurking beneath his midnight dark eyes.

Paloma looked away. She didn't want to think about Bianca and Tomas any more than she wanted to think about Pagan. What purpose did remembering the people she'd lost serve? There came a moment in every assassin's life when enough really was enough. She'd moved on. It'd be smart if Julio did the same.

They sat in silence for as long as Paloma could stand it. Which wasn't long. Tossing her hair over her shoulders, she rolled it into a sloppy bun on top of her head, tied it off with a long strand of her own hair, then let it drop. If she were smart, she'd cut it off. Long hair in this arid climate was always heavy and hot. But so were her girls, and she still had them.

But one day, she might actually *'simplify, simplify, simplify!'* Wasn't that the philosophy that Henry David Thoreau espoused? If he were here, wouldn't he say that she'd 'frittered' her life away on all the wrong things? Yes, she'd been reading more lately. Killing less.

The reading was Pagan Sinclair's mother's fault, but it was okay. The thoughtful works of the American naturalist gave Paloma something productive to do now that she no longer worked the twenty-four-seven job that had nearly killed her. She still needed to touch bases with Vito, though. He and Cabb deserved to know she still lived. Maybe. At least they deserved to know she hadn't died.

But for now, she enjoyed her reprieve from life. From reality. And she meant to enjoy it as long as she could. Thoreau's writings had taught her to stop running and to finally be still. He'd taught her to listen to the insects in the jungle. To finally hear the birdsong up high in the trees. To differentiate the myriad of tweets and whistles, chirps and whirs. To understand which meant danger and which declared that God was good, and all was right in His world.

And God? He'd taught her to look up at the stars at night, to let go and to live and be thankful for what she had. So, she had. Until now.

Sighing, she asked her one and only sibling, "Why are you here?"

Life had been hard on Julio. He'd lost the boyish laugh lines that used to crinkle like little rays of sunshine at the corners of his bright eyes. Then he'd lost the light in his eyes when Bianca walked into the Pacific and took her life. Losing Tomas within the year after Bianca's death was akin to the double tap a sniper blessed his targets with, just to make sure they were dead. Life had done that to Julio. He still breathed, but deep down, he was as dead as his wife and son.

"He still searches for you," Julio said softly, as was his way.

"Who?" she asked. Couldn't be Dane. She'd ended him. She now knew that Cherry Goodwin had survived that shooting, that she was home from the hospital and her husband was with her. For which Paloma was eternally grateful. If she'd accomplished nothing else that day in Washington DC, at least she'd given Cherry the chance at life that she deserved.

That left only two who might be searching for her. Maybe three. Vito. Cabb. Or... her throat went dry at the hope that fluttered to life like a tiny frantic-to-be-set-free hummingbird caught in her heart. *Pagan?*

As if he'd known precisely what she'd thought, Julio nodded. Just once.

He hadn't taken his eyes off her since he'd arrived, and that bugged Paloma. She liked her peace and quiet. It was time Julio left and let her get on with her day. She'd started a business of sorts. Sandwiches mostly. Sangria and pretzels. Small things. But the simple people in this forgotten, out of the way village seemed to like what she made and served in her self-proclaimed diner, which was really just her front porch where Julio now sat. And she liked her neighbors, so there. This was her life now. She had no intention of leaving it. Julio had no business dredging up the past.

"How long are you staying?" she asked, ignoring the elephant suddenly sucking up all the air in her jungle.

Her brother's lashes fell like the thickest, blackest butterfly wings against his darkly tanned cheeks. He'd always ben handsome in his stalwart way. His stubby thumb worried the rim of his mug until it hummed a single, steady note. "The tiniest spark," he said quietly. "That's all it takes, Paloma. One ember. One dream. One single cell joined with another. All it takes is one to change the world. You can be that one. If all you have is hope—"

"Stop it," she bit out. "You're a great one to talk to me of hope. Look at you, hiding in the world as much as I'm hiding from it. Is that why you came to Mexico, just to remind me that all is not lost? As if you know better? Who do you think you are, Don Quixote?"

She would've waved him off like she did the family of geckos that had staked out her humble porch as their 'hood.' But the uncanny sensation of being watched prickled the fine hairs at the back of her neck. Even beneath the tangles that escaped her messy bun, she felt the chill of a sniper's reticle bearing down on her spine. A mere inch below her skull, it would end her. But she wasn't on anyone's kill list as far as she knew, and that sniper out there with eyes on her could only be... Pagan.

She looked over her shoulder, sure it was him, yet hoping it wasn't.

The sight of his hulking body leaned casually against the stone wall outside the front door of the modest chapel, took her breath and stole her heart. Every last beat of it. Just like before.

'He came!' her silly, stupid heart sang. *He came. He came!'*

Not a day went by that she hadn't yearned for him, and after all this time, he still commanded her without lifting a finger. She'd never forgotten the taste of his mouth or the strength in his callused hands. The way he'd held her with so much tenderness when he came. The way he smelled of whiskey, leather and a hard-working man's sweat. The way he'd only ever protected her even though she'd pushed him away. Even when she'd told him she didn't need protection. Even though she had and quite possibly still did.

He's here. He's really here.

Pagan stood with his arms crossed over his magnificent chest and his feet spread wide. Confident, but sad. Massively sure of himself, yet not taking a step toward her. Waiting on her to make the first move.

Julio's warm hand settled over Paloma's clenched fingers. "Chance tells me that if Pagan doesn't start sleeping and eating, he'll die. He's already sick. He cannot go on like this."

She shot Julio a look. "Not sleeping? Not eating? He's sick?"

Julio looked straight into her soul as only a brother could. "It's called failure to thrive, little sister. You've heard if it before. Pagan doesn't want to live without you. He can't."

"But that's what happens to children who..." She slammed her mouth closed as her sweet little Tomas flashed to mind. That was what the doctors said he'd died of. Failure to thrive. It happened when a person lost hope. When they believed they'd been abandoned.

"It's measured by weight loss in little children," Julio said, his voice suddenly tender and raw, his eyes brimming. "But in adults, it's measured by heart. That man over there gave his to you. No one can live without their heart, Paloma. Surely you know that. You understand. Haven't you ever given yours away?"

Which suddenly explained Julio. He had that same failure to thrive syndrome. Paloma knew because she'd been dying of the same thing for months now.

She nodded at her tormented brother as she recalled the exact moment she'd given her heart away. That night she'd been tortured, she'd sent it to Pagan on a wing and a prayer. Oh, how she'd prayed he'd come rescue her then. Now here he was. Standing there. Waiting. Maybe afraid to hope, so he wouldn't get hurt again.

Was he holding his breath the same way she was?

The longer Paloma studied Pagan, the more she knew Julio was right. Pagan had lost weight. His shirt hung off his shoulders, and his sleeves were a titch too long. Sloppy. His shoulders were not nearly so full. His jeans didn't fit nearly as snug as they had before, and his cheeks were pinched. Hollow. She couldn't see his eyes, only his dark glasses. Funny. This was the first time she'd seen him in sunglasses. Was he hiding behind them?

"It only takes one," Julio breathed behind her. "Paloma, you're my only family. Please. He came all this way to see you. Don't throw this man's love away."

She turned in her chair to face the overly-protective man who'd finally caught up with her. "Pagan," she whispered.

When she turned back around to ask Julio how he'd known where to find her, Julio was gone. Only the empty mug remained. That left Pagan still standing across the way. Still uninvited. Still waiting. Still so damned handsome it hurt to look at him. His lips pinched as if he were holding back words he wouldn't let spill.

Paloma rose shakily to her feet, not trusting herself to know what to do next.

But once again... Pagan. Was. There.

Like all those other times, he'd shown up when no one else had. He'd come for her. Julio didn't count.

Tears she hadn't realized she'd been holding back spilled over her cheeks. She dashed them away with the backs of her hands, and Pagan moved. In one lightning fast streak, she was in his arms, crushed against the massive chest she loved so damn hard. So much.

"You came," she cried as she burrowed under his chin, wishing there was a way to crawl into his heart, wrap him around her, and never, ever have to leave.

A terrible growl crawled out of his throat as his hands smoothed down her spine to cup her ass. "God, Paloma," he cried into her hair when he lifted her off the ground. "God, oh God, oh God..." His cries turned to sobs, and once again, Paloma thought, *What have I done?*

Melting against him, she smoothed her fingers over his head and threaded them into his now thick dark hair to soothe him. To love him. To make him want to thrive and live again. To ask for forgiveness for being who and what she was.

"What have you done to yourself, Big Guy?" she chided even as she wiped her face into his cheek to banish her tears. "You're too thin. And you've shaved. What's up with that?"

"I fell in love," he ground out. "With you. But you left and—"

"I'm here now," she breathed into his ear, "and I was wrong to leave you like I did, and I'm never leaving you again, and... and... Hold me Pagan. Just shut up and hold me and never let me go."

"Bed. Now," he commanded.

"Yes," she answered easily. "In the house. To the right. Under the window."

How they got to the bed in her simple, one-room shack in the jungle, she didn't remember. Just his lips on hers when he'd finally laid her down on her lumpy mattress and settled his hulking, trembling body over her. Just the taste of the mouth she'd craved for months without end. Just the scrub of his clean-shaven chin abrading her tender skin and the accompanying trail of fire that burned like an arrow straight to her core.

"You said you'd marry me," he mumbled as his tongue made love to her open mouth. "You promised."

"I did. I will. I promise," she murmured, breathing the intoxicating scent of her man back into her soul.

"Now. The priest is waiting."

"Now?" That startling revelation quelled the fire in her blood, but didn't put it out.

"Yes, now. I'm no good without you. But I'm not here to drag you back to the States. I'm here to stay if you'll have me. If you still—"

"Love you? Was that what you were going to say? That you'll give up everything you love for me?"

Easing his head back enough that she could see him, and him her, Pagan blinked an adorable little boy blink like he'd been caught with his hand in the cookie jar. "Uh-huh."

Only then did Paloma finally let go of everything she'd thought she'd believed. Everything but him. "No. That's not how it works, Pagan. One soulmate does not sacrifice their life, their ambitions, or their livelihood for the other. They don't give up their dreams and change who they are, just to please somebody. Uh-uh."

"But I'm here and I would," he whispered. "For you, I'd give up everything."

*****

And he meant it. Pagan would give up his heart. His soul. His life and every last thing he'd ever thought was important. Because none of those things mattered without the woman he adored at his side. These last months and weeks without Paloma had been hell. He couldn't sleep or eat, worrying where she was and wondering if she were healthy and happy. Still alive. It'd done his heart good the day Julio had finally called and said he'd located her in western Mexico not far from the Pacific Ocean. Did Pagan want to take a little trip?

Hell, yeah.

Now here Pagan was with the woman of his heart finally back in his arms where she belonged. And arguing. As usual. But at least he could breathe again. His heart was pumping hard, but even that didn't worry him. He could swallow without his tongue getting stuck on the lump in his throat—which was just his broken heart.

"What is it you want?" he asked meekly, still ready to do anything to bring a smile to Paloma's sad eyes. They used to twinkle, and when she'd been Vicki Hex, they'd sparked with fire and her passionate zest for life. He'd give anything, do anything, be anything if she sparkled like that again.

"You," she said without hesitation. "All of you. Your dreams. Your heart. And every last one of your aspirations. What is it *you* want?" Her fingertips skimmed his chest, then splayed over his nipples, lighting a fuse down deep in his toes. He found it odd she hadn't stabbed air quotes at him like she used to. He missed even that part of his audacious, in-your-face woman.

"You," he growled as his body hardened under her gentle, exquisite assault.

"You've already got me," she declared as if that were decided and there were no going back. *Sweet.* "What else?"

He honestly had no idea how to answer. Paloma truly was all that he'd ever wanted. He was that man dying of thirst in the Sahara. When you've gone without water for far too long and you're that desperate, all you want and can think of is that one drop of precious, life-giving moisture. Paloma was that single drop of life, and he wanted her more than he'd ever wanted anything. She was his whole damned world. Nothing else mattered.

Until she licked the underside of his chin and ignited the glowing ember in his groin. Okay, that mattered.

Wiggling out of his arms, she crawled down the length of his body, her voluptuous, carefree girls beneath the simple cotton blouse she wore. No bra. All bounce. Against his chest. His stomach. Now *he* licked *his* lips.

The lower she went, the harder his body tensed until he was afraid he'd burst and spoil the make-up sex she obviously had her heart set on.

Yeah no. He couldn't wait. He'd embarrass himself if he did. Plan B. Tipping forward, he snagged her forearms and dragged her wide-eyed and probably annoyed back up to his chest. Before she could complain about women's rights and how she didn't need him telling her what to do, he palmed her sweet backside, grinding her core where it did the most good.

That solved his immediate problem. Well, not *that* one, but it kept her busy while he divested them both of their clothes. Finally skin to skin, she climbed aboard, her legs spread, her palms on his chest, and her knees alongside his hips.

"I can't hold out much longer," he told her frankly as he ran his fingers through her hair and loosed every last one of those uptight, messy tangles. The sight of all that shiny, silky decadence spilling over his bare belly spiked a roaring fever in his blood and—

She impaled herself onto him. Up to the hilt. *Thank you, Jesus!* She knew what she wanted, and she still wanted him. The succulent warmth. The blessed heat of her fire added to his, and he was home at last. Free at last.

He stroked long, possessive caresses down the length of her hair, thinking how once upon a time he'd thought she was everything he didn't like, couldn't have, didn't need. Yet now she was everything. His heart. His soul. His reason to live. And so much more.

She'd become his beach, his safe harbor, and he was the ocean crashing into her sweet body. Together they were the ebb and flow of life and love.

Arching her back, she took one long, languorous slide up. Then down.

Pagan's body responded fiercely. Completely. He barely had time to glove himself before he rolled her over and pumped her full of all he had to give. His seed. His soul. Every last bit of his heart. Paloma was his world. Only her. There just wasn't room for anything else.

She clung to him, her now healed fingertips raking over his broad shoulders as she held on. Easing out of her just enough for her body to draw him back into her slick warmth, and yessssssss...

Pagan bowed his head to her shoulder in utter reverence when she lost control and scraped her fingernails down his back. Her body clenched tight and hard around him, milking him, promising forever as she came with him. They'd always come like this. Together. In melding heat and a fierce kind of forever glory that defied the world. He was so damned addicted. So much in love.

His body tensed as her aftershocks drew out his pleasure until...

Stars. The love of his life had just squeezed the unholy hell out of him, and he was in heaven. Floating on a sea of stars. With her.

Swallowing the tender emotions clouding his eyes and climbing up his throat, Pagan wrapped his arms around his whole world. The village priest was waiting to marry them, but marriage could wait. Pagan had who he'd traveled all night to find. He needed this moment with Paloma more than anything else.

She had no way of knowing she'd been pardoned, or how many other Agency operators had come forward to indict Agent Rich. Paloma had no way of knowing that over the last months, Pagan had read everything he could on women's rights, the power of women, and feminine know-how. Yet none of that mattered.

In the end, all Pagan needed was the incredible thing that had somehow bound them together while they'd been apart. While they'd each been working through their separate issues, it had tugged and pulled, reminded and nagged, until here they were. Lying locked and loaded in each other's arms. Finally ready to take on the world and win. Every time. Together.

They were now the most powerful weapon on Earth. And all because of...

Love.

Epilogue

Julio watched and waited in the shadows until Pagan lifted Paloma up in his arms and carried her into her poor excuse of a house. But the hut she'd called home was sufficient, and she'd seemed to have made a life for herself here. Better yet, the humble people in this small village accepted her. He'd checked. Every one he'd spoken with thought a lot of her. They considered her to be one of them. As it should be. But whether Pagan actually stayed here for any amount of time remained to be seen. Julio suspected not. A man such as Pagan had that bigger-than-life, winner-takes-all persona meant for bigger things than simple, unobtrusive village life. He was one of those Chris Kyle types, born for greatness and grander things than to simply live out his days in Paloma's wooden hut. That would never be enough for Pagan, any more than it would any one of the Sin Boys.

But that was not Julio's problem, and he'd interfered in his sister's life enough for one day. "What do you say, amigo?" he asked the sniper fidgeting at his side. "Are we done here?"

"Yeah. Let's move," Kruze Sinclair grunted as his fingertips toyed with the cigarette he had yet to light. Whether they knew it or not, snipers who smoked had a death wish. If tobacco didn't kill them, their target would, once he or she caught a whiff of that cancer stick. Kruze was in desperate need of a nicotine fix. Yes, they needed to move before Pagan realized he'd been followed.

Kruze faced north. Julio faced west. The Pacific lay just beyond the sandy, grass-covered berm, so close he could smell salt water and seaweed. Paloma had chosen her hideout well. Southeast of the Baja Peninsula and north of Guadalajara, she could've lived out the rest of her days here. Maybe she would, but Julio doubted that. It'd be easier for her to leave with Pagan at her side.

But Julio had a date with the ocean. That was where he was headed. To the Pacific and—Bianca.

"Where to?" he asked his compadre.

Kruze hooked a thumb over one shoulder. "Back to Sonora." Which meant he'd soon be across the border in Tucson, where he'd catch a ride home.

Julio had never understood this calcitrant Sinclair brother. Of the three, Kruze was the tight-lipped, forever-caught-in-the-middle son. Between one domineering older brother and one razor-sharp younger, Kruze was surrounded by family. Yet he didn't seem to know it or understand the richness of having two brothers who loved him like Chance and Pagan did. Julio got the impression that Kruze avoided his brothers. Which was just plain sad. Familia was everything. Julio'd give his soul to have his back.

"Then this is adios," Julio replied as he offered his hand.

"Thanks," Kruze said as he took hold and squeezed harder than Julio had expected. But no problem. Everything with Kruze seemed to be a contest of will or strength. As if he needed to prove he was the harder man of the two, he stared Julio down and held on a fraction of a second longer.

Julio let his friend think he'd won. What did it matter? In the end, they were all losers.

"I will see you around, won't I?" Kruze asked, suddenly more perceptive than Julio had given him credit for.

Playing along, Julio cocked his head. "Of course. Why wouldn't you?"

"Hell, I don't know." Kruze muttered as he let go and ran his fingers over his head. "Just thought maybe you were tired or something. Maybe sick and tired?"

"We are all sick and tired, my friend. But no. I am not that kind of tired. But I do have to visit someone before I leave. Be at peace, brother." Then he lied and said, "If you need me, call. I will always come."

Kruze's head nod said he believed his friend. "Later then," Kruze said as he faded into the fronds and tall grasses that grew along this stretch of the beach.

Breathing the sigh he hadn't realized he'd been holding, Julio turned his back on the direction Kruze had gone and set a steady pace toward the pounding surf. This stretch of the wild Pacific wasn't the exact location, but it was the same ocean, and that was good enough.

He ran his palms over the tips of the thigh high grasses that clung to sandy shores like this one, letting them tickle the husband and father that was left in him. Which wasn't much.

Bianca would've loved this beach. Which was why he was here. The tide was in. The waves off shore were tremendously huge rollers, pounding the surf, demanding to be heard perhaps even miles away. Any one might slip and fall to their death, especially if they were foolish enough to be caught on those massive rock fingers that broke through the sand and reached for the ocean. That took the beating the waves dished out. That waited for him.

Gulls hovered overhead, caught in the brisk breeze like living kites. They squawked. They flapped their silvery gray wings. They screeched and they called. And in the wind, once again Julio heard Bianca's sweet siren call whisper, 'Come with me.' Just like she'd begged him that last day.

Yes. This stretch of the Pacific would work just fine.

Because the greatest regret Julio carried was that he hadn't gone with his wife that last day. Her depression had grown more and more stifling, and that particular day, Tomas had cried nonstop the night before and into the long morning before he'd finally fallen asleep. Their baby hadn't been right since they'd been rescued from Domingo Zapata's hellish prison, and Julio hadn't understood how she could want to run away to the beach when her only child needed her so desperately. So he'd held onto Tomas while she'd walked away and left the two of them behind.

She'd always told him that sitting near the ocean gave her hope, and like a fool, he'd believed her. But hope was not what she'd gone to find that day. Only relief from the demons Zapata's cruelty had embedded deep in her soul. Only the final peace of never having to wake up again.

Ironically, another SEAL had pulled her lifeless body out of the ocean just off Coronado that day. He'd been swimming with his girlfriend when he'd spotted Bianca. But he'd never resuscitated her. Hadn't even tried. You can't bring a woman who'd slashed her forearms from wrists to elbows, back to life. Bianca finally had what she'd wanted. A way out.

As for poor sweet Tomas?

Julio swiped at the tears stinging the corner of his eyes. He hadn't been able to save his son, either. The two people in the world he treasured most were gone. Zapata had taken everything. Even his will to live.

The breeze off the ocean was stiff once he crested the berm, and at last, the dazzling Pacific stretched wide and long, deep and blue ahead of him. He could almost feel its tender embrace wrapping around him. Holding him down. His greatest fear at this pivotal point in time was that he'd struggle when that final moment came. That his body's natural survival instinct would kick in and sabotage him. That he'd have to live one more day without Bianca and Tomas.

Like her, he needed the pain in his heart to end. He needed relief. He meant to find it. Julio steeled his soul and his heart to not fail him in this, his final endeavor.

An old man tottered to Julio's left while a black dog scampered into the waves, chasing sandpipers or fish. Julio no longer cared. He truly cared about so few people these days. Now that Paloma was in good hands, he had one less reason to live.

Tugging his shirt over his head, he tossed it to the beach and began to jog. That way that old man and his dog wouldn't think it suspicious when he dived into the surf. They might think he was crazy, but by then, Julio's powerful strokes would've taken him beyond their reach. He was an excellent swimmer. Every SEAL was. He'd swim until he tired, then he'd roll onto his back and let the Pacific take him the way it had taken Bianca.

Until that buzz in his rear pocket told him he had an incoming call.

His heart kicked an odd beat and a half as his hand slapped automatically over his butt pocket as he stopped short of the beckoning waves. "No," he told himself, but yes. His thumb had by then maneuvered the cell out of his pocket and into his palm, and okay, fine. One last call. This wouldn't take long.

He turned aside from the breeze to better hear his caller. "Juarez."

"Julio, glad I caught you. McQueen here. Got a minute?"

Julio let his gaze scan the distant western horizon where Bianca waited and whispered, *'Come with me. I'm waiting.'*

"Actually, sir, I don't. I'm in the middle of something. Can I call you back?"

"No," McQueen bit out, his cheery Texas twang gone, and his *I-am-the-boss-of-you, do-you-want-a-piece-of-me?* persona radiating loud, clear, and nasty over the connection.

Automatically, Julio snapped to attention. His shoulders squared. His gut sucked in like it had a reason to. And his brain cleared enough that his mouth replied, "Yes, sir. What can I do for you?"

"I've got trouble in Manaus, Brazil, that can't wait."

"But sir, isn't that *Dia de Muertos* territory?"

McQueen had more than just the Sin Boys team in his clandestine league of black operators. While the

Sinclairs handled what trouble they needed to across the far reaches of the world, most specifically the Middle East, a covert team of former Army Rangers, aka the *Lone Wolves,* so named because they hunted alone, also operated out of central Wyoming. *The Panthers*, an elusive group of former CIA agents, targeted the bad guys, gun and drug runners deep in the Florida Everglades, as well as along the southeastern seaboard, both on the Atlantic and the Gulf sides of the panhandle. The *Night Shadows*, a team of former FBI agents who'd seen too much and felt like they'd done too little, worked America in general, from sea to shining sea.

But South American troubles belonged to the men of the deadly *Dia de Muertos Team,* headquartered out of New Mexico. Comprised of an elite team of three USA border guards, they were the ones McQueen should assign this operation to. Not a man on his way to meet his dead wife, who even now called to him with a hushed but persuasive, nearly irresistible, '*Come, Julio. Please, come to me.*'

"No go," McQueen replied tersely. "Lost two of those agents last night. Firefight outside of Tegucigalpa, Honduras."

Julio's heart sank at the thought of two brothers being killed. Honduras was a nation on the brink of all out chaos. "Which ones?"

"Diego and Seb. Santiago's bringing their bodies home today. They'll be at Dover before nightfall. Can you do it or not? This is urgent, and I plain can't wait."

"Yes." Julio answered automatically even as he cast one last look at the ocean.

"Good. I'll email your instructions over our usual secure line. One more thing. I need someone to take over Diego's position. Tag, you're it."

"You want me to lead the *Dia de Muertos Team*?"

"I trust you, Julio. More than any other man on this team, I trust you. Sign on with me once and for all and be the team leader I know you are, damn it. Say yes."

Julio could actually hear McQueen's fingertips impatiently drumming his desk.

"No," Julio replied evenly. He didn't want anything but out of the highly secret, super covert world. Not only no, but Hell to the tenth power, no. He was through with dealing out too much death and never having enough downtime in his life to get his head on straight. Only now that he thought about it, he had nothing to look forward to, and what good was downtime without anyone to share it with?

He glanced one last time at the waiting ocean with its cold, endless embrace. Bianca wasn't really there. Neither was Tomas. Only the ashes of the beautiful bodies he'd cremated and released back into eternity were there. Somewhere.

Damn. He cast a lingering look over his shoulder back to where Paloma's humble little home stood beyond that sandy berm and the waving grasses. Back to where she and Pagan were no doubt happily reacquainting themselves with each other. Back to where another life might just be starting if Pagan finally got his way. The man wanted a family more than any man Julio had ever known.

"Yes," Julio blurted out before he gave himself time to think twice.

"Well, good," McQueen replied as if he'd known all along Julio would accept. "Check your email. I'm sending that encrypted file now. You'll fly out of Houston. Be there by seven tomorrow morning."

And that was that.

Weary to the deepest cellar of his worthless soul, Julio sucked in a belly full of the breeze blowing off the Pacific as he pocketed his cell. Slowly, he let the air wheeze out of him. Was it possible his sister knew something he didn't when she'd chosen to be Paloma over Vicki Hex? Julio wanted to believe she'd found true happiness. Unlike him, she deserved it.

But after his parents' deaths, he'd become an outcast in his country of birth and an undocumented immigrant in America, one who'd only achieved US citizenship through military service. He no longer knew what normal felt like. He was and forever always would be the unlucky bastard who'd lost everything the day Zapata took his family.

Holy Mother of God, he was so tired. It'd been a long time since he'd enjoyed waking up to a new day that Julio couldn't recall if it had ever truly happened.

He'd lost his sense of direction, and he knew it. The way forward was no longer clear. Only the way down.

One op was the same as the next, one day as long as the last. He was empty. Done. The only person who'd mattered was Pagan Sinclair's problem now. Julio had become what all black operators feared. He'd become a ghost. Unseen. Unloved. Unnecessary.

Bianca might have to wait for him to complete this one last job. But she wouldn't have to wait long.

THE END

Thank you for reading Pagan's story

If you enjoyed this book, be sure to check out the sexy guys and gals of Irish Winters' series, *In the Company of Snipers.*

Other Irish Winters' books

King of Hearts, Deuces Wild Series

Joker Joker, Deuces Wild Series

Smoke, Hearts and Ashes Series

Ash, Hearts and Ashes Series

Coming soon

Renner, In the Company of Snipers
Ace, Deuces Wild Series
Damned, An SOBs Novel
Lost, An Sobs Novel

YOU ARE THE KEY TO THIS BOOK'S SUCCESS

Please tell other readers why you liked Pagan and Paloma's story by leaving an honest review at the retail site where you purchased it.

Recommend it to your friends. Lend it.

Most of all, enjoy it!

The best way to keep up with my new releases, giveaways, and actionable intel is to sign up for my spam-free newsletter at IrishWinters.com.

About the Author

Irish Winters is a best-selling author who, when she isn't writing, dabbles in poetry, grandchildren, and rarely (as in extremely rarely) the kitchen. More prone to be outdoors than in, she grew up the quintessential tomboy on a dairy farm in rural Wisconsin, spent her teen years in the Pacific Northwest, but calls the Wasatch Mountains of Northern Utah, home. For now.

She believes in making every day count for something, and follows the wise admonition of her mother to, "Look out the window and see something!"

Connect with Irish online:

On Facebook
www.facebook.com/IrishWintersAuthor/

On Twitter
www.twitter.com/irishwinters1

www. IrishWinters.com

9 781942 895893